Praise for *Ransomed Dreams*
and other novels by Sally John

"This inspirational [story] reminds readers that it's never too late for second chances. And when our hope is in God, nothing is impossible."
ROMANTIC TIMES, 4½-star review

"A thoughtful and engaging novel."
PUBLISHERS WEEKLY

"John has penned an exciting, faith-based story. . . ."
BOOKLIST

"Sally John has penned another moving tale. *Ransomed Dreams* asks hard questions about faith and forgiveness . . . but it also offers hope. It's worth reading to discover the answer."
CROSSWALK.COM

"John's story is surprisingly refreshing and completely upholds biblical truths of faithfulness in marriage. Readers of this book will not only enjoy a good story, but they may also learn valuable truths along the way."
CHRISTIANBOOKPREVIEWS.COM

"*Ransomed Dreams* is another wonderful weave of compelling characters, poignant pacing, and the twin truths that forgiveness is costly but love can meet the expense head-on. Sally John is an insightful, inspiring storyteller."
SUSAN MEISSNER, author of *The Shape of Mercy*

"Sally John has done it again—interesting characters, exotic locations, and a compelling story line. The unexpected twists in the protagonist's life left me evaluating the sources of my own sense of security. Thought provoking."
KATHRYN CUSHMAN, author of *Leaving Yesterday*

"*Ransomed Dreams* is another inspiring story from Sally John that profoundly touches the heart. This novel will captivate readers with its characters, intrigue, and twists and turns. A must-read for anyone who has lost their way and their dreams to discover hope!"
SUSAN WALES, author and producer

"Sally John delivers an intense and emotionally satisfying reminder that our lives can change in a heartbeat."

ROMANTIC TIMES on *In a Heartbeat*

"Talented author Sally John weaves a web around her readers, drawing them into her characters' world. . . . Oh, what a satisfying read—one of the best of the year."

NOVEL JOURNEY on *The Beach House*

"[Sally John] writes an enthralling story with fully developed characters that are experiencing problems that many women of faith face daily. And she does it with warmth, realism, and sensitivity."

ARMCHAIRINTERVIEWS.COM on *The Beach House*

"Once in a very long time, a book comes along that has the ability to touch hearts, change lives, and inspire hope. *Castles in the Sand* is one such book . . . a profound, inspiring read of a family torn apart and the long road home."

READERVIEWS.COM

DESERT
gift

❧

SALLY JOHN

Tyndale House Publishers, Inc.
Carol Stream, Illinois

Visit Tyndale's exciting Web site at www.tyndale.com.

Check out the latest about Sally John at www.sally-john.com.

TYNDALE and Tyndale's quill logo are registered trademarks of Tyndale House Publishers, Inc.

Desert Gift

Designed by Jennifer Ghionzoli

Edited by Kathryn S. Olson

Published in association with the literary agency of Alive Communications, Inc., 7680 Goddard Street, Suite 200, Colorado Springs, CO 80920, www.alivecommunications.com.

Scripture quotations are taken from the *Holy Bible*, New Living Translation, copyright © 1996, 2004, 2007 by Tyndale House Foundation. Used by permission of Tyndale House Publishers, Inc., Carol Stream, Illinois 60188. All rights reserved.

Library of Congress Cataloging-in-Publication Data

John, Sally, date.
  Desert gift / Sally John.
    p. cm. — (Side roads)
    ISBN 978-1-4143-2786-0 (pbk.)
  1. Marriage—Fiction. I. Title.
  PS3560.O323D47 2011
  813'.54—dc22   2011001191

Printed in the United States of America

17   16   15   14   13   12   11
7   6   5   4   3   2   1

For Troy and Elizabeth,
now Mr. and Mrs.

Give honor to marriage, and remain faithful
to one another in marriage.

HEBREWS 13:4

Acknowledgments

As ALWAYS, a team supported my storytelling efforts. My heart overflows with gratitude to:

My readers, for the precious notes that affirm and uplift.

The late Myrna Strasser and the staff at WDLM-FM, East Moline, Illinois, for introducing me to radio.

Jane Hull and Peggy Hadacek, for insightful talks about marriage.

Carla and Chester Genack, for car repair information.

Patti John, for the ticket to Hollywood.

Gary and Millie Heniser, Leanne Payne, and Bill and Harriet Mouer, for teachings.

Christopher John, for the exquisite description of desert quiet.

Elizabeth and Troy Johnson and Tracy John, for research.

Tim, for being Tim for thirty-seven years.

Agent Lee Hough of Alive Communications and editors Karen Watson, Stephanie Broene, and Kathy Olson, for keeping me going.

Everyone at Tyndale House, for bringing it all together.

Blessings to you all.

Prologue

At precisely twelve minutes and thirty-five seconds past ten o'clock in the morning, Central Standard Time, Jillian Galloway's world ceased to exist.

She noticed the time because she was a clock watcher, a habit born of working in radio, where fractions of moments truly mattered. When her mike was on and the clock's second hand swept up toward the twelve and listeners were staying tuned in because they wanted to hear the national news at noon, she wasn't about to introduce a new subject.

But there stood Jackson, her husband, introducing a new subject while at the front door, buttoning his black wool overcoat. An assortment of luggage was at his feet, packed and ready to go. Outside, a cab waited at the curb. Somewhere up in the stratosphere a jet soared, making its way to O'Hare airport, where, in a very, very, very short while, they would board it.

She shifted her gaze from the large wall clock beyond his shoulder and made eye contact with him. "What did you say?"

"I said I'm not going." He repeated the words that simply did not fit into that morning's time frame nor anywhere in her comprehension.

"Jack, what are you talking about?"

With a sigh—the exasperated one he seldom emitted except in the kitchen when one of his gourmet concoctions failed—he lowered his shoulder bag to the floor. "I can't keep this up. I just can't." A wince settled into the lines around his eyes. "I'm sorry."

"Honey, you're not making any sense. We're on our way out the door. What on earth . . . ? What can't you keep up?"

"Us, Jill. Us. I can't keep us up."

Beneath her wintry layers of blouse, sweater, silk scarf, and wool jacket, perspiration trickled down her sides. Her gloved fingers ached around the handle of her laptop bag. Her ears burned from the slap of his words, forcing her to let them inside.

Jack's grimace tightened until his hazel eyes were all but seamed shut. "I'm sorry." He spoke in his professional doctor tone: soft, gentle, giving an unpleasant prognosis to an unsuspecting patient. "I can't explain it. It just is."

She swallowed, gulping around the sudden lump in her throat. "You're tired. You haven't had a real vacation in forever. We both need this trip. A little downtime in the sunshine. A little rest. Then we'll talk. We'll decipher whatever this is all about."

"We *will* talk, but not now. I need some space, some serious space." He shook his head. "The truth is, I want a divorce."

The clock's pendulum ticked and tocked, back and forth, back and forth. It carried off irretrievable moments. It divided time into a before and an after.

Jill blinked. She cleared her throat. The lump remained. She blinked again. "I don't understand."

"Neither do I."

"Try."

"I have been trying since I woke up this morning."

"Since you woke up this morning? So it's out of the blue, this . . . this . . . this need for space. That can't be. People don't wake up and say they want—want . . ." He hadn't said it, had he? Not the *D* word. Not really. He didn't mean it.

"Don't, Jill, please. Don't analyze. Don't stick a label on it. It just is."

His face smoothed, the creases unfolding as if the burden of the prognosis were no longer his to carry. He opened the front door and grabbed hold of her two bags. "I'll walk you out to the cab."

"Jack! This is crazy! I can't leave now."

"Yes, yes, you can. So many fans are counting on you. Let this go for now and focus on your work. You don't want to disappoint them."

"We need to talk!"

"We will. When you get home." He hurried outside, down the porch steps, and along the sidewalk he had scooped clear of snow before breakfast, knowing the whole entire time, with every shovelful thrown aside, that he wasn't going with her.

They would talk when she got home. When she got home.

She wouldn't be home for five weeks.

Jill stood, motionless. Her loving husband of twenty-four years had just announced that he wanted a divorce.

Behind her the clock chimed a quarter past the hour.

PART
one

CHAPTER I

———— ❧ ————

When Jill was a little girl, her father nicknamed her Jillie Jaws. He asked, What choice did he have? Not only were her initials JAW, she was also without question, from birth, a motormouth. When air first hit her lungs, she never even cried. She yammered. Yes sirree, Jillian Autumn Wagner always had something to say.

Until now.

Four hours into it and she had nothing to say.

Not that anyone would have listened. The flight attendants had spent more time buckled in than not because of air turbulence. A sullen thirtyish woman in the window seat wore a headset and kept her nose buried in a novel that sported a strikingly handsome Fabio-type on the cover. The aisle seat remained empty.

Of course it remained empty. It was Jack's.

Her jaw quivered. The movement had no relationship to yammering.

What would her father think? Skip Wagner thought the world of his son-in-law.

Her dad? She was concerned about her dad? What about her audience?

Don't even start, Jillian. Do not even start.

But of course she had started, thanks to Jack's introduction of the subject. He had said her fans were counting on her.

Jack was a kind man, a physician in the classic sense. He was a gentleman who wanted nothing more than to help his patients feel better. That he actually said he wanted a divorce was inconceivable. As if that weren't enough, he had added insult to injury by mentioning her fans. Moments later as they stood at the curb, he'd done it again. At the echo of his voice in her head now, she could scarcely breathe.

"You will be all right," he had said. "This trip is about you meeting your fans." He gave her a quick hug, the stiff-armed sort he used for his elderly, frail mother. Then deftly, one hand under her elbow, the other on the open car door, he ushered her into the backseat of the cab as if she were another scoop of snow tossed aside.

"Jack, I'll go later. I'll get another flight—"

"No!" He shook his head vehemently. "No. I must do it this way. I'm sorry." He shut the car door.

Before the driver pulled from the curb, Jack had scurried away, making it halfway up the sidewalk without a wave or backward glance.

And that was that.

At breakneck speed he had detonated three explosions: He wanted a divorce. He didn't want to talk about it for weeks. He mentioned her fans.

Boom. Boom. Boom.

Her fans were women who listened to her radio show and planned to read her new book. They were women from across the country who trusted her advice on how to prevent a husband from doing exactly what her husband had just managed to do.

More specifically they were women in Los Angeles who had already paid money to eat lunch with Jill Galloway. They had paid money to hear her speak about how to communicate in marriage. They had scheduled it on their BlackBerrys for *tomorrow*.

Before the cab had reached the end of the block, her jaw quit working. Except for the tremble.

She was supposedly an expert in marital discourse. How did it happen that in ten words or less, with absolutely no forewarning, her own husband had exploded their world with *"I want a divorce"* and then sent her off to the airport?

The scene was so totally out of character for him it made her head swim. The Galloways were the poster couple for a healthy marriage. They had worked hard for over twenty years at keeping it healthy. She had taught on the subject for a dozen years. She had a solid grasp of the ins and outs—

A sharp jab against her arm startled her.

Her seatmate moved her elbow from the armrest. "Sorry."

Jill nodded and then shook her head and hoped it was a universal sign for "no problem."

"Excuse me." The woman pushed the headset from her mane of dark hair. "No one is sitting in the aisle seat. You could use it."

Jill gazed at the empty seat.

"Uh, are you all right?"

She nodded, shook her head, and nodded again. *You don't want to know.*

"Do you need the attendant?"

Jill's lungs craved air. Her chest felt like it was on fire. Maybe words were piled up inside. Instead of their usual flight off her tongue, they had lumped themselves together and now spontaneous combustion was occurring.

Maybe she was having a heart attack!

Miss Sullen reached up and snapped on the call light.

Jill blurted, "It's my husband's seat."

"Okaaay." Her voice rose on the last syllable.

"He's in Chicago."

The woman's eyebrows twitched.

"And I think he just left me." Jill unbuckled her belt, snapped off the call light, and moved into Jack's seat, affirming that he really and truly was not coming.

The burning sensation lessened. Maybe speaking aloud had released some of the pressure. Maybe what helped was giving voice to truth, the hard truth that she was on a plane somewhere over the Rockies and her husband for no conceivable reason was not.

She shut her eyes. She couldn't even articulate a prayer. Where was God in all this anyway? A simple answer was that He allowed this situation for a reason. A reason she could use someday. Something like a new insight to share with other women or like material for a lesson plan.

Her chest went all hot again. The simple answer did not resonate. No way, nohow.

She pressed her fingers against her breastbone. Was it heartburn? Not the kind that plagued her when she was pregnant, but the kind inflicted by such emotional pain it felt like her heart was being seared.

"Maybe he didn't leave you," her seatmate said.

Jill opened her eyes.

Miss Sullen shrugged. "You said you 'think' he left you. If you don't know for sure, maybe he didn't."

"Maybe he didn't." Jill sighed. "Out of the blue he said he wanted a divorce."

"Out of the blue?"

"Yes. The thing is, I can't figure out why he would. I mean, of course I've gone over my obvious, most glaring faults. I talk too much. I drag him to events he doesn't give a hoot about. He wanted four kids but I said no after one. I ignore his parents a lot. I don't cook. I really don't like his office manager. I threw his baseball cards into the trash. It was a mistake—I didn't mean to, but I did it. And I spend an arm and a leg every three weeks for this." She grabbed a fistful of frosted blonde hair. Its carefree style cut exactly one inch below her earlobes remained undisturbed.

Miss Sullen's brows inched upward.

Jill went on. "But that's just everyday life, you know? It's what he married. Piled up for twenty-four years with no serious complaint out of him, do they create a motive? I don't think so. But what about the big-deal stuff? the stuff that really matters?"

The woman's eyes were wide open now.

Jill slid into familiar territory, her tone confident. "The big-deal stuff is definitely in the plus column. Jack and I talk openly about everything, and I mean everything. We always have. We like each other. Physical intimacy is very good. We attend church together. We go on dates regularly. We spend time with mutual friends. He loves his work. I love mine. Our son is a mature young adult. As far as I know, that covers it. And trust me, I know a lot about marriage."

The brows disappeared behind Miss Sullen's bangs. "You sure sound like you do."

"Well, I've studied it for years. I speak at women's conferences about it and teach it to a women's Sunday school class. Have for years." Instantly her jaw locked again. Her cheeks flushed. The gush of boldness ebbed, like water circling a drain. She heard its sickening slurp.

"So," the woman said, "you're like an expert."

"Um, sort of." The doubts were piling up faster than last night's snow. She wasn't about to explain that not only did she speak on the subject, she hosted a syndicated radio show devoted to it. And not only that—she had even written a book about it.

"Then you know what this is about."

Jill met the young woman's dark eyes, more somber than sullen, wiser than thirtysome years awarded. Her black cashmere sweater did not quite reach the top of low-rise jeans. Her tall boots were of soft leather. Silver bangles clinked on her wrists; a huge diamond flashed on her left hand.

Jill said, "How do you know?"

"My husband is fifteen years older. We met at the beginning of his crisis."

Crisis.

As in midlife crisis.

On any other day up until this day, Jill would have asked the woman a gazillion questions and taken notes. She must be a gold mine of information. She was the prototype of the Younger Woman whose path crossed the Older Guy's as he bounced around in a confused state of dipping hormones or dying career or diminishing whatever.

But right now Jill was not pulling out her pen and pad. Right now she was imagining Jack grinning at a beauty half his age.

"Then again—" the woman slid her headset over her ears— "maybe he just has the flu." She picked up her book and began reading again.

Jill leaned her head against the seat back and closed her eyes. "Midlife crisis and divorce." She whispered the dreaded words as if tasting a kumquat. Their unfamiliar acidic flavor settled on her tongue. Did she have to get used to it?

Tears stung.

I vote for the flu.

❦

Agonizingly long hours later at the Los Angeles airport, Jill greeted Gretchen MacKelvie curbside with a quick squeeze. "Hi."

"Where's Jack?"

"Home. Flu."

Gretchen held her at arm's length. Taller than Jill's five-two by several inches, she was large-boned with long, wavy brown hair and full lips. "Flu."

"Yes."

Gretchen's left eye narrowed; the other flashed neon green. Her ski-slope nose twitched. She had perfected the matronly glare long before she'd turned forty-two. "What's up with the incomplete sentences, Miss Jaws?"

Jill glared back at her. "It's either flu or midlife crisis. I'm going with flu."

"Jill! What happened?"

"Nothing. Absolutely nothing. He just didn't feel like coming." She shrugged off Gretchen's hands. "Is that your rental? The security guy's heading for it."

"Like I care. Stand still and talk to me."

Ignoring her friend, Jill rolled her luggage hastily toward the car, calling out to the guard. "We're here! We're coming."

"You can't park there, ma'am."

"Got it!"

Nodding, he strode past.

Gretchen muttered to herself, aiming her key ring at the car. "Can't even park for five minutes. Curses on terrorists everywhere." The trunk popped open. Together they loaded the cases. "What do you mean he didn't feel like coming? I just saw him on Sunday. He was looking forward to his vacation."

"Yeah, well, evidently his vacation wasn't this one."

"Is it because of his car accident on Tuesday night?"

"That was no big deal. Few stitches on his head. He put on his Cubs hat and went back to work the next morning. The thing is, he said he . . ." Lockjaw set in again. Jill forced the words through clenched teeth. "He said he wants a divorce."

Gretchen gasped.

Jill slammed the trunk lid shut. "He got sick. Hormones, midlife gear switching, flu, whatever. He'll get better."

"No. Way. You're spinning this, aren't you? You're making it palatable. Next you're going to say God works all things together for good."

"Well, He does. Meanwhile, you and I have our own work to do."

"Jillian Galloway, this is huge. A divorce? Oh, my gosh! Why aren't you bawling your head off?"

"I already did, somewhere over Colorado."

"Malarkey. Your mascara isn't smudged, not even a tiny bit."

"Fixed it over Nevada."

"Oh, Jillie."

"Ladies!" The security guard neared again, making a show of flipping open his ticket pad.

They hurried around to the car doors and climbed inside.

Within moments Gretchen eased the car into the traffic. She sighed heavily. "Don't you ever get tired of squeezing the lemons? We do not need any lemonade, sweetums. Not today."

Jill disagreed. She would have said so, but her jaw was too busy forming itself around a wail.

CHAPTER 2

———— ❧ ————

Jack awoke slowly, like a bear from a long winter's nap, the tickle of spring in his nose.

Or were those icicles forming?

With a groan, Jack rolled onto his back. The bedroom lay in semi-darkness, a sure sign that the afternoon still belonged to the dead of winter. His cold nose reminded him that he had not turned up the thermostat before pulling on sweats and crawling under the covers that morning. Morning? Had it been merely hours ago that exhaustion hit him like a two-by-four?

He glanced at the clock on the nightstand next to Jill's side of the bed. No digital lights glowed.

"Oh, God, what have I done?"

He rubbed his hands over his face. Crusted tear tracks were more prominent than the stubble.

In his entire life, Dr. Jackson Galloway had never been prone to losing it. Too many people counted on his steadiness, his levelheadedness. As an only child, he'd always been there for his parents, more so

11

now as they aged. Then there was his son, his patients, their families, his staff.

His wife.

She would be in L.A. by now, having analyzed the situation ad nauseam and concluded—he would bet his practice on it—that he was in the throes of a midlife crisis. He would soon be pilfering cool clothes from his son's closet, buying a red sports car, and trolling in singles bars for hot babes.

He'd rather eat dirt.

Without a doubt something had snapped inside him. He said words he had not rehearsed, not even imagined. They simply popped out, a horrific announcement to Jill after which he shooed her into the cab. His tears had started before he reached the front door. They continued as he unplugged and removed batteries from every single clock in the house and stopped the living room clock's pendulum.

After a lifetime of diagnosing, Jack just wanted to *not* think for a change. He wanted to put his brain on hold. He had reached the end of some rope that morning. For now, he would follow the age-old prescription to get plenty of rest.

Right after the phone call.

With another groan, Jack flung back the covers and planted his feet on the carpet. He turned on a lamp, picked up his cell, and without checking the time or messages, hit the two and Send.

"Jack!"

"Hi—" He almost added "angel." *Angel?* It was his old pet name for Jill. Ages ago, when he first spotted her across a crowded sidewalk, *angelic* was his impression. She resembled a Raphael-type cherub with blonde curls and rounded cheeks, smiling as if on the brink of erupting with excitement. No wonder he had made it a point to speak to her, a complete stranger. She spoke in return, eyes bluer than the California sky. At the sound of her whispery, musical voice, he was riveted. Her vivacious manner prompted him to ask her to dinner.

"Jack! Talk to me!" The curls were long gone, but not her wired nature.

He pulled on his earlobe. "Hi. Did you get there all right? Is Gretchen with you?"

"Yes and yes. Listen, hon, I understand what you're feeling. Well, as much as a female can anyway. You are going to be absolutely fine—better, even, because of this struggle. We'll work together and get through it. Gretchen and I have been talking. I'll just cancel engagements and be back home Monday night. Then we can—"

"Jill! Stop it. Please." His body felt like a rubber band, stretched to its limit. His fingers and toes tingled. His vocal cords ached. It wasn't the first time he'd experienced the sensation. "What I said this morning, it hasn't changed."

"You can't say such a thing and not discuss it!"

"I just called to check on you. Now I'm saying good-bye."

"Jackson Galloway!" Her voice rose high above its usual pleasantly soft tones. "Talk to me!"

"I don't have anything to say at this time."

"Well, I do!"

"You always do, Jill. You always do. But right now I can't listen to it. I'm sorry."

"And what does that mean?"

He sighed. "Good-bye."

She did not respond.

"Jill, we've always been civil to each other. It's a cornerstone for disagreeing well." Now he was quoting her advice to married people? He rubbed his forehead. "Please, I don't want to hang up on you."

Silence.

"Jill?"

Nothing.

He waited until it became evident that she had hung up on him.

His wife invariably had the last word. *Invariably.* No matter what the subject or situation. She cruised through personal conversations as if she were on the radio, wrapping up an interview or signing off. He'd grown accustomed to the quirk. Now, in its absence, he realized how upset she must be.

"Oh, God, what have I done?"

He closed his phone.

What he had done that morning—without forethought—was to stop denying.

In recent weeks that rubber-band sensation had grown more pronounced, setting his typically calm nerves to crackling. He began to note what prompted it. A pattern developed.

And then he went into denial.

The stress of pretending it wasn't happening intensified the pain, wrenching his nerves from head to toe, until that morning, as he stood at the front door with a travel bag over his shoulder, they snapped, leaving him all but paralyzed.

He had no explanation, no understanding. He knew only that Jill triggered his pain. And now, in her absence, he felt no pain.

Jack sighed again. "I'm sorry, angel. I am so sorry."

He put the phone on the nightstand and padded off to the kitchen, a hungry bear suddenly energized, awash in an inexplicable springlike warmth.

CHAPTER 3

— ❧ —

LOS ANGELES

Breathing was becoming an issue for Jill.

Not an option, she told herself. *Not an option.* In five, four, three, two, one, the live radio interview would begin and for the first time ever, she was not the one asking the questions.

Bouncy praise music faded and the lovely young brunette across the table spoke into her microphone. "It's now six forty-five in the a.m., and here with me in the studio is well-known speaker Jillian Galloway."

As a toddler, Jill had been a breath holder. On several occasions, frustrated at whatever, she had even passed out. Which explained why, when she was seven and pretending to be a mermaid at the bottom of a pool, her father jumped in and yanked her to the surface. Eventually he calmed down and told her about Esther Williams, a famous movie star and swimmer.

The announcer was talking. "You may know Jill from her syndicated program, *Recipes for Marriage.* It's heard on our station Monday, Wednesday, and Friday mornings at nine thirty. Welcome to the West Coast, Jill."

Esther Williams made breath holding a thing of beauty. Jill could

15

do that. She was not a drowning woman in need of oxygen. She was swimming, a mermaid gliding—

"Jill. We're glad to have you here."

She nodded.

"And all the way from Chicago." The announcer smiled.

"Uh, thank you." What was the woman's name? "Kelly! Thank you. I'm glad to be here."

"Folks, this is a big day for Jill. Her first book was recently released. It's called *She Said, He Heard: A Guide to Marital Discourse*. And like her interview show, it's all about healthy communication in marriage." Kelly was a natural on the air. Clad in comfy blue jeans and a T-shirt, she spoke in to-die-for dulcet radio tones. "Right, Jill?"

"Right." She smiled. She could do this. Despite the early morning hour on the heels of a sleepless night on a lumpy mattress in a two-star-billed-as-three hotel, despite *Jack*, she could do this.

"You've been married for twenty-four years?"

"Yes."

"Congratulations. Obviously you have some experience in marital discourse. We are curious, Jill. Tell us, what does a typical day in the Galloway household look like?"

A typical day? Jack's declaration yesterday annihilated *typical*.

On second thought, she could *not* do this.

Gretchen, seated at the end of the table, waved her arms frantically. When Jill looked at her, she touched her Adam's apple and glared. *Talk!*

Jill glared back.

Gretchen mouthed, *Get over it.*

It was what her friend had said last night. After Jill hung up on Jack and finished an ugly crying jag, Gretchen had given an ultimatum. "You know I love you and I don't mean to be all business and harshness, but you have a choice. Invalidate everything you've accomplished and give up all your dreams, or get over it. There's nothing else you can do until Jack is ready to talk. So get over it—not forever, but for this moment in time. For the interview, the lunch, the book signing."

It had sounded like a plan. That was before Kelly's question about typical days.

Kelly was still speaking, filling up what would have become dead air if she had waited for Jill to respond. "You talk and interview guests about communicating in marriage. So what does that look like in real life?"

Jill glanced around the small room. For her, it held all the elements of a security blanket. From the suspended microphones to the computerized control panel that looked like it belonged in the hands of a jet pilot. From the swivel seat to the big headphones that muffled the outside world and honed voices. She was okay.

She said, "What does it look like in real life? Well, some days I just want to slug my husband." She grinned at Kelly's flinch. "Figuratively speaking. I see your wedding band, Kelly. How long have you been married?"

"Four years."

"Bless you, child. You are just getting started. Well, a typical day in the Galloway household is basically twenty-first-century. Jack and I hit the floor running about six in the morning. By seven thirty we're in our separate cars going our separate ways, which is a huge dilemma in today's marriages. If we don't carve out time for each other, we lose touch; we lose that heart-to-heart connection that most likely was the reason we married in the first place. In essence, we lose the reason to stay married."

"How do you and Jack carve out time for each other?"

"In my book, I list the standard fare, such as Date Night. But the point is: how do couples communicate while on Date Night? That's what makes Date Night work for you." Jill jumped into spiel mode. She talked about her book, about what made it distinct from every other marital relationship how-to.

She talked about what she wanted to talk about and she made it through to the final blah, blah, blah of Kelly's wrap-up.

She even made it out of the studio, smiling good-byes, chitchatting with Gretchen all the way to the car, mascara intact.

They got into the car and fell silent.

At last Gretchen spoke. "That went . . . okay. Pretty well, actually.

Kelly looked a little dazed by the end, but hey. You were there to promote your book, not your marriage, which, like everyone's, owns timeshare in a doghouse."

"And visits on occasion."

"Right. You want to get your money's worth."

"Gretchen, when was the last time you and Douglas had a Date Night?"

Her friend blinked slowly. "I don't know. Whenever it was we both happened to be in Chicago at the same time."

"December 22."

"Why on earth would you remember that?"

"Because I study marriages." Even the atypical ones like the MacKelvies', who married after age thirty-five, did not have kids, and traveled to separate destinations most of each month because of their careers. "You were home and he flew in from London, just before Christmas."

Gretchen shrugged. "If you say so."

"And I remember when Nan, Kristy, Cathy, and Phyllis had Date Nights with their husbands because they're all regularly scheduled."

"Have I mentioned that you are really weird?" She started the car. "Let's get some breakfast."

Jill rubbed her breastbone. Breathing hurt again. "The thing is, I can't remember the last time Jack and I had one."

"You might want to keep that bit of information to yourself. How about a Belgian waffle with whipped cream? Carb up and take a nap before the lunch shindig. You could use some rest."

She tuned Gretchen out and wondered when exactly Jack had lost the reason to stay married to her.

❧

The few bites of waffle Jill ate for breakfast only made her stomach hurt. She spent the downtime before the luncheon alone in her room, on the chair in a fetal position, staring out the dirty window at jets approaching the nearby runway.

If Jack were there, they would have been laughing at Gretchen's great hotel deal with its "skyline views" and "classic decor." Wasn't it just the night before last that they had discussed how proud the publicity agent was of her low costs? how in all likelihood they would end up in such a place as this?

Yes, it was just the night before last, Wednesday. She and Jack were packing side by side in their bedroom and she had been looking at the cut on his head. He'd gotten it the evening before when he'd crashed the car. He walked away with only a cut that required a few stitches.

She said, "You probably want a cap to protect that from the sun."

"Got one. Do I need another sweater?"

"Yes. And don't forget flip-flops."

"You think the hotel has scummy showers?"

She chuckled. "It can't be that bad. I'm thinking about eleven days from now when we have our getaway at the beach."

"You're absolutely sure Aunt Gretch won't be joining us?"

"I'm sure."

Jack and Gretchen enjoyed an odd relationship. Maybe *enjoyed* wasn't the right word. Gretchen's driven nature bordered on a pushiness that made him want to shove back. Gretchen loved the sparring. They were like iron sharpening iron, she said. He disagreed. She was a busybody aunt who didn't know when to go home. No, *enjoyed* was not the right word. At least they were open with each other about it.

He gave her his mock-serious pose—tilted head, squinty eyes.

"Jack, she'll be in Phoenix when our vacation starts."

Was that what this was all about? Gretchen?

No. He said the *D* word. That wouldn't have anything to do with her friend no matter how much of a nuisance she could be at times.

That day had been a full one at the office for him. By the time they got around to packing, he was silly tired and in the mood to begin his long-overdue vacation. They'd never taken off for an entire five weeks.

Well, technically they still weren't, but Jill's business wouldn't be 24-7. They would have all kinds of pockets of time for relaxing.

Like right now, this morning. This was to be one of those moments to simply hang together, completely uninterrupted.

Gretchen was independent to a fault as well as a workaholic. She would use these times to be on the phone, probably booking more ugly hotels for other clients, not poking her busybody self into their downtimes. She wasn't on vacation. The Galloways were. She understood that because she was Jill's best friend.

Best girlfriend. Jack was her best friend.

Right?

Then how could she have missed the signs? Surely there had been signs! Midlife crises did not come without signs.

No, there hadn't been any. He was guileless, not at all good at being dishonest. His hazel eyes still sparkled and the laugh creases around his mouth still deepened every time he smiled at her. He was as gentle as ever. If anything, she had been the one to pretend everything was hunky-dory in recent months while she focused more than ever on work.

"Jack." She had sat down on the bed and rolled up his socks as she talked. "I haven't really said how much this trip means to me."

"It's your time to shine, Jillie. First book published. Adoring listeners eager to meet you and become adoring readers. A speaking tour in your home state. I'd say you've arrived."

"That's not what I mean. I'm beyond words grateful for all that, but—"

"Beyond words?" He winked. "Really?"

Yes, he had teased her. Just the night before last.

She smiled. "No, I mean I've been too preoccupied with this whole book business. I've let things slide at home. With Connor. I haven't e-mailed him in over two weeks. But mostly I've let things slide with you. With us."

"Understandable. It was a huge project."

"Well, I'm sorry anyway. And I am happy beyond words that we're taking a vacation."

"Beyond words again?" He sat on the bed and put his arms around her.

Jill imagined his hug now. The rough wool of his favorite old sweater against her cheek. The ever-present faint scent of soap emanating from the doctor obsessed with cleanliness. The slight shudder, as if a chill went through him. The quick release as he stood.

"I'll go down and get the coffee ready." And he was out the door.

To prepare the coffeemaker as he did every evening, as he had already done an hour before.

That shudder was not her imagination. And the tease after her outpouring? She heard now as if with new ears how he had deflected, turning the topic from their relationship, and how she'd let it slide to her work and coffee.

Had he known then that he wasn't going on the trip? that his packing was all for show in order to zing her in the morning?

No. The man without guile did not suddenly develop the art of being devious.

She had to go home. Her so-called time to shine was falling into a black hole.

CHAPTER 4

---- ❧ ----

CHICAGO

Saturday morning Jack pulled his ringing cell from his overcoat pocket and checked the incoming caller ID.

Gretchen, twenty-four hours later than he had predicted.

He let the phone ring as he finished pouring coffee into a travel mug and thought about ignoring it. His heart carried enough of a load, full of Connor. He needed to talk to his son, but he had no idea how to tell him long-distance about a decision he couldn't understand himself.

He glanced at the phone again. Gretchen was with his wife. But still . . .

The woman typified the old spinster aunt who figured she was entitled to meddle in the lives of her extended family. Although not old nor a spinster nor even related, she fit the bill, always dispensing advice that no one sought. Generally speaking, he liked his wife's best friend. The three of them shared a history going back many years. It included holidays and her marriage to a really nice guy.

He gritted his teeth as he answered the phone. "Hello, Aunt Gretch."

"I'm in no mood for your cutesy pet names this morning, Jackson Galloway. What on earth do you think you are doing?"

He tucked the phone between his chin and shoulder and screwed the lid onto his mug. "Is Jill all right?"

"Now what do you think? Huh? Of course she's not all right!"

"Gretchen, I'm sorry. I know my timing is lousy, but it happened and I can't make it *un*happen."

"I could tar and feather you."

"Is she eating and sleeping?"

"Sort of."

"She's a strong woman. Always has been. She'll compartmentalize this difficulty and get through it. We'll address things when she gets home."

"Difficulty? *Difficulty?* Jack, you turned her world upside down and inside out."

"I turned my own upside down and—"

"Just tell me one thing: what is going on? Are you having a midlife crisis?"

Jack smiled sadly and shook his head. "No. Everything about my life is fine, except . . ." Except he was having allergic reactions to his wife. "Except I can't be with Jill right now."

"Oh, that makes absolutely perfect sense." Gretchen's voice dripped sarcasm. "Is there someone else?"

"No, Gretchen, there is no one else and there is nothing else to say."

"Oh, I have a thing or two to say, Galloway. Do you realize you're invalidating everything she's been teaching for the past twelve years? You might as well go on national television and rip pages out of her book and denounce it as so much hogwash." Tears filled her voice and she stopped talking.

Jack felt himself go still. Somewhere in the core of his being, things were shutting down.

He listened to Gretchen sniffle for a moment. Then he said quietly, "Please make sure she eats and don't let her wear high heels all day long. Good-bye."

Silence followed.

Followed by more silence.

She'd hung up on him. That made two for two. With any luck the world would end and then he wouldn't have to talk to any other women about what he'd done.

Fat chance.

❧

Jack entered the hospital's east wing, strode through a first-floor corridor to the set of glass double doors marked The Huffman Medical Group, and entered his home away from home.

Most days, the waiting room greeted him with a veritable welcome-home hug. This was partly due to the passion he felt for his work, partly due to the decor. An interior designer had stripped any semblance of *medical* from the area's ambience. There were lush plants, plush carpet, a large aquarium full of colorful fish, and padded chairs grouped in conversational arrangements. Classical music played softly. Two televisions were on, their volumes permanently at low, no soaps or cartoons allowed. Even the check-in counter could have blended into a private living room. It was long, oak-topped, and no glass separated the business area behind it.

No hug embraced him now. Today wasn't *most days*.

He breezed along the counter, unable to avoid eye contact with Sophie Somerville, the office manager. Ten years ago, when he and fellow podiatrist Gordon Baxter joined the group of orthopedic surgeons, they had brought her with them. A top-notch organizer, she was soon running the place. His partners could easily get along without him, but their lives would fall apart without Sophie.

Nothing got by the thirty-five-year-old. He figured she must have a set of antennae twisted with her dark hair into the bun that always sat at the top of her head. Tireless in her efforts to keep the office running like a finely tuned machine, she was a force to be reckoned with on all fronts. She could have been an Aunt Gretch in the making, if not for her quiet demeanor.

She stood now, eyebrows nearing her hairline. "Dr. G!"

Jack held up a hand and went through the door that led to examining rooms and offices.

Just the other side of it, Sophie leaned over the checkout counter. "What—?"

"I'm not here." He hit the maze of halls at a good clip, a rat that knew its way to the prize.

The prize was his office, a sanctuary in his home away from home. It was a small room with beige walls, hunter green accents, two armchairs. The single window overlooked a parking lot. On one wall hung the requisite paperwork which he hoped comforted patients with its proof that he was licensed. If they didn't like those, they could admire the wide-angle photo of the Chicago skyline that he'd taken early one morning from Baxter's yacht. Sunlight glinted off skyscraper windows.

Jack took off his coat and Cubs ball cap, laid them on a chair, and sat behind his oak desk. It was in vacation mode, cleared except for the lamp and two photos, one of his son, Connor, the other of Jill. He balled his hands into fists, unsure what to do first: put Jill in a drawer or move her book from the bookcase behind him into the trash can?

And why was he having such thoughts?

There was a knock on the door and it swung open. Sophie appeared. "But you are here, Dr. G."

He uncurled his fingers. Usually he smiled at how she stated the obvious, gently calling attention to what others would just as soon ignore. She explained insurance woes to crusty patients in such gentle terms they ended up laughing. Anger over appointment mix-ups evaporated once she got involved. Jack would pause in the hallway to eavesdrop on her just so he had a reason to grin.

At the moment, he did not want to talk to her.

He said, "No, I am not here."

She stepped into the office. "Your cut is bleeding."

"That's why I'm here." He pulled a hankie from his pocket and pressed it against his head. "I called Baxter. He said he'd take a look at it."

"It shouldn't be bleeding. Your accident was days ago." She referred to Tuesday night's minor car mishap. He had braked at a stop sign, slid through the icy intersection, and hit a parked car. "What did you do to it?"

He shrugged and lowered his hand. "Shampooed a little too vigorously, I guess."

Sophie winced and slid into the chair on the other side of the desk. "How do you shampoo off eight stitches?"

"Beats me."

Taller than average, she was a slip of a thing, bony even. Never married, she lived with her widowed mother and two cats. Although she occasionally joined Jack and Baxter for lunches or dinners, she always maintained a certain distance, old-fashioned to the core in work ethics. He'd given up on getting her to call him Jack.

Her close-set eyes above a narrow nose zeroed in on him. "Dr. Baxter is with patients."

"I'll wait."

"Did you see how many are out there?"

He searched his memory but saw only Jill's pouty face. *"Men are not wired to notice,"* she had informed often enough for him to have the words memorized. *"But you can train yourself to see the details better."* Evidently his progress was not all that great.

"No, I didn't see how many are out there."

"The waiting room is half-full, three-fourths of them for Dr. Baxter."

Six doctors, two physicians' assistants, and several nurses were on staff. They rotated on weekends, but there were always plenty available to cover. He and Baxter seldom stepped in for the other doctors, keeping to their own specialty of feet. "Three-fourths for him? How did that happen?"

"It's Saturday, and the temperature is supposed to go above freezing for the first time in three weeks. February spring fever." She cocked her head. "And it's Valentine's Day. Most of the staff found other things to do."

Valentine's Day? He cringed. There had been a hole in Jill's itinerary today. His plan was to fill it with a surprise garden tour at the Getty Museum.

"Dr. G, why are you here? in Chicago? You should be in California."

"Uh." Not expecting to see Sophie in the office, he had not yet rehearsed his reply.

They'd worked together since he and Baxter hired her full-time when she graduated from college. She had seemed all grown-up at twenty-two, a little quirky in some ways. She had excellent people skills but seldom revealed deeply personal information.

Which was fine with Jill. She maintained that such personal openness would have been unprofessional. After all his years with Sophie, Jill kept her at arm's length. Although she was nice enough to her, he suspected she felt threatened by the younger woman mature beyond her years. Why else did she balk at including her on those rare occasions when they entertained his partners and their spouses in their home? Why else did she refuse to invite her and her mother over for holiday dinners?

He chalked it up to the obvious—that he spent more hours a day in close proximity to Sophie than to his wife. Besides that, Sophie was a gem at keeping his life in order, something Jill believed was his own responsibility. She could have her agent and a personal assistant at the radio station keeping her on track, but when it came to his—

"Dr. G?"

"Uh," he said again. "Uh, why am I here? Just a change of plans. Jill went on ahead. She had all that business stuff to do before the family stuff. Doesn't need me out there, getting in the way."

"Mm-hmm."

"And what are you doing here on a Saturday?"

"Filling in."

"Sophie, I wish you wouldn't let that happen. This is your day off."

"It's honestly not a problem for me. And I took yesterday off." She stood and tugged her pink turtleneck over black slacks. At least she'd gone casual and not worn her typical business suit. "I'll see if I can squeeze in an appointment for you."

"Preferably before I bleed to death."

She smiled, a brief lift of lips most often pressed together. "It's not that bad."

"Tell you what. Get me in next with Baxter and I'll stick around."

"You're on vacation."

He shrugged. "Obviously not yet."

"Okay. Whatever you say, Dr. G." She shut the door on her way out.

"Whatever you say, Dr. G." That response was probably what he liked most about Sophie.

❧

"You weren't even supposed to get it wet yet, idiot." Gordon Baxter loomed over Jack, who lay prostrate on the table. He waggled scissors and tweezers close to Jack's face. "I gotta take out what's left of the eight and put them all back in."

"Understood."

"Sure you don't want to go back to the ER? You know I'm not the best at this. There could be twice as many stitches before I'm done. And we're talking huge scar for sure. Wrigley Field size. No hair is gonna grow back."

"Just do it, Bax."

"We'll wait longer, make sure it's numb." He sat on a stool, the light behind him outlining his salt-and-pepper short-cropped curls. For a big guy with a gruff baritone voice, he exhibited the best of bedside manners. "So what happened? And I'm not talking about an overzealous shampooing."

Jack looked at his friend. They first met over twenty years ago in podiatry school. Their paths kept crossing until they eventually opened a practice together. They discussed everything. Baxter did not think God existed; he spoke disrespectfully of his ex-wife; he was not involved in the lives of his twin girls, now seniors at the U of I. But he had always accepted Jack unconditionally and was, hands down, the best doctor Jack had ever met.

He took a deep breath. "I told Jill I want a divorce. Two minutes later, I put her in a cab that took her to the airport. We've talked once since."

Baxter twisted his mouth to one side and then the other. "The numbing agent's gone to your brain. You seem to be talking nonsense."

"Guess that means you can get at it, Doc."

"Right." Baxter stood. "You up for dinner?"

Jack heard the underlying question: *You ready to discuss it?* Not really, but it was probably the smart thing to do. On the short list of men he trusted, Baxter was at the top. "Sure."

CHAPTER 5

———— ❧ ————

Sunday morning Jill rode in silence next to Gretchen. After nearly twenty-five years of friendship with the woman, she should've figured out how to win an argument.

It always came down to their personalities. There was type A, and then there was type A with a kick. Jill's driven nature wilted in the breeze of Gretchen going at full tilt, doing what she decided was best for everyone.

"Jill." Gretchen glanced at her from the driver's seat. "You know how sometimes when you're focused, your lips get all wrinkly? Well, that's not what they're doing."

Jill yanked down the visor, opened its mirror, and saw deep grooves in her face. Crevices from the edges of her lips to the bottom of her chin.

Gretchen said, "You're furious. Got it. But you might want to rethink the pinched, clenched expression for now. Bring it out later, like when you're alone in your hotel room."

Jill pressed her cheeks back toward her ears. Her mouth smoothed out. "I'm nervous."

31

"Not as much as you are mad. Admit it, Jill. Get it out before I start quoting Scripture or your own book, that stuff about the sun going down on one's anger being a major thing to avoid."

Jill snapped the visor shut. "Oh, be quiet."

"I miss my lovable friend."

"How's this?" Jill bared her teeth. "I'm smiling."

"Trust me. This is for your own good."

"Please stop saying that. I should be on a plane, not speaking to another group. Not signing another book. Not giving another interview."

"You're doing great. The women love you."

Jill stared at her. "At this point, do you think that really matters to me? That strangers think they love me? My husband won't answer my phone calls. He forgot Valentine's Day yesterday, probably not a huge deal to some women, but Jack always, always surprises me on that day. Come to think of it, I guess he outdid himself this time, didn't he? Even gave it to me early." Her voice rose. "Gretchen, he's in the middle of a crisis, thousands of miles away. He needs me. I cannot believe I am still following you around L.A."

"You're not. I'm dragging you." She sighed. "Think of Jack's crisis as a pothole in his Guy Road. He's tripped over it and fallen flat on his face. He's dazed and confused. Because he's a guy, this is a big deal. He can't ask his wife for help. It's against Man Rules."

"Jack always stops and asks for directions. He calls a doctor when he's sick. He notices a basket of laundry and carries it upstairs."

Gretchen waved her hand in dismissal. "I admit, Jack is an oddball when it comes to Man Rules. But this is different."

"I should be on a plane."

"Like I already said a few hundred times, we'll work on tweaking the schedule tomorrow when everyone is back at their desks. For now . . ." She pointed at Jill's window. "Look at that."

In the distance, a steeple rose out of the morning mist, a white cross on its top.

"Jill, this is why I've kept you going. Okay? This. You're *there*, sweetums. You've made it to the top of your dream hill."

She gazed at the symbols that had so long energized her work. The cross was all about her faith, the steeple all about a well-known church where she could hardly imagine she'd been invited to speak of that faith. She was indeed at the top of her dream hill, that thing Jack and Jill were supposed to climb together.

Gratitude and disappointment tumbled through her, a surefire recipe for disaster.

⁂

Gretchen parked the car and grinned. "Welcome to Hope on the Coast, apex of twenty-first-century Christendom in America." She chuckled. "Hills don't get any higher than this one, huh?"

Jill pressed at the base of her throat where her breath seemed to be stuck.

The church had something like a gazillion members. Its outreach programs fed, clothed, sheltered, and provided rides to countless homeless, sick, poor, and seniors weekly. It had a school, pre-K through college. The pastor and an associate pastor were quoted worldwide as some of the day's best minds on the Bible. The biggest names in Christian music either had roots in the church or hung out with the choir.

Gretchen grabbed Jill's arm. "It's time to compartmentalize. Put Jack in a back room and shut the door. Okay?"

She nodded.

"Breathe. Smile. I said breathe."

Jill shut her eyes. *God, help me, help me, help me.*

They walked across the huge lot. Scents of eucalyptus and sea salt mingled and filled the cool morning air. People strolled and chatted. The ocean lay off in the distance. From photos she had seen, she knew it would be visible once the fog lifted.

Jill felt dazed. This was one hill she had never set out to climb. Then her work evolved, one thing led to another, and the what-if dreams began. Hope on the Coast? Maybe. Someday. Why not? Gretchen, the quintessential type A, made contact. And now here she was.

Jill stepped through the bank of glass doors and into a foyer that stretched out of sight. On an easel where every eye could see sat an enormous poster board. Plastered on it were Jill's photo and information about her speaking that morning to a women's Sunday school class.

Right there, in that church with a foyer as big as all outdoors.

Gretchen pinched her arm. "Yes, you really are awake."

Jill's entire face softened into a smile and she knew the grooves had smoothed away. "Thank you for getting me here."

"Not my doing. That was all God."

Yes, it was all God. Her faithful, loving, all-powerful God. "Why would He give this to me?"

"Simply because He loves you?"

"All I do is talk to people and write down what I learn from them."

Gretchen leaned in close to Jill. Her left eye narrowed; the right one flashed neon green. "I have one down-to-earth note."

"Only one?"

"Ha-ha. Listen up. You and I are impressed because this is a super big deal to be invited here. The glitter factor is sky-high. But remember, Jill: God works through regular human beings, and everyone in this place is a regular human being just like you and me. Okay?"

"Okay."

"But you do fit in nicely with that gorgeous suit."

Jill touched the short silk jacket, glad she'd chosen the orchid one, her best color. "Thanks."

"So no ecstatic squealing, okay? You are not meeting George Clooney."

"Okay, got it." She winked. "What do we do if people squeal ecstatically at me?"

Gretchen raised her head and chuckled. "You're going to be impossible to live with after this."

Jill's eyes stung and she turned away, blinking rapidly. She smiled at

SALLY JOHN

a stranger and felt the weight of disappointment again. Jack should have been there with her at the top of the hill. He should have been there.

❧

Jill managed to avoid squealing as she met people at Hope on the Coast. She shook hands with authors of books she'd read and reread, even of two people she had interviewed by phone. She replied in a lucid manner to a well-known singer's hello. She did not faint dead away as she was invited up to the podium during the main service to be introduced.

Her head agreed that her reaction to the glitter factor was silly, but the rest of her was tickled pink. She could have simply basked in the environment and not said a word all morning long.

But they had asked her to speak to a women's class.

Somehow in that classroom, though, between coffee, music, prayer, and introduction, the program had skated from speaking into answering questions.

Personal questions.

They were written on index cards, a thick stack of them in the hands of the teacher, Danielle. She and Jill stood on a slightly raised platform at separate podiums as if they were having a debate. At least a hundred women sat at round tables, their faces awash in sunlight streaming through large windows at one side of the room.

Danielle looked at a card. "Okay, here's one I'm sure we're all curious about." The woman was totally California coast with long blonde hair, a surfer's toned body, and a toothy smile. She could have been anywhere between twenty-five and forty-five. "What does Jackson Galloway look like?"

Jill blinked. What did that have to do with anything? "What does he *look* like?"

"Yes. You often talk about him and you've written so much in your book about him. Like they say, a picture is worth a thousand words." She held up *She Said, He Heard*, Jill's photo on its back cover facing out.

35

"We had hoped to meet him, but since he's not here—" she shrugged—"imagining what he looks like helps bring your dialogues with him to life."

"Those dialogues are samples of what any couple might engage in. Jack just looks like an average Midwesterner."

"Define 'average Midwesterner.'"

From the corner of her eye, Jill saw Gretchen stand up about halfway back, near one of the windows.

Her friend cupped a hand at her mouth and called out, "He's way cute."

Women chuckled and Jill's cheeks felt hot.

Danielle grinned. "From someone who knows him. So, Jill, cute as in 'hunk' or as in 'farm boy'?"

The heat spread to Jill's neck. "Cute as in pleasant-looking with light brown hair and hazel eyes. Laugh creases. Five-eleven. Trim." Except for the two new inches at his waist since he'd added baking to his gourmet-cooking hobby. But that didn't seem any of their business.

"Somewhere in between, then. All right. Tell us, how did you two meet? He's a Midwesterner, but you're a California native, correct?"

"Yes, I grew up in Sweetwater Springs." She named her hometown, a small place out in the desert that Angelinos liked to visit in winter. "We met in Hollywood, at Grauman's Theatre. Uh, I mean Mann's."

"Really?" Danielle's eyes sparkled. "Love at first sight and you moved all the way to Chicago?"

"Something like that." Jill used up every last ounce of self-control to lift the corners of her mouth. "Danielle, I'd hoped to talk about the book, about ways to improve our communication skills with husbands and significant others. I—"

"But this is so much more fun!" Danielle looked out at the audience. "Isn't it, ladies?"

The group applauded enthusiastically.

Too enthusiastically. Too ecstatically.

Danielle said, "We can get all that technical information from your book. I've read my advance copy and I highly recommend it. I'm sure many others here will read it. They'll glean from your insights, and believe me, they will apply them. But they'll crave more personal information. You don't have nearly enough for my satisfaction. And you know what?"

Jill shook her head. *No idea.*

"Today, Jillian Galloway, we have you right here with us, in the flesh." With wide eyes and a pleased-as-punch tone, she went on to sing Jill's praises.

Praises to Jill.

Jill, a regular human being.

As if glitter surrounded her.

Meanwhile, her husband was back at home, considering a divorce.

The second hand on the wall clock jerked forward at half speed and the bizarre interview continued. Replying to questions that Danielle read from the index cards and made up impromptu was like tottering on a balance beam. To keep her focus, Jill held her breath. She drank water. She homed in on Gretchen. She fiddled with a button on her jacket, resisting the desire to rub her chest, which burned like it had on the plane, as if words piled up inside of her, trying to find a way out.

Those words had nothing to do with her wedding twenty-four and a half years ago, her son, Connor, Jack's work in podiatry, or what she watched on television.

Danielle flipped through several index cards. "Time is running short. It has been so great having you here, Jill. . . ." She paused at one full of small print, front and back. "Here's a situation: 'On your radio program an expert said that sometimes we get blindsided in a relationship. You said that was impossible if we stay open. My husband and I stayed open for sixteen years, through thick and thin.'" Danielle turned the card over. "'Last week he moved out. No warning. No explanation. So why don't you just—?'" Danielle cleared her throat and looked up. "Obviously this woman is in a great deal of pain. Dear, whoever you are, I hope that you'll talk to one of our counselors here. They—"

"Why don't I just what?" The words burning in Jill's chest jumped into complete sentences and found their way out. "Why don't I just keep my big mouth shut? Great advice. I totally agree." She looked out over the women, trying to find Gretchen, but saw only wavy lines as if the air itself churned as much as she did. "Four days ago I would have said we can't stop the birds from flying over our heads, but we can most certainly prevent them from building a nest in our hair."

"Jill—"

"I would have said, honey, if you'd kept your eyes and ears open, if you'd dotted all your i's and crossed all your t's, then you would not be in this predicament." Her voice rose into tremor territory. "If you'd taken ownership of your relationship, he wouldn't have left. He couldn't have. He would have had no reason to. But now?" She paused, caught a breath, and lowered her voice. "Now I say that's a bunch of cow manure. Pardon my French. And I am truly sorry for feeding you such false hope."

The women's faces still floated before her. She heard their heavy silence.

She turned and tried to bring Danielle into focus.

"Jill, I'm sure you'll agree there is always hope when we invite God into a situation. I do apologize for not censoring that card. In this class we are all about being real and this dear woman is—"

"Being real? Try this one on for being real, Danielle: the way-cute Midwesterner wants a divorce." She blew out a breath. How was it that she hadn't told anyone close to her except Gretchen and now she could announce it to the world?

A speechless Danielle stared, her mouth half-open.

"It's true. After all I've done, the birds have built a nest in my hair. You might want to reconsider recommending that book." Anger engulfed her, an onslaught of rage that nauseated her. She had to get out of there.

Gretchen touched her elbow.

Jill grabbed her friend's hand and stumbled along beside her, down from the platform, down from the top of the hill.

CHAPTER 6

———— ❧ ————

Sunday morning Jack sat in his basement nook, a home office Jill had created for him, a space located between the laundry and family rooms. He rarely worked in it, really didn't need it, but had grown to appreciate it.

From her undying determination to do things correctly—*"A doctor should have his own professional space in the house, not a corner in the dining room!"*—came a place of solitude. In recent months he had rediscovered that aspect and sought it out often. With Connor seldom at home, the dryer thumped only occasionally and there were no male teen voices booming around the pool table or at video games.

Jack stared at the e-mail on his laptop, reading it for the umpteenth time since he'd first seen it on Thursday, the day Jill left. It was from their son, copied to both his and Jill's addresses.

Hey, Mom and Dad. Well, you're probably in sunny SoCal by now. Just wanted to let you know Prof Isola is taking us to Prague. I've told you what a fanatic she is. Free time? E-mail? Phone calls? Not on my watch! So I'm OOT for about ten days. Later.

"OOT" was Connor's shorthand for "out of touch," a phrase he made frequent use of. Jack figured it was code for "love you guys, but hey, I'm twenty-three, in Europe, got better things to do than chitchat."

Jack smiled. Connor was all Jack could ever hope for in a son. He was a great kid, a good human being, never a source of grief or despair. A graduate of the University of Illinois, he was now studying in Italy for his master's in art history. What did it matter he would never make a dime working in a museum? So what if most of his study time now meant touring Europe and discussing art in every café from Paris to Prague?

His smile faded. Like Jack, Connor was an only child and close to his parents. As it did for Jack, the word *close* meant taking on too much responsibility for their well-being. Divorce would hit him hard.

Jack moved the cursor over the Reply tab and hesitated. Tell him in an e-mail? Pretend all was well? Just a quick "luvya"?

He shook his head and signed off. Connor's schedule had granted him a reprieve.

❧

Not up to a public airing of his dirty laundry, Jack felt no qualms about skipping church. His solo presence would have provoked questions. Jill's Sunday school women would have bombarded him for answers he did not have.

He opted instead for a private airing. His parents lived at an assisted-care facility in a neighboring suburb, a short drive.

"Jackson, dear." Katherine Galloway stretched across the couch and laid a shaky hand on his head. "You can brush your hair over and people will hardly notice this horrid laceration."

Jack smiled at her attempts to finger-comb his hair. "It's too short."

"Oh, it's long enough. What is this? Silver?" She yanked out a strand.

"Ouch!"

"Good grief, Kate." Charles spoke from the padded rocker. "Our son is old enough to have gray hairs."

"He is not. He's only forty-five. No, that's not right. Forty-six."

"And how old was I when I went completely bald? Hm? Forty-two."

"You were not."

Jack tuned out his parents. He'd given up refereeing them soon after they moved into this small apartment. Their forced togetherness escalated a nitpicking hobby into a full-time activity.

Was that why he wanted a divorce? Because he did not want to end up bickering with Jill, day in and day out?

But he and Jill never nitpicked. They liked each other.

Didn't they?

"Jack." His bald father set the rocker in motion. "Weren't you supposed to go somewhere?"

Good news, bad news. One of them remembered the plan he'd informed them of last week. "Yes. I was going to go with Jill to California for her book tour. But here I am, considering a divorce instead."

They gazed at him, two sets of uncomprehending, rheumy eyes.

"I thought you should know."

Even if they had not recalled his schedule, Jack would have told them. In spite of their failing health, Charles and Katherine remained his first line of offense and defense. They had provided a stable, privileged life for him. The three of them had honestly enjoyed his growing-up years. Although his mother had snooty tendencies, she and his dad were always fair and open with him. Their list of ultimate taboos was short: do not live with a girl before marriage and do not loan money.

Naturally he had committed both crimes during college and not shared that information with them. The girlfriend living arrangement was a semester thing when he was an undergrad. The money was a large sum, never repaid, to a friend in med school. Jack recovered from both, no worse for wear really. Why upset his parents? The past was the past.

And besides, his self-imposed responsibility to keep them happy dictated that he keep his mouth shut.

A choice he did not now have the privilege of making. They would notice Jill's absence eventually.

Katherine pursed her lips. "Jackson, dear, Galloways do not divorce. No matter what she's done, you make it work."

Jack expected that. His mom had never wholeheartedly approved of Jill. "Mother, she hasn't 'done' anything. It's not like that."

His dad put his elbows on his knees. "What'd *you* do?"

"Nothing."

"Jackson." Katherine squeezed his arm. The morning sunlight shone in her neatly curled, stiff hair, casting shades of blue. "There is no such thing as a midlife crisis."

He couldn't help but smile at how his mother's conclusion mirrored Jill's. "Well, there is evidence for it, but I feel fine. There's no crisis in my life. There's nothing I need or want except not to live with Jill anymore. I want the best for her, wish her all the success in the world. But I'd rather not be with her."

His dad nodded. "I felt like that on occasion. Not about Jill. About—"

"Oh, Charles. You did not."

"I did, Kate. I most certainly did."

Now he and his mom stared at his dad.

"Each time, I had a good stiff drink and it went away." Charles chuckled. "You'll get over it, Son. Odd feelings and daydreams are just part of life. You don't want to start messing with wills and trust funds and dividing up property and bank accounts." That was his dad, the former bank president, speaking.

His mom said, "Perhaps this separate vacation time will help. Now before we go down to the church service, tell me about my grandson. He sent us a postcard last week."

"Kate, it was this week."

"No, I distinctly remember. What is today?"

"Sunday. Which explains why we're going to church."

Jack went deaf again. *Good grief.* Was their entire relationship built on disagreement? Granted it was always civilized, no shouting or throwing things, no swearing or crying. But he remembered plenty of stomachaches as a kid. Jill had been the one to finally help him see that it was not his job to keep the peace between his parents.

And yet . . . he had kept the peace in his own marriage, hadn't he? He had kept it by sticking to a promise he'd made to himself as a teenager: he would never relate to his wife like Charles and Katherine did to each other.

Which basically meant that the first time he knowingly introduced conflict into his marriage was three days ago.

❧

Jack went with his parents to the church service held in the common room. He ate lunch with them in the dining room and said his good-byes before their naptime.

Now he sat in his car, warmed by bright sunshine streaming through the windows and glinting off the snow piled around the parking lot, and debriefed himself.

There had been no further mention of his situation with Jill until they parted, and then it was only cursory.

His mother had held his chin in her hand, looked him straight in the eye, and said, "Make it work." Then she kissed him on the cheek.

His father hugged him and suggested the brand name of a good Scotch.

Jack had not expected or wanted more from them. He just wanted to keep them in the loop. He owed them that much.

What took him by surprise was his intense reaction to their bickering. It hadn't affected him for years. He heard it, of course, but no longer internalized it.

He pressed on his stomach. The ham and scalloped potatoes were not setting so well. He knew better than to have eaten two helpings of the cafeteria food.

His thoughts turned again to Connor. Imagining how he himself would have felt to be told on the telephone that his parents were splitting, he cringed at the thought of putting his son through that.

Could it wait until May, when he was due home?

Where would Jack be in May? Single?

Obviously they could not tell Connor after the fact.

Jack glanced at his watch. If he correctly recalled Jill's itinerary, she was at that very moment speaking to a women's group at a megachurch. She would not be answering her phone.

Perfect timing for a coward.

He pulled out his cell and hit the speed dial. "Hi. Uh, I assume you got Connor's e-mail? About being out of touch? I'm just wondering how to, uh, tell him about, um, us." He took a breath. "About what I've done. It just seems that we shouldn't tell him long-distance. Do you mind if we hold off? He's busy anyway. And he thinks we're busy. I hate to not answer his e-mails or a call. Not that he calls all that much."

Jack heard his incoherent rambling and paused to order his thoughts. "Let me think on this for a week, okay? Or tell me if you have a better idea." Like she wouldn't. "I hope things are going well. I'm sure the women there at that big church think you're the cat's meow." He rolled his eyes. *Lame.* "Be safe. And take off those heels."

Jack closed the phone and sighed. He should have skipped the inside joke.

But how did one start skipping inside jokes with a close friend of twenty-five years?

Probably as slickly as he'd skipped mentioning the past seventy-two hours. Grocery shopping, cooking a new recipe for salmon, getting upset enough to inadvertently scrub open the gash on his head, working on a Saturday with Baxter, visiting his parents . . .

He'd always told her the minutest details.

Except . . . except about the accident that totaled his car. There were a few particulars that seemed irrelevant at the time. Or something.

He shook his head and started Jill's car, cracked open a window to air out the scent of her perfume, and mentally put *car shopping* on the agenda.

⁂

Later that evening Jack picked up his ringing cell from the kitchen counter, saw Gretchen's number, and stirred the risotto in the saucepan.

He had spent most of his life answering telephones and pagers at inconvenient times. His service would call when he was off duty because even patients with nonemergency foot problems needed his attention. He was always on duty for his aging parents. Ditto for Connor, of course. Typically Jill phoned him several times a day.

He had never minded. Being available was a doctor's way of life. But Gretchen, two days in a row? Overkill.

The phone's doorbell chime ring continued.

He sighed, set down the wooden spoon, and put the lid on the pan. She was calling because Jill wasn't. Had Jill listened to his voice mail? "Hello."

"We're in the middle of a crisis here."

"It's my fault. Blame me."

"No question about that." Gretchen exhaled loudly. "Jack, she lost it today. Totally and irrevocably."

He turned off the stove. Today was Jill's big day, the most important one in her schedule, the one she'd been giddy about for months. That big church, Coast something or other, was a feather in her cap. "I already said it's my fault. What else do you want from me?"

"Your help."

"Gretch, you two do just fine without me. You always have. Please, I don't want to be involved."

"She was talking at that big kahuna of a church to maybe a hundred women and she announced that you want a divorce."

He closed his eyes. *Dear Lord, I'm sorry.*

"Tell me, Jack, how am I supposed to fix it? Huh? With one little sentence she blew every speck of her credibility to smithereens."

"How is she?"

"Galloway, give me a break. She's a mess. I've never seen her so furious. She—"

"What is she doing right now?"

"What do you think?"

"Working out in the hotel's fitness center." At least that was his hope.

"Yes."

"Then she's okay. She's handling it. If she were comatose in a corner and not eating, then we might want to consider—"

"Oh, stop being a doctor for one minute and be her husband!"

At Gretchen's high-pitched voice, he held the phone out from his ear.

"It hasn't hit her yet that her future is over! She ended it today."

"That's ridiculous. She knows how to interview. She knows everything there is to know about communication skills. None of that involves me or—or us."

"Where have you been for the past twenty years, Jack? That's the whole premise of her work! You two communicate and you make marriage work. You know the secret of keeping each other happy."

"Now that is totally ridiculous. Nobody makes someone else happy or sad."

"Then why have you left her? Huh? Because you are not happy with the status quo, which is being married to her. Living with her. Dialoguing with her."

"You can't reduce my decision to that."

"Whatever. I don't know how much longer she can keep up this charade. She may not have to. Once the gossip gets going, people are either going to cancel her appearances or gawk at her like she's a circus freak and want to ask questions like 'What all can you do with that third arm?'"

"Gretchen, you're being absurd."

"Just trying to catch up with you. And oh, by the way, you will always be involved. She's your wife and no papers will ever change that fact. Good-bye."

The line went silent.

He slid onto a stool, laid his phone on the countertop, and crossed his arms.

"You two communicate and you make marriage work."

It was true that he and Jill thrived on talking about everything under the sun. But was that the same as communicating?

People always commented on how well Jack and Jill got along. They noted that their many years together were an anomaly. But was that the same as making marriage work?

Given the present circumstances, he'd have to answer both questions with a no.

CHAPTER 7

———— ✤ ————

Given the speed of the treadmill and the time spent on it, Jill figured she had jogged to Omaha. She should reach Chicago by midnight. Who needed a plane?

The hotel fitness center was empty. No surprise. It was small, smelly, and state-of-the-art 1982. She wouldn't be there if her choices had been anything but lose her mind or get on a treadmill.

She wiped her brow with a damp towel and kept going, elbows pumping. The room blurred from view, replaced by her reflection in the large dark windows. Correction. The reflection of herself as an overweight twelve-year-old.

Techno blasted through her earbuds, the wild music compliments of Connor, who liked to leave surprises for her on her iPod.

Connor.

What was this going to do to him? Oh, it was too awful to think about. Did he even have to know? It wasn't like she and Jack were sitting down with a counselor yet. Things had not progressed beyond Jack's *"I want a divorce"* statement. Which could be construed simply as an opening to a new dialogue. Why bring Connor into an unfinished conversation? It did not concern him, unless . . . unless . . .

Well, she was not going to imagine *that* outcome.

Still, Jack's voice mail suggestion to avoid Connor over the next week was outrageous. She wasn't about to ignore her son. And if they talked, he would learn of Jack's absence. There was no getting around that. One thing would lead to another and then—

"Mrs. Galloway!"

At the shout and sudden appearance of a woman, Jill jerked and nearly lost her balance. "Oh!" She grabbed one handle and reached for the power button with the other hand. Her hand and legs bounced like an out-of-control marionette's. "Oh!"

"I'm sorry!"

"Oh?" Jill finally connected with the controls and clung tightly as her legs steadied and the belt slowed to a halt.

"Are you all right?"

She wiped her face again and pulled out the earbuds, gasping for breath. The woman came into focus. "Danielle?"

The teacher from Hope on the Coast stood before her, blonde hair pulled back in a ponytail, her toothy smile hesitant. "I'm sorry I startled you."

Jill nodded, still catching her breath. Her mind raced faster than her heart. All the shame and distress of the morning hit her like a freight train.

Danielle said, "I called Gretchen. She said I could come to the hotel. Do you want some water?"

Still mute, Jill nodded again and stumbled to the bench where she'd laid her things. She sat heavily and opened her water bottle.

"Mrs. Gal—"

"Jill."

"Jill." The woman sat beside her.

Up close to the teacher, without a hundred pairs of audience eyes watching her, Jill studied the athletic, healthy face. There were more crow's-feet than she remembered. The woman was nearer forty than twenty-five.

"Jill, I want to apologize. I—"

"I'm the one who needs to apologize."

"You already did. This morning."

"I did?"

"Yes."

"It wasn't Gretchen?"

"She did, but so did you."

"I can't remember much except that I came unglued and said some horrid things."

"I goaded you."

"Trust me. I was on the verge of jumping off the cliff when I walked into your church. The earth was already giving way before we met. Goading didn't push me—"

Danielle grasped her wrist. "I goaded you and I am so very, very sorry."

Jill met the intense gaze of emerald green and realized the woman felt almost as bad as she did. "You were doing what you thought best for your audience. I do it all the time on the radio. Except I prefer to call it *prompting*, not *goading*. I *prompt* people to dig deep."

"I had an agenda."

"Same thing."

Danielle shook her head. "I told Gretchen and now I'm telling you. My ladies promised not to talk about your meltdown."

Jill's laugh came out a strangled noise. "But it's so juicy! I mean, granted, I'm not known like half the people in your congregation are. Still, though, it seems worthy dirt to dish out. 'Marriage expert's marriage falls apart.' That's way too rich to pass up."

"All right." Danielle squeezed Jill's wrist and let go. "Some of them will elaborate to outsiders, but most of them won't. After you left, we talked about what our respectful response should be. Someone even suggested that we call our class hotline if we feel an irresistible urge to gossip. At least that would keep it in-house."

"I appreciate that. I don't know that it matters. I can't continue with other engagements, pretending that I have a healthy marriage."

"You don't have to. Talk about what you know, like about your recipes that give insight. Just leave out the guarantee."

Ashamed all over again, Jill pressed the towel to her face. It wasn't that she'd brutally shared her pain with a hundred strangers. It was the ridiculous guarantee she had offered up for years and years as if God Himself were speaking. *"Do it this way, and that will happen."* How could she have been so amazingly presumptive as to put God in a box like that?

"Jill, I believe in you, in what you're doing. Please don't give up."

Jill lowered the towel, looked at her, and shrugged. A thank-you stayed stuck in her throat.

Danielle said, "About that agenda I mentioned."

"Prompting."

"Not exactly." Her eyes filled. "You know the last index card I read, the one that put you over?"

Yes, she knew it literally. The words had branded themselves into her memory. *"On your radio program an expert said that sometimes we get blindsided in a relationship. You said that was impossible if we stay open. My husband and I stayed open for sixteen years, through thick and thin. Last week he moved out. No warning. No explanation."*

"What about it?"

"I wrote it." Tears spilled over and down Danielle's face.

"You . . . you made it up? To prompt me?"

She shook her head and the ponytail swung about.

"Oh. Oh, my." The truth dawned. Danielle had not made it up. She was traveling the same nightmarish road.

"Jill, please keep going. Remind women that the only guarantee we have is that God will never leave us. That He will never, ever give up on us."

Jill could only wrap her in a tight hug. Danielle didn't seem to mind the sweat.

❧

Jill peeked at her wristwatch. Monday, 7 p.m. Pacific Standard Time. Her day of public breath holding neared its final hour and she was still standing. Hallelujah.

Danielle's admonishment the previous night had convinced her to follow the schedule as planned. Gretchen danced a jig but kept her promise and called key people, all of whom were not at work or answering cell phones. "Cupid must have sent out a memo," Gretchen reported. "Evidently Valentine's Day is a three-day weekend this year."

Jill felt the proverbial crush of being between a rock and a hard place. She was booked through next Tuesday. The day after would begin a week off. It was to have been her and Jack's vacation at the beach and the anniversary of the first day they met, twenty-five years ago when their paths crossed in Hollywood. She had hotel and restaurant reservations.

Now what? Should she try to get a ticket for home tomorrow and not bother telling her publisher and all those other people who were expecting her? Or should she leave Jack alone for a week to wallow in the throes of midlife crisis?

"Hey." Gretchen nudged a chair against the back of her knees. "Sit before you keel over."

"I'm fine." She sank onto the padded seat, put her forearms on the table, and ducked behind two stacks of *She Said, He Heard*. By closing one eye, she blocked the huge bookstore from view.

It was a crowded place, people in every aisle and at the coffee shop, but the steady stream toward her had finally ceased. The whole scene felt unreal.

Gretchen sat next to her. "You're doing great, Jillie, just great."

"Can we leave?"

"The manager asked us to stay a little longer. He's ecstatic. Do you have any idea how many books have sold tonight?"

"No."

"I don't either." She chuckled. "But the manager is ready to throw his arms around you. He said he's never seen such a turnout for a first-time author."

"That's all your doing, Ms. PR."

"Well, yeah, I am pretty good with advance work." She grinned. "But that was a cakewalk. You're the one who blazed the trail. Eight years on the radio, syndicated out here for three, interviewing well-known personalities. People know you. Of course they want to meet you in person. Of course they want you to sign their books."

"I'm just a curious, high-strung loudmouth who wanted to put some new handles on some tired old principles and then tell everybody."

"And surprise! You struck a chord with a lot of us. We needed new handles."

"I made up guarantees. I messed with God's teaching."

"You stayed true to it, Jill. You did! Our Sunday school class has prayed forever that you not stray from God's message of love and healing in marriage. We've had you covered through your entire career, sweet-ums, and God is faithful."

Jill leaned toward her friend and lowered her voice to a hiss. "Then why does my husband want a divorce?"

"Oh, Jillie."

"We need a new subtitle. *Want to chase hubby out the door? Try this version of discourse.*"

At the sound of a discreet cough, they both turned. Across the table stood a middle-aged woman. Thankfully she was not close enough to have overheard Jill's anxious whispers in Gretchen's ear.

She smiled at Jill. "Excuse me, are you Mrs. Galloway?"

"Uh, yes."

"Are you still signing books?"

Jill nodded.

Gretchen said, "Yes. Yes, she is."

"That's wonderful! I have a few friends with me." She moved aside. About six women stood in line behind her. They smiled and waved. "We're members of a book club, and since we all listen to you on the radio, we planned to read your book next. Then when we heard you were going to be just an hour from us, we were thrilled. We thought, why not treat ourselves to our own signed copies? So here we are!"

Jill said, "You drove an hour to see me?"

"More like two. Freeway traffic." Her eyes glistened.

Jill knew what was coming. How many women had she seen that day whose eyes glistened with unshed tears? There had been countless at the luncheon where she spoke earlier and several more at this table since five o'clock. Next came the gratitude.

"Thank you, Mrs. Galloway."

"Jill."

"Jill." The stranger smiled. "Thank you for changing my life and my husband's. We'd been married thirty years when I first heard your teaching. Honestly, until then we were not on the same page at all."

Jill stood. Despite her tiredness she had to stand and she would remain standing. Otherwise she would not be able to reach across the table to hug these women who heaped on the affirmation that for the moment was the glue that held her together.

She only hoped that when they heard about her own failed marriage, they would not feel hoodwinked. Maybe, just maybe, they would be as gracious as Danielle and the women in her class.

Maybe, just maybe, Jill was not responsible for infecting marriages with foolishness.

CHAPTER 8

――― ❧ ―――

Jack eyed Baxter over a forkful of porterhouse steak. The toothy smile creasing his friend's boyishly round face signaled something. "What?"

"Apparently your appetite has not been affected by the situation."

"No, it hasn't." Jack ate the bite of meat, grilled to red perfection. Chewing slowly, he evaded the topic they had not yet broached.

The day had been a long one. Flu was making its rounds, leaving the office understaffed. Technically still on vacation, Jack was called in anyway by Baxter. Sophie protested, but Jack figured staying occupied was a good thing at this point. He had missed Valentine's Day, the first time in his married life, and Jill had flaked out on her most important speech, no doubt due to him. He didn't quite know what to do with those facts yet.

Baxter cut into his own steak. "You're feeling all right then? eating and sleeping?"

"Better than I have for some time."

"That's telling."

"I thought so."

57

"It's only been, what? Five days? The euphoria will fade."

"I'm not euphoric. There's plenty of guilt and shame inside, but I am oddly . . . I don't know. At peace. Relieved, I guess, is the word."

"Relieved because she's away? Maybe you only needed a break from her?"

Jack shrugged. "I haven't gone to deciphering it all out yet."

They ate in silence for a moment.

Baxter said, "So where have you gone?"

He rubbed his head.

"Besides to reopening that gash? Leave it alone, bud."

Jack lowered his hand and gripped the knife. "Anger. I've gone to anger. I shampooed in anger. Isn't that the most ridiculous thing you've ever heard?"

"Not even close. What took you there?"

Jack felt hot inside. Avoidance was no longer a choice. "Chapter 7 took me there—Sizzlin' Spinach. I was thinking about last week. There I was, standing in the big bookstore at the mall, reading a description of flickering candles in my bedroom." He shook his head. "It could've been worse. In this day and age she could've gotten away with a whole lot more. Call me a namby-pamby fuddy-duddy, but she didn't have to go that far. This was enough to violate something sacred between us."

"That was quite a speech." Baxter slid his fork into his mouth.

"Yeah. You don't seem surprised."

He shrugged a shoulder and chewed.

"You read the book then?" Jack had given him a copy some weeks ago.

Baxter nodded.

"You didn't say anything."

He swallowed, set down his fork, and took a deep breath. "You and I don't meddle when it comes to the wives. When Stacey and I were in counseling, you listened to me. You pointed out when I was being a jerk, but you never bad-mouthed her. This book business is between you and Jill."

"Right. You mean besides the hundreds of reviewers who have already read it or the thousands who are probably reading it right now?"

"Yeah, besides them."

"You'd be angry too?"

Baxter barked a short laugh. "I blew a gasket with *Easy Eggs: Interacting in Everyday Life*. I could have gone a long time without knowing how you fold your underwear. *Sizzlin' Spinach* is almost grounds for divorce." He paused. "Almost."

"I gave her carte blanche. Years ago when she started teaching about communicating in marriage, I said, 'Use whatever.' If she and I learned something in the way we relate because of the unusual way I fold underwear, I had no problem with her talking about it in her women's Sunday school class."

"And the bedroom stuff?"

"I guess carte blanche means no boundaries in any area." Jack clenched his jaw. "There were about twenty-five women listening to her at the time, most of them over the age of fifty-five."

"How'd it all go from talking to her aging women friends to bookstores across the country?"

"Things evolved. They just rolled from church into other speaking engagements. Then she started writing it all down."

"What about the radio program?"

"Not so much. It's interview and call-in, generally about someone else's work. There are times, though . . ." Jack shook his head. Of course Jill used personal stories on air. "I put it out of my mind, you know? I don't listen to the program much. Once in a while somebody at church makes a coy reference to what she's said about me in the class. It never seemed like a big deal."

"Doesn't your Bible say something about respect being a good thing? Maybe that doesn't apply to married couples. Maybe it's okay for a wife to treat her husband like a gnat. I'm sorry." He held up a hand. "I'm sorry, Jack."

"Of course the Bible speaks to that. I suppose a case could be made for me disrespecting her by not paying attention to her work. Jill's book revealed that there's a disconnect between us."

"Hold on. Are you telling me you had no clue what was in the book until you read it in the store?"

Jack looked everywhere but at his friend's eyes, bugged out in disbelief. "I guess."

"How could that happen?"

"Because she gave me the manuscript and I ignored it. I had helped her with the recipes, but as far as what else was in it . . ." He shrugged. "It was her gig. It was geared for women. I figured I'd misunderstand some part and then I'd upset her by not saying anything or saying something critical."

"Oh, man. You don't pay attention to her and now you're livid because of what she's been doing all along, right under your nose, things which you actually gave her permission to do?"

"It's not quite that simple. There's a disconnect because we're not who we were when we got married. This is not the life I signed up for. We've both changed too much."

"Well, now you're being a jerk. You don't leap from 'We're fine' to 'I want a divorce.'"

His words stung, but Jack figured he deserved them. Still, they did not diminish the sense of relief produced by his leap from "fine" to "divorce." Relief? More like exhilaration. It wasn't right, but it was what it was. He could not go back to the status quo.

He had made an appointment with his attorney. He had made an appointment to see an apartment for rent. He imagined he would keep both.

❧

Getting a car could wait. Housing could not. There were always taxis, but the optimum time for moving out might soon be gone.

He figured Jill might come home during the lull in the schedule.

But after Gretchen's phone call he wondered if she'd wait until then. No way did he want to give her a front-row seat to watch him pack up and walk out the door. Allowing that scenario seemed crueler than what he'd already done.

By Tuesday afternoon he had signed a three-month lease on a furnished, second-story, one-bedroom apartment. He invited Baxter over to see it.

"Furnished?" Baxter wrinkled his nose and did a slow turn on mud-brown carpet in the living room of sparse, mud-brown plaid furniture. "Why not take your time and buy your own new stuff?"

Jack stood at the island that separated the living room and kitchen, unpacking a box. He pulled out his cherry red Le Creuset skillet. "I brought my own pots and pans."

Baxter ducked momentarily through the bedroom doorway. "Did you bring your own clothes?"

"I'll get them later tonight."

His friend sat gingerly on the edge of the couch. "Again, why not take your time?"

"Jill might be coming home sooner than expected."

Baxter's brows rose in question.

"Gretchen called. Things are not going well." Jack removed the last of his favorite kitchen utensils, all of them things Jill did not use nor would she miss. He tossed the empty box toward the door that led out to a hallway.

"Jill's probably pretty upset?"

"Yeah." He put his hands on his hips. "The message I got from Gretchen was that I want out because I'm not happy, which means Jill has nothing to talk about."

Baxter cocked his head. "That's what she talks about? Your happiness? Guess I missed that part in the book."

"It's convoluted. Bottom line, I didn't want her to have to watch me move out."

"You're such a nice guy."

"Yeah. Happy, too."

"You know you could have moved in with me." He chuckled. "For a short time anyway. The swinging bachelor and the churchgoer who actually talks about God now and then. We could have handled a few days together."

Jack smiled. "Thanks anyway. I don't know what's next, Bax. I need some time alone to sort it all out."

"And see your attorney?"

He nodded.

"You seem to be moving pretty fast, bud. I can give you my marriage counselor's number."

"For a swinging bachelor, you're kind of gung ho on me not divorcing."

"The key word is *you*. It wasn't supposed to happen to you." He shrugged. "You guys were different."

That was what they all said.

CHAPTER 9

———— ❧ ————

Vivian Kovich closed her laptop with a decided thump. "Date Night, schpate night. Give me a break, Jill."

"*Schpate?*"

She looked up and saw her nephew Dustin in the doorway to her office. "You heard me. *Schpate.* It's German for 'my sister is goofier than ever.'"

The young man laughed. "Was that her on the radio, the real Jill Galloway?"

"Don't you have somewhere else to be?"

"Not for half an hour."

Viv shook her head. "Yes, that was her. She was interviewed on an L.A. station the other day. I found it in their archives."

Dustin slid into a chair on the other side of her desk. "She's a famous whatever, right?"

"Yep." Famous whatever. Loudmouth, mostly. Viv loved her sister like crazy, but she refused to let that make her delusional.

Dustin pointed at the book on her desk. It lay upside down with Jill's photo on the back cover in full view. "She doesn't look like you."

As always, the camera loved Jill. Her dazzling smile lit up her face like lights on an aluminum Christmas tree. The trendy hairstyle suited her. She resembled their short, blonde mother. Viv took after their dad, rangy with medium brown hair and eyes and a splash of freckles. The same went for their personalities, flighty versus grounded.

"I think she looks much older than you, Aunt Viv."

"Mister, you are not gaining any points with that remark. You've got a twenty-minute drive ahead of you. Old folks are always ready early. And why am I telling you this for the umpteenth time?"

He grinned. Beneath thick curly lashes, his dark chocolate eyes twinkled. The kid was a charmer.

"I swear, Dust, if you were not related—"

"You'd hire me anyway. You know you would."

Yes, she would hire him in a heartbeat. He was an asset to her business, which catered to senior citizens. Totally unflappable with a ready smile, dimpled cheeks, and broad shoulders, he was every elderly person's dream grandson.

"I was like twelve last time I saw your sis." He was also a chatterbox.

"Her visits are infrequent and short. This time will be no different. She and Jack will pop into town and pop right back out."

He cocked his head. "I detect a sour tone. Bad blood between you?"

"Dustin Kovich, you are a nosy little bugger. Go to work."

"Right." With a smile and a wave, he left, probably because he realized he'd pushed her buttons long enough. Docking his pay for lateness had never been a problem for her.

Viv sighed. Young people were a challenge. Not having a child of her own, she had never developed the gift of patience. She enjoyed her many nieces and nephews on her husband's side. Long-distance, she adored Jill's son, Connor. He was a good kid, but when he was little, she'd made a tongue-in-cheek pact with God. She would be a nice person as long as He kept Connor's parents safe. If Jack and Jill's will ever went into effect and she became Connor's guardian, she could easily become a very, very difficult woman.

She walked out to the front office of her small tour agency and watched through the large windows as Dustin drove off in her sunshine yellow van. The lime green lettering on its side caused the usual fluttery catch in her throat. Encircled with palm trees, sun rays, and foamy ocean waves, it read "Vivvie's Tours ~ Adventures for the Young at Heart" along with the phone number, 1-800-VIVVIES.

She had come a long way. She was married to a great guy and had her own small business. Not only was it a hoot, it had just paid for her very own minibus to be delivered next week. Life was good. What did it matter that her sister was married to the sweetest man on earth and had a loving son and owned a big house and had met Oprah and was becoming famous for speaking Christianese? What did it matter that Jill was two hours up the coast and had not called yet and probably would not find time to come by the office? None of that should matter.

But it did. It always did.

❧

Seated in his recliner, feet up, Marty shifted his gaze from the television to Viv, who stood beside it. He said, "Why does it matter?"

"It doesn't." She had just unloaded on her husband all the angst about her sister that had been building since early that morning.

"Sounds like it matters." His eyes strayed toward the screen again. The Lakers game had been muted for her whiny speech but Marty didn't need audio to follow any athletic event. "Block it. Yes! What! What? Foul? Are you kidding me? Foul? Idiotic call, ref! Idiotic." He turned to her. "Viv, you know Jill loves you. She's just different."

"Then you're fine with her and Jack staying here instead of a hotel?"

"Sure."

"For four nights?"

Marty's double take made her smile.

He said, "They never stay that long."

"No. But this trip is a huge deal for them. Besides the book tour, they're celebrating the anniversary of when they met up in Hollywood twenty-five years ago."

"Who celebrates when they *met*?"

"My sister. I think it's partly an excuse to get Jack to join her. It's been more than two years since we've seen him. And they haven't vacationed since I don't know when."

"Jack's a good guy." Marty tucked in his chin and grunted a short *hm*, his announcement that he'd reached a decision. "Sure, four nights is fine with me."

"You're a peach."

His nod swung into a vehement shake at the television. "No way!" He turned the sound back on.

Marty loved his sports almost as much as he loved his work. He built ships, big ones that the Navy bought. He was a welder—one of many, of course, but he spoke of it with such enthusiasm that she almost believed he was responsible for the entire enormous vessel. He looked capable of such a feat with his square frame that remained as rock solid as the day she first saw him.

Like him, she adored her work. Somewhere in between their other passions she and Marty loved each other. It drove her sister crazy how they lived their marriage. Viv knew without reading Jill's book that her and Marty's relationship would not be touted as a model.

"Oh, rats rats rats," she muttered. Had theirs been used as an example of how *not* to do it? She really should read the thing before Jill showed up.

"Vivian." Marty muted the volume again. "Wanna go out for dinner?"

She stared at him, wondering if she heard correctly.

His face unreadable, he stared back at her. He didn't have his nephew Dustin's lashes but the chocolate color of his eyes was the same. It ran in the Kovich family. Marty's were the darkest of everyone's though, probably an 80 percent cacao shade. His hair, still military cut, matched.

He said, "Not Mickey D's. Maybe the Blue Crab down on the harbor."

"Really?"

"Really." Every once in a while, he surprised her like this. "You could wear that black dress."

She smiled. "We'll have ourselves a schpate night."

"A what night?"

Laughing, she turned on her heel. "Give me twenty minutes."

CHAPTER 10

——— ❧ ———

LOS ANGELES

Jill lay on the lumpy hotel bed, curled into a ball, cell phone in hand. She'd spent the past hour in that position, hoping for Jack to call, dreading that he would, vowing not to call him first, and then calling him twice and leaving messages trying not to sound like a basket case and knowing she missed the mark by a long shot.

She tried her sister's number again.

"Hey!" Viv greeted her. The sound of her familiar, strong alto instantly comforted Jill.

"Hey, yourself. You answered."

"I saw your missed calls on my cell. Sorry, I was taking a phone break."

"When was the last time you did that?"

"I have no idea. Marty and I went out. We had a schp—a dinner out. What's wrong?"

Jill moved the phone from her mouth and sighed. This was why she had delayed the call. Viv could read her like nobody's business. With only ten months between them, they'd been like twins on some

69

deep-down level, connecting almost eerily. At every other level they were night and day, black and white, fire and ice. Some of their teachers never caught on that they were sisters by birth.

She put the phone back to her mouth. "I'm just tired. Gretchen has me going nonstop. We just got back to the hotel. Tomorrow we'll—"

"I've got your itinerary, Jill. Tell me, how did everything go? You sounded great on the radio."

"You listened to that?"

"Sure. I wouldn't miss my opinionated sis spouting off on L.A. drive time for the world. So how was this luncheon and that luncheon? the signings? and Hope on the Coast? Is that as wow of a place as they say?"

And some people thought Jill was the only Wagner sister with magpie jaws. "It was."

"I bet everyone is getting a kick out of meeting you."

"Some of them seem to appreciate me."

"Oh, come on, Jill. You know women resonate with your stuff. Jack is probably strutting like a peacock."

"Yeah. Listen, I just wanted to touch base. I better get to sleep. We have an early—"

"Back up. What's wrong with Jack?"

"Noth—" She shut her eyes. This was Viv, zeroing in on undertone and nuance. She could be like a terrier when Jill held back. She'd hang on and pull until something broke loose. "He didn't come."

"He didn't come? He didn't come! Why not?"

"He just didn't want to. You know what a homebody he is."

"And overworked. I'm sorry, Jill. You were counting on vacation time with him. You must be in a major funk."

"I'm okay. These things happen. And Gretchen has me going—well, you know all that. I-I'm not sure if I'll get down there to San Diego. I may head home earlier than planned."

"But you have umpteen things scheduled here. I'm even bringing some of my seniors to your signing up in Carmel Mountain. And I'll have my bus by then. I want you to see my bus."

"I'll call, okay? It depends on . . . on . . ." On how long she could compartmentalize Jack's announcement? "On what Gretchen comes up with. I really miss Jack."

Jill promised to call again soon and made it through a quick good-bye, grateful that Viv had not yanked the rest of the story from her.

She put her phone on the nightstand and turned out the light. The clock read 10:45 p.m. Numbers danced in her head. The day had begun at 6:45 a.m. at a prayer breakfast with a businesswomen's group. Following that were a midmorning coffee chat, a luncheon, a book signing. The day ended with dinner with two other speakers, clients of Gretchen's who, like the businesswomen, had their acts together.

There had not been one whiff of gossip. She did all right sidestepping what felt like an albatross, The Guarantee. No one asked impossible-to-answer questions. Still she held her breath. For roughly sixteen hours she'd held her breath. It was a record.

Numbers probably danced in Gretchen's head too. She would be counting how many books had been sold, how many potential buyers might have had their interest piqued.

Jill on the other hand counted how many people she had misled, beginning with her sister and going backward.

CHAPTER 11

———— ❧ ————

"AND LAST BUT not least, we come to Sizzlin' Spinach." From the dais, Jill looked out over the audience and paused for their reaction.

Almost fifty women smiled at her and a wave of chuckles swept round the room. From the far back, Gretchen gave her a thumbs-up.

Jill stretched her mouth into a smile, hoping it didn't look as fake as it was beginning to feel. It had started out genuine but was fading fast. Danielle's pep talk had lost its oomph.

As had yesterday's phone conversations. Her publisher and the radio station manager had both been hugely sympathetic. They said similar things. *"Oh, Jill, I am so sorry. We will pray for you and Jack. No, don't concern yourself just now about gossip. If and when it becomes necessary, we'll help you put out a statement. Meanwhile, if you're uncomfortable talking about some particular aspect of the book, don't say it. For now, we'll keep airing the recorded shows. It's not like you claimed to have a perfect marriage."*

Still, business was business. *"Can you just hang on through Sunday? We'll talk again."*

Today was Wednesday. Gretchen had canceled two minor appearances earlier in the day and one for tomorrow. Jill had decided that she would buy a ticket for an early Monday morning flight home. Those things should have given her another dose of oomph. Recovery, though, was not happening. She felt emptied inside, as if she were in the process of uncleaving. The part of her that was one with Jack had shut down for want of oxygen.

Lord, help me.

With her last ounce of energy, she refocused on the women before her. The event was a tea, an elegant affair in Beverly Hills. Linen table-cloths and napkins, fresh flowers, bone china, sparkling crystal and silver, cucumber sandwiches, scones and jam, the whole whoop-de-do. It should have been fun.

She glanced over her shoulder at the screen. Some saint at the control booth had kept her PowerPoint presentation on target for the past thirty minutes, never missing a beat. They'd gone through six recipes, literal and figurative. On the screen she shared Jack's recipes, the ones he had created to go along with her chapter titles. She also shared highlights from the book on how to relate to a husband in every sort of situation.

Like she and Jack had? She truly thought he had enjoyed their joint project. He loved to cook. He was always making up dishes. He seemed to like the challenge of throwing together a spinach concoction. He didn't bat an eyelash when she explained the sizzle reference.

She put the microphone back up to her chin. "God's gift of intimacy reminds me of spinach." She smiled. "It's natural. It's good for us. And sometimes, just as the flavor of spinach in this recipe is enhanced with garlic, lemon juice, olive oil, and a quick sauté—" she pointed over her shoulder—"we might want to enhance our times of intimacy. Music does wonders for romance, especially the classics. A little Vivaldi, Bach, whatever. Then there's candlelight. The older I get, the more I adore candlelight. You know what I'm sayin', right? In the shadows I'm still the twenty-one-year-old he married."

There was laughter, though some in the audience would doubtless be uncomfortable with her openness. Over the years her enthusiasm to be straightforward got her into trouble. She stepped on toes without meaning to and people let her know it. Terribly upset whenever that happened, she would hold herself together until she got to Jack. Then it was Niagara Falls. He'd listen with a knowing smile and suggest cutting back some on the zeal.

It seemed a long time ago that Jack had taken such an interest in her work. Or in her.

Suddenly Jill hit a wall and her jaws slowed. With an effort she wrapped up the talk before its technical end, no doubt confusing the saint at the controls but sending the message to Gretchen, who in turn nodded.

There would be no question-and-answer session. As Gretchen put it, Jill's ability to hold it together these days had a shelf life of about ninety minutes. Her internal clock ticked toward the time limit. She was about five minutes away from laying her head down on the nearest flat surface.

A podium in front of fifty lovely women from Beverly Hills was probably not the ideal spot.

❧

"It's all my fault." Jill looked at Gretchen's profile as she maneuvered the car through freeway traffic. "It feels good to confess that out loud."

"That's swell, sweetums, but it can't all be your fault. It takes two to tango."

Jill ignored her comment. "Rule number one is to stay current. If I'd stayed current with Jack, he wouldn't be in this emotional mess. The past six months I've been caught up in work like never before. You know how things were taking off. Seven new stations picked up the program. My interviewees were reading advance copies of the book and loving it. Poor Jack. I was the one who kept putting off Date Night. I was the one who didn't make eye contact and listen to him. I was too busy talking about dates and eye contact and how to listen."

"Not to rain on your parade, but wanting a divorce does not happen because of a crazy-full six-month period."

"Where's the umbrella? I am not letting your rain touch me."

"I just don't want you to lose sight of who you are, Jillie. Remember when we first met at church? You were a newlywed and new to Chicago. I was single. I wanted to be your friend because your husband had this all-American smile. I put up with your enviable, whimsical cuteness so I could hang out with Jack in hopes his friends were clones. I got to play doting aunt with Connor. Then of course you became my best friend mostly because I wanted your faith to rub off on me."

Jill had heard the story more than once. It always ended with them being a dynamic duo, encouraging each other to get to where they were today. That was true. Gretchen had introduced her to radio people. Jill had introduced her to key people who helped her get her public relations agency off the ground.

"You still are whimsical and cute and married to Jack Galloway, the kindest, most handsome doctor imaginable. Connor is still a doll and the two of us even have inside jokes. And you still have a deep, abiding, enviable faith. It's really hard to like you some days." She shrugged. "But I never would have wished this on you."

"There is a purpose to everything, and the sooner I get home, the sooner I can get a handle on it."

"Starting Monday. For a week."

"We'll see."

They rode in silence, the unspoken disagreement hanging between them. Gretchen wanted her to return to the tour after a week back in Chicago. Jill, obsessive planner, refused to commit.

Gretchen said, "We need prayer support. Are you ready to bring in the prayer chain?"

"No." Jill shuddered at the thought of her entire home church hearing about her and Jack's situation via e-mail.

"We can say it's an unspoken request—"

"No!"

"Not even the private chain for our class?"

"No."

"How about your dad?"

"Not yet."

"Jill! Skip Wagner is the first guy we always call for prayer backup."

"No, Jack is."

"Yeah, well, Jack isn't himself. The more I think about it, the more I think it was that car accident. He bumped his head. Something got knocked out of whack. You know, this whole thing could be the result of that accident. It shook him up more than he admitted or even knew. It's coming out now in this strange behavior. So stop blaming yourself. It's not all your fault."

Jill thought back to the previous Tuesday, the evening it happened. They'd both been running late, tying up loose ends so they could pack Wednesday evening and leave town early Thursday. A frozen pizza was in the oven when Jack phoned from the ER.

He had said, "I'm fine," and described sliding through an icy inter-section, sideways into a parked car. The impact rammed his head against the edge of his window, which was partially open. It was open? On a cold, sleety winter's night? He said he needed air and no, she needn't come to the hospital. His car was not drivable, probably totaled. He'd hitch a ride with somebody, right after X-rays and a few sutures on the top of his head.

She remembered seeing him come through the door at home. He tilted his head to reveal bloodied hair and an ugly raw spot on the part line. The hair had been shaved for the gash to be sewn. He'd gone straight to bed, complaining, not surprisingly, of a headache.

Eating pizza by herself, she thanked God that Jack was all right. He'd broken his crown, but he was all right.

She had hummed the "Jack and Jill" nursery rhyme, a ditty she'd always figured was a smile sent from God. After all, how many couples had their own personal rhyme that came with the happy connotations of childhood?

Their real story came with happy connotations as well. They had made it up the hill and filled their pail. In October they would celebrate their twenty-fifth wedding anniversary. They could rest assured that so many years together proved they were at the top, that their buckets were full of everything they needed.

Puh-lease. Was she naive or just plain stupid? Nursery rhymes were full of horror. Humpty Dumpty fell to his death. Georgie Porgie was a mess. Little Miss Muffet met a spider and was never heard from again. London Bridge—a huge, entire *bridge*—fell apart. And Old Mother Hubbard? All about heartbreaking tragedy.

Jill turned now to Gretchen and quoted. "'Jack and Jill went up a hill to fetch a pail of water. Jack fell down and broke his crown.' That's where this ends. Mark my words, no matter what pushed him down the hill, I am not tumbling after. I will skip to the bottom and pick him up."

CHAPTER 12

——— ❧ ———

Jill eyed the pleasant young woman seated in the rattan chair next to hers in the hotel lobby, and she suddenly felt very, very old.

Lindsay was a journalist, interviewing her for a local newspaper's religious section. She had long, straight dark hair and wore red-framed glasses and a happy expression. "You grew up in California, right?"

"Yes, in Sweetwater Springs." When had her own happy expression turned sour? Last Thursday? Or had it been a slow, ongoing squishing of her features?

"My favorite hiking trails are there."

Mm-hmm, she thought. Right smack in the middle-of-nowhere desert. Which described how she felt at the moment—nothing like Lindsay must feel. She had her whole life ahead of her. The girl most likely had regrets already, but nothing like what the next twenty years would bring. It wouldn't help to warn her.

Lindsay said, "Did you visit Palm Springs much as a kid?"

Jill tried to answer coherently. Gretchen had tugged her through the last three days, but they'd taken a toll, and this Sunday didn't feel very restful, let alone worshipful. Her mind drifted. She was eighty miles from home. She should call her parents. The plan had been to visit them in a few weeks. With Jack. After their vacation. After the last item on the itinerary was checked off.

Obviously none of that was going to happen.

Her dad, Skip, would be hurt, but he would console; he would offer insight; he would be there for her and Jack in whatever way benefited them. Her mother, Daisy, was another story.

She just wasn't up to Daisy.

And besides, she and Jack were at the *start* of a dialogue. There was nothing to report.

Jill's phone rang in her pocket and she rudely pulled it out. Jack's name appeared. "Lindsay, I am so sorry but I have to take this. Family issues. Be right back." She threw her a smile and walked across the lobby. "Jack."

"Hi." His voice was hesitant.

As it should be. She had left him several voice mails that he ignored.

"How did this morning's interview go?" he said.

"It's still going." She strode through the hotel's entranceway, made a beeline across the stone drive, and silently thanked Gretchen for dragging her to Palm Springs the previous night.

"I don't want to interrupt."

"We come first, Jack. No matter what I've made it look like in the past, we come first. Did you get my messages?"

"All six of them. Look, Jill, I'm sorry for not getting back to you. I'm sorry that I can't just talk this through with you. I'm not ready."

Jill sat on a stone bench beneath a lone palm tree, part of a mini oasis with bushes, flowers, and trickling fountain. Gretchen had lived up to her promise of a resort with all the amenities, including pools and spa and restful quiet. She had even thrown in a massage. It was an out-and-out bribe to keep Jill on the tour for as long as possible, but it was also a friend's concern for her well-being.

And it helped. Her lungs did not burn. Her tone was even. "Jack, this long-distance business isn't healthy. We need to be face-to-face. We can talk face-to-face."

"I don't want to talk. How many times do I have to say that until you get it?" His irritable tone snapped open a red flag in her mind.

Jack never ever displayed irritability. He might be angry at circumstances sometimes, but never grumpy or moody or crabby. A quick apology always accompanied the rare bark at her.

This out-of-character temper was a symptom of midlife crisis.

Like the fatigue? Like the lack of interest in her? Like his weight gain?

Had the signs been there all along, masking themselves as rhythms of every day, as ups and downs of life's seasons?

She shook her head. It was asking what came first, the chicken or the egg? Did the way she ignored him create the crisis or enhance its effects? Either way, it just was.

"Jack—"

"Hold on." His voice sounded as if he tilted the phone away from his mouth. "Sophie, I'll be right there."

Jill said, "You're at the office?"

"Yeah—"

"Jack!" Her tone lost its evenness. "Good grief! You need a break!"

"The office is not my problem."

"Meaning I am."

"Jill, I don't want to say any more."

"Say more! I need to hear what you're thinking."

"Okay. Bottom line, our marriage is my problem. It's not how I want to live my life."

"How can that be? What do you want? What's changed?"

"What hasn't?" He breathed heavily. "I refuse to get into it right now. Sophie needs me. I have to go. Give me some space, Jill. That's all I ask. Okay? Just a little space for the time being. All right. Good-bye."

"Good-bye." Jill spat the word and smacked her phone shut. How dare he do this to her, to them! How dare he say everything had changed between them and then refuse to get into—

"Sophie needs me"? Sophie needed him?

Obviously he meant workwise. Sophie had a question. She wondered about a file. She—

She was always right there beside Jack, day in and day out, efficient, thoughtful, *single*. Year after year after year taking care of his needs.

What needs exactly?

If they were having an affair, then Jack's behavior pretty much expressed every last symptom of a midlife crisis.

Familiar fears sprang to mind. She had always been wary of Sophie. The woman had never married, never even dated as far as Jill knew. She made no attempt to mask her adoration of Jack. Oh, Jack couldn't see it, but Jill could. It was quite obvious in the way Sophie looked at him and talked to him.

Jill had always trusted Jack. His middle name might as well have been "Old Faithful." That didn't make Sophie's attention to him any less a threat. It didn't make Jack's free offers of information—where and when he and Sophie went out to eat, what gifts he gave her at Christmas and birthday times—easy to accept.

They had a history, innocent or not, and Jack's speaking to Sophie just now set off new alarms.

It was time for Jill to go home. As in *now*.

※

LOS ANGELES

The unflappable Gretchen was decidedly flappy. She hadn't stopped gesturing since Jill made an airline reservation the previous day.

They stood near the security line at LAX. Or rather Jill stood. Gretchen paced in tight circles, most of her hair falling out of a French twist, her lime green silk blouse wrinkled and untucked.

"Gretch, I'm fine."

"Yeah, right. You're going against everyone's wishes, including Jack's, and you think you're fine. You've lost touch with reality."

"I'm going through security. Give me a hug."

"No. Way. Get over it already. Neither of us are leaving until the last possible minute. I may even get permission to go to the gate with you. I'll explain how you're a menace to others. That you need constant supervision." The glare did not quite hit the mark, though she put up a good bluff. "You may yet come to your senses."

"I did. I am going home to save my marriage."

"Have you seriously weighed all the issues here? This is not only about you and Jack. I'm talking radio, publisher, audience. Have you given one thought to how much time, energy, and money so many people have invested in you?"

Jill stared at her. "I can't believe you said that. Of course I have. Do you honestly think I've stayed here for this worst week of my life in order to feed my ego?"

"We should talk about it."

"Gretchen, I'm done talking."

"Then we'll drink coffee. I'll go get some. Sit there." Gretchen pointed at two empty seats nearby. "Do not move." Her eyes filled and she hurried away, soon out of sight in the crowd.

Jill dropped her carry-on bags to the floor and sat. In truth she was as unnerved as Gretchen. She had spent the equivalent of two mortgage payments on airline charges. She was letting everyone down, from publisher to audience to her sister, and she could not imagine returning in a week to placate them. She was responsible for Jack's condition. She ignored his insistence that he was not ready to talk and purchased a very expensive ticket.

She should tell him she was coming.

"Hi." Jack answered his phone.

She inhaled, surprised that he had actually answered. "Jack." She exhaled and took another deep breath.

"What?"

"I'm coming home. Today."

A silent moment passed. "Hm." He hummed in his doctor tone,

alert, waiting for more information, not wanting to comment until he had the whole picture.

"I'll be in late tonight. The rest of the itinerary—none of it matters. Not really." She bit her lip, trying to slow down. "The PR stuff and . . . and . . . and everything . . ."

"Of course it matters. It's what you're all about. It's your life's work."

"No! I'm telling you it does not matter. It's all going on hold. I'm coming home to work on us, Jack. *Us.* We're what matters. Our marriage. I've been telling others for years how to stay in relationship. Why would I not explore that with you for ourselves?"

"You're putting your work on hold."

"Yes."

"You'll get back to it."

"Eventually. There's always something to glean from our real life that I can use to help others. Aging couples are going to stumble into midlife issues."

"We're a lesson plan in the making."

She swallowed. His retort stunned her. What happened to the Jack who saw God in everything from little toes to plantar warts to coq au vin and told her about it so she could tell others because he was not an up-front sort of guy?

He sighed and in that familiar sound of frustration she imagined him pulling on his earlobe. "Jill, what did I say yesterday?"

"That you don't want to talk. I can't believe you really mean it. You might think you do, but—"

"I meant it."

"Fine." She found her voice. He was not getting off easy this time. He was not shoving her into a taxi. "I hear you, Jack. Now hear me. What I need is to be there. I need to find a counselor for us. I've got a list of the best ones I recommend to couples, but for us . . . I don't know. Maybe we can start with Lew." They'd known Pastor Lew Mowers for twenty years. "Have you told him yet?"

"Jill." In that one syllable his tone went from an empathetic doctor to one with the coldest of bedside manners. "I moved out of the house."

The sound of a rushing wind filled her head, as if a jet whooshed right through the terminal. "What?"

"I have an apartment."

An apartment?

"And I spoke with a lawyer."

A lawyer?

"What about a counselor?" she whispered. "We need to see a counselor."

"I disagree. That would only prolong the inevitable." He dropped the bombshells in a calm voice as if rattling off steps in a surgical procedure. "I didn't want to say this on the phone, but in your typical driven manner, you've forced things to a head. The bottom line is we don't have a future because I don't love you. I'm sorry, Jill, I really am, but that's the way it is. I want the best for you, and our marriage is not it, not for either of us."

She could not follow what he was saying. The noise in her head drowned him out.

He sighed again. "I'll send a car to the airport for you and put a house key in the mailbox. Which flight are you on?"

"Jack! You can't end a marriage on the telephone."

"I didn't. You did."

Jill shut the phone and made a beeline for the restroom.

CHAPTER 13

———— ❧ ————

"Rock 'em, sock 'em, Jillie!" Viv giggled and flipped a page in her sister's book. "Marty, you have got to hear this."

"Trust me, I'm hearing." Across the kitchen table, her husband lowered the newspaper enough to peer over it. "I can't tell if you like it or not, though."

"Oh, I love it. Jill is totally crazy and it comes through loud and clear."

"And that's a good thing?"

"Yes! It's a wonderful thing. This book will appeal to a lot of women who think like she does."

"I'll take your word for it."

"Come on, just let me read one part to you." She pushed aside breakfast dishes to make space for her elbows. "You want to have some idea what it's about before she gets here."

"Why?"

"So you two have something to talk about."

"Why?"

Viv caught the tease in his eye and gave him her best glare.

"Seriously, Viv. You said Jack's not coming."

"Right."

"Then she'll hang with you at the office and you'll do girlie things. I don't foresee us interacting all that much. I need to put in some serious overtime, probably the week she's here."

Viv shook her head in resignation. In the early years she would get mad at him for disliking Jill; then she would be mad at Jill for disliking Marty. She finally decided it was their problem, not hers.

"Martin Kovich, you are such a chicken."

"When it comes to your sister, you bet I am." He raised the paper and she was looking at a Lakers guy, both feet off the ground, hands above the basket.

"We're not supposed to end the conversation at this point."

"You know I'll talk to Jill. I'll even spring for dinner at the Prado."

"With or without you?"

He chuckled.

"Anyway, that's not what I meant. It says here in her book that we should end a conversation with a recap to make sure we both come away having heard the same thing."

The basketball player folded. "You want me to listen."

"Please. I can't figure out if we're having Rockin' Roast or Easy Eggs."

"Huh?"

"Do you think we're disagreeing or conversing about everyday stuff?" She glanced down at the book. "Then again, maybe we're working through a difficult time? Given the fact that we view Jill as synonymous with difficult, we'll go with that one. Which means we're into Crunchy Casserole."

Marty snapped the paper shut and laid it aside. "Give me the short version." He needed to leave for work soon. They made a point of having breakfast together most days because it was the only time they could count on. She often worked late into the evenings. He often coached boys' rec ball, whatever the season, after work.

Viv smiled. He was listening. "You have a good heart."

He grunted and folded his arms.

She picked up the book. "Okay, short version. *She Said, He Heard* is all about how married couples don't always really hear what they say to each other because they miss the message that is behind the words."

"I could have told you that."

"But how do you fix it?"

"Talk louder. Make frequent use of exclamation points."

"Mr. Finesse."

He smiled. "So the book tells you how to fix it."

"Yeah. It's based on recipes for communicating. She put them in an acronym for *recipes*. Cute, huh?" Viv read from a front page. "The *R* is for Rockin' Roast, how to disagree. *E* is Easy Eggs, how to interact in everyday life. *C*, Crunchy Casserole, covers difficult times. *I*, Indigo Ice Cream, for the blues. *P*, Pristine Pie, is for beautiful moments. *E*, Ecstatic Eggplant, for happy times. And *S*, for Sizzlin' Spinach—physical intimacy."

"Cute."

"There are actual recipes at the back." She turned pages. "I bet they're Jack's."

"So what's in the spinach chapter?"

She looked at him.

He shrugged. "I'm a guy. It's my love language."

Viv skimmed a page. "It looks like romance stuff. Candlelight, dinner out. Hm. Evidently Jack likes music in the bedroom."

"Hold it. That's too much information. What's in the blue ice cream?"

"Let's see. Besides blueberries—" Viv found the section—"she talks about when she and Jack had to move his parents into an assisted-care place, how it was such a sad time, how she and Jack made a scrapbook together about his mom and dad. It was how they did 'blue' together."

"That's what I wanna do. Cut and paste and draw."

"What if we used stickers?"

"Nope."

"Marty, she's not saying everyone should do the same thing. It's an example. She gives broad guidelines for how to really hear each other."

"We both know she's been using examples from home for a long time in her classes. Jack Galloway, GP, is cut from a different cloth than me."

Viv winced at Marty's nickname for Jack. *GP* did not refer to *general practitioner*. *Guinea pig* struck closer to the truth than to a joke.

He pushed back his chair and stood. "Babe, if you told a bunch of women what you and I said to each other in private when my dad died, I would've moved out." He gazed at her for a long moment, conviction in the line of his thin lips, warm love for her in his brown eyes.

"You're saying you don't want to read the book?"

He walked around the table, kissed her cheek, and whispered, "You heard correctly."

Curious. Marty and Jill were so much alike but would never admit it. Refereeing the two bullheads without Jack's help was not a happy prospect.

Maybe she had serious overtime to put in at work that week too.

⚘

Later that day Viv stood inside her very own, brand-new slice of heaven on wheels: the minibus. She wiggled and jiggled her version of a happy dance down its aisle. She sang off-key, making up words to the tune of "My Girl."

"Talkin' 'bout my bus. I've got a Turtle Top Odyssey. And it's brand-new and I am so happy. My bus, talkin' 'bout my bus. My bus. Ooo-ooo." She snapped her fingers. "I've got a turbo diesel engine, six-speed transmission, and a sixty-gallon tank. And when all fourteen guests sit in the double-high recliners, they'll like the wide, wide seats. And a whole . . ." She twirled. "Lot . . ." Another twirl. "More. Talkin' 'bout my bus."

She slid her hand along a seat back. "Carnival rainbow pattern on gray. All the colors in a gorgeous spray." She touched the luggage space above and sashayed toward the back. "Rear-contoured overhead luggage with light. So, so bright. Ooo-hoo. And in the back, a loo!"

Viv opened the restroom door, reached inside, and flushed the toilet. "Woo-hoo!"

Laughing, she strode to the front, climbed over the console, plopped into the driver's seat, and admired the control panel.

"Wow."

The only thing missing was someone to share the moment with. Blame that on midafternoon timing. Marty was at work. Her driver, Dustin, and the two women who helped part-time weren't in the office. Her friends were doing their own thing. Maybe she could drive this most magnificent machine over to one of the senior complexes where many of her regular customers lived.

"I'm whining. Good grief." She smiled, traced the steering wheel with a finger, and inhaled deeply, filling her lungs with the intoxicating, chemically heavy scent of *new*. "By the way, God, thank You. I love it."

At least Marty was coming later, if not sooner. He said he'd try to get away early. Unless a game with a ball was involved in some way, Marty did not get away early. But this was a special occasion, and he wanted to be there for her.

Be there for her.

Viv did not take that for granted. She whispered, "Thank You that he understands the hugeness of this moment for me."

At the thought of her excitement over a stretch chassis, steel wheel wells, and seat fabric upgrade, she grinned. Her peaks were not exactly in the same realm as Jill's, whose included radio interviews, talks at megachurches, meeting fans. She actually had fans. How sad she couldn't share it this week with Jack.

How *odd* that she couldn't. Why wouldn't Jack . . . ?

Marty's words came back to her now. After he heard what Jill had written about Jack, he had said, *"Babe, if you told a bunch of women what you and I said to each other in private when my dad died, I would've moved out."*

Marty would have moved out. Marty. Solid-as-a-rock Marty, who was, in some ways, far more grounded than Jack. Beautiful a man as Jack was, inside and out—not to mention truly Jill's other, better half—he sometimes gave in to Jill's opinion too easily.

She replayed Jill's voice from their phone conversation. Her articulate sister had stuttered. She had relayed nonsense about Jack's not coming. *"He just didn't want to."* What was that all about? He had missed one of the major highlights of Jill's life.

It was both un-Jack and un-Jill-like. Jack was loyal to a fault and Jill would have wanted him there. What was going on?

Viv pulled her phone from a jeans pocket. Jill was in her Cleopatra mode, playing queen of "da Nile." If denying and spinning truth suited her, she used it. *"You know what a homebody he is."*

"During a week like this one? Give me a break." Viv scrolled through her contacts to Jack's name. She stared at his numbers for home, mobile, office, private line, hospital. At last she decided the cell was her best bet.

It rang several times. As she prepared to leave a message, he answered.

"Jack Galloway."

"Jack, it's Viv."

"Hi. Viv." His voice was . . . off.

She adored her brother-in-law. She and Jill had met him by accident on the same day. It was love at first sight for both sisters. It took Viv about five minutes to intuit that he was the perfect match for her pain-in-the-neck sister. It took Jill less time than that to fall head over heels. By day two she believed the man hung the moon.

She still thought that.

Viv said, "What happened?"

Silence filled the line.

Which meant she was right. Something had happened.

Jack cleared his throat. "Can you put that question into context?"

"You really need context?"

He sighed. "What did she say?"

"Nothing. Come on, Jack. This is my sister's coming-out party and you're not here. It's as simple as that. I don't need to be a rocket scientist to figure it out. What happened between you two?"

"I told her I want a divorce."

Stunned, Viv had no reply. Jack and Jill, divorced? It was as inconceivable as having grown up and never sung the silly rhyme. Her sister and Jack were made for each other. Since that first day she saw them together, Viv could never think of one without thinking of the other. Splitting them up would be like ripping apart superglued fingers.

At last she said, "Why? What's going on?"

"I don't really want to talk about it."

"Well, that makes two of you."

"She'll fill you in when she's ready. You know she will. You're two peas in a pod."

"So are you guys." Or like superglued fingers. "Are you okay?"

"Am I . . . ?" He went silent. After a long moment, he whispered, "I was okay until you asked that." His voice cracked. "I feel like I'm having a tumor cut out and they got the anesthetic all wrong."

"Then why did you say—?"

"Because the pain is still less than it was before I told her."

"Oh, Jack! It's the book, isn't it? Marty said if I told everyone stuff like that about us, he'd move out."

"It's not the book. It's not even that she's talked about these things for years. You know I gave her permission to do that, right?"

"Yes, but this is too much."

"But it's not the root of things. The book is just the proverbial straw on the camel's back. Our marriage was positioned to break."

"How did it get there?"

"I don't know, Viv. I just know that it has."

Tears were spilling over by now. "What are you going to do?" She wiped a sleeve across her cheeks.

"Move on."

"Move on? You can't do that. You have to stay and fight!"

"That describes the past twenty-four and a half years." He exhaled. "And I'm tired of it. I moved into an apartment. I saw a lawyer. Thanks for calling, Viv. I appreciate that. Tell Marty hi."

Unbelievable. When had Jack Galloway turned into an A1, bona fide creep?

❧

Marty pointed a plastic fork at the white carton. "You want this?"

Viv shook her head. Dinner was Chinese takeout in the kitchen. "Why doesn't she return my calls?"

He speared the last egg roll. "Under normal circumstances, I would have no idea how your sister's mind works. Tonight I can't even begin to pretend a guess."

"Maybe she's hurt or lost."

"Don't worry. You said Gretchen was with her and the Palm Springs bookstore Web site has her listed for tonight. So that's where they are. That's what they're doing."

"Oh, Marty, why didn't she tell me?"

He popped a forkful of garlic chicken into his mouth, reached across the table, and squeezed her hand.

"How can she keep on going like nothing's wrong? speaking and signing books?"

"What's really wrong," he said around the food and swallowed, "is that you've gotten sidetracked from this momentous day." He picked up his soda can. "Cheers for the minibus."

She stared at him.

He grinned and took a swig. "It really is beautiful. Just like you."

"I don't deserve you." Her voice caught. "Why doesn't he fight for her? for their marriage?"

"I don't know, babe. Maybe guinea pigs have a shorter life span than the average guy."

"That's mean."

He replied with a grunt, his version of *whatever*.

"You're mad, aren't you?"

"Yeah. Don't get me wrong. She deserves it on some level and Jack

94

deserves his say at long last. But when she hurts, you hurt. That's what I don't like. That's what makes me mad."

Viv watched him polish off a carton of rice.

Marty had been a bruiser. His aggressive nature had scared her in the beginning. He had to ask her out five or six times before she said yes. Fresh out of the Navy with minimally tattooed Popeye arms, he enjoyed conflict, both verbal and physical. It wasn't that he sought it out or created it. He just never backed down from defending whatever or whoever needed it.

Through the years he mellowed. The physical got worked out on a ball field or in the welding shop. When he started coaching little kids and he overheard seven-year-olds mimic him to a T, four-letter words and all, Marty cut back on the verbal arrows. Deep inside him, though, his core motive remained to defend all that was good and right.

"Marty."

"Hm?" He drained his soda can.

"Thank you for fighting for me. For our marriage."

His dark eyes shimmered and he gazed back at her.

"Maybe you could call Jack, give him some pointers."

He barked a laugh. "Right. Kovich the therapist."

"Seriously, you could—" Her phone rang and she grabbed it. "It's Jill!" She answered it. "Jill!"

"It's Gretchen, on Jill's phone. Hi, Viv. Listen, we have a little situation—"

"Where is she? Why didn't she tell me? What is going on?"

"You know?"

"I called Jack today."

"Okay. Well. Jill and I are parked outside at your curb and—"

Viv dropped the phone on the table and raced through the house and out the front door. Within moments Jill was out of the car and in her arms.

"Oh, Vivvie." Tears streamed down her face. "I did it wrong. I did it all wrong."

CHAPTER 14

———— ❧ ————

"I MISS HIS cooking." Jill opened the lid of the pizza box in Viv's kitchen. "I've been gone twelve days, and of all things I miss his cooking."

Viv set plates on the table and sat across from her. "I promise to cook tomorrow."

"I wasn't saying . . ." Her voice trailed off. It had been doing that a lot, like a train going by and disappearing into the trees. "Maybe I'm missing it forward. Like a part of me senses what's coming if he goes through with . . . Life is never ever going to be the same. We can't ever go back to what we were."

Viv studied her face. "Look, I understand why you fell apart at the airport. I understand why Gretchen dumped you here last night. I'm family. Fine. I realize your marriage is in the sewer. I'm sorry. But, Jill, we did not get to bed until two this morning and the office was nonstop crazy today. I need ten minutes off from the counseling session. Okay? All the analyzing." She pulled off a slice of pizza and put it on her plate. "The introspection."

"Well, excuse me for fighting for my sanity here."

Viv held up a warning finger. "Eat. This used to be your favorite pizza."

"Venetos? They're still around?"

"Yep."

Tears stung. They had stung throughout the day. How could Jack say he did not love her? He knew as well as she did that love was not a feeling. So he was just choosing to quit on them?

She felt paralyzed. She couldn't eat, sleep, or even call Jack to tell him where she was. It didn't seem to matter. He hadn't called her to find out if she made it home.

At the airport yesterday, hearing Jack's news that he'd moved out and seen a lawyer knocked every last breath of hope from her. Why bother going home? He didn't live at their house. He wouldn't have to see her face-to-face if he didn't want to and he obviously did not want to.

She'd waded through the red tape of retrieving her luggage and finally come to terms with the choices before her. The thought of staying in another hotel turned her stomach. The thought of seeing her mother felt almost as bad, bad enough to give up the idea of hugging her dad. Viv would welcome her, but Marty wouldn't be happy.

A tear slid down her cheek. Was this her future? Burdening others with her problems?

"Jillie, please eat something."

"You're as bossy as ever." She picked up a breadstick and pulled it apart. "I should call Jack."

Viv finished her slice and took another from the box. "I called him and told him you were here."

"You *talked* to him?"

"Yes. His office lady put me through. He was between patients."

"He was at the office? And he talked to you but didn't bother to call me?"

Viv shrugged. "He didn't answer the cell, so I tried the office. He mentioned something about flu going around and being understaffed."

"Maybe he has the flu after all."

"Jillie, don't get your hopes up. Anyway, before Gretchen left this morning, she and I agreed he should be told that you were safe and sound out here, not there. She said if she talked to him again it would be the last time ever and it would not be pretty. So I offered."

Jill nodded. It was best Gretchen had left for Phoenix to meet a client. She took away a large amount of agitated air with her. While Viv empathized, Gretchen discussed how she planned to slug Jack.

"Viv, how did he sound?"

She took her time chewing and swallowing. "Like a doctor in between patients. Preoccupied and professional, but he thanked me."

They ate in silence for a few moments, Jill majoring on the bread. Her stomach was not ready for green pepper or sausage.

Viv said, "I told him that you didn't have plans yet."

"I can't even think about going home. The thought of Jack not living there—" fresh tears collected—"I can't face that."

"He was angry that you didn't do what he asked, to stay put. He hasn't stopped loving you."

"But he said—"

"Shh. On another subject, you're welcome to stay here for as long as you want."

"Oh, Viv. Marty's avoiding me. It's Tuesday night and he's not home."

"Bowling league. No worries about him, okay? But you have all your friends in Chicago. Maybe you'd be more comfortable with them."

"What would I say?"

"Not much. This is when you just cry together."

Jill imagined those women closest to her. Besides Gretchen, there really was no one else. Of course she enjoyed downtime with coworkers and lunch with church ladies occasionally. Except for social outings with Jack, she spent her time either doing shows or preparing for them, not nurturing friendships. She shook her head.

"You think people are going to judge you."

"Of course."

"So? That will puncture your pride. Not a big deal."

"But pride goes before a fall, and I am not ready for a fall yet, Viv.

All I've been able to do is get myself through the day. E-mail has gone by the wayside. I need to figure things out, maybe salvage some dignity."

Viv chewed, tilting her head one way and the other.

"You're not buying that."

She swallowed. "I understand. What about the show?"

"I'm covered for a while. We prerecorded several. They're running old ones too."

"What did you tell the station?"

"That Jack and I hit a bump in the road and the PR trip was put on hold." A sinking sensation came over her. "They should cancel the show immediately. They shouldn't be broadcasting all that stuff I'm not even sure comes anywhere near the truth. I don't care if it is touted by *experts*."

"Hey! Knock it off with the *should*s. There is truth in what you teach. The point is you don't have to think about the show yet, right?"

"Okay, okay. Right," Jill agreed begrudgingly. "Are you sure you don't mind me staying for an indefinite time? I can't imagine it will be long, but . . ."

Viv reached across the table and squeezed her hand. "Yes, I am sure. It's smaller than you're used to but I hope you feel at home."

"Thank you. It's comfy."

The one-story bungalow Viv and Marty had lived in for twenty-plus years was pleasant. It sat on a busy hill, close quarters with neighbors. Marty kept the small backyard with its patio and fruit trees well manicured. One could even catch a slim view of the airport runway and harbor three blocks away.

She missed her sprawling Chicago suburb and roomy house. She missed Jack. She missed the life that was—in the blink of an eye—no more.

Viv grinned. "The downside is we don't cook much."

"That makes three of us." Jill looked around the compact kitchen with its old-fashioned tile countertops. Blinds covered the many windows and the sliding door behind Viv's chair, masking the winter night's cold and dark. "I don't know what else to do. Where else to go."

"Don't worry, Jillie. We'll get through this. Do you want me to call Mom and Pops? Do you want to see them? We could run over there tomorrow, spend a few hours, come back."

Jill shuddered. "I can't face Mom yet."

Viv's eyes beamed with understanding. Daisy Wagner was so far off the path of nurturer they couldn't even tease about her.

"Okay. Do you have work to do, e-mails and stuff?"

"Yeah." Corresponding with listeners had been a highlight of her week, but now the thought filled her with dread.

"I was thinking that if you have time tomorrow, maybe you'd like to see the office?"

Jill met her sister's medium-brown eyes. As usual they twinkled, hinting at fun. The corners of her wide mouth were, also as usual, slightly turned up, hovering on the verge of a grin. Her medium-brown hair, long and layered, was a mass of natural waves seldom styled or even brushed. Freckles still sprinkled her nose.

Viv said, "It'll be like the old days."

Like the old days. Those would be the days before Jill had met Jack Galloway. Given the fact that nothing was the same, those days might be a good place to visit.

She nodded.

❧

Jill went to bed early that night. Viv thought it a good respite for her. To Jill it felt like sheer coping. If she shut out the world long enough, maybe everything would change.

The next morning Jill awoke without her chest afire. That was a change.

As the day wore on, though, it felt heavier and heavier, like a bag of solid concrete, as if the unspoken words had piled so densely they died of asphyxiation.

Maybe God was telling her just to shut up.

Which made no sense. Her gift was the gift of yap. Exhorting, encouraging, cajoling, explaining, teaching. Communicating.

She went with Viv to her office, a mute tagalong.

"Ta-da." Viv spread her arms wide, grinned, and took a twirl in the middle of Vivvie's Tours. "What do you think?"

Jill rubbed her chest. "A trip down memory lane is easier in theory than reality."

Viv lowered her arms. "Come on, Jillie. Give it a try."

Lord, please help.

Eons ago she and Viv were business partners in the agency. When they were barely nineteen and eighteen years old, their aging grandmother offered her business to them lock, stock, and barrel. Ellie's Tours catered to senior citizens, taking them on simple day trips all over Southern California. The sisters skipped straight from high school into self-employment, had a blast, and made enough money to support themselves. Then Jill met Jack and . . . everything changed.

And now it was all changed again.

"Jill, forget memory lane. Start with the here and now. Tell me it's nice."

She heard the anxious note in Viv's tone and focused on the scene before her. The place was nice. Extremely nice. A storefront in a strip mall, it had windows facing the parking lot and morning sun. There were overstuffed chairs, a love seat, wallpaper, and carpet, all in desert colors of tans, corals, and turquoise. Framed colorful posters depicted Southern California's highlights: ocean, mountains, and desert. Scattered about on low tables and the single desk were plants, brochures, and maps.

"Viv, it's wonderful."

"Thanks." She smiled. "Remember my other place?"

Jill cringed inwardly. No, she did not, not really. Her last visit to San Diego had been too brief to visit this office, new at that time. Before that—well, she wasn't sure when she last saw Viv's place. It had been sometime after she'd moved from the original hole-in-the-wall where they started.

Viv said, "This is a little larger and heaps better locationwise." She set a bag of fresh croissants on a side table and flipped on a coffeepot. "Come see the boss's office."

They walked into a small room at the back, tastefully furnished too but messier than the front.

Jill smiled. "Obviously your space."

"Bet your desk looks the same."

"Well . . . yeah."

"We are a couple of hurricanes, huh?"

"The trick is in knowing where the eye is."

"And staying in it when necessary." Viv gave a thumbs-up. "That was our motto. The problem was we never seemed to be in the eye at the same time."

"We clashed so much. Grandma Ellie thought we were nuts to try to work together. She was so surprised when we made money. She would be proud of you now."

Viv laughed. "I do look legitimate, don't I?"

"Definitely."

"And you haven't even seen the new minibus yet."

"I'm so proud of you too, Viv."

Her sister stared at her for a moment, a somber expression on her face. "Thank you."

"I should have told you sooner. Years ago."

Viv shrugged.

But Jill knew she didn't mean it.

She walked over and embraced Viv in a long, silent, overdue bear hug.

❧

A short while later Dustin Kovich breezed into the office. Jill still remembered him as a toddler at Viv and Marty's wedding. He'd grown into movie-star cute with dark eyes like Marty's and none of the machismo.

"Aunt Viv, that was so cool." He spotted Jill behind the front desk.

"Hey. You're Jill, the famous sister." He stepped over and thrust out his hand. "Hi."

Jill shook it. "You're Dustin, all-grown-up famous right-hand guy."

He glanced at Viv. "You said that?"

Viv smiled. "I talk nonstop about my right-hand guy. So what was so cool?"

"Breakfast at the Del. The ladies ate it up, and I don't mean the eggs. The food was out of this world but it was the ambience. You know how our Casitas Pack love their upper-crust moments. The old hotel was perfect."

"Pack?" Jill looked at Viv.

"That's what they call themselves. They live in the Casitas senior complex and take at least one outing a week with us. Now they've started a breakfast club and asked if we'd provide transportation." She chuckled. "With Dustin of course."

When he blushed, Jill figured the elderly women doted on him.

He said, "Now can I drive the bus?"

"No way."

"Come on, Aunt Viv. You promised."

"I said when I can go with you. Today is not a good day."

Jill said, "Why not, Viv? You two go. I'll stay. I'm a little rusty with booking a tour, but I know how to answer a phone and take a message."

Viv hesitated.

"I'm fine. Really."

"If you need to, you know, like emotionally shut down or something, just lock the door and turn out the lights."

Jill wanted to crawl under the desk. She didn't care if Dustin was a relative of Viv's, he was a stranger to her. Why should he be privy to her emotional state? Why should he think anything other than that she was there on vacation?

She held up a hand and plastered on a smile. "Go."

A few moments later they were out the door and walking toward the beautiful white minibus Viv had shown her earlier. A wide, flared racing stripe in yellow flowed around lime green lettering: *Vivvie's Tours*. In smaller fonts were the phone number and Web address. The whole thing was splashy, yet sophisticated—very Viv-like.

Her sister had *arrived*.

Jill felt a stab of envy.

She swiveled in the desk chair, turning her back to its source.

A couple weeks ago she never could have imagined such a reaction. She was the one who had arrived. She was the one with a public ministry growing by leaps and bounds. She was the one in a truly communicative marriage. She was the one with a faithful husband who never forgot a birthday or anniversary or Valentine's Day or Christmas. She was the one whose son graduated at the top of his college class and was working on a master's.

Now none of that mattered.

None of it mattered.

"Really, God? It doesn't matter? It's what? Suddenly null and void? Was it just a sham? What exactly do You want? I gave it my best shot and my husband left me. Is this the end—of my marriage and my career?" She exhaled a frustrated breath. "It can't be. You made it clear this was my path. Okay, I get it. You put me on a side road so I can get a different focus. Like men in midlife. I line up experts to interview. Hint here and there that Jack and I are entering the danger zone. Meanwhile I tell him—no, I insist—that we see a counselor. Lew is my first choice, our initial step. He knows us."

She nodded. Yes, it was a start. She had to believe Viv's version, that Jack did not mean what he said.

"Excuse me?"

Jill jumped at the soft voice behind her and spun the chair around.

A short, plump woman stood a few steps inside the door, her eyes hidden behind dark wraparound sunglasses. "I am so sorry. You must not have heard the jingle." She pointed a gold cane upward at the small bell attached to the door. Bracelets on her wrist sparkled and clinked.

"No, I didn't." Jill's heart still pounded. At least the surprise visitor appeared harmless. She wore a hot pink velour jogging suit. Straight white hair hugged her head like a bowl, enhancing the chubbiness of her face.

She slid the glasses off. They dangled from a sporty elastic strand. "I didn't want to interrupt your conversation."

Jill gave her a blank look. "Conversation?"

"You sounded rather upset and you were waving your arms. But then I noticed that you didn't have one of those blue teeth in your ear." She pointed at one of her ears, its lobe hidden behind a cluster of pink rhinestones. "I suppose you're like me. You process verbally. You think better if you hear your thoughts expressed out loud."

Jill had no response.

"Oh, where are my manners!" She stepped to the desk and held out her hand. "You're new here. I'm Agnes Smith. Vivvie knows me. I'm with the Casitas Pack."

Jill stood and shook the woman's hand, noticing the firm grip and many rings. "I'm Jill, Viv's sister."

Agnes grinned. "Yes! Yes, you are! You're that famous lady. I saw your picture on the book cover. I must say, you're even prettier in person. I am so happy to meet you." She rummaged inside her large handbag. "I take it Vivvie is not here. No matter. I wrote down some new ideas for our breakfast club and wanted to give them. Here we go." She handed Jill a slightly crinkled envelope. "If you'll just give that to her, angel, I would appreciate it."

Angel. The name startled her. It was Jack's pet name for her. A long, long time ago.

Agnes said, "I do hope I see you again. Perhaps you can join us old-sters on one of our little jaunts? We're going to the zoo tomorrow."

"I-I'm not sure. I have a lot to do." Find a counselor, get back home, fix a marriage.

"Well—" she shrugged, an exaggerated up and down motion of her shoulders—"you never know, do you? God may have something else in store for you."

Jill smiled politely.

Agnes laid both of her hands atop the cane and leaned slightly forward. "I did not intend to eavesdrop, but you were talking rather loudly. Might I suggest something?"

Jill enjoyed old people. As a child she helped her grandmother with her business during the summers. She had learned from Ellie that seniors were simply young people in weathered skin. Their quirks had grown more pronounced with age, but underneath they had the same needs and desires as anyone. Food, shelter, clothing, and love pretty much summed it up.

Once in a great while, though, an odd one came along, an elderly person who did not have those generic needs and desires—someone who seemed to have moved on, who already had one foot planted solidly in the next world.

Those were the ones who intimidated Jill.

Agnes Smith belonged to that group.

The woman smiled. "God loves to draw us closer to Himself, close enough to hear His heartbeat." She gave a slight nod, turned, and went to the door. "I will see you, Jillian," she called as she walked through it.

The door eased shut, its bell tinkling.

Jill sat down.

Why would anyone want to hear God's heartbeat?

CHAPTER 15

———— ❧ ————

JILL PULLED A cloth bag of groceries from the back of Viv's Jeep. "Oh."
She stopped unloading and looked at her sister.

"What's wrong?" Viv hoisted a bag onto her shoulder and reached
for another.

"I just got hit with this flash of normalcy."

Viv handed her a sack and shut the back of the car. "That's a good
thing, hon."

"No, it's not. I'm standing in your garage unloading groceries and
it feels *normal.*"

"Uh-huh." She stepped up to the door that led into the kitchen and
hit the automatic button to shut the overhead door. It rattled down.
"You could do with a little normal."

"I don't know." Jill followed Viv into the kitchen. "Cloth bags,
warm sunshine in winter, living at your house. This isn't any which way
normal."

Viv smiled and began putting away groceries. "It's the rhythm. Work,
eat, sleep, go to the market. Time and place don't matter. And what's

wrong with my cloth bags and warm winter sunshine?" She pointed to the pantry, a floor-to-ceiling, built-in cabinet next to the refrigerator. "Take this bag and unload it in there."

"Bossy, bossy." Jill opened the double doors, saw the disorganized shelves, and added to them. Jack would never let theirs get in such a state, but she didn't mind.

Maybe Viv was right. A day of routine and helping at the office had calmed Jill. Although she incessantly checked her phone and e-mail for messages from Jack, she had cried less than the day before and her chest did not feel full of concrete or burning lungs.

She shut the cupboard doors. "It's only been two weeks, Viv."

"I know."

"I shouldn't feel normal."

"Jillie, you're just taking a breather. It's a release valve."

"Jack and I should be working on things."

"You're working on things by stepping away from the situation. Which is what Jack proposed at the beginning. For now you can help me cook. Ha. That's probably what you call the blind leading the blind." Laughing, she walked toward the living room. "I'm going to ask Marty what veggie he wants."

The elusive brother-in-law was home. Jill hadn't exchanged ten words with him since she arrived because he hadn't been around much. She trailed after Viv, folding a bag, and stopped in the doorway between the rooms.

Marty sat in his recliner, his eyes on the television.

Viv stood next to him, hands on her hips. "It's so kind of you to show up."

He didn't bother to shift his eyes from the screen. "Kind of you to notice."

"You're missing my scowl, Martin. I've got a good one going." She creased her eyes to mere slits. "How's this? I learned it from Gretchen."

"Yes!" He was talking to the TV. "Nice shot." He looked at her. "Nice scowl."

"Thanks." Viv leaned down, kissed him, and turned to Jill. "That Gretchen is a pro at it, isn't she?"

"She's got nothing on you, though."

Marty turned his head to look at her. "Hey, Jill."

"Hi."

Viv said, "We bought roasted chicken from Ralphs."

"The little lady is cooking tonight. I love your chickens. You always choose just the right one."

She punched his arm. "Shut up. Do you want asparagus or green beans?"

"That's my choice?"

"No, I'm withholding veggie information."

Jill went back into the kitchen. As usual, she bristled at Marty's attitude. She didn't know why Viv put up with the way he spoke to her.

A short while later, the three of them ate the half-take-out, half-home-cooked meal at the kitchen table. Jill wondered if Viv had given orders to Marty to be amiable. They chatted about the new minibus, Viv's software that Jill was attempting to learn, Dustin, and even that odd woman Agnes Smith.

Marty said, "She's kind of like a car wreck. You can't take your eyes off her, but you want to because sooner or later she's going to bring up God and give you the willies. As a matter of fact, she brings God up more than you do, Jill."

Viv rolled her eyes. "Marty."

"What? It's true." He looked at Jill. "Don't get me wrong. Faith is a good thing. I only get the willies when someone shoves it down my throat."

Jill had had this conversation with him once or twice in the twenty-plus years they'd known each other. "By faith you mean going to church regularly."

"Yeah. I don't care to broadcast it."

"That's fine. I think God wants us to talk about Him, though."

"Communication doesn't have to be verbal. Or published in a book."

Viv groaned.

Jill said, "Everyone is different. I talk and write. And you do what, Marty? How do you communicate about God's reality in your life besides sit in a pew?"

He smiled but his dark eyes didn't crease. He set down his fork and knife and leaned back. His large forearms looked bigger as he crossed them. "The recipe is for beef, but this is a Rockin' Roast *chicken* we're having, isn't it?"

Jill started. "You read it?"

"Of course. My sister-in-law wrote it." He threw Viv a glance. "Changed my mind."

Jill opened her mouth and closed it. No need to ask what he thought of her book. She could imagine and it wouldn't be positive.

"I thought it had some helpful hints in it."

She blinked. "Really?"

"Yeah. Probably for a different crowd, though. Like a goody-two-shoes kind of female crowd. I mean, Viv and I have our Roasts and Crunchy Casseroles and Easy Eggs, but our 'recipes' aren't anything like the ones in your book. Sometimes we swear."

Viv groaned again. "Oh, Marty."

"Okay, I swear. Once in a while your sister does too, but not much. We've been known to yell at each other and then not talk for days. What was our record, babe? A week? 'Course the Sizzlin' Spinach is extra good after not talking—"

"Martin!"

He held up a hand. "Sorry. TMI, as they say. Then there's the regular stuff, like I'm sure you noticed. I don't get out of my chair to greet her. And like any self-respecting misogynist, I call her 'the little lady' and 'babe,' which are both on your no-no list. I also doubt, since there are two women in the house, that I will help clean up the kitchen tonight."

Jill had never really minded Marty's sarcasm. The two of them usually had at least one go-around per visit over some subject or other. But his tone strayed into personal territory. She had no comeback.

Viv said, "Marty, that was downright disrespectful."

"Sorry. I forgot the kid gloves." He turned to Jill. "Look, I am sorry you and Jack are having a rough time of it."

"You blame me for him leaving."

"I think you trusted in a bogus formula." He shrugged. "In all of our years of disobeying the so-called rules, Viv knows I love her. She knows beyond a shadow of a doubt that I am not going to leave her. Period."

"How . . . how . . . ?" She swallowed. "How does Viv keep you from leaving her?"

Marty frowned. "She doesn't. It's my choice."

"But . . . but . . ."

"You want it to work? You want your marriage to work?"

Jill nodded.

"Because you love Jack and not because of the book and your reputation that got flushed down the toilet?"

Tears seeped from her eyes. She couldn't answer. Of course she loved Jack, but her career was who she was. How could she turn her back on what she was called to do?

"Figure it out, Jill." Marty shoved his chair back and stood. "I need to take a walk." He stopped next to Viv, put his hand at the side of her head, and leaned over, holding her against himself for a long moment and whispering to her. He kissed the top of her head and went out through the garage door.

By then Viv was crying.

Jill wiped a napkin at her own tears. "Viv, he said that you know. How do you *know*? How do you know he won't leave you?"

Viv gave her a sad smile. "Because he had a reason to and he didn't."

CHAPTER 16

Stretched out on his mud-brown plaid couch, Jack pointed the remote at the television, hit the Mute button, and smiled. He'd discovered a great thing about not being continuously stretched like a rubber band at its snapping point: he could do absolutely nothing and enjoy himself.

It was Wednesday evening, nearly two weeks since he had snapped. Aside from the decor, life was all about new. He had new stitches, a new home, a new car, a new routine.

His fussy pal Baxter sat on the recliner, which he'd first insisted on covering with one of Jack's new towels. "You want to tell me about it?"

"My visit with the lawyer?"

"No, the weather forecast."

"Not much to tell. You've been there, done that. It's a simple division formula, right? 'Theirs' becomes 'his and hers,' most of which can be 'hers' as far as I'm concerned. I've got everything I need."

"Except decent furniture."

Jack chuckled.

"Property splitting is only one side of the divorce coin, Jack. Have you thought about all the other stuff you'll lose?"

He had. "You mean stuff like the incessant sound of ticking, chiming clocks? or the rubber band feeling?" He had told Baxter about that one. "Or the analyzing of every conversation?" He raised his voice to a falsetto. "'Jack, that was brilliant. Let's back up and figure out what we just did. What exactly are we communicating about? We're not really discussing scooping snow off the walk, are we?'"

Baxter stared as if in disbelief. "Yeah, stuff like that."

"My brother-in-law calls me the GP, short for *guinea pig*."

"Ouch."

"I overheard him say it one time. He's got this deep voice that carries. It ticked me off at first, but the more I thought about it, the more I realized it was pretty accurate. And then I realized I didn't mind. I served as a GP for a decent cause." He paused. "Jill gets mail and e-mails by the thousands. The majority are full of nothing but praise and gratitude. The other 10 percent are heartbreaking stories from women who wished they'd had the information years ago. How do you argue with that?"

"The question is, why are you arguing with it now? It's not just because you read about your candles in a bookstore aisle."

"No?"

"Nah. That was embarrassment. Just cause, for sure, but still. Why the sudden problem with your pride?"

"You sound like Jill."

Baxter did an eye roll. "Lord, have mercy."

Lord, have mercy. Lord, have mercy. Yes, Lord, have mercy.

It was an easy phrase that tripped lightly off the tongue, even one of an atheist. But it resonated in a new way. In essence it was a prayer. A prayer that he had lost sight of and now most desperately needed answered.

Baxter said, "You want my opinion before this intermission is over?"

Mercy. What he wanted was mercy. Compassion, kindness, relief, forgiveness. He wanted forgiveness.

"Jack."

"Yeah, okay. What's your opinion?"

"It's the concussion."

"I didn't have a concussion."

"Of course you did." Baxter shoved the footrest down and leaned forward. "Humor your doctor here and describe the accident again."

"What can I say? I proved what I learned long ago in driver's ed: brakes don't work on ice. When I saw the stop sign, I should have slowed to three miles per hour instead of eight."

"Where were you coming from?"

Jack glanced at the television. The hockey game was back on, but Baxter was clearly not interested. Disliking the position of psych patient lying on a couch, Jack sat up. "I told you. The dry cleaner's."

"On Ash, four blocks from home. The accident was a mile away."

"I took the longcut to avoid traffic."

"Jack, this is where your story breaks down. Four blocks of traffic? What were you doing?"

He sighed. "Procrastinating. Taking my time getting home."

"Okay, that I can buy."

"The weather was bad, but I had errands that could not wait. We were leaving town the day after the next. I remember braking. I remember sliding, turning the wheel, seeing a parked car. I remember calling 911 and being glad the passenger seat airbag deployed and not mine because it would have hurt a whole lot."

"You did not mention remembering the crash impact itself. And you noticed the airbag while you were calling 911, not the other way around. You should have seen the airbag while getting out your cell phone and then called 911."

Jack rubbed his forehead. "You haven't experienced an accident. It all runs together."

"At the least you were dazed and confused. I believe you were knocked out. Nothing showed up on the CT scan that night. Since then, Sophie and I have not heard you complain about headaches, dizziness, insomnia, or inability to concentrate."

"Because I haven't had any problems."

"Except all of a sudden you can't stand your wife."

"We've discussed that. Things have been building up for a long time. I've been in denial. It's why I took the longcut."

"The way you've solved the problem is totally out of character and out of line. Even I left my wife with more courtesy than you've shown Jill."

Jack winced. He could not deny what Baxter said.

"Listen, bud. I can't get a handle on you. Neither can Sophie. It all points to post-concussion syndrome."

"What? Come on, Baxter. You're chasing windmills. I have good reason to be acting a little weird."

"I want to do an MRI to rule out physiological causes. Sophie set it up. Lunchtime tomorrow. If your brain is okay, I promise to give it a rest." He smiled. "Because I trust you'll be seeing a counselor one way or the other and he can dig into emotional causes." He motioned to the television. "Turn the sound back on, please."

With a shake of his head, Jack picked up the remote. If Baxter the Bulldog and Sophie the Whiz had joined forces, there was no doubt he'd be having an MRI tomorrow.

❧

Jack awoke with a start, his heart booming like a kettledrum. The bedroom was pitch-dark. He didn't bother to turn on a light and find his watch.

Lying still, he took deep breaths and grumbled. If Bax had not tried to diagnose him earlier that evening, he would be absolutely fine. By speaking about post-concussion syndrome and tests, Baxter had sown all kinds of disruptive seeds.

Were symptoms honestly in play?

Irritability? Yes. It was growing against Baxter.

Stubbornness? Growing as well.

Insomnia? As of this moment, yes.

Change in personality? Yes. The accident was a wake-up call, not the cause of it. His eyes had been opened to the rut he and Jill were living in. The brush with serious injury energized him. The point was, they did not have to continue living in it.

Loss of memory?

Jack sat up, piled pillows behind himself, and leaned into them. He drew up his knees, pressed his forehead against them, and covered his head with his arms.

Loss of memory.

Yes.

Yes.

That was the worst. That was the most telling.

He'd avoided explaining to the cop, the ER doc, Jill, Baxter, and anyone else who asked that he did not distinctly remember seeing the stop sign or braking. He'd simply read the clues. Given the location of the accident and the policeman's reference to the stop sign, it was an easy conclusion. Less obvious was why he was there in the first place. Clothes covered in plastic from the dry cleaner's hung in the back. Evidently he had picked them up before the accident. He did not know why he'd taken such an indirect route home. What he told Baxter was a stab in the dark, though it could have been the truth. He had not been eager to go home for a long time.

But why was the car window open during a sleet storm? The impact jerked his head and smacked it against the edge hard enough to slice it open.

He imagined driving his car. Chicago's long winters meant it was common for him to drive home from the office in the dark during inclement weather. Grateful that he did not need to take an expressway, he often avoided even main thoroughfares and instead followed a maze of neighborhood streets. They were less congested. They were more interesting and calming even if snowplows did not get to them. They prolonged the trip home.

Sometimes he listened to Jill's radio station—if they played uplifting music. If they chitchatted or got stalled in hip-hoppy rock, he switched over to the jazz channel.

He remembered leaving the office later than usual that night. Most likely there had been music on the radio at that hour, the sort he liked. Maybe Michael W. Smith or Matt Redman. Maybe—

"Oh." The word escaped him like an expulsion of a breath held too long.

From the recesses of his memory came a tune, unfamiliar, something about *come to Jesus, come to Jesus.* Something about living, singing, dancing, flying. Sophie had introduced it to him. In the same roundabout way she helped patients see the uncomfortable reality of their insurance issues, she talked about her faith. It wasn't an in-your-face or a dogmatic black-and-white expression of God. There was a gentleness and subtlety about it.

He liked that about Sophie. The song was gentle and subtle too. He enjoyed listening to it in the car that night and thinking about Sophie.

The song had faded out and Jill's voice came through the speakers. It was a recorded commercial on her station for her program. She also mentioned the recent release of *She Said, He Heard* and an upcoming interview with some PhD she had quoted in the book. She said the title three times.

Three times.

He remembered distinctly.

He didn't slow down. He sped up to twenty-five miles per hour, the maximum on that street for a dry, sunny day. It was an inadvertent push on the gas pedal. An unconscious reaction . . .

To an in-your-face, black-and-white expression of a God who offered no mercy.

Lord, have mercy.

CHAPTER 17

———— ❧ ————

Jill gazed straight ahead at the back of Dustin's longish dark hair. He was driving the new minibus and Jill was ignoring her seatmate.

Somehow she had ended up on this outing rather than Viv's trip to a shopping mall. Somehow the zoo invitation had become an expectation. Somehow she had become an honorary member of the Casitas Pack.

Perhaps it was for the best. Viv had gotten testy last night when Jill asked more about Marty's cryptic words. Viv refused to explain why he had a reason to leave their marriage.

Like Jill couldn't guess. The Other Woman fit that scenario. What was with Viv's reticence? She seldom held back. What was the big deal for her to admit that Marty, like a huge percentage of husbands across the nation, had had an affair?

The hard part always came after. Jill could not guess at the timing of Marty's indiscretion, but surely he and Viv still lived with that cloud hanging over them. Kudos to them for forging ahead, but how could Jill minister to Viv if her sister would not let her inside?

"Everything all right, angel?"

Jill jumped at the voice.

Her seatmate, Agnes Smith, smiled. The palest of pale blue eyes gazed at Jill. Up close her complexion appeared translucent, as if the rounded cheeks were lit from within.

Suddenly Jill understood she could no longer hide from the intimidating ringleader of the Casitas Pack. The woman had blatantly coerced her into joining them for today's visit to the zoo. She had finagled her peacock blue velour–covered bottom into the seat next to Jill's.

And now she glowed from within and suddenly it all became too much for Jill to hold inside.

She shook her head vigorously. "No. Everything is not all right."

The story poured from her into the listening ear of a stranger who dug into a peacock blue backpack and pulled out a hankie for her.

Jill wiped her nose. "I'm sorry to unload on you, Agnes. You don't even know me."

"No worries, dear. Apparently you needed to unload on someone outside your circle of acquaintances. I just happened to be here."

"I doubt you believe in 'just happened.'"

Agnes chuckled. "You're right. It's my euphemism for 'God arranged this.' People tend to hang around longer if I don't hit them over the head with the God talk right off the bat." She squeezed Jill's hand. "I have two observations. Do you care to hear them?"

Jill smiled. "I've been gleaning advice from experts for years."

"I'm no expert."

"Oh, I suspect you are."

"Well, I was married for forty-five years and I'm eighty years old. I guess one could say I've been around for a while."

"Those are impressive credentials."

"It's just life." She shrugged. "I'm wondering what you think about God."

The release from telling her story to this elderly woman was palpable. Jill's chest did not hurt. But at the question, she squirmed. "I think He loves me and wants the best for me. I think He hears my prayers. I think Jesus was God with skin on and came to show us what God is like."

"I used to see Him as a distant king sitting on a throne, concerned only with rules, ready to rap our knuckles with a yardstick if we disobeyed. So I made sure I dotted all my i's and crossed all my t's."

Jill winced at the echo of her own words.

"As a young wife and mother I did everything according to what I thought God wanted." Agnes chuckled. "Even if it looked prissy and persnickety. Heavens to betsy! I was pigheaded about some things."

"None of us are perfect."

"No, we are not. But I thought I was close enough in order to have earned all the perks like a happy marriage, perfect kids, and no major problems. Guess what? My husband struggled with leukemia for years. One son was so embarrassed by me he left home at sixteen and didn't talk to me for ten years. The other son became a pastor and he's got the 'holier than Christ Himself' act down pat. My daughter married a gambling addict. My twenty-year-old grandson was killed in Iraq." She sighed deeply. "At first I questioned God's existence. Eventually I began to question my image of Him. Finally I concluded that God loves me." She smiled.

"And?"

"And that He is crazy about me. That He actually likes me."

"And?"

"That's all." She clapped her hands once. "Everything else follows from that, from living in the mystery of His wild love."

Jill blinked. "I am sorry for all your pain."

"Thank you, angel." She patted Jill's arm. "So as I was saying, I have two observations. One, you remind me of myself at your age."

"I do?"

"Yes. The black-and-white formulas about keeping rules in order to earn God's favor."

"I don't think that way."

"I read your book." Agnes winked. "You do think that way. Most likely not consciously."

"My method is to put handles on how to live a better way. That might look like a formula, but I only want to help people."

"Of course you do. And there is hope that you have succeeded."

"Hope?" Jill hoped they had succeeded in reaching the zoo.

"Yes, hope. Which brings me to my second observation. There is truth in what you've written, in what you teach, in what you believe. Therefore I trust you have helped people see differently. But it's not the end-all."

"What do you mean?"

"Dear, simply that God wants you to lighten up. Let go of your tight grip on the need to have all the answers. Let Him show you how much He adores you."

"I know He loves me."

"There you go with the pat answers. Oh, look!" She pointed toward the windshield. "Here we are at the zoo. Maybe we can learn something from the animals."

"The animals?" Marty was wrong. The woman wasn't like a car wreck. She was like a carnival worker who ran the roller coaster and sent people careening and screaming.

Agnes leaned in close to Jill, almost nose-to-nose. "One look at the warthog and you'll get an idea how much God must love His wacky creatures." She settled back in her seat and hummed softly, looking out her window.

Letting her words find their mark in Jill.

They stung. Jill had admitted to God and Gretchen her role in pushing Jack down the proverbial hill. If she had taken time out from her pursuits, they would have stayed current. He would not have tumbled so far down the path as to say he did not love her.

Okay. Take ownership, make repairs, move forward.

But this . . .

Lord, this is too much. It's too much.

She shut her eyes. *Not only did I do* it all wrong, *I am* all wrong.

Her boisterous brother-in-law and this oddball stranger—two people who would not see eye-to-eye on anything—basically agreed on what was wrong with the Galloway marriage.

Jill pressed on her burning chest. Her breath became ragged.

No, Lord. Please.

Were Marty and Agnes right? Did people see her as a persnickety Goody Two-shoes who trusted in keeping rules rather than in God? Was that the message she promoted?

If so, then she was everything she had always abhorred.

Silent sobs wracked her body. The oddball stranger held her hand.

༜

At the sight of the warthog, Jill smiled. She could not help herself.

She stood at the low chain-link fence in front of the wild hog's pen, absolutely transfixed. Weighing in at over two hundred pounds, the animal might have been the figment of a child's bizarre nightmare. Top-heavy with legs too small and head too large, he had curvy tusks and warty protrusions on his face. His noncolor of browns and grays blended into the surrounding rock and dirt. Guttural snarls and grunts came from him, ghoulish sounds.

How had Agnes tied such a thing to the love of God?

When Dustin had stopped the bus curbside at the zoo entrance, Jill disembarked with the others. She could not recall her feet actually touching the ground nor handing her ticket to the gatekeeper.

Her body ached from the recent sobbing, a release of pain so deep it had been inaudible. It subsided, leaving her with a sensation of moving in a bubble that only Agnes could penetrate.

"Jill, go see the warthog. Get a glimpse at what real love is." She pressed a map into Jill's hand and traipsed off.

As Jill had gotten her bearings, the bubble melted away, gently, peacefully. A riot of flowers and pink flamingos came into view, their colors vibrant. People filled the walkways, their voices and faces and clothes distinct to her senses. Odors mingled and separated—eucalyptus, animals, sweet waffle cones.

Now, after a long trek to the hog exhibit, she wondered at the almost-unbearable beauty surrounding her. Even the ugliest animal she had ever seen in her life expressed it.

She noticed a family of four near her. Mom and Dad laughed loudly. Big Brother roared, pointed at the hog, and mimicked him. Little Sister burst into tears at the others' reactions. They moved on, still chuckling and hugging each other.

Agnes Smith would say that little girl was like God, full of compassion for the unlovely.

"Right. Okay, God. I get it. I am the unlovely and You love me. But this is not a news flash. I've been around the block a few times."

Her throat tightened as the news flash presented itself.

Yes, she was like that warthog. People who learned the truth about her and her failed marriage were either going to laugh, ridicule, or feel pity. But . . . God loved her.

God. Loved. Her. Prissy, judgmental, plank-in-the-eye, warts and all. If she dotted a t and crossed an i, He would still love her.

He would still adore her.

Jill watched the warthog for a long time, basking in God's love, trying to get her mind around the fact that she could really and truly dot a t.

CHAPTER 18

———— ❧ ————

CHICAGO

"Dr. G?"

Jack glanced up from the computer and saw Sophie in his doorway.

"Call for you, line two."

"Intercom broken?"

She turned beet red.

He smiled. "Sophie, the MRI showed nothing. I am absolutely fine. You can stop checking up on me."

Flustered, she gave a businesslike nod. "It's your wife." She backed out, shutting the door as she went.

Jack noticed the red light blinking on the desk phone and scratched his chin, stalling.

He owed Jill more than the lowlife he'd been channeling.

The red light blinked—patiently, accusingly.

"You're being a jerk." Baxter's voice played in his head. *"Even I left my wife with more courtesy than you've shown Jill."*

He took a deep breath and picked up the phone. "Hello, Jill."

"Hi. I'm sorry to interrupt your day. Do you have a moment?"

Huh? "Uh, sure."

"I—"

"Wait. I need to say something. I apologize for what I said on the phone."

"It's all true, though, right? You moved into an apartment. You talked with a lawyer. You don't love me."

Jack winced. "Yes, but—"

"But nothing. It's true and it kept me from coming home, which has turned out to be a positive thing."

Obviously an alien now inhabited his wife.

She said, "A good dose of Viv and a few other things were exactly what I needed to gain some perspective."

"You sound different. Calm."

"I am and I want to make amends."

"I'm the one who wants out. It's not up to you to make amends."

"Jack, there's too much to explain over the phone. I'm taking a long, hard look at myself and I do not like what I see. I want to change. I want to be a new kind of wife. I want us to start over."

He leaned back in his chair and rubbed his forehead. Her voice was not racing at its typical warp speed. The words, however, echoed those of Jill the expert, Jill the counselor, Jill the answer bearer.

Why couldn't she hear it in herself?

She said, "I don't have a formula in mind. This is all new territory."

He bit back a retort about fodder for a lesson plan. New territory was an elixir to her.

"So I'm wondering," she went on, "why don't we do what we originally planned to do this Saturday? Go to Hollywood and remember how we met."

He envisioned the title already: *She Said Remember, He Heard Let's Rewrite History.*

"What better way to focus on us and find our way back to each other? It's perfect. The timing. The place. I mean, how often can you commemorate the twenty-fifth anniversary of a day that changed your life forever? What do you think, Jack? Hm?"

He thought she was analyzing and serving up Crunchy Casserole, the dish for how to communicate during difficult times.

"You can hop on a plane and be out here Friday. Or even take the red-eye and get here Saturday morning. We'll start at Grauman's, just like we did the first time."

"Jill, listen, please. I am not playing this scene."

"But playing the scene at Grauman's, where we met—"

"I'm talking about Crunchy Casserole."

"You can't go on ignoring this situation, Jack, honey."

"I'm not."

"I think you might be. Crunchy Casserole has always been the dish you avoid at all cost. Even the recipe you created for the book is full of water chestnuts, which you hate and never eat. Did you hear what I said? I want to start over. I want to change. We can fix this. I know we can."

"I heard." He sprang from his chair and banged his thigh against the corner of the desk.

"Then come out here so we can work on it together." Her breath became audible, several deep inhalations and loud exhaling.

His head reeled. He did not want to go out there. He did not want to be *fixed*.

She was sorry. So what? What did that mean? That he should ignore his allergic reaction once again and sit back while she spun yarns about a reconciliation? about how to do it the right way?

"Please, Jack. Take some time and think about it. I will be there in Hollywood on Saturday, at the spot where we met, at noon. I know you remember where it was."

He paced. Two strides covered the room. He swiveled on his heel. "Jill, I can't—"

"You can at the very least think about it. Right? Don't decide now. Don't promise anything except that you'll give it some thought."

He turned again, ready to pop. "I'll give it some thought."

"And come to your senses. Just kidding! Bye, Jack. Thank you."

He mumbled a good-bye and hung up without breaking his stride. It took a few spins before the taut rubber band of his nerves loosened and eased into place.

"Whew."

He sat down and gave it some thought.

Despite Jill's conciliatory tone and declaration that she wanted to change, she had launched a familiar script. Jack knew his lines forward and backward. He offered differing opinions, asked questions, and then he gave in to exactly what she wanted.

By agreeing to think about it, he really agreed to do all he could to make himself meet her needs. She would expect him to show up in Hollywood because in that way he would do what he had always done: kept the peace.

Jack shook his head. Why had he listened in the first place? Better he continue with the lowlife in charge when it came to conversing with Jill.

No, that was unfair. Jill was a spark plug that propelled them along wondrous roads of life. Keeping the peace was the price he paid to travel with her. It had been worth it.

Had been.

Still . . . he missed her. No, he missed the friendship they had enjoyed.

Maybe he should get a dog, one that did not like casseroles.

***

Assuring that sufficient thinking time passed, Jack waited until late that night to phone Jill. "I can't make it."

"Hon, it's still only Thursday. By Saturday your 'can't' may change to 'won't' and then to 'well, why not?'"

"I'm not coming."

"Okay. But then you won't hear about the warthog or Agnes Smith or Viv's new minibus."

"I am not coming. End of discussion."

"Well, I am." Her voice lilted and she rushed her words together.

He recognized the cover-up for tears.

"So," she went on, "if you change your mind, you'll know exactly where to find me at noon on Saturday."

Once more he would try. "Jill—"

"Do what's best for you, Jack. I need to go. I want to remember us when things were good. Bye!"

Jack loathed himself like never in his life.

CHAPTER 19

―――― ❧ ――――

"You're obsessing, babe." Marty pulled gently at Viv's waist, easing her from the recliner's arm onto his lap. "Relax."

She snuggled against him, her head on his shoulder, watching him watch the muted television. Being close to him like this was her safe harbor, one she hadn't sought for far too many days. "Why didn't I see it coming?"

He chuckled. "You did. You just didn't want to think about it. Mix up Jill with Agnes and you've got a humdinger in the making."

"But a spur-of-the-moment trip to Hollywood with the Casitas Pack just so Jill can be there when Jack doesn't show up?"

"It must be one of those ooey-gooey female things, right?"

"It's signing up to get stabbed in the heart again, and this time in front of an audience."

Viv had tried in vain to talk Jill out of following through with this ridiculous idea. Her sister and that stubborn streak of hers refused to back down, even after Jack said he would not be there.

Viv overheard her sister's side of the conversation. To her credit, Jill

133

did not whine or cajole but simply said, "Do what's best for you, Jack. I need to go. I want to remember us when things were good."

Huh?

Somehow Agnes Smith had gotten into the act. She insisted Jill should not go alone, that she and her regular band of six or so angels as well as five nonregulars would accompany her, and asked Viv if she needed the minibus or Dustin on Saturday. Saturday as in *tomorrow*.

Double huh?

Marty said, "I hear your brain waves. Stop obsessing. You said you'd drive them. Leave it at that."

"I wasn't about to let Dustin drive my new bus in L.A. traffic."

He looked at her and smiled. "Nor were you about to miss seeing your goofy sister flip out at a Hollywood landmark."

"She is not going to flip out."

He kissed her cheek. "She's going to hurt and you want to be there when it happens."

"She knows Jack won't be there. Why doesn't she give it up already? That's her problem. She won't let go. She keeps on pressing, which serves her well until it's a person she's prodding. Now he's running and she's going to get hurt all over again. Deep down she's hoping he'll change his mind and surprise her by showing up."

"Jack needs space right now. She has to wait until he's ready."

"Does that mean you're not going to call him and tell him that she needs a hero? that she needs him to come out and fight for their marriage?"

Marty grunted. "Not my job, babe."

"But if he'd just show a little interest. How can he keep putting her off, ignoring the whole—?"

Marty put a finger to her lips. "Not your job either."

"But—"

"Shh."

Viv gave in at last to the respite Marty offered just by being available. She took his callused hand from her lips, held it tightly, and went back to watching him watch the Lakers.

Once again she was struck by her sister's plight. Jill and Jack liked each other. She knew that. She had seen evidence throughout the years in how they related to each other. It was no act. That Jack was now unavailable to Jill broke Viv's heart.

It might not be her job to tell them how to fix their marriage, but there were things she could do. Pray, for one. Drive the minibus, for two. And for three, join that band of angels who would be hugging Jill when she began to cry.

CHAPTER 20

——— ✯ ———

ALTHOUGH JILL AND Marty spoke cordially to each other, she gave him and Viv their space as much as possible. Of course not joining them to watch basketball was an easy choice.

The small guest room with its television, radio, and desk provided a welcome haven. Pop music played as she worked on e-mails.

Connor had not yet responded to her note, a bland string of uncommunicative sentences. *How was Prague? No snow here! Ha, ha.* She and Jack need not have been overly concerned. Their son's creative head noticed beauty in a dried-up oak leaf, not the passage of weeks between his calls or e-mails.

Her cell rang and displayed Gretchen's name. They hadn't talked since Jill met the warthog.

It was the first thing Jill told her about.

Gretchen said, "I don't get it. You know God loves you unconditionally. Shoot, if I didn't believe that, I'd never get out of bed in the morning."

Jill rolled her eyes. "Maybe my delivery needs some work. What I learned was that I'm prissy and judgmental and proud and I have a plank in my eye."

"I could've told you that."

"Why didn't you?"

"I figured you knew."

"Seriously?"

"Yeah. It's part of your charm. It means you're warty like the rest of us."

"That's the most convoluted thing you've ever said."

"Thanks. So what else is new besides the Revelation according to Warthog?"

Jill gave up. Some days Gretchen wore her agent persona like a suit of armor. Jill couldn't blame her. She was on the road, working 24-7, out of touch with that inner self who was Jill's friend and would get the story.

She turned her attention to work and looked at the laptop. "E-mails are up. I guess people are still listening and reading the book."

"And still loving your advice."

"Not this person. Subject line says, 'Die.'" She clicked to open it. "'Dear Idiot. You should be shot.'" Hm, *idiot*. Another word to add to her growing list of nicknames.

"Delete it. Anything to indicate the gossip mill is going?"

"'Going yet,' you mean. You can say it out loud. Oh, here's something. This woman, Mrs. Anonymous, says my teaching is smelly garbage."

"Yikes."

"She says it's wrong to reduce God's Word into algebraic formulas. She's praying for me."

"Prayers are always good. Don't lose heart, sweetums."

Well, she was losing heart. The writer's admonition resonated. She herself had said not long ago that she had messed with God's Word.

"Jillie."

"What?" she snapped.

"Long live the warthog!" Gretchen chuckled. "Bye."

Jill closed her eyes. The animal really was filthy as well as ugly. It was probably stupid too. Identifying with it was losing its appeal.

❧

HOLLYWOOD

"Vivvie, I should have told Jack more." Jill heard the edge in her tone but could not refrain from examining the situation with her sister again. Or still. "Like about the warthog, how I can see where I've been wrong."

"Umpteenth time you've said that," Viv muttered through a clenched jaw. She was driving the bus, both hands on the wheel, eyes behind sunglasses darting back and forth as quickly as the freeway traffic surrounding them. "Enough already. You've strayed into blather territory. And please sit down."

"I am sitting." Actually she was leaning more than sitting. Sprawled sideways on the console, she was partially in the cab, a lower section of the bus that contained only one seat, the one Viv occupied.

"Jillian Autumn, I am serious." Her voice carried a threat.

Jill pushed herself up and stepped toward the passenger seats. Senior women filled fourteen of them, quite a turnout for a last-minute decision to take a day trip to Los Angeles. She knew they had canceled other plans, not because they wanted to visit a tourist site they'd seen several times over but because they wanted to support her.

Agnes motioned for her to sit beside her. Today she wore a black velour pantsuit and white T-shirt, glittery silver bangles, necklace, and earrings. Her white hair looked freshly downsized to a smaller bowl.

Car wreck or not, in some indescribable fashion the woman offered hope. Jill would sit with her and try not to worry about the crazy journey she had concocted after spending time with that warthog. She truly wanted to go down another memory lane, and she wanted to explore it with Jack. Instead she got a pack of sweet old ladies.

When Jill sat, Agnes took hold of her hand and squeezed it. Without a word she turned to look out the window. No doubt she was saying a lot in silent prayer.

Jillie Jaws considered taking notes. Maybe her gift of yap needed tweaking.

Within two hours they arrived in Tinseltown. Suddenly their bus seemed as enormous as a semi. Jill held her breath as Viv maneuvered the vehicle along Hollywood Boulevard absolutely filled with other buses and cars.

Agnes said, "Your sister is a confident little bugger, isn't she? Drives this bus like it's a two-seater Mercedes."

"Mm-hmm."

Agnes chuckled. "She really is a magnificent driver. We've never had any qualms about her ability to get us to and fro."

Viv braked at a stoplight and Jill gawked at the scene that lay outside. It wasn't the ride or her sister's driving or the traffic that had her nerves crackling. Nor was it the glitzy energy that usually struck her. It had nothing to do with the fifteen blocks of the Walk of Fame, charcoal-colored sidewalks featuring over two thousand pink stars with famous names embedded in brass. It had nothing to do with the Kodak Theatre situated high up in a multistory open-air mall waiting for the next Academy Awards night. It had nothing to do with the street performers and ticket hawkers mingling with the crowds of visitors.

Nope. It had everything to do with the huge red pagoda-style building right there on the sidewalk in the middle of the city. Streams of tourists strolled about in front and in the forecourt. Grauman's Chinese Theatre had always struck Jill as so Hollywood, both stunning and tacky at once. Its details were endlessly ornate. Dragons were poised to climb onto the copper roof. Lion-dogs guarded the main entrance. The most famous part was the forecourt with hand- and footprints of movie stars immortalized in the concrete squares.

And right there on one of those concrete squares, twenty-five years ago on this twenty-eighth day of February, Jillian Wagner and Jackson Galloway met.

Today they would not meet there.

Jill muttered to herself, "This is the most stupid idea I've ever had."

Viv swung the bus around a corner and braked in an unloading area. The wide side doors swished open.

Women made their way past Jill, down the two steps, and onto the sidewalk.

Viv was turned in her seat up front, smiling, chatting with them. "Yes, I'm coming, as soon as I can find a parking spot. Careful, Martha. Have fun, ladies! Watch it there, Lila." She looked at Jill, who wasn't budging. "Go."

She shook her head.

Viv cocked an eyebrow and shifted her gaze to Agnes, still seated beside Jill next to the window.

Agnes hooked her arm with Jill's. "What I like about this place is its history. Do you know what movie they first premiered here in 1927?"

"No."

"*The King of Kings*. A Cecil B. DeMille silent film. Isn't that fascinating?" Agnes winked. "Because we know the King of kings, don't we? And He is all about healing our hearts that get so overfull with our own histories. Come on; grab your pocketbook and let's go. I want to hear all about how you met your Jack."

If those pale blue eyes had not been gazing at Jill, she doubted she would have taken one step toward hiking down this memory lane and reliving one single minute of her history.

But they *were* gazing at her.

She stood and helped Agnes to her feet.

❧

It had been the type of winter day that gave Southern California its reputation for year-round balmy temperatures, blue skies, and swaying palm trees. It was a perfect day to shuttle a group of seniors up to L.A. for a visit.

"Like today," Agnes said.

"Like today." Telling her story, Jill strolled beside Agnes, slowing her pace to stay even with her and her cane, trying not to bolt through the crowded court to her and Jack's spot.

"You and Viv didn't have a minibus back then, did you?"

"No. We had a nine-passenger van. Grandma Ellie started the business as a lark. But it grew to the point where she couldn't run it alone. She brought us on board full-time when we were still in our teens."

"What was your grandmother like?"

Jill smiled. "She was the queen of fun and touristy bargains. Viv and I grew up out in the desert. Not much to do there except hike and watch television and movies. Our parents still seem contented there, but Viv and I could not wait to leave. We loved our summer visits with Grandma Ellie. I especially loved our treks to Hollywood to see anything and anyone connected with all the TV and movies I watched."

"And here we are."

"Yes, here we are." Jill pointed to a square just ahead and they walked to it.

"Shirley Temple." Agnes read the name and smiled. "Why her?"

"Grandma Ellie said I looked like her when I was little."

"Let me guess. Your bubbly voice and pretty features."

"Nope. The curly hair." She touched her head. "It went straight when I got pregnant."

"So on that fateful day twenty-five years ago you stopped here at your favorite square. And then what?"

Jill stared at the prints and the writing. Shirley Temple had signed her name and written *Love to you all* in 1935. She would have been about seven years old.

How beautiful that a young girl felt so much goodness in her soul she wanted to share it permanently with the world. Jill felt drawn to that. She wanted to be like Shirley Temple on the inside, not just the outside curly hair. On her first visit she knelt and tried to fit her hands into the prints. The first time they fit.

But even after she outgrew them, she continued to touch them whenever she came. She would always kneel, place her hands into the prints, and pray that God would give her the opportunity to love the world in a big way.

On that fateful day as she knelt and prayed, a male voice above her had said, "They almost fit."

She remembered looking up and into the kindest eyes she'd ever seen. His smile finished her off, though. It was absolutely perfect with lips not too thin or too full, the corners of his mouth dimpling inward and upward just so.

At the memory now her breath caught. She could not voice her thoughts to Agnes. Instead she sank to her knees and placed her hands over the prints. The sun beat on the back of her neck. People shuffled by. Conversation and laughter filled the air.

Lord, I wanted to love the world in a big way. You sent Jack. Then teaching, radio, and the book, all so I could tell the world about Your love. I am sorry. I tried. I honestly tried.

She wiped at the corner of her eye.

Can I just have Jack back?

He wasn't coming. Deep in her heart she had hoped that despite his declaration to the contrary, he would revert to his old self and pull one of his off-the-wall surprises and show up. Now deep in her heart she sensed that was not going to happen. Why had she allowed herself to hope? Disappointment cut like a knife.

She sat back on her haunches and willed herself not to cry.

"They almost fit."

Jill whipped around and looked into the sun. The outline of the man was tall. Too tall to be Jack.

He moved and blocked the sun. "Did I get it right, Mom? Is that what Dad said?"

"Connor?" She jumped to her feet and into her son's arms. "Oh! I don't believe it! What are you doing here?"

"Term break. Thought I'd surprise you guys." He gave her an extra bear hug and then held her at arm's length. His smile was the same as

Jack's, his eyes blue like hers, his dark blond hair a combination of both of theirs and pulled back into a ponytail. "Where's Dad?"

Jill's smile vanished.

Connor had no idea where Jack was. She wasn't so sure herself about where he was. Off the deep end? Wallowing in the murkiness of some vague crisis? With another woman?

Who knew?

CHAPTER 21

———— ❧ ————

AFTER PARKING THE bus, Viv wove her way through milling tourists in front of the Chinese Theatre. Most likely Jill was already at Shirley Temple's spot, reminiscing with Agnes about how Jack first spoke to her.

She saw Jill now. She was reaching out to—Connor?

Viv's nephew grinned and wrapped his mother in a hug. Taller and lankier than Jack, he was a cute kid with Jill's delicate features. He looked very Bohemian in sandals, jeans, and T-shirt, his long hair tied back. What was he doing there? He was supposed to be in Italy for several more months.

Viv groaned. "Oh no." He was surprising his parents. If he'd known about the separation, he would not be there.

She noticed Agnes standing off to one side and hoped the saint was praying her socks off.

Viv neared as Jill and Connor parted.

"Where's Dad?" Connor glanced around as if searching for him and saw her. "Aunt Viv!"

"Hi." She embraced him and yanked his ponytail. "Still got that." She had seen him the previous spring, after his college graduation.

He grinned. "Hey, it's great to see you. I didn't think you'd be here."

She smiled and shrugged. *Long story. Long, long story.*

"Is Uncle Marty here?" he said, animated as usual like his mom. He waved his arm, beckoning behind Viv. "You can all meet Emma."

Emma? Viv exchanged a look with Jill, whose face was scrunched up as tightly as it had been twenty-three years ago when she was in labor with this son.

A lovely young woman with flawless skin stepped to Connor's side. There was an obvious European flair about her. Black hair straight across her forehead, diagonal at the sides. Black pencil skirt, black-and-white striped shirt. Chunky necklace and bracelet. Chunky heels. Square handbag. Except for the silver hoop earrings and large brown eyes, she seemed all angles.

"Mom, Aunt Viv—" Connor's face lit up; Viv imagined she heard a drumroll—"this is Emma Trudeau."

Emma's face did not light up. She resembled the proverbial rabbit in the lettuce patch, every nerve on alert.

But she did not run. *"Bonjour."* She shook Jill's hand. "I am very pleased to meet you, Mrs. Galloway." Her accent was French, her voice low and surprisingly confident.

Jill appeared still lost in the birthing process with cheeks too rosy and forehead damp with perspiration. Spoken words were not imminent.

Viv nudged her aside and shook Emma's hand. "She's Jill. I'm Viv. Nice to meet you, Emma. Welcome to Hollywood."

"Thank you." The girl almost smiled.

Connor said, "So is Dad coming or not?"

Viv looked at her sister. *Nah.* Vocalizing the news to her son was a ways off for Jill.

So Viv took charge. "Actually, he's not, Connor. A problem has come up." Concern lined his face. "Nothing to worry about. He's fine." *Well, so to speak.* "Let's go somewhere else to talk. How about the Roosevelt Hotel? It's not far."

Not waiting for anyone to reply, Viv grabbed hold of Jill's elbow and made a beeline to the street with her in tow. She glanced over her shoulder and gave Connor and his friend an encouraging smile. Behind them Agnes thrust her cane high as if it were a sword and she was shouting, *Charge!*

Familiar with the old woman's wild imagination, Viv figured Agnes was seeing angels. Good. Her sister and nephew needed all the help they could get not to fall into total despair.

She noticed the young couple. Connor's expression was still worried. Emma's left arm still looped around his elbow. Something flashed, a glisten of sunlight on her hand.

On her third finger, to be exact. Her ring finger.

Viv groaned to herself. Did Connor have big news of his own? Jill would have told her if she already knew. What was it with the Galloway men jumping to the grand finale without a gradual buildup?

Beside her, Jill shook her head vigorously. "Jack should have told him. I can't do it. I cannot do it."

"Well, you have to. First, though, you better start breathing. Inhale. Do it, Jill."

She produced a raspy noise.

"Deeply. Deeper. Blow it out now, really hard. Harder. There you go. Do it again. Pretend you're in labor. You're about to give birth. Come on. You can do it, Mom."

"He wasn't there then either."

"What? Breathe, honey."

"Jack." Jill struggled to catch a breath. "He missed most of the labor. He got there just as Connor came out."

"I remember." Of course she remembered. She was there; Jack wasn't.

Viv checked for oncoming traffic but didn't slow. She hurried them off the curb into the crosswalk as the Don't Walk warning flashed. "You delivered early. He was in surgery."

"It ticked me off."

"It should have."

"He knew I was close. It was elective surgery. The woman's bunions weren't that bad. She could've lived with them another week."

"Jillie, shh."

"It was our first real Rockin' Roast meal, you know. We learned how to argue on that one. I was so mad."

"That's great."

They stepped onto the curb and scurried down the sidewalk.

"I put it in the book."

"Mm-hmm." She had read it and cried for Connor. As a baby he would have overhead their row, first from the womb and later as a newborn. Helpless and vulnerable, he must have been affected in some way by the discord.

Jill said, "As a matter of fact, I do believe I'm still mad about it. Which probably proves I should keep my trap shut."

"Not today, you don't." Viv steered her through the hotel doors. "Today you talk to your son."

"How do I do that without making his father look like a—like a . . ."

"Like a creep? a scumbucket? a reprobate?"

Jill scowled at her.

Viv admired her loyalty but there was no time for that. She changed the subject. "Isn't this lobby gorgeous now? You haven't seen it since the latest renovations."

Her arm still linked with Jill's, she marched across the polished tile as if she owned the place. Dead ahead was a vacant corner of buttery soft, tufted leather seating. She stopped there and turned to watch Connor and Emma. Somehow they fit in the 1927 ambience. Artist and foreign beauty.

When they reached them, Viv said, "Emma, are you an artist too?"

"I like to paint, but no. I am not an artist. I do as Connor. I study the history of art. It is much more satisfying."

Connor said, "Aunt Viv, you know I'm not an artist either."

"But you are. I still have that watercolor you painted for me when you were fourteen. It's framed in my living room. Someone who knows art offered me a lot of money for it. I figure if I hold on to it long enough, it'll pay for my nursing home."

Connor couldn't hold his smile and his eyes kept darting to Jill. "Mom."

"Yes." Jill took a firm grasp of the hand Emma did not hold and pulled him down beside her on the love seat.

Emma had no choice but to sit elsewhere. Viv pointed to one of two wingback chairs and they sat. The girl crossed her legs and arms, tucking the telltale diamond ring out of sight.

Jill cleared her throat. "Dad didn't come. At the last minute, when we were leaving the house to go to the airport, he said he didn't want to come." Holding Connor's hand in both of hers on the seat between them, she looked directly at him. "Honey, he said he wants a divorce."

Connor flinched. "What?"

"I know, it's just out of the blue, completely out of character. We've talked since. He says he's not ready to address things yet. He wants time and space. I suspect we're into a midlife crisis here. There weren't any typical symptoms, but we are at a certain age when we start to question what's next in life. Perhaps it was the car accident that—"

"Car accident?" His voice rose. "What car accident?"

"Oh. Well. That's right, you don't know about that either. We didn't call you because there was nothing to tell you, not really. It was two days before we were to leave. He braked at a stop sign, hit a patch of ice, and slid into a parked car. He bumped his head. The ER put in a few stitches and x-rayed. I think it shook him up more than either of us realized at the time."

"Back up, Mom." Connor slid his hand from hers and massaged his temple. "Dad announces he wants a divorce and then you get on a plane and go to California?" His tone was incredulous.

Jill sat up straighter. "You weren't there. It's impossible to imagine. He practically carried me from the front door to the taxi that was waiting and dumped me in the backseat and told the driver to go."

"And you didn't tell the driver to stop. You didn't get to the airport and turn around and go back."

"I was so upset I could hardly breathe, let alone make a sensible decision like turn around and go back. I came here today hoping he would show up and we could start working on things. I'm sorry, honey." Jill pulled a tissue from her shoulder bag and dabbed at her eyes. "We'll get through this; I promise. It's one of those unplanned detours on the marriage road."

"Mom, why don't you just go home?"

"Home? Home?" Jill nearly squeaked the word.

Uh-oh, Viv thought. Her sister's jaw wiggled, not exactly a tremble, not exactly a clench. It was, however, a definite signal that meant trouble.

She stood. "Jill, let's—"

"Home? I don't have a home, Connor." Words gushed from Jill. "For your information, I tried to go. I called your father from the airport, and guess what he said. He moved out. He moved into an apartment. There is no home to go to."

"Why do you always have to be so literal?" His voice resonated with more maturity than twenty-three years' worth. "You have a hometown. You have a husband in it. How can he talk to you unless you're there? Obviously something is seriously wrong, and you expect him to travel all the way out here to do what? Talk on a sidewalk next to some handprints?"

"You can't possibly understand."

"No, I can't. You two still treat me like a kid."

"You are a kid, compared to us, and yes, we probably spoiled you to some degree but why would we burden you with things you don't have to carry?"

"Things like my parents splitting up? Like that's got nothing to do with my future? You've kept me in the dark about everything except how wonderful your marriage is. Which, apparently, was all smoke and mirrors."

"It was not! We do have a wonderful marriage. Your father is going through a midlife crisis and that happens to the best of men. And it hurts the best of marriages."

"But I bet you have all the answers for it, don't you?" He stood abruptly and held an arm out toward Emma. Everything about his body language indicated he was distraught.

The girl moved to his side and he draped an arm around her shoulders. They exchanged a few quiet words in French.

Jill's cheeks shone with two bright pink spots. The rest of her seemed drained of color and energy. She did not stand. "Connor, I appreciate that this news disturbs you, but I do not appreciate your attitude. If you want to be treated as an adult, then act like one."

He turned from Emma. "You're right, Mom. I apologize for the attitude. As an adult, I'm here to say that I came all this way to introduce my parents to my fiancée. I thought it would be a happy occasion. Obviously it's not, so we're going to leave now. I'm taking Emma home to meet Dad. That gives you another reason to go home."

Jill stared, speechless.

"You know, so you can spend time with your future daughter-in-law?"

Her jaw went from slack to rigid.

Connor shook his head as if disgusted. "Maybe by then you can tell us congratulations."

Jill said, "We just met."

"Oh, forget it." He turned and gave Viv a quick hug. "Bye, Aunt Viv. Tell Uncle Marty hey."

She whispered in his ear. "Congratulations. I'm sorry."

"Not your fault."

As Viv returned Emma's hug, she saw Jill stand.

Gentle Connor, fury written on his face, hugged his mother. He released her and, to his credit, made eye contact. "We're traveling with Emma's parents. I'll be in Chicago March 23."

"Okay," she whispered. "I'll come."

Viv breathed a quiet "Yes!"

Jill held out her hand to Emma. "I am sorry we had to meet under these circumstances."

The girl nodded politely. "I am also. Good-bye."

Viv watched the young couple walk away. They did not turn around before disappearing from view.

She plunked back down on the chair. A lifetime ago she had

suffered three miscarriages and an early hysterectomy. She and Marty were sad, but deep down she was all right. She wasn't so sure she was cut out to be a mother. She probably would have been like Jill. In her sister's enthusiasm not to be like their mother—a bystander at best during their childhoods—Jill smothered Connor with attention, all sorts of unnecessary, overbearing attention. Viv marveled at his ability to fly the coop.

Jill said, "I should go home."

Viv sighed to herself in relief. "Okay. We can get you on the red-eye tonight or a direct flight first thing in the morning."

Jill shook her head. "Viv, I blew it with Jack. I blew it with Connor. I blew it with my career. I ruined it all. Where would you go if you ruined it all?"

Viv didn't even need a heartbeat to ponder her reply. "To Pops."

"Yeah. I'm forty-five years old and I want my daddy."

Viv watched the pink spots fade from Jill's cheeks. Her complexion turned grayish. The light in her eyes went out.

Viv bit her lip. They were in the middle of Hollywood, hours of busy freeway traffic from home, with a group of seniors who were probably looking for her by now. Her tears would have to wait.

CHAPTER 22

———— ✿ ————

Jack admitted to himself that he had not considered the ramifications of his actions, not really, not in the comprehensive, exhaustive manner that one would expect of a physician. In many ways he was still too caught up in the moment, adjusting to the everyday how: how to begin the day, end the day, eat and sleep without that *other* who had been there beside him for the past twenty-five years.

Now, though, as he sat at his desk and listened to his son vent and grieve on the phone, he began to sense the ripple effects of his actions.

"Dad, I just wish I'd known before I showed up to surprise you guys."

"I didn't know myself until it happened."

"But that was over two weeks ago! I left Rome last night! And it's not that hard to reach me!"

Well, that was debatable, given that the kid seldom checked for messages on his phone or e-mail. But Jack did not go there. "Connor, the truth is I don't understand what I'm doing. I only know I don't want to be married any longer. I couldn't bring myself to say that to you."

"Because you're embarrassed that you and Mom are not the picture-perfect couple everyone thinks you are?"

153

Jack tugged on his earlobe. He'd always encouraged Connor to speak his mind. It was the thing he himself most appreciated about his own father, who never belittled Jack because he spoke out of inexperience.

Or because he spoke a disconcerting truth.

"Yes, I am embarrassed to some extent. I liked being a poster husband."

"'Liked.' Past tense, meaning up until now."

"I suppose."

"Until what? Your car accident? Which brings up another point."

Jack gave him a brief overview of that night. "It wasn't a big deal. The cut is healing fine." He heard a discreet knock on his door. "Hold on a sec."

Sophie poked her head inside, a question on her face.

He nodded in reply and mouthed his son's name. Yes, he realized his patients were stacking up, but Connor came first.

She gave him a thumbs-up, supportive as ever, and shut the door.

"Connor, I am sorry you were blindsided. How did you leave it with your mother? Are you going down to San Diego with her?" There was no response, and Jack thought he heard a muted sniffle.

This was why God hated divorce.

"Son, are you okay?" Such a dumb question.

Connor inhaled shakily. "I have some news too. Good news, but Mom . . ." He cursed softly.

Jack shut his eyes. Connor's pain did not stem from Jack's actions alone. Like Jill, he was sociable, well-liked, straightforward, confident. He even resembled his tall and lanky Grandpa Wagner. But there had always been an underlying tension between mother and son.

Like between husband and wife?

"Dad, I met a girl."

"Emma."

"Yeah." There was a grin in Connor's voice. "How'd you remember? I only mentioned her once."

"It must have been your tone when you mentioned her." The kid had been obviously enamored of a fellow student. "She's French, right?"

"Right. From Paris. Smart and beautiful. We have the same interests, et cetera, et cetera. Anyway . . ." He paused. "Anyway . . ." He stopped talking again.

"You love her."

"Oh, Dad." Regret was in his tone. "I wanted to tell you in person. We're engaged. And we want to get married soon, in Chicago. April 11 will be our last Saturday in the States, so sometime before that date."

An avalanche of reactions hit Jack. *Don't be ridiculous. You're too young. Didn't you just meet like five months ago? Think it through. Marriage is not all it's cracked up to be. Look at your mother and me. What a waste of time and effort! The only good, lasting thing about us was . . . you.*

The only good, lasting thing was Connor, his son, who at twenty-three understood only that he did not want to live without the woman he adored. She was the only person on the face of the earth who made him feel good and right and accepted and worthy and able to leap tall buildings in a single bound.

Jack chuckled. "Wow! Connor, that's wonderful. Congratulations. Is she there with you?"

"Yeah."

"Put her on."

"She's kind of shy." There was a muffled exchange. "Here she is."

"*Allô*, Jacques."

"*Bonjour*, Emma. I'm afraid that's the end of my French. Congratulations."

"Thank you very much. I love your son."

"I do too." He spoke briefly with her, listening to the voice that had captured his son's heart. It was a pleasant one, shy and confident at once in its mix of languages and accents.

Connor came back on the line. "We're meeting her parents in San Francisco tonight and doing some touring between here and there. I'll be home the twenty-third. They'll arrive later that week." He offered more details of what they had in mind for a small wedding. "Okay?"

"Great."

"Dad—" his voice broke again—"Mom hardly spoke to her."

"Oh, Con. Tell Emma not to take it personally. Your mother is hurting. I've hurt her badly."

"No. She would have been like that anyway. She always told me she'd have a hard time giving me up to another woman."

Jack thought of his own mother's relationship with Jill. It wasn't pretty. "Moms are like that. No other woman is good enough for their son. Vice versa is true. If you were my daughter telling me about a guy, I'd be googling him already. I'd be asking you for bank account information, fingerprints, family history, genetics."

"Got it." Connor blew out a breath. "Thank you for your support."

"Emma sounds like a good match for you." He heard the *but* in his own voice. "I'd be remiss, though, not to ask the obvious. Are you sure?"

"Yeah, I'm absolutely sure she's the one. You always taught me that marriage is a good and honorable thing. Has that changed?"

Good question. He loved Connor more than anything in the world. Jack wanted to revisit every moment he had lost his temper with him or made a bonehead parental decision or missed an opportunity to spend five minutes with him. He would redo those moments. He would make everything right so that his child never experienced wounds that he had unintentionally inflicted because he was, like every father before him, enrolled in on-the-job training. Mistakes came with the territory.

In this moment now—could he protect Connor from further harm? Of course not. All he could do was tell him the truth.

"No, Con, I still believe that marriage is good. When I met your mother twenty-five years ago, my world changed. She made it a better place. If Emma makes your world a better place, marry her. Live in that better place."

A silent moment passed and then Connor said, "What happened to your better place?"

Jack rolled his eyes. "I'll get back to you on that one."

Connor groaned. "Big help you are. See ya, Dad."

"See you, Son. Give your Emma a hug from me."

After he hung up the phone, Jack sat still. Stronger than the pull on his conscience to get back to work was the pull of his son's question.

What had happened to his better place?

A litany of responses sprang to mind. They all began with *Jill*.

Jill did this. Jill did that. Jill did not do this. Jill did not do that. Jill wanted this. Jill wanted that. Jill. Jill. Jill.

And what was Jack doing the whole time?

Evidently not caring about the disintegration of his better place.

CHAPTER 23

———— ❧ ————

In the passenger seat of her sister's car, ignoring the desert landscape zipping by them, Jill lifted her cell phone high and checked its screen for the umpteenth time. "Godforsaken country."

"Which you are totally missing." Viv reached over and poked her arm. "Look out the window."

Jill looked. "I see dirt, rocks, sticks that call themselves bushes, and an empty two-lane highway going nowhere. What's your point?"

"It's beautiful."

"And God hath forsook it. There is no cell service." She sighed, lowered the phone, and bit a fingernail. "I can't believe I let you convince me to bring my bags. All I want to do is spend a few hours with Pops. I need a Pops fix."

"Give it a rest, Jill. You need serious time off. You cannot take care of Jack, Connor, your friends, and your fans right now. You need to take care of yourself. Famous people do this all the time." She threw her a grin. "Think of it as rehab."

"With Mom and Pops."

"Right. Well, with Pops, anyway. He is the ultimate rehabber. I'll run interference for you with Mom."

"Do I have an addiction?"

"That phone."

Jill straightened her sunglasses and leaned against the seat. *Rehab* felt like an apropos term.

Yesterday's events were the icing on the cake of despair. Jack's no-show at their special place in Hollywood on their special anniversary deeply pained her, although it had not been a complete surprise. But add the encounter with Connor, and she was brought to the end of herself. She was left with no choice but to face a brutal reality about her family and friends.

Her husband and son had shut her out of their lives. Her career was either on hold or nonexistent. Viv, Marty, Gretchen, and other friends with whom she'd talked or e-mailed in recent days all had their own lives to get on with. She really had nowhere to go except back to the warthog's pen or to her dad. If she chose the animal, she wouldn't have to contend with Daisy; but Skip won out anyway.

Viv had called him and relayed the lowdown on his elder daughter's life. She said Jill would be coming for an indefinite stay.

He replied, "No problemo, kiddo," and insisted that Jill not wait to come next week with Viv's scheduled senior trip. She needed to get home ASAP, as in *now*.

Skip Wagner's fatherly track record put every *Father Knows Best*–type dad to shame. The sisters trusted his opinion.

Viv offered to drive her the two hours over to Sweetwater Springs. Then, practical as ever, she cautioned Jill against unnecessarily spending money. Although Jack made a decent living, their monthly expenses had increased with his move out of the house. Women in Jill's position—separated with little or no income of their own—counted pennies. Jill should not even consider renting a car or staying in a hotel or even paying for Viv's gas.

That was when Jill burst into tears. Marty left the house. Viv congratulated her on the emotional display. It was far better than the zombie she'd been mimicking since Connor's good-bye. Not even Agnes had been able to crack Jill's exterior during the bus trip back from Hollywood.

"Yee-haw!" Viv let out a squeal now and the car shot forward like a cannonball.

They barreled down a familiar stretch of highway, Viv's lead foot firmly in place. Jill's stomach tickled as they hit a series of smooth roller-coaster dips at full speed.

"Vivian! Slow down!"

Her sister only laughed.

It was Wagner tradition to drive NASCAR-style into and out of Sweetwater Springs. Their father was not a reckless driver, but he'd fly along fast enough to make his little girls giggle and their mother fuss. Jill couldn't find her giggle today.

A few moments later the road flattened out and stretched like a ribbon before them, disappearing into a mirage of billowy silver curtains. The town was close now, although it lay hidden from view, behind those curtains.

At the age of eighteen, Jill had hightailed it the other direction, hitting those dips far above the speed limit. With a population of two thousand, her hometown did not resonate with her dreams. In San Diego she lived and worked with her grandmother. The following year, just as eager to live in the city, Viv joined her.

Since then, Jill had visited Sweetwater sporadically. Sometimes Jack accompanied her. Connor loved the desert and as a teen often went during school breaks by himself.

Odd, Jill thought, how as a girl she couldn't wait to leave the small town in the middle of nowhere and how her big-city son could probably live in it happily ever after.

But with a French wife?

A chill went through her. Wife.

No. Connor and what's-her-face were engaged. That did not mean imminent matrimony. It did not even mean certain matrimony.

Where was he now? Had he called? Had he listened to the apologetic voice mail she left last night? Should she leave another?

Jill checked her phone again. "I have a message!"

Viv gasped. "Oh, happy day! Sweetwater is connected to the outside world!"

Jill ignored the gibe and keyed into her messages. "It's a text. From Gretchen. She says, 'Someone from Hope Church wants to talk. I gave her your number 'cause you really need to listen to her. Love you.'"

"You don't *really need* to do anything related to work, Jillie." Viv glanced at her. "Get that through your thick head."

"Fine. I don't really want to talk to anyone about work anyway."

"Put the phone down."

"I have to see if Jack or Connor called." She scrolled through a few missed calls from friends. One unknown number; maybe it belonged to that teacher. Nothing from her husband or son.

Nothing.

Viv reached over and snatched the phone from her hand. "This only makes you feel worse. From now on anyone who wants to reach you can go through me or Pops. Until you're ready, this cell stays with me."

"Do you want my laptop too?"

"Nope."

Then Jill remembered. "They don't have Internet, do they? They don't even have a computer."

Viv smiled gently. "You'll live through the withdrawal."

Jill wondered if she would even notice. She felt like the landscape looked—all grays and browns, sticks pretending to be live plants. Both Sweetwater Springs and her future were ahead somewhere, out of sight and unimaginable.

❧

The instant Viv parked the car, Jill's door opened and she tumbled into her father's waiting embrace.

"What took you so long, Jaws?"

Her ear pressed against his chest, she listened to the rumble of his deep voice. She shut her eyes and caught faint scents of Old Spice, desert air, and automotive grease.

"Huh?" He held her at arm's length and gazed at her with brown eyes squinted nearly shut. His narrow, rugged face hadn't changed all that much in the forty-plus years she had known it.

She felt ten years old. It wasn't exactly a bad feeling to be called on the carpet and expected to spill whatever painful truth was undoing her. "Pride."

"Yep. That would do it." He tilted his head and gray bristles on his chin caught the sunlight. "You know you never need to hide from me and your mother."

"Oh, Pops! I look like a fool to everyone who's ever heard me teach. I couldn't stand to have you two see me like that."

"Nasty thing, pride." He squeezed her shoulders and let go. "We love you, foolishness and all."

Her bottom lip trembled. "Jack doesn't. He doesn't love me anymore."

"Sure he does. He just doesn't like you."

"Thanks. That helps a heap."

Skip grinned, the familiar gap between his two front teeth endearing and comforting.

She realized Viv must have gone inside to greet their mother and was glad for the chance to receive Skip's comfort before Daisy's typical *tsk* and head shake.

"Jillie, I aim to say one thing straight off and be done with it."

She winced. She knew what was coming because she'd heard it all her life. It was his answer for everything from a hangnail to slow business at his service station. It had become her answer for everything as well. It was why Gretchen accused her of making lemonade from life's lemons.

"Pops, I don't want to hear it. All things do not work together for our good. Two and a half weeks ago my life got split into *before* and *after*. Before and after Jack left me. I don't believe in Romans 8:28 anymore."

"Doesn't take away its truth. You're in a rough spot right now, but shake-ups remind us we are not in control. We need 'em, and by my calculations, you haven't had one in a mighty long time."

"My husband wanting a divorce is a little more than 'a rough spot.'"

"Then God must love you extra, darlin'."

"You are not going to make me smile."

He chuckled. "Don't expect to. Not today. Just glad you're here, Jillie. Just glad you're here." He turned and began walking up the driveway.

She watched him go, his gait as loping as ever. He wore, like always, a ball cap, white T-shirt, blue jeans, and cowboy boots. When he was a small boy, his family had moved to Sweetwater. It was scarcely a village back then, but on the cusp of expanding into a town that catered to tourists more interested in nature than glitz. His father opened the first service station, which her father ran until five years ago. Figuring his girls were never going to be interested in it, he sold it.

Jill looked beyond him toward the house. The home she'd grown up in was a small ranch-style with attached garage, the stucco still the color of dirty beige. A scrub oak and a sycamore provided scant shade in the rocky dirt yard. Hardy perennials grew willy-nilly, some in full spring bloom. A red blossom sat atop a fat barrel cactus. An ocotillo cactus soared at least twenty feet high, its spindly arms sticking up and out every which way like Medusa's hair with tiny orange flowers. Sagebrushes gave off their sharp scent.

The best part of Sweetwater was the mountains. They surrounded the town like an embrace, a ring of colorful, steep, boulder-laden peaks. Some were purple, some pink, some blue, some gray. They rose to meet the sky's blue vault and seemed to hold between them a hush, a quiet so deep it sometimes made her ears ring.

"Jillie." Skip waited for her by the house. "Mom baked pies."

Pies. Ten o'clock in the morning and her mother would offer them pie and sweet iced tea. Like the house and the gap between her father's teeth, some things never changed.

Suddenly it felt good to be in a place where things never changed.

❧

Jill laid her fork on the yellow dessert plate. Not even a crumb of crust remained. Not even a trace of blueberry blue or raspberry red marred the surface. Nope, she'd all but licked it clean in the middle of the morning in her mother's kitchen.

Daisy pointed a spatula at it. "Want some more?"

"Oh, Mom." She groaned. "No. Thanks." Why had she eaten the entire huge piece of pie? Was she into comfort food now? Until thirty minutes ago, the thought of food turned her stomach. If this was her reaction to the warm fuzzies of home, she was in trouble.

"Don't you like it?" Across the table Daisy batted her blue eyes. Differentiating between her tones had always been a challenge. Was this one a tease or an accusation? "I got up at the crack of dawn to bake it before church."

Looking at her mother was like looking at a prune version of herself. The eyes and mouth were the same, the creases around them just a little deeper. The blonde shade of her short hair was more platinum than ash. Although no taller than Jill, Daisy was tinier.

Jill glanced at her family seated around the kitchen table. Some gene had gone haywire. Viv and their father were tall and rangy, their mother short and skinny; she herself was short and counted calories. The three of them could sit around and eat pie until the cows came home and not store one fat cell.

Jill said, "Is that gym still in town?"

Daisy said, "I'm going to need the car every day this week. Your father works on cars day and night, but you know we only have one now that we actually drive."

Jill tuned out the ensuing monologue about schedules and the woes of one car for a retired couple in a stoplight-free town that took three minutes to drive across.

At last her dad mentioned that he'd been restoring an old car, a Chevy 396 Super Sport convertible. "It's red."

Daisy rolled her eyes. "Can you believe it? The man is seventy-one years old. I asked him, why bother with a midlife crisis now?" She paused and her eyes bulged. "Jack doesn't have a red sports car, does he?"

"No." Not that she'd heard of, anyway. Maybe he did though.

"Connor sure liked his grandpops's car."

"Connor? Connor saw it?" Jill saw a look pass between her parents. "When was that?"

"This past week." Skip reached across the table and patted her hand. "I was getting around to that bit of news, darlin'. He and Emma spent a few days here before they went over to Hollywood yesterday to surprise you."

Daisy said, "Naturally, since you and Jack didn't see fit to tell any of us, we didn't know a thing about you two and neither did Connor, so we all just had a gay old time. That Emma is a beauty, isn't she? Kind of hard to understand sometimes with her accent, but she's real personable."

"I have no idea. I spent less than thirty minutes with her."

"Well, one thing at a time, I guess, and you got your hands full with this other business. Viv had her turn at it. Now you got yours. Like we told Viv, you stay as long as you need to. Kind of funny how you both skedaddled out of Sweetwater and then had to come crawling back to sort out your problems. Guess your pops and I did something right, huh?"

Viv had stayed with them? Curious she hadn't mentioned that to Jill. It must have been when Marty had an affair.

Daisy made a face. "You didn't catch me going back home to your grandma Ellie's."

Skip chuckled. "That's because there was no need. You married Mr. Perfect."

Daisy hooted as she always did when he referred to himself as the ideal husband. Jill wondered if her mother truly appreciated that it was not an exaggeration. Her dad *was* Mr. Perfect, the role model for the guy Jill fell in love with.

Or so she thought until two and a half weeks ago.

How Skip put up with her mom was nothing short of miraculous.

The woman must have been born thorny. Daisy and her own mother, Grandma Ellie, never got along. Like Jill and Viv skedaddling out of Sweetwater, Daisy had escaped her hometown of San Diego at first chance, which was soon after she met the boy from the desert.

Kind of like what happened when Jill met the boy from Chicago?

No. No way, nohow. Jill had enjoyed living and working with Viv at that time, yet always with an eye on Something Else, which came along when Jack entered the picture.

It was nowhere near similar to her mother's situation.

❧

A short while later, Jill walked with Viv out to her car and said more jokingly than she felt, "I'm rethinking this visit. Maybe it's not such a great idea after all."

"Mom's just being herself."

"I really didn't expect any sympathy from her, but good grief. Would it kill her to say she's sorry for me and Jack?"

"That's what the pie was for, Jill."

"I wonder if rehab groups take women who just need some time to pray and think and be *alone*."

"That would be called a retreat center, and you can get that here. Mom and Dad will leave you alone. Give them a chance."

"And eat the pie?"

Viv smiled. "Eat the pie."

"You're speaking from experience, aren't you? Why didn't you tell me you stayed with them?"

"I don't know. It was just for a long weekend one time when I needed to get away."

"And why didn't you tell me that Marty had an affair, hon? I would have cried with you."

Viv opened the car door, crossed her arms on its frame, and stared at Jill. She pursed her lips.

"It happens," Jill said. "It happens a lot even in Christian marriages."

"Jill, Marty did not have an affair."

"But you said he had a reason to leave you and didn't. What else besides another woman would give him a reason?"

Viv blew out a loud breath. "Me. I had the affair."

Jill felt like she'd been punched in the stomach. Vivian? Her sister had cheated on Marty?

Tears welled in Viv's eyes. "I know; you can't believe it. I was stupid. I turned forty and fell into this emotional cesspool. I kept asking, 'Is this all there is?' Lost in a trite, 'poor me' syndrome. Marty was just being Marty. All work and sports. He is the original husband in that old joke: 'I told you I love you when we got married. If anything changes, I'll let you know.'" She shook her head. "I'm not blaming him. I had the business, but it doesn't make eye contact or give hugs."

"Didn't you tell him you were lonely?"

Viv's jaw tightened and her eyes cleared. "I told him, Jill. It fell on deaf ears. So I told the CPA in the office next to mine. He heard."

"Oh, Viv. Of course you needed someone to hear you. It's understandable how things went from your vulnerability to his attention to . . . to . . ."

"To sex, Jill. It went all the way to there." She waved a hand in dismissal. "Okay, enough. It's over."

Jill winced and quickly tried to smooth out the reaction on her face. Viv had actually slept with another man? The image horrified her. She understood the physical need, she knew it happened, but *Vivian*? Her sister had never been a prude and yet she was the most moral, upright person Jill had ever known.

Viv said, "The rest of the story is Marty came into the office one day for something. The CPA stopped in at the same time. After he left, Marty said, 'End it.' Just like that. I don't know how he knew; he just did."

"Have you . . . have you gone to counseling?"

"Yes. We're in a good space now. Marty took it as a wake-up call. He pays attention to me and I don't begrudge him his time with sports. It's not like I need to be with him constantly, but he makes a point to keep eye contact and listen to me. It works."

"Did the counselor take you through forgiveness? Without that—"

"We covered it all."

"That's wonderful. You're walking it out now, the forgiveness in the day-to-day. Marty realized he could lose you if he didn't change. He made the choice. And you didn't give up on him when—"

"Stop it, Jill. Stop analyzing my marriage."

"I don't mean to—"

"This is why I couldn't tell you. You'd figure everything out and give us all the answers. Worse yet, we'd end up being an example on your program. And then you started writing that book, putting everything in print. No. No way."

"I wouldn't—"

"Of course you would. Not by name, but you would reference us. We're a textbook case. We'd fit into your rigid, black-and-white scheme perfectly. You just outlined the entire scenario in under sixty seconds."

"What do you mean?" A sinking sensation filled her. When Agnes Smith had talked about the book, she accused Jill of having a black-and-white attitude. Now Viv echoed her words.

Viv sighed. "I have to go."

"Tell me what you're talking about!"

The hot noonday sun beat directly on them. They were both tired and needed a break from each other. Their voices were rising.

Still Jill pressed the issue. "You criticized my work. Agnes said the same thing. Yes, I'm judgmental and dogmatic. I think we are called to be better people, but I do not have a rigid, black-and-white scheme or attitude or anything. I know grays exist. I account for grays in everything I teach."

"You could've fooled me."

"Viv, I said I understand why you cheated on Marty."

"Because it fits into one of your a plus b equals c equations. Besides that, you've always considered him a horse's patootie, beneath your standards, someone you would never, ever fall for. A tattooed welder isn't even good enough to be your brother-in-law."

"Vivian, how can you say that? I like Marty just fine. Twenty-five years ago I couldn't figure out what you saw in him. He got into fistfights and he cussed like a sailor."

"He *was* a sailor! And I was nuts about him because he was nuts about me. He made me feel like a special woman. I can't believe I tried to throw it all away. But you know what? We both made mistakes, yes. But he fought for me. He fought to get me back. What I don't understand is why Jack won't do that for you. Why he sits in Chicago and ignores your calls. Talk about a horse's patootie." She slid quickly into the car. "I gave your phone to Pops."

With that she started the engine, slammed the door shut, and sped off.

Jill's heart raced.

Why didn't Jack fight for her? Why was he just quitting on them?

The sun beat down on her. Its heat seeped into her bones, her lungs, her heart. It burned her skin and dried up whatever that place was that stored tears.

She had alienated Viv, the last in a long line of broken relationships. The real question was, why on earth would Jack bother fighting for her?

CHAPTER 24

———— ❧ ————

NIGHT FELL AND with it the temperature. Forty degrees in winter in Chicago would have felt balmy to Jill. Not so in the desert. Despite the afghan and heat from the gas fireplace, she shivered.

But maybe that had more to do with situation than climate.

After Viv's abrupt good-bye, Jill unpacked, ate food she'd avoided for years, and tiptoed around Viv's unsettling observation that set off a swirl of self-indictments.

Her father had sensed her unease. He told her to go sit in the backyard and be still, like she used to do as a kid. "Remember?" he said, his eyes full of tenderness. "You swore that God filled up your jaws with words."

The memory startled her. She had buried it so deeply. At age twelve she had quit listening in that way because her mother ridiculed her nonstop.

Well, she wasn't a kid anymore. She sat in a lawn chair in the middle of the dirt yard and waited. Desert hush enveloped her, a silence so thick it seemed a thing to be touched. She remembered how when she was a child, she heard God's voice in the airy whispers that floated on the stillness.

Her attempt to recapture the experience had lasted about three minutes. She heard only pings against her eardrums, the echoes of a loud silence.

Now she kept her mother company in the living room and tried to stay warm. The television was tuned to one of Daisy's favorite game shows; Jill was tuned again to Viv's hard words.

"Jill." A commercial came on, Daisy's cue to speak. "You should talk on your show about how your dad makes love to his car. I bet he's not the only old guy who does it."

"Mom!"

"He even hugs the thing. And he's out there in the garage day and night like some eager beaver with a hot chick."

Jill rolled her eyes. "Cars have always been his passion. Just because he doesn't have his service station doesn't mean he's suddenly going to take up golf."

"You said Jack doesn't have a red car?"

"Right. No, he doesn't."

"So what do you think? Does he have a girlfriend?"

"N-no."

"You don't know for sure though, do you? He must have a bevy of nurses eyeballing him day in and day out. He's a good-looking man."

An image of Jack's staff flashed in her mind. There were several attractive nurses and office workers. Many more worked with him at the hospital. Female doctors too. But . . . those would not catch his eye. No, it would be Sophie, the one he spoke of like a friend. Jill understood too much of how things worked. It was in relationship, not physical attraction, that vows were broken.

Vows were broken. Marriage vows that even Marty determined were to be kept. How could Jack have fallen so far from their roots?

Daisy said, "Your dad wasn't all that innocent, you know."

Jill had heard this one before. "Pops never so much as flirted."

"'Course he did. You think he's some kind of saint, but there were plenty of women he ogled. They'd come to the garage and show a little leg to get special attention. He used to pump the gas for them and give them deals on car repairs."

"Mom, he treated everyone the same." Jill had worked side by side with her dad from the time she could walk. If she wasn't in school, she was at the station doing homework or changing spark plugs. "And besides, he worships the ground you walk on."

Daisy's crooked smile was an odd mix of humor and disgust. "Which is why I did not go out of my mind worrying over those no-good, flashy seducers. I kept him happy at home. Not like you and Viv out there running your own businesses. Good night! You two both signed up for trouble. Why do you think my dad ran off? Hm? Because my mother was too busy with business to give him the attention a man needs."

That wasn't exactly the way Jill's grandma Ellie described it, but she was too tired to rehash the old argument.

Daisy went on. "I wasn't about to give your dad a reason to run off. Maybe you ought to quit that radio business and take care of Jack."

"Mom, it's a different world than it was fifty years ago."

"The Bible still says *wives, submit to your husbands*."

"It doesn't mean what you were taught."

"It doesn't mean to treat your husband with respect?"

"That's not what I'm saying. It doesn't mean you can't work outside the home."

"If it cancels out respect, it does."

"Working outside the home has nothing to do with . . . Never mind." *You win.*

Arguing was not worth the effort.

Nothing had changed between them. At least there was no possibility of alienating her mother. The woman thrived on conflict.

"You're sort of like your mother, Jill."

A chill went through her. Jack had said that once. She talked him out of the comparison, blaming it on her work. She was totally caught up in developing the Crunchy Casserole and Rockin' Roast concepts. Jack let it go.

But . . . she was sort of like her mom. She pecked at Jack's opinion until he changed it or until he must have decided, as she did now, *"Never mind, you win."*

It sounded like one more obnoxious trait to add to her list.

❧

Jill retreated to her old bedroom with her laptop.

Although no trace of her childhood remained in the room, memories surrounded her all the same. They were not unpleasant. Overall, growing up in Sweetwater had been okay. Competition at school was nil, which meant a short, chubby girl could make the cheerleading squad and a so-so student could be student council president.

Somewhere along the way she had picked up on the idea that the God who gave her words in the desert also gave her dreams to follow. Marrying her high school boyfriend and simply repeating her parents' life never appealed to her. That Something Else beckoned her first to San Diego and later to a totally new life with Jack. It beckoned her to teaching and radio and writing.

Midlife crisis simply did not follow suit.

A whimper threatened, but Jill pressed her lips together and climbed onto the bed. She leaned back against a pile of frilly pillows, flipped open the laptop, and flipped it shut.

No Internet.

Not that she had any interest in reading or writing e-mails or blogs.

But sooner rather than later she had to get back to corresponding with her listeners. Despite the chaos of her life, she could not give up on her work and disappoint those who counted on her to be there for them. Despite the fact that her book had no legs to stand on, she was responsible to continue what she could. Taped programs still aired, women still wrote to her, still appreciated a personal note. True, assistants at the station covered for her, but not full-time, not for weeks on end. Things would be piling up.

And it was only 8:22. The night stretched before her like a black hole. If she didn't accomplish something, she would lose her mind.

She could write a lesson plan about what it really felt like when a husband checked out.

No.

All that talk with Viv about wanting to think and pray and be alone was a bluff. Right now she felt ready to go find Internet service and e-mail that person who said she should be shot and set up a time to meet.

"Oh, God, I cannot handle this! I am not the person I thought I was. This stupid list in my head of how stupid I've been just keeps growing."

An image sprang to her imagination of a full-size plastic trash can strapped to her back. The stench of rotting garbage filled her.

The list had morphed into something much worse.

Her whimper began softly, a dry mewling. Then the tears came. This time they weren't angry ones nor sorrowful ones nor ones of confusion. They had nothing to do with Jack or Connor or work.

No. They were tears of surrender.

❧

"Jillie?" Skip's voice through the closed bedroom door carried over the sound of blowing her nose.

"Come in." Jill tossed a wad of tissues toward a wastebasket and grabbed another handful from the box on the bed. Before her dad stepped into the room, they were damp with tears.

"You okay, kiddo?" He ruffled her hair.

"I'm a mess."

"Yep, I can see that. Your face is redder than my sports car." He glanced at the armchair next to the nightstand, brushed the back of his jeans that were always greasy, and sat on the carpeted floor. "Mess is good every once in a while."

"Why?" She hiccuped.

Skip drew up his long legs and crossed his arms over his knees. A toothpick dangled from his mouth. His gray hair was matted down as if he still wore a ball cap. "All I'm saying is that when we're at the end of ourselves, we finally let go of the reins. That frees up God to do some major steering. He'll bring you through this."

"I don't see how. I'm more than a mess. I'm a major screwup."

"You won't get an argument from me." He chuckled. "You do realize faith is not about seeing the outcome before you get to it."

"Pops, I'm giving up pat answers."

"Well, darlin', maybe you can try living them out instead." He reached into his shirt pocket, pulled out a cell phone, and tossed it onto the bed. "Jack called."

Jill stared at the phone as if it were a tarantula.

"I told him I'd tell you."

"You talked to him?"

"Phone's in my pocket and rings with my son-in-law's name on the screen, I'm going to answer it."

"Pops!"

"We talked about cars. He didn't seem all that interested in my 396 Super Sport. 'Course I s'pose he's got a few things on his mind." Skip rubbed his bristly chin. "I ought to go and shave."

"Pops! What else?"

"What else what? Jack wants to talk to you."

"He said that?"

"He called you. Same thing."

All right. Jack had called her. Was that the same thing as fighting for her? "Pops, would you fight for Mom?"

"What do you mean? Like if somebody tried to hurt her?"

"No. That's a given. I mean like Marty fought for Viv. He didn't give up on their marriage. He even went to counseling."

He nodded once, a quick down and up. "Sure."

"How do I get Jack to fight for me, to keep us together?"

"Not possible, Jaws."

"Then how do I fight for him?"

"Not a woman's job."

"Mom already gave me the submission lecture."

"Picky, picky. First you don't want to hear about God's faithfulness. Now you don't want to hear about His divine order."

"Women and men are equal."

"That's not my point. They are different."

"Which means?"

"Jillie, I'm talking about the partnership you and Jack have. You're in it together, but he's wired one way, you're wired another. I don't give a fig who decides what's for dinner or which car to buy. The thing is, your fighting for him involves yapping and that only makes him dig his heels in deeper."

"I don't yap. I do not nag!"

"Darlin'—" he paused for a long moment, his warm brown eyes focused on her—"what do you think that book is?"

Jill's face crumpled. She could almost hear the trash can lid open and the splat of one more piece of garbage as it hit the pile inside.

Skip slid quickly toward the bed, reached up, and took her hand. "I'm sorry. I know it hurts. You wrote some wonderful stuff. Helpful stuff. But Jack has a different set of ears than a stranger has."

"But I talked about what a good husband he is!"

"And how he's flubbed along the way. And a whole lot else."

"I used other people's stories. I made up examples. It's not like he's on every page."

"Doesn't take every page."

"What did he say?"

"Nothing." Her dad smiled in a sad way and flicked one of his ears. "That's just what I heard with these husband ears."

"But Jack always told me I could use whatever personal illustration I needed if it might help others."

"Well, the book will help others, mostly women is my guess."

Jill looked at her father's worn, thoughtful face. He was old, friendly, and giving. He lived in a summertime furnace that most of the world ignored. For almost fifty years he had been married to the queen of naggers.

"Pops, I talk all the time. I press. But I swear I have deliberately avoided nagging. I never wanted to sound like Mom."

He gave his curt nod. "The way anyone hears depends on their heart condition. If a heart is filled with God's peace and forgiveness and love, then it beats so loud it drowns out any nonsense others say to us."

Jill took a deep breath. Her dad did not hear her mother's nagging. He knew it was spoken, but he did not hear it.

"Pops, how do you keep on loving her?"

He grinned. "Hey, I read about that one in your book. Love isn't a feeling; it's a verb. I just choose to do it." He stood, leaned over, and kissed her forehead. "Jack called. That was his choice. Now you choose whether or not to call him back. Night."

Jill watched him shut the door.

The question was not whether to call Jack. It was why should she bother if all he heard from her was nagging?

Splat. Add *nagger* to the pile.

CHAPTER 25

———— ❧ ————

If Skip Wagner were not his father-in-law, Jack would have called the guy for advice. The man was a unique blend of gearhead, cowboy, and mystic. But he was his father-in-law and therefore off-limits as an unbiased counselor.

Odd that within moments of deciding this, Jack found himself talking to him.

Jack sat now at the small kitchen table in his apartment and rehashed what had just transpired. He had called Jill's cell phone number and was confused when Skip answered, confused to the point of being tongue-tied.

After Skip's brief explanation about why he had the phone, Jack stumbled over his reply. "I-I don't know what to say."

"Son, you don't have to say a thing. Did Connor tell you about my car? She is a beaut."

Jack could not recall what was said after that. Conversations with Skip were often like that. The particulars did not matter so much as the tone. No hint of condemnation came through. Skip's gravelly voice oozed only acceptance and forgiveness.

Those were the things that settled into Jack's psyche. Like a dried-up plant on its last leg on a rainy day, he soaked it in.

Jack enjoyed a good relationship with his own dad, but it never quite entered into the realm he sensed with Skip. He couldn't describe it without sounding weird. The truth was, his connection with Skip seemed timeless. If God revealed Himself to Jack as a father loving his son, he would talk like Skip. He'd probably even wear cowboy boots.

His cell rang now and he stared at it. Jill was returning his call, probably bouncing as crazily as his phone was against the table.

But he had to talk with her. Connor was getting married.

"Hi, Jill."

A half beat of silence passed. Then she spoke. "Hi."

"Hi. So. You're at your parents'."

"Yes."

"How long will you stay?"

"I haven't decided."

"Don't you want to come home?"

"I told Connor I'd be there when he was."

That didn't answer his question. "Something's come up. It's, um, it's a little bigger than us."

"What's wrong?"

"Nothing. It's . . . well, it's good news. You know about the engagement."

"Mm-hmm."

Jack felt a stab of anger. Jillie Jaws could talk the paint off a wall. What was up with the sudden mime routine? "Naturally Connor's upset about us. About me. I've upset everyone and everything, but he's still our son and his plans involve us. He and Emma are getting married. Early April, in Chicago. So we need you here soon. They want simple, bare bones, but there are still arrangements to make before they get here. You've got a better handle on this sort of thing. Can you set a date to be here, please?"

No response.

"Jill, listen. I realize this is not what we envisioned for him. She was supposed to be from Chicago, maybe from downstate. We were supposed to get to know her. But we raised him to be his own person. We gave him our blessing when he went off to Europe. This is who he is. And now he needs you here. All right?"

"I'll see."

"You'll see? What's to see?" Jack's voice rose. He had never in his life yelled at Jill, but now he could not stop himself. "Your son needs you! What's to see?"

"Good-bye."

The line went dead.

Jack smacked the tabletop with one hand and with the other dropped his phone before he threw it at the wall. Swearing loudly, he sprang to his feet and paced the apartment.

Several laps later, he picked the phone up and called Viv.

"Hello."

"Viv. I'm sorry to bother you."

"You sound out of breath. What's wrong?"

"Nothing. Everything. Sorry."

"Stop apologizing."

"Sor—Okay. I just talked with Jill. Anyway, I'm calling to invite you to Connor's wedding."

"His wedding! Ha! He only said they were engaged. I knew there was more. Ha!" She giggled. "Little Connor. And Emma. She was so intriguing looking."

At least the aunt was happy about things. "I just told Jill. I don't know anything about planning a wedding but I know things need to be done right now, and she refuses to commit to getting here before Connor does."

"Oh, my." Viv sighed the words.

"What is wrong with her?"

"Besides your other news?"

"Yeah, besides that. This is totally unrelated. This concerns our son.

She's strong enough to step away from our situation for a while and throw together a small wedding for him."

Viv chuckled. "Just a small wedding."

"Family only. Emma's parents, my parents, your parents, you and Marty. Not that we expect you to drop everything and zip over to the Midwest on such notice."

She laughed out loud. "Jack, don't be such a freaking moron. Nothing is *unrelated*. You started a chain reaction with your little announcement. Jill's whole world came crashing down. Everything she's accomplished went kaput. On top of all that, Connor shows up with a complete surprise of a girlfriend-slash-fiancée. Then yesterday I got so ticked at her we're not on speaking terms. And now she's living with Daisy. For goodness' sake, she can't plan a *wedding*. Her emotions are completely zapped. She has nowhere to shove in even one more iota of stress. Do you get it?"

He shook his head. People thought Jill was the sharp-tongued sister. "Yeah, okay, I get it. But what do we do? Connor wants to get married in early April because they fly back to Italy on the twelfth. We need her here. She says she can't commit to that. Can you imagine she would miss his wedding? That I do not get. She didn't sound at all like herself."

"Isn't that what you wanted? For her not to be herself?"

Jack literally drew back. "What do you mean?"

"You said you want a divorce. That translates into you don't want to be with her as she is."

"I-I'm not sure what I want."

"Well, that might be a good thing to figure out. Are you talking to anyone?"

"Baxter. And Sophie, our office manager." Sophie knew something was amiss and had hovered like a mother hen until he finally told her. "My parents."

"You know what I mean." She paused. "Marty and I went to a marriage counselor, a couple years ago. It can be a positive experience. It's nothing to be embarrassed about."

"You and Marty? Really?"

"Yep."

"*Really?*"

"Yes, *really*. I can see how it might be hard to get your brain wrapped around that bit of information. You thought we were the perfect couple."

"Actually I did."

"Get real, Jack."

"You two always—I don't know—you always meshed. Like you're on the same team. A winning team."

Viv went quiet for a moment. "Thank you." Her voice was soft. "We all need a little help in the game, though. A coach of some sort."

"I suppose." He scratched his head. "I don't know who that would be. I've considered the pastor, but to tell you the truth, I'm embarrassed."

"You gotta get over that."

"Maybe. He's a good guy but I know what he'll say. He'll cite me chapter and verse to prove what I did was wrong and then tell me to fix it. I can rebuke myself without any help from others."

She sighed. "When you're ready, you'll find the right person. I have to go." She promised to put the wedding on her calendar and they said their good-byes.

Relieved to have the two phone calls behind him, Jack went to bed. When he turned out the light, an emptiness enveloped him along with the darkness.

It was a new feeling. He missed Jill lying beside him. He missed *them*. He missed their entity. He missed what he had described to Connor as that "better place" where he once lived, back when he and Jill were teammates.

"Dear God."

Yes. *Dear God.*

Jack listened to his heartbeat slow.

"Lord, forgive me. I forgot You were here all the time. Waiting."

A Jesus story came to mind, one about Him healing a man. The pastor's version had stuck because it emphasized not how people in need went to Jesus, but how Jesus responded to them. He would look at them tenderly and ask, "What would you like Me to do for you?"

Jack knew he was accepted and forgiven not only by Skip and probably Viv, but by God as well. He understood that Jesus was always asking that same question down through the ages to anyone who came to Him for help.

What would you like Me to do for you?

"Please take care of Jill. Please bring her back for Connor's sake."

But what about you, Jack? What can I do for you?

For himself? He could not begin to imagine.

And then he began to cry.

CHAPTER 26

———— ❧ ————

Viv sat at her kitchen table, cell phone still in hand, Jack's voice still echoing in her head. *"You always meshed. Like you're on the same team."*

"Okay." She inhaled deeply and blew out a long, noisy breath. "Okay."

She had told her brother-in-law that she had to go because she simply could not listen to him anymore. Next Jill would be calling with her rendition of the latest in the Jack and Jill saga.

With quick decisiveness Viv opened her cell, turned off the power, reached down, unplugged the house phone at the wall, and muttered, "No more Galloways tonight."

"Viv?" Marty's voice surprised her. She looked up and saw him in the doorway, nowhere near the television. "You okay?"

"Sure." Her vision blurred and she knew she was in trouble.

"Was that Jack?"

"Mm-hmm." She blinked rapidly.

"I heard you laugh and say something about being a moron. What's up?"

Viv shook her head and then Marty was in front of her, pulling

185

her to her feet and into his arms. She said into his T-shirt, "It hurts so bad."

"I know, babe; I know."

He held her tightly and rubbed her back and didn't ask any more questions, didn't offer any solutions, didn't ask what he could do, didn't escape to a televised game.

She cried as if in physical pain. Her front-row seat to the splintering of her sister's marriage was too close. Shards flew and cut into her flesh.

And Marty just held on to her more securely.

The reality of their oneness seeped into her. It permeated her entire being. His strength became hers. His touch was like a kiss on every wound, binding it with his love.

They were indeed on the same team.

Maybe Jack should be the one with the radio program.

CHAPTER 27

--- ❧ ---

SWEETWATER SPRINGS

The three-week anniversary of Jack's unimaginable announcement landed on the fifth day after hearing of Connor's plan to wed. That morning Jill ate key lime pie for breakfast and went with her mother to the beauty shop.

She squirmed now, the backs of her thighs sticking to the vinyl chair. Wrapped in a gold plastic cape, she watched the scene behind her unfold in the mirror's reflection. It promised fiasco.

She did not think the sense of doom was totally due to her personal mess.

One chair over sat her mother, with stylist Bella Carlson behind her. Behind Jill stood Stella Carlson, Bella's identical twin sister. Or was it the other way around?

Stella ran her fingers through Jill's hair. "What are we going to do today, sugar?"

Jill eyed the sixtysomething twins. The only change she noted since she last saw them was that they both wore glasses, fancy ones with rhinestone silver frames. They had put on a little weight too.

But some things remained the same. Neither sister had married. Their shop still smelled of Juicy Fruit, White Shoulders, and thick aerosol hairspray. Their identical poofy pinkish-red curls had not changed in length, style, or color since as far back as she could remember, which would have been when she came in for her first cut at the age of three.

"Shampoo and blow-dry?" Jill cringed at her voice that had been swinging upward at the end of every sentence ever since she felt the weight of the trash can strapped to her back and gagged on its odor. She doubted every single thing she said, wondering if her words or tone nagged.

Had Jack always heard her that way?

Daisy said, "Oh, honey. You need a haircut. You said you're way overdue."

That was before. *Before my husband left me. Before my son went off the deep end and decided to marry a stranger from* France. *Back when I had a career and it mattered what I looked like.*

Stella pulled at several strands. "Looks like you're about ready for some highlights."

"It's fine? I just had it—"

"I always thought you'd be cute in one of those buzz-cut styles." Stella smiled and looked at her twin. "We both said that, didn't we?"

"We did," her sister agreed.

Daisy slid from the chair and followed Bella toward the sinks at the other end of the small shop. "She couldn't have gotten away with it when she was a teenager. Cheeks were a little too chubby. They would've shown up all the more with no hair."

Stella said, "If I remember correctly, a certain young doctor thought those were angelic cheeks."

These women did not forget a thing. They had done her hair for her wedding, back when all she could talk about was Jackson Galloway.

Stella patted her cheek. "They're not as chubby now, sugar, but you're just as pretty as you were back then."

"Thanks?"

Daisy called out, "You both know why we had Vivian, right?"

Stella groaned. "Daisy Wagner, you've been telling us that story since you first got pregnant with her."

Daisy cackled.

Yes, her mother cackled. Like a crazy hen.

Jill hoped she wouldn't tell the story. She'd heard it for as long as the twins had, since she was a newborn and her mother got pregnant.

Daisy said, "But I haven't told it in ages. This is the God's honest truth. When Jillian was first born, she looked exactly like a Martian."

"Green?" Bella said.

"No, don't be ridiculous. I've told you before. That's an old wives' tale. Martians are not green. They're just weird-looking, like nothing you've ever seen before. Not really human even. So Skip and I figured we better try again and get it right." Daisy thought it was a joke. She didn't want people imagining that her second baby born a mere ten months after the first was a *whoops*. Vivian wasn't the *whoops*. Jillian was.

"Sugar—" Stella leaned down to Jill's shoulder and met her eyes in the mirror—"you know how long I've been cutting hair. I saw the photo on your book cover. I can follow your hairdresser's lead, no problem, and get you back to your sassy do."

"All right?"

Stella's penciled brows rose above her glasses.

"Yes." Jill tried for a more decisive tone and lowered her voice. "All right. Let's do it."

Stella smiled.

Daisy proceeded to introduce the subjects of Jill's marriage on the rocks and Connor's wedding.

"Mom."

"Oh, don't get all bent out of shape. We're in the beauty shop. This is where we talk about anything and everything. Right, ladies?"

"Whatever is said in here, stays in here," Bella said.

Jill closed her eyelids and wished there were such a thing as ear lids.

She managed to keep her mouth shut, a practice that seemed on its way to becoming a habit.

Would that make Jack happy?

Was it really her responsibility to make him happy?

The twins deftly moved the conversation into other areas and Stella deftly worked her magic.

"There you go, Jillian." She whipped off the plastic cape. "What do you think?"

Jill opened her eyes and looked at a stranger. It was her hair but her face no longer matched it. She tried a smile. It helped. "Perfect, Stella. Thank you."

"I'm Bella, but you're welcome." She laughed and began sweeping up the clippings.

Jill turned to her mother sitting under a hair dryer, her head full of curlers. "Mom, I need a walk. I'll meet you at home."

"You go ahead." She shouted to be heard above the noisy dryer. "My treat today. Divorce is expensive, you know."

Jill wondered how much a bus ticket out of Sweetwater Springs cost.

❧

Jill left the beauty shop, clomped along a side street, and rounded a corner onto Saguaro Avenue, the main street of the downtown area. She tried to convince herself that exercise would rid her of the desire to pack her bags.

She had cried, slept, cursed, and moped long enough. Admitting that much had been the catalyst to get her out the door with Daisy and over to the Carlson twins' shop. Now it pumped her legs.

"Just keep moving? I mean, yes, I should keep moving. Lord, I trust You for what's next?" She murmured to herself, skimming along the sidewalk, hearing the question mark. "I mean, I do. I do trust You. I need to make some decisions." *And I don't have anything left in me to do it alone.*

She stubbed her toe on a sidewalk crack. "Ow."

Going against every urge in her body, she slowed down.

And then she slowed some more. She forced herself to pay attention. She forced herself to notice her hometown.

Except for increased traffic, nothing had changed about the downtown area. She passed stores that catered to tourists and townspeople alike: grocery and hardware alongside souvenir shops of pottery, paintings, and sculptures created by local artists. A Mexican restaurant appeared packed, as did the old-fashioned hamburger joint.

There wasn't a free parking spot in sight. Springtime came early to the desert with seventy degrees and potted flowers in bloom, heaven for campers and hikers.

Beyond the low buildings, beyond the flat expanse of dirt and cacti, were those mountains filling 360 degrees of horizon.

Her energy flagged and she headed to the town square at the end of the block. Encircled by a roundabout, it was the hub of traffic. Four main streets fed into it. There were no stoplights, only yield signs.

She waited for a break in traffic, crossed the street, and plopped onto a park bench dappled in shade from a newly leafed sycamore.

The square wasn't a green space or even a square. It was a dirt rectangle. Not a blade of grass sprouted, only patches of wildflowers in rockscapes. There were a few picnic tables and a gazebo. A group of children and mothers played at the small playground in one corner.

Children and mothers.

"Jillian was a whoops *and an ugly one at that."*

Her mother's words had most likely been the first glob of garbage shoveled into her little girl's heart. Jill was a mistake and therefore not worth much.

Much later in life, she understood that although Daisy had not meant to harm, her joke did indeed harm.

It was why Jill left Sweetwater Springs at eighteen.

It was why she hesitated about having children.

It was why she had a tubal ligation.

It was why she was a driven perfectionist.

And after all was said and done? She was still her mother's daughter: a nagging wife and a lousy mother. Jack wanted a divorce and Connor had not been able to tell her he wanted a wedding.

She could not imagine her life being more of a total failure.

Layers of regret wrapped themselves around Jill as snugly as a shroud. Combined with the afternoon warmth, which suddenly felt oppressive, it was not a good situation unless she was ready to quit breathing altogether.

Which maybe she was.

"Lord, if You want to smite me this very minute, count me in. Go for it. I do not deserve to stay here on this earth, telling others how to live."

Traffic continued to flow by. The children still squealed in delight. A tiny lizard darted across the sidewalk and up onto a rock. He stopped, looked around, did a few jerky push-ups, and raced away. At an intersection a bright yellow minivan loaded down with camping gear veered north.

God did not seem to pick up on her smiting suggestion.

"Are You sure?"

Jill watched the minivan continue down the block. Its right turn signal flashed and the brake lights lit up. The vehicle slowed and disappeared behind a tall white fence. The campers in the van probably needed gas or air or water or soda or an oil change because they had pulled into her father's old service station.

Which was now owned by Ty Wilkins.

Regret slithered into the garbage can. Suddenly its weight was too much. She got up off the bench, checked for cars, crossed the street again, and walked toward the station.

Ty Wilkins represented her first major life decision, made with the unparalleled wisdom of an eighteen-year-old.

She reached the tall white fence and paused to gaze beyond it at a familiar sight. The property had been her father's pride and joy. Its tall sign that rose above the posted gasoline prices still proclaimed in sky-blue letters, *WAGS, Full-Service Station.*

The new owner had not needed to update or spruce up a thing. He merely maintained the white stucco building, four sets of gas pumps, overhang cover, soda machine, and ice bin. Like when her dad owned it, everything was incredibly spotless for a place that majored on oil and grease.

From what she had heard, Ty also maintained the station's excellent reputation. She noticed that the three garage bays held cars, two up on lifts, a couple of mechanics at work. More vehicles were neatly parked nearby, awaiting an oil change or some repair.

Since Ty bought the business from her dad seven years before, Jill had not set foot near it. Somehow she was never in a car when it needed gas, never walking that direction on the busy four-lane, never craving the bubble gum available only at Wags.

Never feeling the need to revisit that memory lane.

Two men emerged from the building. Ty, still tall and lanky, was easy to recognize. He helped the other guy load cases of water into the van, chatting the whole time.

His eyes strayed her direction and he stopped talking. He lifted the ball cap from his head, raked his fingers through his hair, replaced the cap, placed his hands on his hips.

Maybe she should greet him. He wasn't the first person she had alienated, but he was in the top tier of significant ones.

CHAPTER 28

———— ✢ ————

CHICAGO

Jack sank his teeth into a sandwich and savored the blend of peanut, pumpernickel, and banana.

"Dr. G." Sophie slid onto a chair across from him at the lunchroom table and shook her head. "Peanut butter again?"

He swallowed the first bite. "But with a twist. Banana slices instead of jam, and the pièce de résistance: pumpernickel bread. *Homemade* pumpernickel bread."

Her brows rose above the close-set eyes. "When did you have time to make bread? You were here until eight last night."

"Bread machine," he said. "It counts as homemade."

"It doesn't count as a vegetable serving." She pulled a plastic container from a cloth bag and set it before him. "Have some salad."

"Salad again?"

She smiled, removing more things from her bag. "Arugula this time, with raspberry vinaigrette."

He accepted a fork, popped the lid, and did not fuss as he had the first time she shared her lunch with him. That was last week, the day after he'd told her about the separation and the apartment. "I've always packed my own lunch, Sophie," he had said a little too aggressively.

Like today, they had been alone in the break room, the result of staggered lunch times for the staff. She had replied calmly, "But your lunch used to be balanced." End of discussion.

"The banana is not enough," she said now. "I'll share my apple."

He grinned in anticipation.

Sophie rolled an apple around in her hands, searching for the right grip. In one swift motion, she split the fruit in half. "Voilà."

"Bravo."

"Thank you. Thank you." She handed him his share. "How is your week going?" It was a casual question, her way of hovering from a distance.

"It's going well." As a matter of fact, it was going great. Sunday night's crying jag released and rejuvenated. Besides his own well-being, he had learned the secret to women's handle on emotions: not being afraid to bawl when necessary.

Jack figured that wasn't something to announce to his office manager. Instead he talked about Connor. "He keeps calling. The wedding plans change by the hour. He and Emma are definitely dancing to the beat of a different drummer and her name is not Emily Post or whoever the etiquette expert is these days." He took a bite of salad to stop the flow of chitchat. *Jill is going to have a fit. Con doesn't want Pastor Mowers doing the ceremony. Maybe she won't show up. What is wrong with her?* "Mmm, great salad."

"Thanks. Is he having a good time with Emma's parents?"

"A blast. They sound like interesting people."

"Anything I can do to help with the wedding?"

A piece of apple didn't want to go down his throat. "Uh, he seems to be doing pretty well by himself. He booked his favorite restaurant for the reception."

"That has to be Giorgio's down the street."

He nodded.

Sophie smiled. "I remember whenever he worked here at the office, he'd eat lunch and dinner there. He wished they served breakfast."

"I think it was more the food than the art that beckoned him to Italy." Jack chuckled. "He reserved Giorgio's banquet room. Can you believe it? For a Saturday, only weeks in advance?"

"I'm not surprised they would make it work. They know him."

"And he does have a gift of persuasive speech." *Like his mother. Maybe he doesn't need Jill here to talk anyone into anything.* But he needed his mother here at home, available.

"Well, I am happy to help, Dr. G. Make phone calls. Address invitations. Whatever."

A week ago Jack would have thought nothing of Sophie's offer. It was totally in character for her to step up to the plate and take care of things in an efficient and unselfish manner, whether it was related to business, family, or community.

But Baxter had alerted him to womanly wiles that even the likes of prim and proper Sophie Somerville engaged in. His friend said, "She's nuts about you, Jack. You know that much." He seemed surprised at Jack's hesitancy. "Don't you?"

Well, he didn't, not really.

Sophie was loyal and kind and the perfect manager. She deflected attention from herself and heaped praise on him and Baxter and the other doctors alike. She even dressed appropriately.

Baxter's eyes had bulged. "You missed the extra unbuttoned button on the soft, silk red blouse yesterday."

Jack had also missed the yellow in her hazel eyes until last Friday when she got in his face about something because he hadn't been paying attention.

Not paying attention was becoming the bane of his existence.

"Dr. G." Sophie was leaning across the table toward him now. The yellow flecks shone. Her dark hair swung down, partially covering the left eye. "You let me know if there is anything I can do to help."

When had she taken her hair out of its bun? For years and years, as long as he could remember, she had worn it in a bun.

Jack cleared his throat, found his teasing tone, and pulled up an old joke. "You could start by calling me Jack."

Sophie's cheeks were supposed to turn pink. Her hands were supposed to flutter. She was supposed to say, in a flustered voice, "I-I can't do that. You've always been and always will be Dr. G."

None of that happened.

"Jack." She smiled and moved sinuously to a standing position. "Please tell me if there's anything else I can do . . . Jack."

"Sure."

She gathered her things and, with a little wave, walked out the door.

Jack gazed at the tabletop and pulled on his earlobe. Paying attention was not necessarily a positive thing.

❧

"Nip it in the bud," Jack muttered to himself as he approached the front desk later that afternoon. "Just nip it in the bud."

He made it through the door to the outer waiting room before Sophie noticed him.

"Dr. G! You're leaving?" She stood.

He stopped at the counter opposite her. Behind him a few patients still waited, but not for him. Behind her, nurses and office staff were busy at work.

"Yes, I'm leaving," he said. "Last night caught up with me."

"Well, you caught up on paperwork too, and you do have a 7 a.m. surgery tomorrow." She flipped her long hair over a shoulder. "I guess you can be excused a little early today."

His smile felt feeble. "See you tomorrow."

"Don't forget." She lowered her voice. "I am available, Jack."

For what? he wanted to snap at her. *For what?*

Instead he spoke calmly. "Thanks, Sophie. I'll pass your offer on to Connor and Jill."

A few moments later, as he strode down the hall toward the exit, Jack wondered if Sophie's crestfallen expression meant that Operation Nip It in the Bud had succeeded.

He hoped she would not despair. He liked her very much as a friend. He highly respected her as office manager. He did not want to lose the relationship.

What if he were attracted to Sophie? Could he have been so cavalier about ending something before it began? Or would he have flirted with her?

Those questions did not matter. The truth was he couldn't think of any female he cared to flirt with, dead or alive, acquaintance or stranger. He couldn't imagine ever being attracted to another woman besides Jill.

Jill. Jillie Wagner. Spunky, cute, bubbling over with joy, totally convinced God loved her exactly as her father Skip did, delighted to do whatever was before her. Happy to cart a bunch of seniors around Hollywood or talk on the radio or eat his gourmet concoctions.

Or wash his shorts or iron his shirts.

Or meet him for a late dinner after surgery or include him in a birthday party for a station staff member.

Or plan a speaking, book-signing tour, him by her side.

He doubted, though, that she had been delighted to cancel that tour and stay with her parents.

Jack sighed, got into his car, and turned his thoughts to cooking.

CHAPTER 29

——— ❧ ———

Ty Wilkins reminded Jill of her father. He was not quite as tall, not quite as lanky, but he was both. Her father had strong shoulders and a wide smile. Ty's chest was broader, his grin a stretch from ear to ear. The two men lived in blue jeans, T-shirts, cowboy boots, and ball caps, but the true similarity lay in their character, a rare blend of solidness and generosity.

As the bright yellow minivan pulled away from the gas pumps, Jill walked across the concrete to where Ty stood in the shade of the canopy. "Hi." She held out her hand.

He grinned his wide grin and shook her hand with his rough one. "Awkward as always, huh?"

She smiled at his reference to class reunions. They tiptoed around each other at those occasions, as if not quite sure how to relate now that they weren't going steady.

He let go of her hand. "You were missed at the last reunion. All sixty-seven of us agreed it would have been more fun with you there."

"I'm sure."

"It's true." He took off his red ball cap and wiped his forearm across his brow, brushing aside black curls. "You always were the life of the party." He replaced the cap. "How are you, Jillian?"

She wondered—not for the first time in the past twenty-eight years—how it was that a heartstring that should have long been tied up elsewhere could still be tugged when Ty Wilkins asked her the most mundane of questions.

"I've been better," she said.

"I'm sorry to hear that. From what Daisy tells me, you're sitting on top of the world."

"I thought I was." Why on earth would her mother talk about her to him? "How about yourself?"

His eyes narrowed, not enough to hide the willow green color.

She flashed back to one particular sleepover in eighth grade. She and her girlfriends spent half the night discussing the eye color of every boy in the middle and senior high schools. They concluded that the only one with eyes the color of springtime willows down in the canyon was Ty Wilkins, which probably explained why—although he was not especially cute or an athletic standout—he took first place as a major heartthrob.

That was before girls recognized abstract qualities like solidness and generosity in boys.

Ty said, "I'm all right. Business is great."

"It looks like it. Two mechanics?"

"And two high school kids help out in the afternoons. Once in a while your dad even lends a hand."

"How's Mandy? and your boys? Last I heard, they were at UCLA."

"Yep." He rubbed the back of his neck. "Nobody told you?"

"Told me what?"

"Mandy and I are divorced. About eight months ago."

"Oh, Ty!" Of all the nonsense news her mother passed along, she hadn't bothered to inform her of this heartbreak? "I'm so sorry."

"Thanks." He shrugged. "Probably for the best. She hated this place and my grease and grime." He splayed his calloused fingers, the nails and tips stained as her father's always were. "Anyway, the house is more peaceful now."

"I'm sorry."

"We grew apart. It happens, right? You should know. You're the marriage expert."

It was her turn to shrug. "I'm thinking of giving that up." She twisted her lips, trying to keep them together, but his pain yanked her own to the surface. It came out. "Jack left me. He wants a divorce. I guess we grew apart too. I just didn't know it."

"Whoa. I'm sorry."

"Thanks." She took a deep breath. The Sweetwater memory lane unearthed yet another ugly wart from her past. "Ty, I'm sorry for being so mean to you."

He studied her face. "That was a few lifetimes ago, and you apologized on your way out of town."

"I don't think it was all that heartfelt. I had one foot on the brake and the other on the clutch."

He laughed. "We were eighteen. Two crazy, stubborn kids with different agendas. I was going to be a mechanic here and nowhere else. You were going to be anywhere else, changing the world."

It was the main thing they had argued about throughout their two years of going steady.

He said, "I never expected you to move back. A card would've been nice." His tone teased, but his expression was tender. "For the record, I stopped being mad at you after the tenth reunion."

"That quickly?"

He smiled. "Mandy got tired of the attitude."

"I deserved your anger."

"Well, you were one snotty, determined girl, but you had every reason to be mad at me too. I refused to move to San Diego. I could have been a mechanic as easily there as here."

"But it wouldn't have been what you wanted."

"Nope. There's no place like Sweetwater. I wanted your dad's life probably more than I wanted you."

"You thought I could be a bookkeeper like my mom."

"Took me a while, but I finally caught on you were better at working on cars than number crunching."

"Or baking pies. I still don't even cook." Jack baked pies and cakes, and he cooked. He spent more time in the kitchen than she did. Was that an issue with him? Although he knew when they married that she was clueless in the kitchen. Not to mention totally disinterested—

"Jillian, I'm sorry about Jack."

His words startled her.

"All of a sudden you had this faraway look on your face." He smiled briefly, sadly. "I used to do that, in the beginning. It feels less like an ambush as time goes by."

She should be taking notes. "Thanks. I'm sorry about Mandy."

"I appreciate that." He paused. "Good to see you."

She smiled and breathed out a thank-you. A handshake didn't feel like enough. Jill closed the distance between them and they exchanged a quick hug. "Good-bye, Ticonderoga."

He laughed at the old nickname.

She walked away, toward the street, much lighter than she had felt a short time before.

Maybe the banter the other day with Viv about rehab and addiction had not been a joke. Whatever her problem, Jill was apparently engaged in one of the twelve steps—the one about making amends.

She had never regretted leaving Ty or Sweetwater Springs, but she had regretted her despicable behavior toward him. In high school they were best friends as well as romantically attracted to each other. She wore his ring; he wore hers on a chain around his neck. They attended every homecoming and prom together. Everyone believed they would marry. Then she left without a backward glance, lumping her boyfriend in with everything else she did not like about Sweetwater.

Halfway to the street she stopped and turned. Like her dad would have done, Ty chatted with a driver at the self-serve pump. He probably even washed windshields for pretty women who smiled at him.

He was a good guy. He seemed happy.

Jack would probably be happy too without a wife around.

※

"Pops—" Jill crouched near the shiny red sports car and talked to her dad's legs protruding from beneath it—"I need my phone."

"Hold your horses. Be out in a sec."

She glanced at her wrist for the watch that wasn't there and rubbed the skin. It itched for the feel of a stretchy gold and silver band. After her awful conversation with Jack Sunday night about Connor's wedding, she cried to her parents only to find out they already knew. Connor had sworn them to secrecy because he wanted to be the one to give the happy news to his parents.

She'd stolen that from her son.

She whined her remorse to her dad until he threatened to escort her straight back to Chicago if she didn't give him her phone and watch and *be still*. She relinquished her things but could not physically be still. For the next three days she moved, spending hours on the trails, walking and jogging, dodging hikers, stones, lizards, and one time, a rattlesnake.

Eventually a stillness crept in.

"Pops, please."

Skip rolled out on his creeper from beneath the car and sat up. "Hair looks good."

"Thanks." She sat on the concrete floor. "The Carlson twins send their love."

He wiped a kerchief across his face, smearing a grimy streak. "So you think you're ready for the phone?"

"Yes, sir."

He closed one eye.

Jill smiled at his puzzlement. "Yes, Sergeant."

"Oh, come on. I wasn't that bad."

"No, sir." She laughed.

"Stop."

"Yes, sir." She saluted him military-style. "Anyway, I want to call Connor."

"Okaaay." He paused. "What if he doesn't answer?"

Her grin faded and she took a deep breath. "No problem. I'm apologizing. Voice mail works."

"You told me you already did that."

"Pops, can we do this without the devil's advocate?"

Now he smiled. "Nope."

"I wasn't sincere before. I mean, I meant it, but I didn't really embrace the whole picture." She bit her lip, hoping to avoid further explanation.

"You mean you didn't confess to the whole mothering issue."

Why did she think her dad missed any detail? She shrugged.

"Darlin', I know you did not want more babies after Connor. I suspect you weren't so crazy about having even one. The main reason you would feel that way is fear. What if you were unable to nurture him? Your own mother didn't do so hot with you and Vivvie."

"Pops, I don't want to blame Mom."

"You're not. It's just the truth and she admits it. It's too bad, but that's just the way life was. I could see it way back when, her hesitancy, her withdrawal from you girls. Not much a dad can do except fill in the gaps as best he can." He grinned. "I wasn't so hot at being sweet and tender."

"No, but—"

"Nope. No excuses. You and I have touched on this in the past and I know you've forgiven us. Trust that Connor will forgive your mistakes, whatever they were. He's learning that family members hurt each other unintentionally. Sooner or later he'll figure out what to do with the fallout from his dysfunctional mother."

"Ha-ha."

"In the meantime, I imagine he'd appreciate some crow eating." Her dad winked. "Phone's in with the wrenches." He lay back down on the creeper and pushed himself under the car.

She hesitated. "Pops, I'm ready for my watch too."

He rolled right back out. "Going somewhere?"

"A wedding. If he'll have me."

"He'll have you." He smiled. "It's in the kitchen drawer with the spatulas." Chuckling, he disappeared again.

"Hey, Pops."

"Yeah, Jaws?"

She heard his tone of exasperation but knew that he was teasing. "After I call Connor, can I work with you?"

He didn't reply immediately. "Sure," he said in a quiet voice. "I'd like that."

Jill would like that too.

CHAPTER 30

———— ❦ ————

SEATED AT THE small desk in her bedroom, Jill stared at her phone and traced a finger around its sleek sides.

Twenty-one missed calls. Thirteen new voice mails.

Jill scrolled through the missed calls and saw several from Gretchen, her manager at the station, and coworkers. Not one from Jack or Connor.

What had she said in her last voice message to Connor? *"I'm sorry, Con. I was so rude to you and—and Emma. I was reeling from everything else. From your dad not showing up at our special spot. Not to mention his surprise announcement. It wasn't you. Please call me."*

No wonder Connor hadn't been eager to return her call. It didn't matter that she had been in the depths of despair. He would have only heard that his mother blamed his dad for her inability to enthusiastically respond to him and Emma and their surprise arrival.

"Time to eat some crow, Mom."

Jill pressed the five and hit Send. A moment later Connor's phone rang.

When his voice mail picked up, she shut her phone.

Maybe she'd listen to her messages first.

As she flipped the phone back open, it rang. Connor's name appeared. "Connor."

"Hey, Mom. Sorry, the phone was buried in my backpack."

"Are you busy?"

He chuckled. "We're in Napa at a coffee shop. My French fiancée and her French parents are making fun of California wines."

"I suppose since they're French, they drink wine."

"Mom." There was exasperation in his tone.

"It wasn't a moral judgment."

"Hold on. I'm heading outside."

Jill's resolve turned to doubt. They were off on one of *those* conversations. He would misunderstand whatever she said because his head was elsewhere.

"Okay. Dad tell you our news?"

"Yeah." She gathered enthusiasm and tried again. "Yeah! That's quite the surprise."

"It doesn't top yours."

"Yes, it does. Oh, honey, I don't know where to start. I'm sorry."

"That I'm getting married?" He was definitely on a short fuse.

"Connor, give me a chance to talk. I'm sorry for the way I behaved in Hollywood."

"I heard that on your voice mail. What do you want me to say?"

"Nothing. I needed to say it to you. I hurt you. What I did was inexcusable." *And I hope you can forgive me.* She kept the obvious to herself.

Connor would know what she was thinking. She had schooled him enough in the significance of letting others off the hook for his own well-being. This was not the time for another lesson. With his edgy mood he'd only hear coercion. He had to figure it out for himself.

"Honey, you're not a child anymore. I need you to be grown-up about this. Dad and I are in the middle of a life-changing mess. The timing couldn't be worse, but what's done is done. We move on. I am happy for you. Emma must be an extraordinary young woman." She spoke around a lump in her throat. She wanted to be happier for him.

She wanted to have gotten to know the girl, to have a front-row seat to their growing relationship, to give them advice.

Given her current situation, that would not have been a good thing.

She swallowed. "Now, what can I do for you? Dad says you want small."

"Yeah. We have to get back to school and we want to do it while her parents are here." He rattled off the very, *very* short guest list, the plan for dinner in the back room of his favorite Italian restaurant.

It wasn't Jill's mother-of-the-groom dream wedding. Nope. Not even close.

He said, "Did Dad tell you about the ceremony itself?"

"No."

"Okay. Now don't freak out."

She counted to five. It was a reflexive reaction to the phrase that always prefaced something she didn't want to hear. "Honey, I'm sure Pastor Lew will accommodate you. We can use the chapel. It's smaller—"

"Mom, the thing is, we don't want him to marry us."

"What! What? Connor! Pastor has been an integral part of your entire life! Why on earth would—?"

"Why on earth would I even try to talk to you?" His voice rose. "You want me to grow up, but the minute I make a decision you don't like, you go off the deep end."

"Good grief. I'm only confused, that's all. Help me understand. Don't you like him?"

"Not really."

"But why—?"

"Look, I can't do this right now. I'm having a nice time with Emma and her parents. And oh, by the way, yes, they do drink wine, and as a matter of fact, so do I."

"Oh, Connor! How could you! You're playing with fire. Your great-grandfather Galloway—"

"Was a raging alcoholic. I know and I know all the genetic possibilities."

"Then why—?"

"Probably because you pounded into my head 'Don't do it.'"

"I also told you not to run into the street."

"It's not the same thing."

"Connor, my only intention was to protect you. To keep you from doing something that would hurt you or that you might regret later."

"But it's *my* life. I have to make my own choices and figure things out for myself. *C'est la vie.*"

"But—"

"But nothing, Mom. Let it go. Let's just say *au revoir* for now and finish this later. Okay?"

She placed her free arm across her middle and squeezed tight, holding back an emotional explosion. "I apologize for freaking out."

He exhaled loudly. "I'm sorry for raising my voice at you. We good to go now?"

"Who do you want to conduct the ceremony? And where?"

"Later. Say *ciao*, Mom."

"*Ciao*, Mom."

He snorted, the sound falling somewhere between a chuckle and a locker room phrase.

Jill closed the phone and wished with all her might that she could stick her son and his independent streak and his smush of languages in a corner for a long, long time-out.

Jill did not rejoin her dad in the garage. Instead she walked. She walked hard, regret and confusion coursing through her, jamming each footfall against the rocky earth until at last she felt drained.

What was all this? First Jack, then Connor. A wall had been built between her and the two people closest to her and she had no idea how to tear it down.

It took the entire three-mile round-trip trail to the waterfall plus the two-mile round-trip trek from the house to the trailhead to work out her twisted knot of emotions. The western sky was all pinks and purples above the mountains before she got back to the center of town, the sun long gone.

She did not make a conscious decision on which route to take home but found herself passing Wags Service Station. She slowed and then stopped.

Beyond the pumps, Ty was visible through the open doorway and picture window. He moved about the shelving units, perhaps organizing the few groceries he carried.

Exhausted, she watched him, her breath condensing in the cool evening air.

And in her imagination she began to play a game.

What would it be like to chuck her life? Just start all over. Give Jack his divorce. Let Connor do what he was going to do anyway without a cautionary word. Get a small, cheap apartment in Sweetwater. Wander the trails. Volunteer at the nature center. Be a help to her aging parents. Do anything but teach. Never, ever give an opinion on communication or puzzle out a relationship.

Fall in love again with Ty Wilkins. Taste his kisses that by now would be full of the manliness only hinted at when they were teens. Be his right hand at the station.

He stepped through the door now, a trash bag in his hand. He caught sight of her and paused.

They gazed toward each other in the semidarkness, the area between them brightly lit by the overhang's lights. The air fairly crackled with electricity. It was not part of her fantasy.

She wondered if he played the same dangerous game.

They stood like that for a while, a minute or two. Maybe half an hour. Maybe longer. Time ceased.

Jill lingered in the tantalizing scene that played out in her mind. She tingled from head to toe. She felt like a child whizzing down a playground slide.

She heard the silence, the hush of the desert.

And then she heard the whisper.

She wanted to run from it, from the words that spilled into her heart.

This is how it happens.

No! she argued.

This is how it happens.

No. I'm just . . . I'm just—

This is how it happens.

Everything faded from view, real and imagined. The gas station. The pink sky. Ty's lips on hers. An abyss pushed them all aside. It yawned, a great widening blackness that wrapped around her, seeping into every pore of her body.

"No," she whispered.

Jill turned and quickly walked away. She began to jog. Her muscles protested and her heart pounded.

She wanted to sleep with Ty.

This is how it happens.

It happened out of the blue. Out of pain and loneliness. Out of being human. Out of the declaration of a husband who hurt so much he wanted a divorce. Out of a son's rejection.

"Oh, God." She panted the words as her feet hit the concrete. "I had no idea."

Of all the pithy suggestions she had spouted about how to avoid adultery . . .

"This is too easy. I could have. Oh, God. I wanted to. Help me. Help me. Help me."

Who did she think she was? Temptation was alive and well in the desert, in the heart of a woman who condemned others and thought she knew better.

The garbage can creaked and groaned, its weight unbearable.

"Come to Me, all of you who are weary and carry heavy burdens. Come to Me."

Jill slowed to a walk and let herself dwell on the familiar words. She replayed them over and over. The cool night air touched her skin and she knew it was full of acceptance.

God loved her, warts and all, trash and all.

CHAPTER 31

———— ❧ ————

"Jackson, dear." Katherine Galloway's voice warbled through the cell phone. "Is this an inconvenient time?"

Jack touched his chest, willing the boom in it to quiet. His mother never called in the morning on a weekday unless his father was having a heart attack. Of the four times that had occurred, even the refined Katherine had not inquired politely about convenience.

He said, "I'm just out of surgery and walking to the office."

"Oh, tell me, what did you do?"

Jack grinned at her enthusiasm. She still believed that doctors walked on water. "I reconstructed an ankle."

"How marvelous! Will he or she be able to dance?"

"If he wants." The hockey player he had worked on did not seem the dancing type. Jack prayed he would find something, though. Ice-skating was no longer in the kid's future. "How are you?"

"Peachy keen."

Turning into a rabbit warren of back hallways, Jack chose to avoid the easy route to his office. And Sophie.

His mother said, "Did you want something?"

Uh-oh. "You called me."

"I did?"

"Is Dad okay?"

"Your father? Well, yes, he's fine. As fine as a coot can be, anyway. I must add that caveat. He seems a bit grumpy. I don't think he slept well."

As his mother rambled on, Jack entered the back entrance of the main office. A few more steps and he would be home free, inside his private—

"Dr. G."

He spun on his heel, gave Sophie a fake smile, and pointed to the phone at his ear.

Sophie smiled sweetly and pointed at the coffee mug in her hand. She passed him and went into his office.

Her hair was pinned back in its bun.

She emerged, no mug in sight, smiled, and passed him again.

The coffee would be on his desk because she would have checked upstairs with the OR and learned when he had left. She would have perfectly timed the delivery of the coffee she knew he enjoyed after early-morning surgery.

Katherine was still chatting about his father's attitude.

Jack shut his door and sat at the desk. "Mother, do you remember why you called?"

"Jackson, you know better than to ask me that! It addles me. I do believe it sets the Alzheimer's into motion."

"You do not have Alzheimer's and you are less senile than 98 percent of other women your age."

"I don't suppose that says much, considering my age. Have you told me this before? I can't seem to recall."

He laughed. "Very clever. Now, I really need to get to work."

"Yes, of course. This won't take long. Your father and I were listening to Jillian's program on the radio. Until today they've been running pre-recorded interviews. But this one is from a few years ago. Why is that?"

"They only made so many new ones. Since when do you two listen to Jill's show?"

"Why, Jackson, we've listened to it for, oh, I don't know. Ages."

"You never mentioned it."

"I'm quite certain we have. Perhaps you've got a touch of senility yourself."

Jack would bet the new blender he bought last night that his parents tuned into the Christian radio station the day after he informed them about the separation. Gearing up for battle, Katherine would need to arm herself with ammunition, tidbits to shore up her position. *"Galloways do not divorce."*

"At any rate," she said, "this was an especially well-done presentation and rather poignant given the present circumstances. The topic was husbands in midlife crises. According to the expert she interviewed, there are enough documented cases of similar situations that doctors believe it is a real phenomenon. Then women called in with the most heartbreaking of stories. Jillian was absolutely tender with them and pressed the expert for answers. He didn't seem to have any."

"Mother, do you mind jumping to the point of this story?"

"Oh, sorry. I *forgot* it's a workday for you. The point is, Jillian was asked what she would do if faced with this. She said communication is the key and that at the first warning signal, she would insist that you both clear your schedule, sit down, and talk. She said above all, she would be right beside you as your helpmate, not the enemy."

Jack pinched the bridge of his nose.

"And then," Katherine went on, "she said this went way out of her league, that it might be necessary to see a counselor. I guess my point is, maybe you should do that."

"Do Galloways see counselors?"

"It is a new day, dear. Good heavens, it's a new century. Do you have a new red sports car?"

"No, only a new blender. It's white."

"Perhaps it's the same thing."

Blender as a chick magnet? "Mother—"

"I hear the exasperation. May we have a copy of Jillian's book?"

"I gave one to you."

"You did? Well, we'll check the bookshelves. I don't remember see-ing it."

"I'll bring one on Sunday. Good-bye."

"She also said that Christian counselors are listed in the Yellow Pages. Good-bye, dear." Click.

Jack shook his head. Where had all that come from?

There was a quick rap on the door and it opened. Sophie appeared. "The natives are restless, Dr. G."

"Coming." He stood and gulped the still-hot coffee. Sophie did know how to make a perfect cup.

He better not tell her about his new blender. She might unleash the bun again and call him Jack and suggest smoothies at his place.

❧

Jill's distinctive, whispery voice flowed through the laptop's speakers and filled Jack's small apartment.

It didn't belong there.

He closed the computer and chided himself for allowing that other voice to speak in his head and convince him to listen to Jill's archived radio program.

He really did not want to listen to either his wife or his mother.

As newlyweds, he and Jill had clashed over his preferential treatment of Katherine's opinions and feelings. Jill helped him see that he needed to respond first to his wife rather than to his mother. It made sense, of course. It was part of God's practical "leave and cleave" plan. With Jill as his loving partner—her heart even back then was passionate about good communication—he slowly but surely tuned out his mother's voice.

He did not know that the transition had been overly difficult until he read a well-documented account of it in Jill's book.

Had he simply traded his mother's voice for Jill's? He sometimes wondered. It seemed impossible. He first fell in love with Jill's voice because it was not condescending or strident or bossy.

But somehow along the way her voice had become louder than his own.

I'm living my father's life. Which was exactly what he had meticulously avoided.

Or so he thought.

Jack squinted at the clock on the microwave. It was after ten, but his dad was a night owl, unlike his mother.

Jack checked his head. The spot he had banged in the accident throbbed as if it were a fresh wound and not a red line of new skin. He should tell Baxter about it, but what could he do for psychosomatic symptoms? Jack had been listening to Jill's voice when he lost control of the car. End of story.

Or just the beginning.

He called his dad, who answered on the second ring.

"Jack, I am so ticked at the mayor. Guess what he did today."

"Watching the news is not healthy for you, Dad."

"Yeah, yeah. You sound like your mother."

"I'm sorry."

"For what?"

"For sounding like Mother."

"Why would you say that?"

Jack sighed to himself. "Is she asleep?"

"Is the pope Catholic?"

"Dad, I have a serious issue here. Just listen a minute. Why do you let her rule the roost?"

"Her? The pope is a woman?"

Jack waited.

"Okay, okay. Turning off the television and getting serious. Now, what's on your mind, Son? I'm listening."

He couldn't hold it in any longer and he couldn't rearrange the words.

"All at once I'm so angry at you, Dad. So angry. I needed a masculine voice when I was growing up and all I got—all I've still got—is her voice in my head." His throat closed in. He loved his father. How could he even insinuate that he'd been let down by him?

"I taught you how to fish and golf."

"Dad, please. Don't you get it?"

"Nope. Try again."

"You let Mother rule the roost."

"Yeah, so? She was better equipped than I was to run things. More vocal about it. Smart as a whip. Kind of like Jill."

"Exactly. I married my mother."

"Son, that sounds a little sick."

"I mean Jill can talk me into anything, like Mother does with you."

"Nah. No comparison. You're a different generation. In my day, husbands didn't concern themselves with what wallpaper went up or who had the best deal on pork roast. We were all about making hay. What is it you're mad about?"

Jack's frustration fizzled and he laughed. "I don't know. Right now I'm feeling like I want to hear more from you. I wished I had all along."

"Well, thanks. Can't say that I heard much from my own dad, you know. Now that I think about it, I guess I married my mother too. Mom was a strong woman who could single-handedly take care of her family and stand up to a drunken fool. Goodness, you don't think history repeated itself?"

"Dad, you never got drunk and you made a good living."

"Details aside, I'm sorry if I let you down in any way."

Jack smiled. "I know. I'm just venting. I want out of my marriage but I'm going about it all wrong. I don't know the right way. There probably isn't one, is there?"

Charles cleared his throat, uncomfortable as usual when talk slanted toward heavy. "I've always loved and admired Jill. She is an honest-to-goodness honey. But I can see how she'd get you all twisted into knots."

"That about sums it up. Any pearls of wisdom? I've seen changes in how you are with Mother."

His dad barked a short laugh.

"It's true. You let her win the bickering contest more often."

"That's because we live in this eight-by-twelve-foot hole in the wall, and I don't have the office to go to and she doesn't have her clubs to occupy her time."

Jack smiled at the exaggerations. Their condo had two bedrooms and his parents attended all sorts of activities at the facility.

"Jack, I let her win because I simply don't care anymore about life. I'm tired. There's my pearl for you. You're too young to be tired. Fight for whatever is important, which probably ain't the wallpaper."

He said hesitantly, "That's a good pearl, Dad."

"Well, don't ask me how you do it. I don't know—hey! What about my grandson? He's getting married! What's his girl like?"

"Emma sounds very sweet. She's soft-spoken and considerate."

"She could be a rooster in chick clothing." He laughed.

Jack doubted it. But then . . . would he have believed it of Jill years ago?

"Jackson, you're thinking too much. Grow up and get on with it."

"Is that supposed to help?"

"I don't know, but it sure felt good to say it." He laughed again.

Jack joined in. Before long his side hurt and he doubled over. His dad's uproarious howl filled the line.

He'd always liked his dad's laughter.

Lord, I need this guy for a while. Please don't let him have another heart attack.

CHAPTER 32

———— ✦ ————

Viv spotted her sister across the wide expanse of the lobby and waved.

Jill waved back, a good sign that they were once again on speaking terms.

Sisters. Viv smiled to herself. They were thrown together simply because they had the same parents. How wacky a basis for a relationship was that? No wonder they could be inseparable one day and distant as foreign enemies the next.

"Hey." Viv stepped into Jill's hug. "I told Mom I'd come by the house."

"I couldn't wait to see the Casitas Pack." She winked. "And you."

"You look great." Viv eyed Jill's baggy capris and glowing skin. "Pie must agree with you."

"Pecan this morning." She puffed out her cheeks. "I've power walked to the moon and back. Can we sit?"

They went to a corner couch, its upholstery a splash of Southwestern colors. Artificial cacti of every variety were displayed in colorful clay pots situated around the Sage Resort's lobby. Viv had brought a small group over to spend a few days in the desert. It was her treat, a way to celebrate their loyalty and the new bus.

Jill said, "Mom thinks you're being absolutely ridiculous to pay for all those people to stay here four nights."

"Maybe I am. I did charge them a small fee for transportation. And I got a really good deal on the rooms. I'm hardly losing money." She did a quick calculation and smiled. "Not a lot anyway. Dustin is working overtime back home. And there is gas for the bus that fees from seven ladies don't quite meet."

"Seven?" Jill laughed. "The bus that seats fourteen."

"Up to fourteen." She grinned. "This is not simply a thank-you to my special pack. It's our celebration of that bus. I couldn't *not* use it. So." She eyed her sister closely. "How goes it?"

Jill gave her a thumbs-up. "I passed the state of 'okay' yesterday. I'm into good, very good. Who would've thought? Mom and Pops and pie equals a winning combination. Well, I guess you did think of it."

Viv shook her head. "Nope. Not until after the fact. I came here because I was desperate and couldn't imagine anyone else taking me in. Parents have to, you know. It's their job."

"Yeah." She wrinkled her nose. "I'm so sorry for hurting you, Viv."

Unsure how to respond, Viv shrugged. Since childhood, their apologies to one another tended to be off-the-cuff, a natural conclusion to a sibling spat, no big deal. This one was . . . a heartfelt adult version.

"Jill, I'm sorry for not trusting you."

"Good golly. Why would you trust me? I wouldn't trust me. I'm all about black-and-white answers. No grays allowed in my paradigm. No place for mystery or unknowns or even human nature. I'm sure you thought that if you had told me your story, I would have told you that your behavior was morally reprehensible and you should know better." She paused. "Whoa. I didn't plan on that full confession. I was hoping you'd just forgive me."

Viv smiled. "I can do that."

"Thanks." Jill rubbed her hands on her thighs in a nervous gesture.

"While I'm at this, uh, confession business, I may as well get it all out. The other day I wanted to have an affair with Ty Wilkins."

"Ty Wilkins?" Viv held in a laugh and nearly choked. Tall, skinny Ty, uncoordinated beyond belief unless he was wielding a wrench? "Sweetwater Springs is a lonely place."

"Viv! I'm dead serious. I talked with Connor and about lost my mind. He's getting married, by the way."

She nodded. "Jack called to tell me after he told you."

"Well, by the time I finished talking with Jack and Connor, I realized I've been one lousy wife and mother. Why bother trying to be good anymore? I was ready to . . . Did you know Ty is divorced?"

Viv shook her head and widened her eyes.

"Nothing happened, but seriously, I was ready to commit adultery and do whatever else would make me feel better. I swear I will never judge another person again for anything. I will never, ever say again that God does not live in the grays of this world. He knows it's a dreadful, confusing place and He won't abandon us when we turn away from Him!" She gestured wildly. "He is in the air we breathe. How do you get away from that?"

"You look feverish, hon."

Jill stilled her arms and her shoulders relaxed. "I'm a little upset with myself."

Viv smiled. "You should be."

Jill frowned.

"But at least now the expert Jill Galloway empathizes with me and all of humanity. She is one of us, hallelujah."

"Viv, this isn't funny!"

"Hopefully she'll learn how to lighten up too." She held up her hand to ward off another protest. "Okay, I'll quit. Any news on the Jack front?"

"I don't know. I have to get home ASAP. I have to plan a wedding and try to get us to a counselor. We simply can't do this alone. That's assuming Jack even wants to do this. If he chooses to throw in the towel like he said, then, well . . ." She blinked back tears.

Viv took her hand and squeezed it. "One step at a time, Jillie."

"That's what Pops keeps telling me. Which reminds me, he gave me the mail you sent."

A heavy box, chock-full of letters addressed to her sister, had been shipped to Viv's house from Jill's radio station. "I had no idea so many people write to you, hon, and that was just for the past month and on paper. I can't imagine the e-mails you must get on top of that."

Jill took a deep breath. "It's not me. It's the work. I study marriages and tell others what I learn. It touches a chord. A heartstring. But I can finally admit that I did make up formulas and guarantees that won't always help and may even hurt. I have to fix that part, Viv. I have to tell people that persnickety dogmatic doesn't equal right."

"You'll still twang heartstrings, maybe even more."

"Maybe. I read all the letters. And I listened to voice mails. There was one from a woman in that class where I fell apart. She was so incredibly kind. She said they've been praying for me. At first it all affirmed my work. So much admiration and even concern from the ones who know what's really going on." She paused. "Then I thought about how I have these deep heart connections with thousands of strangers and yet I don't with my own husband or my own son. I'm exactly like Mom."

Viv sat up straight, surprised at the comment. "You're not."

"Think about it. The neighbors love her. Customers loved her at the station. The town loves her. You and I lived with her and could not wait for summer to visit Grandma and to turn eighteen and move away. To this day we'd rather not hang out with her."

"That's common enough. Mothers and daughters usually don't see eye to eye."

"Viv, we don't have a deep heart connection with our own mother. We don't communicate on that level. We don't tell her certain things."

"She's prickly."

"So am I, to Jack and Connor and you and Marty and who knows how many others."

Viv shrugged. "I've always told you you're a pain in the neck and I wasn't joking. It's your personality, but it's not like Mom's."

"Oh, Viv. You've always accepted me."

"Not always. You can be difficult."

"And I bet you thank God every day that we don't live together. Poor Jack. He's had to live with me. He is so kind and generous, just like Pops. But he's had enough. He is obviously not going to hang in there like Pops has with Mom."

"You'll fix it, Jillie."

"I don't want to fix it. I want to change. I want to be different. I want to be a brand-new person."

Viv stared at her. She noticed the trimmed hair, clear eyes, stilled hands. "I'd say you're on your way."

"Really?"

She nodded. "It shows, hon."

Jill smiled, not the professional, photo-ready smile, but the one from childhood, lopsided and crinkling a side of her nose. She said, "It's just a little something I picked up here in the desert."

CHAPTER 33

─── ❧ ───

TABLE LEAVES HAD been added to accommodate the Casitas Pack, Viv, Jill, Daisy, and four pies in the Wagner kitchen.

Jill raised her brows at Viv. *See? What'd I tell you? Miss Congeniality.* Viv only winked.

Inevitably the conversation between gabby older women, all mothers, drifted to their children and birth stories. Inevitably Daisy retold her silly story about nonexistent aliens from outer space who were not green.

The Dutch apple pie on Jill's tongue disintegrated into a vinegary pulp.

Daisy finished her story and grinned. "And that's why we had Vivian." Two women chuckled politely.

Two touched their ears, a nifty gesture often employed to indicate the hearing aid was on the fritz again.

One feigned a sudden onset of dementia by slackening her jaw and gazing toward a ceiling corner, an equally nifty way to bow out of a conversation.

Another said with vehemence worthy of a courtroom drama, "There is no proof that aliens exist on other planets!"

And Agnes said softly but firmly, "Oh, Daisy, you are a card. I bet Jillian was so perfect you couldn't wait to have another."

Jill exchanged a glance with Viv and imagined her thought echoed Viv's. *Can we adopt Agnes for a mom?*

When Daisy burst into laughter, Jill looked again at her sister. *Huh?*

Daisy said, "Agnes, the little runt scared me to death. She was so precious. Imagine such a thing coming from me. This will sound crazy but every time Skip walked by, I got all hot and bothered. I just didn't let up until we made another one."

"Mom!" Viv cried out and clapped her hands over her ears.

Daisy said, "I suppose you're old enough to hear that version, now that you're in your forties."

Viv said, "I'll never be old enough to hear that version!"

Jill laughed until tears ran down her cheeks. "Please! Stick to the green Martian story."

"How many times do I have to tell you, Jillian? Martians are not green."

The conversation flowed easily after that, mothers talking about babies. Even the deaf and dementia-stricken joined in with clarity.

When Jill's laughter slowed, she knew something had changed between her and Daisy. Her mother's declaration that she had been precious was music to her ears. It drowned out the old tapes. *I was a* whoops, *unwanted, ugly, a thing to be avoided.* She heard instead that she was adored. By her mother. God was one thing, but her mother? up close and prickly Daisy Wagner?

Until that moment Jill would not have believed how deeply the *whoops* had embedded itself into her psyche. Now, as it loosened its grip, she felt peace flow into its place.

She caught Agnes's wink and smile. Agnes, the instigator of mind-blowing conversations.

Whatever that woman had, Jill wanted it.

❦

Twelve days after she had arrived, Jill rode out of Sweetwater Springs with a first-ever twinge of sadness.

She was convinced it had nothing to do with the sight of Ty Wilkins standing outside the station, waving at the minibus.

Viv tooted the horn and seven seniors waved as if he could see them through the tinted windows.

Agnes said, "Your high school boyfriend seems like a nice man, a *very* nice man."

Jill stared at her seatmate. "How do you know?"

"We met him, dear. Yesterday. We wanted Vivvie to take us on a tour down her memory lane. Of course yours often crisscrossed with it." Agnes's pale blue eyes did their sparkly dance. "He reminds me of your father. Is your Jack like Skip and Ty? Is he a nice man, a *very* nice man?"

"Yes, he is a very nice man. His patients and staff think he's wonderful."

"And you must too."

"Except for his behavior the past few weeks, I do."

She patted Jill's arm. "You two married so quickly. Didn't you tell me it was only six months after you met?"

"Yes. And my parents and Jack's were as upset as I am with Connor. I need to remember how crazy in love we were at first sight. Jack was kind of shy, so sweet, really good-looking. He was intent on becoming a doctor and taking care of people. I felt safe with him."

"You gave up your business with Vivvie for him."

"Grandma Ellie's company was more a means for me to get out of Sweetwater than anything. It was fun, but not what I wanted to do the rest of my life. For Viv, it was a passion. It still is."

"Any regrets?"

"Goodness, no. Life has been a dream." She frowned. "Maybe that's the problem. I've been off in my own make-believe world without paying much attention to reality. Why didn't I see this midlife crisis, or whatever we call it, coming?"

"Dear, surely you understand that marriage is like an automobile. It needs regular tune-ups. When was the last time you adjusted the carburetor? changed the spark plugs? put air in the tires?"

Jill chuckled. "You've been talking to my dad."

Agnes did her odd little shrug, a quick movement of shoulders to ears and back down. "Do you and Jack sit down regularly and have heart-to-hearts?"

"All the time. That's how I test everyone's theories and ideas about communication. The book is based on our personal experiences."

"Hm." Agnes, in the aisle seat, shifted her eyes beyond Jill's shoulder toward the window.

"Hm what?"

She looked at Jill again, but her eyes darted and seemed unfocused. "It sounds to me as if you and Jack carry on other people's heart-to-hearts. Like doctors in a morgue doing an autopsy, examining how someone's liver failed, hoping to figure out your own liver but you can't, not without examining it. And yet you tell other people what their livers are like."

"Every liver performs certain basic functions in the same way."

"Yet you must take into account all the variables. Age, weight, diet, heritage . . ."

"But the basics do not change."

"And where have the basics gotten you?" Agnes smiled. "I believe I need a little nap." She lay back against the seat and shut her eyes.

As usual, the words of Agnes Smith provoked uncomfortable questions.

Did Jill know—truly know—Jack's liver?

"By the way," Agnes said, her eyes still closed, "in ancient times the liver was thought to be the seat of our emotions."

Well, okay. An honest liver-to-liver conversation it would be then, first thing after she got home. Before any wedding plans she and Jack would talk, really talk. Their marriage was still the priority. They would get to Connor's but not until they had a handle on their own.

The bus hummed along the two-lane highway. Muted strains of rock and roll came from speakers near Viv in the driver's seat. She took the roller-coaster dips at a reasonable speed. The landscape stretched, a carpet of wildflowers and cacti all in their full spring glory. In the distance rose steep, rocky mountains. Slowly they changed in the morning sun from shadowy purples to light browns.

It all faded from view as Jill imagined one scenario after another of herself and Jack dialoguing. He had always been willing to engage with her, sometimes even role-playing, other times pausing midsentence to give her time to jot down notes of their conversation or even record it.

Maybe she should not take notes or record this time. Maybe she should inform Jack that this exchange would be solely for them. She would not use it for a lesson plan or for an on-air topic.

Was that bothering him? He had always said . . .

What she wanted him to say?

"Angel." Agnes grasped Jill's forearm and scooted to the edge of her seat. "If you orchestrate a conversation beforehand, it won't be a heart-to-heart."

The woman's ability to mind-read was downright unnerving.

"But," Jill said, "there are points we need to cover. If I don't—"

"Nonsense. You just pray, expect the Spirit to show up, and then listen more than you yammer. It will be taken care of." She smiled. "You've learned something here in the desert. Else you wouldn't be going back yet."

Jill laughed. "How do you do that?"

Agnes pointed up. "I listen more than yammer. You don't mind telling me, do you?"

"No. What I learned was that my mother always loved me. Which means I can stop trying to prove to her that I am worthy of being loved."

"To her or anyone. Your mother and God love you for who you are, not for what you accomplish."

"I am not what I do. I've never seen myself in that way."

"Freeing, isn't it? Makes you want to go out and dot some t's."

Jill giggled. "And cross some i's."

Agnes bobbed and clapped her hands, a little girl on Christmas morning. "Yes. Tell me what else happened."

"What do you mean, 'what else happened'?"

"I saw something in your eye when we first arrived, days before your mother's story."

That thing about Ty showed?

"Something good, Jill. A new insight."

The garbage can. "I admitted I'm not perfect."

"Was this a rather long time in coming?"

"I guess it looks that way. Of course I thought I knew that, but it was only a vague suspicion. Ever since I saw the warthog, every time I turn around it's like scales fall from my eyes and I see some new awful thing about myself."

"Hallelujah."

"I haven't said that yet."

"Try it."

Jill took a deep breath. "Hallelujah! I am judgmental, dogmatic, persnickety, prissy, a nagger with a black-and-white attitude, et cetera, et cetera."

"Very good. Now what?"

"It was all in a garbage can strapped to my back. But now I've only got one hand on it. God's helping me carry it."

Agnes stared at her, a smile tugging at her mouth. "Oh, dear."

"That is worth a hallelujah, isn't it?" Jill grinned. Between the wash of unconditional love and the assurance that she needn't carry her burdens alone, she wanted to dance. She was ready to tackle whatever was thrown in her path. Jack and Connor were not going to recognize her.

Agnes chuckled and then burst into laughter. "Jill, God wants you to *give* it to Him."

"What?" Jill wanted to pack the woman in her suitcase and take her to Chicago.

"God doesn't want you to carry that garbage around. Isn't that what the Cross is all about? Dump it out, my dear. He has forgiven every thought, word, and deed against Him and you."

"Dump it?"

"All of it."

"But it reminds me—"

"Of who you used to be." Agnes grasped her arm and gave it a gentle shake. "You are a new person, Jillian Galloway. Don't dwell in the old. Now dump that rubbish this instant!"

"Agnes, I'm just getting the hang of being honest about myself. I need some time to think this through."

"Time is short." The pale blue eyes lost their focus again. They moved almost as if Agnes were watching some activity above Jill. She cocked her head and touched her ear, listening. Her skin appeared cottony soft. "Yes, time is almost up."

"Are you all right?"

"Never been better." She refocused and met Jill's gaze. She smiled. "This has been grand, my dear. Wouldn't have missed getting to know you for the world, but now I must go home."

Jill felt a sense of dread at the sudden attack of senility. "Agnes, we're on the bus."

"Yes, I'm aware of that." She kissed Jill's cheek, undid her seat belt, and quickly stepped into the aisle.

Unbuckling her own belt, Jill reached out to grab Agnes's arm. The bus lurched and Jill clutched a handful of air.

Time slowed. One moment unfurled. An hour passed. Another moment opened as gently as a blossom welcoming the sun. Jill's mind recorded it all.

Viv nearly stood on the brake pedal, elbows akimbo, hands on the steering wheel.

Agnes twirled, a graceful spin of daffodil yellow velour.

Women screamed.

The bus rammed something, bounced up. And down. Up. And down. Bone-rattling, teeth-jarring jolts.

Agnes's body bounced off the silver pole at the stairwell. It smacked against the partition at the front. It tumbled onto the floor.

The bus hit down a third time. Wham.

The overhead compartment descended, its gray molded frame coming to meet Jill's forehead.

The world went black.

CHAPTER 34

————— ❧ —————

Viv respected dust storms.

She first met one at the age of six as she played alone in the backyard, not far from the house. It whipped at her without warning and too quickly for her mother to reach her. For several minutes it pelted her, driving sand and dirt into her eyes and mouth, stinging her arms and legs. She searched blindly for the house, her screams lost in the wind's roar, unable to find the back door or hear her mother's voice until the storm had passed.

Which made her overly cautious when it came to driving her tour vehicles across the desert. Except for that roller-coaster stretch outside of Sweetwater in her own car, she drove like a little old lady determined not to bump a lizard. No matter if skies were clear and the wind calm, she monitored forecasts.

As she had that morning.

The thing was, haboobs did not always announce their intentions.

It was a beautiful spring day, dry, not too hot, clear skies, calm wind. A yellow carpet of wildflowers lined the two-lane.

Viv enjoyed driving. Traffic didn't bother her, but long stretches of empty roads through an ever-changing landscape were a special treat. She especially liked the vastness of the Sweetwater desert, a mismatched puzzle of valleys, dry creek beds, canyons, overlooks, and ridges.

Low scrubby bushes, cacti, rocks, and beige sands filled the space as far as the eye could see. Surrounding it all were hills like great piles of unfolded laundry, soft towels of earthy colors. Mountains rose, inverted ice cream cones with three-thousand-foot peaks. Deep quiet reigned, louder even than her music.

It made her feel small and big at the same time, an ant who moved along the whorls of God's fingertips.

The ribbon of highway dipped and curved and squeezed itself between rock walls near enough it seemed she could reach out her window and touch them. In some places the right or the left wall gave way to boulder-strewn drops and panoramic vistas of valleys and mountains so magnificent they snatched her breath away.

Red Gulch Canyon was just such a pass. Viv slowed going into the rock-wall-enclosed S-curves, anticipating the burst of beauty on the right side as she pulled around the final loop.

Wham.

Without warning, the storm roared at her. It struck the bus head-on at thirty miles an hour. Its mass of dust and debris would reach upward thousands of feet high and outward far enough to engulf the valley.

Visibility instantly went to zero.

Viv instantly slammed on the brakes.

Her mind automatically registered several things at once. The storm itself would most likely last only a few minutes. There had been no traffic behind her, but she had to pull off the road, beyond the narrow shoulder, and turn off the taillights so no one would follow them.

Where was the shoulder?

Viv turned the steering wheel slightly. The bus skidded. *Oh, God!* It bounced and banged and careened down the embankment. It went down. And down.

An eternal moment passed. Cries from the women and the rat-atat-tat of sand peppering the windows filled her head. With a sudden, violent jolt, the bus stopped.

And stayed put. Right-side up. No rocking. No teetering. No creaking. Solid on the ground.

They hadn't hit a rock wall. They hadn't plunged over one of the steep drop-offs. They hadn't broken apart or flipped over or crashed onto the boulders.

Thank You, God! Viv set the brake and turned off the engine and almost laughed. *Like I'm parking in a lot! Thank You. Thank You.*

She unbuckled her seat belt, trying to turn around. A sharp pain shot through her left arm and yanked her back. The wrist angled in an odd way and caught in the harness loop, slowing her. She jerked it free and scrambled over the console into the back of the bus.

Six of her ladies were struggling to get free from seat belts, calling out to one another. *Thank You, God, that they wear the belts.* Jill was crawling toward Viv, or rather toward a figure slumped partially in the aisle, partially in the stairwell.

A figure clad in yellow.

Agnes.

What was she doing there?

Jill reached her first and gently touched her cheek. "Oh, Agnes!"

Viv knelt and took hold of the motionless wrist. She checked for a pulse. Jill's fingers were on Agnes's neck.

"Jillie?"

Her sister looked at her and nodded. A trickle of blood from her forehead disappeared into her collar. "I think her head hit the divider."

"There's not a scratch on her."

"But her neck . . ."

Viv noticed then the crookedness of Agnes's body, the head not aligned as it should be. "Oh, God! I'm sorry!"

Jill reached over Agnes and hugged her. "She knew, Viv."

"Knew what?" Another pain ripped through her arm. "Oh!"

"You're hurt."

"We have to get out! We have to get out!"

Someone touched her back and she turned to see Martha, tall with salt-and-pepper hair. "My phone isn't working. Let me look at your wrist, Vivvie." She knelt and gently felt along the arm. "It might be broken. Try to relax now. We have enough first aid supplies and food and water for an army. We'll be fine, honey. Remember I was a nurse and Iris was an aide."

Viv started to blubber. "Agnes."

"Dearie, Agnes is just fine. You know where she went. She just stepped into the unseen world and she's happy to be there. That blissful smile on her face says it all, don't you think?"

Viv collapsed into Martha's arms.

CHAPTER 35

———— ❦ ————

Jack pulled a pen from the chest pocket of his lab coat and grabbed a pad from the counter. "This is what I'm trying to say." He wheeled his stool over to the patient seated on a chair in the examining room and began to sketch.

The young woman chuckled. "What is that?"

"Your leg bones. It's the way they've probably always grown. See how that throws off your balance? Orthotics will correct it. No more pain in your feet."

The door burst open and Sophie appeared.

At the sight of her pinched face, Jack felt the room tilt.

"My dad?"

"Your brother-in-law." Her voice was low, her words rushed.

Jack's thought processes slowed. His brother-in-law? Who?

Sophie beckoned to him and apologized to his patient. "Sorry, Mrs. Collins. He really needs to take this call. A nurse will be right with you."

Getting himself into the hall was like swimming through molasses. Something was wrong. Something was very wrong. He had a

241

brother-in-law. He lived in California. Why would he call him in the middle of the day? Why would he know about Jack's dad?

Sophie handed him the phone and shut the door behind him. "Jack, there's been an accident," she whispered. "Talk to Marty."

Marty. His brother-in-law. He put the phone to his ear. "Marty?"

"Hey, Jack. Listen. Viv and Jill had an accident. They're okay. Just happened. They're still in the bus."

"Bus?"

"Viv's tour bus. They're okay." He sounded as if he were talking himself into believing his statement. "I'm pretty sure they're okay. Viv called me so . . . Hold on."

Sophie was pushing on Jack's back, steering him toward his office. Through the phone came the sound of a blaring horn followed by muttered cussing.

"Marty!"

"Yeah. Yeah. Viv called, maybe twenty minutes ago? Dust storm. Bus went off the road. Thank God not a cliff. It's right-side up. Nine of them on board. Everybody's okay. Well, almost. Hold on."

Again came the noises. Sophie shoved him into a chair and sat in the other one in his office.

"Stupid drivers! Get out of my way, jerk! Sorry."

"You said *almost*!"

"Agnes. One of the old ladies from—"

"Jill! What about Jill?"

"Viv says she's okay."

"What does *okay* mean?" Jack nearly screeched.

"She's walking and talking, Jack. That's all I know. I figure if they're walking and talking, they're all right."

"Okay. Okay." He leaned forward, elbows on his knees, hand against his forehead.

Sophie touched his shoulder.

Jack lowered his voice, tried to get his mind around what Marty was saying. "Where are you?"

"Ninety minutes out."

"Ninety!"

"I'll do it in forty-five."

Jack imagined Marty in his man truck with its big tires and powerful engine, traffic parting for him like a curtain.

Marty said, "They're at Red Gulch Canyon."

Jack shook his head. He'd never heard of Red Gulch Canyon. It sounded like some godforsaken desert hole. Where was Jill? Last they talked, she was at her parents'. What was she doing on Viv's bus? Viv had a bus?

He hated feeling ignorant.

Marty went on. "So they're still closer to Sweetwater than the city. First responders are heading out from there now. Volunteers for the most part, but they know the terrain."

"Skip's a volunteer!"

"Right. Which means our girls are in good hands. I gotta warn you, though. It's going to take them a while to get at the bus. The storm might have dumped junk on the highway. There might be other accidents along the way. And . . ." He went quiet.

Jack waited.

Marty cleared his throat. "Viv couldn't tell how far down they went. There's some steep terrain heading into the valley. But they didn't roll or hit anything major."

"Oh, no. What about that woman? Who did you say?"

"Agnes. She . . ." He paused. "She died. Apparently she didn't have her seat belt on. I didn't get any more details. The cell signal is iffy. Viv gave me what I needed to call emergency and got off."

"*You* called 911?"

"Yeah. Goofy broad." How he managed to say that lovingly was an exclusive Martin Kovich talent. "She wasn't thinking or talking too clearly. I doubt a dispatcher could have deciphered a word. I better pay attention to the road. I'll call you soon as I know more."

"Thanks. Thanks, Marty."

Jack looked at the phone. He couldn't find the Off button.

Sophie took it from him. "Is Jill all right?"

"He, um, he thinks so."

"What happened?"

He blinked and she came into focus. He repeated what Marty had told him.

When he finished, he pressed his hand to his mouth. Visions of Jill came to mind. Injured? Scared? Going into shock?

Dying?

He was a physician. He handled emergencies. He stopped bleeding and stitched skin back together. He fixed bones.

But Jill had always handled Connor's gushing wounds and bruised knees. Connor had even bandaged Jill's cut finger once. He was five years old. Jack had watched, silently nauseous.

"Jack, don't go there."

"What?" He saw Sophie again.

She stood. "Don't go to the worst. Try to call her. If Marty talked to Viv . . ." She shrugged. "Connor needs to hear from you too. I'll go cancel the rest of your day." She walked out the door.

He'd never wished his wife harm. Never wished her off the face of the earth.

He'd only wanted not to be with her.

He reached for his cell phone.

CHAPTER 36

—— ❧ ——

RED GULCH CANYON

Jill huddled in row five, seat one, reclined position, left side of the bus, wrapped in a blanket, a cold pack pressed to her forehead.

In row five, right side, Viv lay across both seats, her legs propped on pillows and dangling into the aisle.

In row one, left side, both seats in full recline position, the body of Agnes Smith lay under a blanket. From head to toe.

It was the only thing they could do.

The six other women of the Casitas Pack sat scattered about. Martha, Iris, Ruthie, Cynthia, Yolanda, and Lila had made her and Viv comfortable. Martha had strapped Viv's arm to a board to immobilize it. They somehow managed to lift Agnes onto the seat and then prayed, different traditions meshing to honor the dead. Now they sang and kept up spirited conversation, mostly stories about Agnes.

"Viv." Jill's head pounded with the talking effort but she wanted to keep checking on her sister, even if the others were also. Her sister was in the worst shape.

"Mm."

"If I were stranded on a desert island and could choose six others to be with me, this is them."

"You didn't count me."

"Nope. You have wimped out on us. No one else even has a bruise. Not counting my bump."

"What were you doing out of your seat?" Viv had already asked that twice. Either the shock was dulling her mind or she just could not believe her sister would do such a stupid thing.

"Going after Agnes." They had all talked about the woman's odd words, which of course the pack did not find odd in the least. "Great timing on your part, braking and swerving right at the moment she stood up." The teasing did not quite come across. "You know I'm joking."

"Mm."

"Keep talking please."

"Can't."

Jill caught Martha's eye. The woman reached over the back of Viv's seat and laid a hand on her forehead and murmured. From what Jill had observed over the past two hours, she was praying for the shock to recede, for medics to arrive soon.

Viv had hung in as long as she could. Hers was the only phone with a signal and she used it to call Marty. Jill had groaned when she overheard Viv talking to him and not an emergency operator. But after listening to her incoherent screeching, she figured it was for the best. Her phone lost its signal then. It never came back.

But Marty could be counted on.

Jack was . . . far away.

Outside, the storm was long gone. It was their nature. Blow in, blow through, blow out. Wreak havoc, pitch every loose bit of rock and dirt and plant against whatever was in the path. Screaming meemy winds deafened and then went quiet.

But the women were not going anywhere. The bus had come to rest wedged between boulders as tall as the turtle top Viv loved so much. The driver's door would not open. The window of the back exit door was completely covered with dirt and rock. From the size of the rocks, the debris was not simply dust stuck to the window. There was a pile of it against the door. Cynthia and Lila confirmed that when they were unable to budge it.

A younger woman might have kicked out the windshield. Jill did not volunteer. It would mean hiking up to the highway—and who knew how far that was?—and waiting there instead of here. Her entire body ached from being thrown about.

And besides, Marty knew where they were. Unglued as she had been, Viv read him the coordinates from the GPS. Even if the bus were not visible from the highway, he knew their exact location and would have immediately notified Sweetwater Springs emergency.

Jack was . . . far away.

Jill closed her eyes. What was she going to do without Agnes?

❧

They found them.

Once the driver's door was wrangled open, Skip was the first one through, a distraught father, not a volunteer EMT. Ty came on his heels, followed by two others, medics and firemen with equipment, unprofessional worry on every face. They all knew Jill and Viv.

And then, wonder of wonders, Daisy climbed in, tears streaming down her face.

"Daisy!" Ty nearly barked. "Wait outside."

"These are my babies. Get out of my way."

He stepped down into the stairwell.

Skip and Daisy took turns clinging to Viv and Jill.

"I'm fine, Mom. I'm fine."

"Look at that goose egg on your head, child."

"Let them take care of Viv. Something's broken. Her wrist or her arm. Move over, Pops. I'm fine."

Everyone talked at once. From outside came digging noises and shouts. A helicopter whomped overhead. Sirens joined in. Marty showed up, barging in like a bull.

Jill wasn't so sure the scene felt like a rescue. She preferred the earlier peace of waiting.

Ty stepped over her and sat in the window seat beside her. "You Wagner sisters and your splashy exits from Sweetwater." He took her wrist in his glove-covered hands.

"Viv needs help."

"No worries. We got her covered." He nodded toward her sister. "See? IV is already going. We'll get her out first, soon as the exit's cleared, and up to the ambulance. How you doing?"

The willow green eyes blurred. Her voice refused to work. Her body shook as if she'd been dunked in Lake Michigan on a January morning.

"Not so hot, huh? You're the second one out. How'd you hit your head?"

She gave up and let the tears fall. She let them soak Ty's navy blue T-shirt, let her face rest against the shoulder that had been there for her in the past.

CHAPTER 37

———— ❧ ————

Jack did not reach Jill until many hours later.

He called Connor to let him know. After his son's distress over not knowing about Jack's accident, he needed to keep their son in the loop. He was skiing in Idaho with Emma and her parents and offered to leave. Jack told him there was nothing to do yet.

Late that evening, Marty phoned him from a San Diego hospital. Viv was in surgery for a broken wrist. All six seniors were being held for observation. The bus was going to be towed to Sweetwater Springs as soon as they dug it out and taken to Skip's former garage to determine whether it could be repaired.

And Jill?

Back at Skip and Daisy's.

Skip and Daisy's? After spending over a week there already?

Marty reminded him the accident happened near Sweetwater. That sense of being ignorant had filled him again.

She answered their house phone. "Hello?"

"Jill!" He exhaled a long breath of relief. "Are you all right?"

"I'm good."

"I've been trying to reach you for hours. Marty said you were there but the line's been busy. You didn't answer your cell."

"I was talking with Connor. He was checking on Grandpops, the famous Sweetwater EMT, and found me. Maybe he can find my phone too. It must be on the bus, which is still knee-deep in rock and dirt."

The way she was running off at the mouth she must have been shaken up. "You're really okay?"

"You're really worried."

"Of course I'm really worried. Why wouldn't I be sick with worry? You're riding in a bus that goes off a cliff in the middle of nowhere and a woman gets killed."

"Jack, relax. I'm fine. Well, except for this bump on my forehead. I guess I fell down and broke my crown too. I didn't know Jill broke her crown, did you? Here I always thought it was only Jack."

"How could that happen? Marty said everybody had seat belts on because Viv insisted on it."

"She does that. But Agnes got up . . . Oh, that's another story. Anyway, I undid my belt to help her and then . . . then I don't know. We went off the side of the road and bounced around and my whole body bounced around."

"Were you knocked unconscious?"

"Do people remember that sort of thing? I don't remember it."

Déjà vu. "Jill! You need tests. You should be in a hospital. You may have a concussion. Internal bleeding. All kinds of things! Why aren't you at the hospital with everyone else?"

"The ambulances had to transport Agnes and Viv. Poor Viv. Her wrist was broken. Did you know that? She had to lie there on that bus for hours with a broken bone. And—and where was I?"

"Are you on pain meds?"

"Yes."

"You're a little loopier than normal."

She giggled.

He grinned. Jill had a silly side that produced the same effect. "So if you're on meds, you've seen a doctor. Right?"

"Righto."

"But you didn't go with the others to San Diego?"

"No. There was a van, but the Casitas Pack and all their luggage filled it up. Mom and Pops came, did you hear? But they were absolutely no help. Hold on, Jack. Sorry, Mom. I meant medicalwise. Your hugs were a huge help."

Jack rolled his eyes.

"Anyway," she said, "Ty said I could just go home with them if I promised to stop by the ER. Which I did, Dr. Galloway. And Pops will wake me up in the night. Meanwhile Mom keeps feeding me and tucking blankets around me on the couch. She makes the best hot cocoa."

"Ty?"

"Tyler Wilkins. He's the one who bought Pops's place, remember?"

The high school boyfriend. Standoffish guy.

"He's an EMT too." She yawned.

"Jill, how are you really? Please talk to me."

"You want me to talk?"

Jack winced. Yesterday he would have said no. "Yes. Tell me what happened with Agnes."

She sniffed. "Oh, Jack, I've never met such a warm, wise woman. I want to be like her when I grow up."

He smiled. Jill was always meeting women she wanted to emulate, as if she herself weren't a model of warmth and wisdom. "What made Agnes so special?"

And then she talked for a long time.

"I'm so sorry, Jill."

"Thank you for listening. Mom and Pops are getting tired of hearing it."

"I'm sure they're not. You're in good hands. Do you have any idea when you'll be home?"

"Uh, no. I haven't thought about that at all."

"Of course not. Okay. Well, you need some recovery time. Connor won't be here for a while, so don't worry about it. Do you need me out there?"

She didn't reply.

And he knew he had flubbed. Somehow, something he had said offended her.

He waited for her instruction.

A tide of resentment grew and then he berated himself. Circumstances were not typical. She was under incredible stress, on meds, thousands of miles from home. Perhaps he wasn't in the doghouse.

At last she said, "No. No thanks. I don't *need* you. Thanks for calling. I should go. Mom's favorite cop show is starting and she wants me to watch it with her."

"Sure. Talk to you later."

"Bye. Love you." The line went dead.

"Love you," he said to his kitchen.

What was going on? The last thing on earth he would have imagined Jill doing was extending her time in Sweetwater and watching television with Daisy.

But she had bumped her head.

He bumped his head and wanted a divorce.

She said she did not need him. Did she mean she did not need him to go out there?

Or that she did not need him . . . . at all?

CHAPTER 38

———— ✣ ————

"Jillian." Daisy spoke harshly from the recliner. "Why didn't you tell your husband to come out here and get you?"

"Your show's on. Unmute the volume." Jill rearranged the pillow under her head on the couch.

"You are still the most stubborn girl I have ever met." Daisy turned on the volume, increasing it as she continued to talk over the program, explaining the story line to Jill.

During the first commercial break, Daisy scooted to the kitchen and nuked popcorn for them. At the next pause she fetched Jill's pain medication. Another time she retucked the comforter around her, murmuring about what a special person Agnes was.

Deep inside, Jill mourned the loss of her new friend. She would carry the woman in her heart forever. She had a gazillion new lessons gleaned that she could share. The most significant one was how Agnes brought about a healing between Jill and Daisy.

Agnes would want her to soak in this time.

And so Jill soaked it in. She was lulled into a most wondrous mommy moment. She had known daddy times, but this side of her mother soothed like warm oil, softening old protective calluses.

When the show ended, Daisy sat on the edge of the couch. Jill looked at a wizened face that would no doubt be hers one day and she smiled.

"Jillian, I have to ask you something and I am dead serious. Are you taking up with Ty?"

She grinned. "No way, José. He is just an old friend."

"You thought about it though, didn't you?"

"It crossed my mind and kept on going."

"You're a good girl."

"I'm your daughter."

"Why didn't you tell Jack that you *want* him to come out?"

"Because I've been telling him what to do for twenty-five years."

Daisy harrumphed and gave a quick nod. "Time he figured things out for himself then."

"My thoughts exactly."

"Could take some time."

That was the scary part. Jill prayed it would not be a lifetime.

PART
two

CHAPTER 39

——— ❧ ———

Jill checked her watch for the umpteenth time. Jack was late. She had been standing at the pickup curb outside the airport for twenty-eight minutes in the cold night air, her luggage neatly stacked beside her.

She should have told him she would take the train. No. She should have stayed in San Diego and gone to Agnes's funeral and delayed this reunion.

"Oh, God." The abbreviated prayer braced her for yet another wave of uncertainty and doubt. Since leaving the desert, the reality of facing Jack had loomed, a growing black cloud in her mind.

She believed she had changed. But would Jack see it or even care? Today marked the fifth week of separation. Would he talk now about them as he had promised he would?

The cloud overshadowed the goodness everyone had packed into her. Her parents had driven her to Viv's, a two-hour flow of encouragement and love from their lips. Viv had continued where they left off. Even Marty had been thoughtful.

Jill pressed at the base of her throat. The tension of being unable to pray more than two words ached like a vise gripping her vocal cords. "Oh, God."

Agnes would be proud of her brevity, for not informing God about what exactly needed to happen, for not preplanning a conversation with the estranged husband.

Estranged. It was such an ugly word. How did people acquainted intimately on so many levels for twenty-five years get to being estranged?

When he'd asked if she needed him to come out, it had felt like a slap. She could have died. Viv could have died. Agnes did die. And he had to ask if she needed him to be with her in the aftermath of such a nightmare?

Two days later she was back at Viv and Marty's house, sitting in their kitchen, on the phone with Jack. He repeated his question. Stunned and hurt, she again said no thanks.

After Jill hung up the phone, Viv glared, her eyes almost hidden in dark circles. She removed her arm from its sling and set it on the table. The cast made a decided thump. "I want you to write something here." She pointed to her forearm. "Write: 'Jack does not fight for me because I won't let him. I am stubborn and foolish and always have to be in control, and I get off on being hurt and self-righteous. Love, Jill.'"

Marty had seconded the motion, adding his own steely look. "He might try harder if you gave him half a chance."

Now Jill doubled over the suitcase handle. "Oh, God."

She *had* needed desperately for Jack to come and be her knight in shining armor. Why had she denied herself?

Because a true knight in shining armor would make the choice himself without asking. She wanted it to be his choice, his determination, his spontaneous reaction.

Squealing brakes jerked her attention to the street. A black car had stopped in front of her. Its door opened and Jack emerged.

"Jill!" He hurried around the car she did not recognize.

He had a new car. It wasn't red.

Of course he had a new car. He'd totaled his own the previous month.

"Jill!" He wrapped his arms around her and held her tightly. "The traffic was—Are you all right?"

She lifted her chin, began to nod, and then burst into tears.

❧

The initial hugs and expressions of relief over, her tears abated, Jill and Jack rode home. After all that had occurred in the past five weeks, it comforted her to feel an old sense of camaraderie with him.

Maybe the bus accident was the cause. Although Jack had failed her ridiculous litmus test for knight status, he had been exhibiting his gracious qualities. He sent flowers, phoned often, was overly concerned about her well-being, and talked to the doctor who had seen her.

The underlying stressful tone had disappeared from his speech, as if he no longer thought about divorce. Maybe the accident had knocked him right on through the midlife crisis.

The thought warmed her. Recalling his tenderness while she cried and his welcome-home kiss after filled her with hope.

She twisted around in her seat to face him as he drove, her cheek against soft leather. "The car is nice."

"It's a set of wheels." He reached over and touched her hand in the dark. "Jill, I'm so glad you're home, safe and sound. I can't tell you how scared I was when Marty called."

"He should have waited until he knew more."

"No, I needed to know as soon as he did. And he kept me updated." Jack squeezed her hand. "It was the longest day of my life. I can't imagine how awful it was for you."

"Off-the-charts awful. But there were amazing things too. I cannot believe that not one of those seniors needed so much as a Band-Aid. But Viv . . ." Jill's voiced trailed off.

"Is going to be fine. A broken wrist. Bruises. She will be good as new in no time. Head injuries are a different story. We still need to be on the lookout for repercussions."

Repercussions. Ty had used the same word as he sat next to her on the bus, examining her forehead.

He had said, "The skin isn't broken but there's a knot, I'd say jumbo egg size. Cage-free, no hormones added."

She talked about Jack, looked straight into Ty's willow green eyes and talked about her husband. "Jack was in a car accident and cracked his head open a few weeks ago. He needed stitches." *Jack fell down and broke his crown.*

And now Jill had finally tumbled down after him. The very thing she had vowed not to let happen.

"Any repercussions?" Ty asked.

He wants a divorce. "He, uh, he hasn't been himself since."

"Hopefully that won't happen with you. I kind of like you the way you are." Ty held her hand, fingers on her pulse. Checking it or trying to calm her? "Except for the shivering, but that will go away soon."

Jill eyed Jack now by the light of the dashboard. She remembered how throughout the years his gentle touch quelled her shivering. He knew feet secrets and massaged her soles to quell distress.

"I need one of your foot treatments."

He threw her a small smile.

They arrived at the house and she knew immediately that no way on earth was that going to happen.

She knew it because the house was dark. It was dark because Jack had not been there to turn on welcoming lights. He had not been there because he did not live there.

A pallor of awkwardness fell over Jill. Their marriage was floundering. That fact pounced front and center, in-her-face ugly.

As she walked inside, that fact resounded like crashing symbols. The pendulum on the wall clock was not ticking.

She flipped on lights. Jack set down her bags and went into the hall bathroom.

She headed upstairs to their bedroom, to their closet, into their bathroom. All traces of Jack were gone. His cologne, his hairbrush, his toothbrush, his clothes . . .

"Oh, God!" she cried out. Her chest tightened.

She returned to the kitchen. The rack above the stovetop was empty. His favorite pots and pans no longer hung there.

"Jack!"

"Back here," he replied.

She found him in the small family room off the kitchen. The cozy nook held only two recliners, a television, and a bookcase. They had built it as their getaway when it became apparent that the house had become the main gathering hub for Connor and his twelve-year-old friends.

Jack stood before the gas fireplace. His face was tired, his clothes rumpled, his light brown hair in need of a cut. The light caught his left hand on the mantel.

His gold wedding band was gone.

The flames behind glass threw off enough heat to warm the small space, but it did not touch the sudden chill in her heart.

"Have a seat," he said. "Are you hungry?"

She looked at her chair, a fresh cup of tea on the end table. She looked at his chair, at his end table that should have been piled with books.

"Jack, I can't do this."

"Can't do what?"

"Live here without you."

"Sit. Let's talk."

She shook her head. Her chest ached. She had no words to speak. They were dying inside of her, beaten to death by one blow after another proclaiming unabashedly that Jack had moved out of their home, out of their marriage.

"Jill, I know this is beyond difficult, but we need to talk and get through Connor's—"

"How dare you! How dare you do this! Get out. Get out right this minute, Jack."

He held his arms out at his sides. "I'm sorry."

"Now!" She turned on her heel and hurried back through the empty kitchen, up to the empty bedroom.

Deeply ingrained, oft-repeated phrases sprang to mind. *Don't let the sun go down on your anger. Reclaim your marriage. Take ownership of your relationship.*

She did not have the foggiest notion of how to heal a marriage.

The looming black cloud engulfed her. She crawled into bed, clothes on, under the covers, and wondered if she would ever crawl back out.

CHAPTER 40

———— ❧ ————

SEATED ON HIS stool at the end of the examining table, Jack kneaded Mrs. Bengsten's right foot and smiled to himself. A patient's foot before him, life resumed its balance. He could set aside Jill's deserved anger. He could anticipate Connor's return with delight. He could even laugh at his concerns about Sophie.

That morning he had noticed her hair hanging loose to her shoulders, free from the bun. He skirted around someone at her desk, but not fast enough.

"Dr. G! Do you remember David?"

He paused and greeted a vaguely familiar pharmaceutical salesman.

Sophie had leaned across the counter, her hand on the guy's forearm, his hand on top of hers, and whispered, "David, this is the one who's like a dad to me."

Later Baxter confirmed Jack's suspicions: Sophie and the salesman were an item, had been for some time. Baxter had slapped his shoulder. "So sue me for thinking it was you."

Jack turned his attention back to the thick ankles and swollen feet protruding from black knit slacks. "Massage like this, a few minutes every day. It will help the circulation."

"But Olie hates to touch my feet, Dr. G. They're not the prettiest things. Maybe if I got him some of those latex gloves, he wouldn't mind so much."

"Well." Jack looked at the gray-haired woman propped upright, her face a road map of a difficult life. Was that Olie's fault? Would lines crease Jill's face someday because of him? "Some people are like that about feet."

"Not you, though, Dr. G."

"Feet have always intrigued me." He smiled. "The things they do for us, and we usually take them for granted."

"I should tell him we can't take mine for granted, right? Not with the diabetes."

"Right."

"I'll pay the grandkids. They'll do anything for a few bucks, even touch Grandma's old feet." She laughed.

Jack smiled and hoped the jerk Olie had a good pension. "We'll get these calluses trimmed and—"

A loud thump on the door interrupted him. A conversation ensued just the other side.

He excused himself and opened the door. Baxter and Sophie were nose to nose and fussing in loud whispers.

"What's going on?"

"Jack!" Baxter grabbed his elbow. "One minute."

Sophie frowned. "This is so unprofessional. You both have—"

"Yeah, yeah." Baxter pulled Jack quickly down the hall, into his private office, and shut the door.

"What—?"

"Shh. Listen." Baxter reached across his desk to a radio.

Jill's voice filled the room.

"So except for this knot on my noggin, I am fine. Absolutely, positively fine."

She didn't sound fine. The *angelic* was missing from her voice, replaced by worn-out, stressed-out, overworked, hesitant, and grating tones.

A familiar male voice said something. It belonged to either Sam or Don, the morning show guys, brothers in their forties. Likable on air and in person.

"Yes," she said. "I'm scheduled to do live interviews next week. We have a great lineup of local marital counselors who'll talk about their special areas of expertise."

"Jill, from what I hear, you probably hope one of them knows how to plan weddings."

"Don, bro—" Sam's tone reprimanded—"sometimes you talk too much."

"What?"

"Well, take a look at her."

Jill must be at the studio, not on the phone with them.

Sam went on. "Jillian Galloway is speechless. That wedding info was on the q.t. Way to go, Donno."

"Oops!" Don said. "Seriously, I didn't know that, Jill. I apologize. Too personal."

She chuckled, a strained noise. "I'm all about personal. You guys are stealing my thunder, that's all."

"At least we didn't say *who* is getting married," Sam said. "It's not you, is it? And there she goes. See you!" he called out as if Jill were walking away. "That was Jillian Galloway, folks, just back from her home state of California and author of *She Said, He Heard*, available at bookstores everywhere."

"She'll be here at the mike next week," Don added. "Monday, eleven o'clock in the a.m. Meanwhile she is recovering from a tour bus accident, so we thank you for your prayers. Hey, Sam, let's give a shout-out to those volunteer medics in Sweetwater Springs, California."

Baxter reached across his desk and turned off the radio. "Fun guys."

Jack locked eyes with his friend. "Mind telling me why you insisted I listen to that?"

"Thought you'd want to."

"Why would I want to?"

"She doesn't sound so good."

"She was exhausted last night. Good grief. She was in a crash where a woman died. She should have stayed home today."

"What are you going to do?"

Jack sighed. "Call a truce. Get Connor married. After that, she and I will talk. We'll figure something out."

"Bzz! Wrong answer. You need a game plan. You need to speak up."

"And say what?"

"Say what you want. You can't keep Jill in this no-man's-land any longer. I don't care how many weddings you have to go to. What exactly do you want, Jack?"

"To trim Mrs. Bengsten's calluses." He turned and walked out the door.

CHAPTER 41

———— ❧ ————

Jɪʟʟ ᴘᴏᴋᴇᴅ ᴀ fork at her lunch salad and avoided the concerned expressions aimed at her from across the table. The wincing women in the restaurant booth were Gretchen and the station manager, Nan Zimmer.

Jill had just described last night's screech owl routine aimed at Jack.

"My opinion?" Nan spoke first.

Jill met the tawny eyes. Nan was about ten years older, the most *together* woman imaginable with smooth mocha-colored skin and natural curls clipped very short. Her stylish clothes flowed on a well-toned body. Beneath the lovely outward appearance beat a lovelier heart.

"Jill," Nan went on, "you've got too much on your plate. It happens to all of us. Even you. Superwoman is the creation of some misogynist who got a sick kick out of dumping a load of guilt on us. There is nothing sinful about not being able to fix your marriage, arrange a wedding, entertain the in-laws-to-be, promote a book, conduct live interviews, correspond with listeners, and recover from trauma and bruises all within a week's time."

"The wedding is two weeks away."

"Jillian." Her tone reprimanded. "I just told you there is no guilt or shame in this situation. Something has got to go."

"Work."

Nan nodded.

"But work is my sanity."

Gretchen barked a laugh. "Which is at an all-time record low. I'd say it's down to the lockup level. But there's no cause for alarm. Nan and I promise to find the best facility for you."

Jill blinked back tears. Gretchen had no idea how close to the truth she spoke. Or that Jill already had her facility chosen. It was back in Sweetwater with her mom and dad and ring of mountains and hairdressing twins. But . . . "I can't quit."

Nan said, "Then I'll fire you. *Temporarily*, Jill. You'll get through everything else on your list and come back better than ever, wiser than ever."

Gretchen nodded. "Full of lemonade stories. Like how God gave you a whole bushel of lemons when you had to go live with your parents, as an adult, in Backwater Springs."

"Sweetwater Springs."

"Water whatever. It's the desert for crying out loud. Why do they call it water anything? Anyway, it's like Moses, banished from Egypt, working for his father-in-law for forty years in the middle of nowhere. Then he sees a burning bush and hears God's voice. And there you have it!"

"Have what?"

"Lemonade!"

Nan burst into laughter. "You skipped the burning bush part of the analogy. Where does Jill get that?"

Gretchen drew back and gazed down her ski-slope nose at Nan. "Do I look like God to you? How should I know?"

Grinning, Nan turned to Jill. "She's right. All we know is that God is faithful. He will give you your own burning bush. He'll reward you with a gift from the desert, a story to tell others to encourage them in their own journeys."

Gretchen leaned forward. "All journeys are strewn with lemons, you know."

"You stole that line from me."

"So sue me, sweetums."

Jill tried to rest in their banter, in their loving care for her well-being.

They weren't even aware of the debilitating fear that had struck her that morning and yet they provided a way out. By allowing her to take a leave of absence—no guilt, no strings attached—she could breathe more easily.

Earlier she had been doing fine. Considering that she had kicked her husband out at the exact moment he seemed ready to sit down and talk about *them*, the fact that she got out of bed feeling clearheaded was in itself a miracle.

Then there was the mishap in the garage. Any other day the crumpled garbage can under the right rear tire would have caused her to fuss and fume. With her heightened awareness of the role of trash cans, however, she calmly asked herself what it meant. She decided it meant that she did not belong behind the wheel of a car. She took the train downtown.

She arrived at the studio in time to catch up on work-related items before lunch with Nan and Gretchen. While she chatted with the receptionist, one of the announcers greeted her with a bear hug.

That was when clearheaded and calm went out the window. Her grip on reality began to wobble and the debilitating fear circled, looking for a way inside.

Sam and his brother Don were the luvvies of the staff, their morning show a longtime listener favorite. Sam had ducked out and a moment later she heard the two of them on the lobby speakers, discussing her.

"Guess who I just saw in the lobby. Hey! Let's get her in here."

Before she could protest, they had her seated before a microphone, headset on. Her eyes went to the control panel and she panicked at the sight of it. It was all she could do to sit still and not whimper.

At that moment, deep in her heart, she knew there was no way on earth she was ready to return to her job on the radio. How could she ever be ready to sit in that chair again, flip switches, watch the clock, and talk about how to succeed at marriage?

She said now to her friends, "All right. I need a break. I'll take it."

❧

Bolstered by Nan and Gretchen's confidence that a recipe for lemonade was in the works, Jill phoned the man she'd been avoiding.

"Jill, how are you?" Lew Mowers had always been the quintessential pastor—kind, caring, friendly, never condescending or harsh, wise beyond his fifty years. Why she had hesitated before talking to him pointed, as it had with her dad, to her stupid pride.

"I'm . . . I'm . . . I don't really know how I am."

In short order he wove the conversation around recent events and her state of mind. Gretchen had filled him in on the highlights, so he was aware of her and Jack's separation and the accident. He did not know about Connor.

Jill said, "I'm sure I can talk him into having you perform the ceremony."

"Jill, hold it right there. Connor is a wonderful young man. I've known him his entire life, but that doesn't mean I'm the one he wants for his wedding. My feelings are not hurt in the least. He and Emma need to make their own choices and you, Mama, need to let them."

Things went downhill from there. She suspected it was the only way up. God's convoluted take on how to mold His people into the best possible versions of themselves seemed, at times, perverse. Lew's words sliced through her. They filleted her soul.

The conversation eventually got around to Jack. She said, with too much heat in her voice, "He won't agree to see you for counseling."

"Again, Jill, not a problem. Just because you hear God speak through me does not mean everyone does. Trust that God will provide others to minister to Jack. If you want to talk with me and Lindsay," he mentioned his wife, "we are available. You know that. And you know we're praying for you and Jack and Connor and Emma."

"Mm-hmm."

"Now, what do you want to do about your ladies' class?"

An image came to mind of another ladies' class. She stood before it, spouting off about the demise of her marriage.

Lew said, "Would you like an extended sabbatical?"

She shook her head and nodded and shook it again.

In the wake of her silence, he answered his own question. "Yes, I think that's a good idea. We will see you when we see you."

CHAPTER 42

JILL SPOTTED CONNOR standing curbside at the airport in almost the same spot she had waited the night before. She parked nearby and sprang out of the car.

"Mom!" He hurried to meet her and wrapped his arms around her. "Are you all right?"

She looked up at him. "I told you I was. You didn't need to come home yet."

He studied her face exactly like his dad the doctor would. "You're really okay?"

"I am fine." She looked behind him, away from those blue eyes that knew her too well. "Where's Emma?"

"She and her parents stayed in Denver. They have more sightseeing to do."

"Oh, Connor." Jill spoke with remorse. "Why did you cut your time short with them?"

"I figured it was time to stop putting myself first. It's obvious you and Dad need some moral support ASAP. Mom, about that other phone call, I am sorry for being—"

"Truthful? For being real?" She shook her head. "I'm grateful for your honesty."

"My delivery needs some work."

"And so does my receptivity."

"I know you disapprove of things I've done, but it's my life." Evidently he needed to get some things off his chest right then and there, curbside at O'Hare.

"Yes, it is your life, Connor. And you do not have to earn my love or my approval. All right?"

A slow grin spread across his face. "All right."

She smiled and handed him the car keys.

He made bug eyes and opened his mouth wide. "No way."

Jill shrugged and walked toward the car, consciously choosing to let him gather his luggage by himself without her instruction or muscle. Like allowing him to drive, it was an act of letting go of the old, controlling Jill. Baby steps, for sure. But movement all the same.

His silly reaction to the keys indicated he noticed her effort. Of course, how could he not? Except for the season when he was required to practice in order to get his license, she had been driving the kid around for twenty-three years.

Kid? Connor was a young man, about to be married, whose gaze discomfited her because it saw right through her and shed light on every mothering flaw.

But earlier that day he had phoned her rather than his dad. He had asked her to pick him up at the airport after a seven-month absence. Maybe that added up to something akin to forgiveness.

Maybe it meant it wasn't too late to be a better mother.

❧

"Mom, did you grow up eating pie for breakfast?" Connor set the rolling pin on the countertop and surveyed his work, a paper-thin circle of dough.

Jill laughed. "No." She set down the vegetable peeler and flexed her fingers. "How many apples do we want?"

"Grandma's recipe calls for five more. You can't stop yet." He grinned and picked up the peeler. "I'll work on them. Why don't you slice?"

They stood across from each other at the counter where the bottom of its L shape cut across the kitchen, dividing workspace from eating area. They were trying to re-create his favorite "Daisy Breakfast."

The hour was late. They hadn't arrived home from the airport until after ten o'clock. Despite their clearing of the air earlier, they tiptoed around the obvious: Jack's absence. How should Connor reunite with him, the father who no longer lived at home? Should they invite him over? Did Jack even have to wait for an invitation? Should Connor leave his mother and go to Jack's place? The questions remained unspoken.

This was new territory. Jill wondered if she would research it someday, draw from personal experience, and air a program about it. The thought made her cringe.

Jill bit her tongue and offered no solution.

Eventually Jack and Connor resolved the issue without her input. Connor got off the phone and said something about his dad's early surgery in the morning, the lateness of the hour, when they could touch base tomorrow.

Jill bit her tongue some more. She hated these new complexities. What was Jack thinking not to see Connor after all these months?

"Voilà!" Connor held up an unbroken strand of apple peel. "Four more to go."

"Con, you know Grandma will have a different recipe for this tomorrow. She makes them up as she goes along."

"Yeah, she told me, but I made her write down the basics. What is it with her and pies anyway?"

"Aunt Viv and I think it's her way of showing she cares. She puts a lot of energy into her baking and then offers it to everyone." Jill sat on a stool, less energetic than she wanted to admit, and began slicing apples.

"Unfortunately if you don't eat her pie, she gets offended and thinks you don't love her."

"She seemed fine when Emma only ate a little."

"That's because Emma is your fiancée and young and beautiful. Grandma would understand that she wants to keep her figure for you and so she wouldn't take it personally."

"You really think that?"

"I've known your grandmother for a long time and—"

"No, I mean about Emma. You think she's beautiful?"

"Of course. She looks like a model. Her skin is flawless. Her French accent is lovely-sounding as well as a lovely expression of her willingness to enter your world of English, which means she adores you. She seemed confident and kind." Jill peeked at him through her eyelashes, wondering how open she could be with him. "All that said, I don't like her."

Connor grinned. "Now you're bluffing."

"Mostly." She sighed. "First your father leaves me and before I can get used to that situation, you leave me. Yes, it's irrational. I mean, you're supposed to leave and cleave but my first reaction is *sss*!" She made a catlike hiss and clawed the air. "I'm being replaced by another woman."

"Yes! There is a God." His eyes twinkled.

She laughed. "You probably wanted me replaced long ago."

"Only now and then." His grin softened. "I'm glad you think she's beautiful."

She studied him for a moment. His long fingers worked gracefully with the fruit. He had Jack's hands, an artist's hands. "Connor, beauty attracts beauty. You would not want to marry someone with a shriveled-up heart."

"Thanks." He scooped the parings into the trash bin. "Mom, uh, about Dad. Is he, you know, uh . . . ?"

"Seeing someone?" Jill slid the bowl of sliced apples toward him. "I don't think so."

"I hope not."

She shrugged. If another woman had replaced her in that relationship,

Jill would just want to sit down and die. "I am happy you found Emma. I promise to be nice to her the next time we meet."

"You are such a wise woman."

"Ha-ha. Now show me how you pick up that dough and put it in the pie pan."

He proceeded to do so without a misstep. "So what are you going to do in place of baking pies when you get old and gray and need to feel the love?" He poured sugar on the apple slices, sprinkled cinnamon and nutmeg, not measuring a thing. Then he began to mix it all with his hands.

She said, "I doubt I'll bake. I do like to talk. I could start a new show. A call-in format." Jill lowered her voice to its soft radio tone. "Call 1-800-L-U-V-F-E-S-T. Tell me how wonderful I am and I'll tell you how wonderful you are."

Connor laughed so hard he clutched the edge of the counter and tears ran down his cheeks.

She hadn't seen him do that in such a long time.

It reminded her that they had indeed laughed together during his growing-up years. There had been joyful moments of connectedness between mother and child. Maybe there weren't enough of them to cast a rosy glow on the fact that she had smothered him with instruction, and yet they were, without a doubt, real.

Even as she had returned to her mother, Connor had returned to her. Like her, he needed a good dose of God's compassionate, motherly side. *Come to Me and I will give you rest.*

She prayed that, like her, he would receive it from a not-so-ideal mommy in human form.

CHAPTER 43

—— ❧ ——

"Your mother *what*?" Jack nearly yelled into the phone. "She *quit*?"

"Chill out, Dad." Connor chuckled. "It's not a money issue, is it?"

"No, it's not a money issue." Jill's income was slotted for special vacations and rainy days, neither of which had yet occurred. Two frugal workaholics did not cruise, nor did they have time to put up with rain. "It's just—what about her class?"

"That too. She's not going back to teaching either."

"How can she give all this up?"

"It's all temporary. She really does sound fine with taking a break. You know she could use one."

"But these things are her *life*."

"Like she said to me, when you factor in a marriage on the rocks, there's not a whole lot she has to offer on the subject."

"She said that?" A load of guilt hovered over his head yet again, ready to dump on him. It was his fault that she was doing this.

"Dad, I'm not blaming you."

"I did get the ball rolling." He tried to hit a neutral tone. "I'm sorry, Con. You're in the middle of a major mess here."

"Dad." There was a gentle reprimand in his tone. "You guys have to let me in. I'm a big boy now."

Jack looked at the photo on his desk, a favorite that he never managed to replace with one more recent. Connor was five, his blond hair almost white. His chubby hand gripped a fat crayon, his face intent on the sketchbook in his lap. Jack even recalled what the little boy had said after he'd taken the shot. *"Mommy says I can be an artist."*

Mommy says . . .

Jill says patients will love me. Jill says I exude trustworthiness. Jill says . . .
Jill said a lot.

"So what do you think, Dad?" Connor asked. "Dinner here tonight? Talk wedding?"

"Your mom's okay with that?"

"It was her idea. We have apple pie."

Jack chuckled. "Anything else?"

"Takeout?"

"I'll bring dinner."

❧

Jack carried a cardboard box through the front door and felt ridiculous. They should have gone out to a restaurant.

Connor shut the door behind him, sniffing. "I don't smell dinner."

"We have to bake it." He set the box on the floor and hugged his son for a silent moment. Seven months was a long, long time. He chucked Connor's shoulders, let go, and looked up to make eye contact. "You've grown."

"My waist has. It's the pasta." He grinned and bent to pick up the box.

Jack glanced around the living room. All the lamps were lit. The giant clock's pendulum banged out its ticktock. Classic rock music rumbled in from the kitchen stereo.

The hen was back in her roost.

His feelings—which usually did not register so quickly—went from embarrassment about bringing a casserole into his own home to resentment for being put in such a predicament to tension, as if every nerve in his body were being stretched to the point of snapping.

It was that rubber band sensation. He hadn't experienced it in . . . weeks.

This is not good.

Jack blew out a breath. He followed Connor into the kitchen, chitchatting, catching up. As they unpacked food containers from the carton, Jill walked in.

"Hi."

"Hi."

Connor let out a low whistle. "Awkward moment between the 'rents."

Jill cocked her head to one side.

Jack shrugged.

He wondered if Jill's masklike face mirrored his own. They were two strangers standing in a kitchen packed full of shared memories, with the child they had reared together, with no idea how to relate to one another. The thought hit him again as it had weeks before, just after he'd made his awful pronouncement: what had he done?

Connor lifted the casserole lid and peered at Jack's tuna and noodle concoction. "Mm. Nice, Dad."

Jill peered over his shoulder. "Your favorite." She flashed a smile at Jack.

Okay. With their son between them, they could be normal.

"Uh." Connor wore a sheepish expression. "Well. Hm. Awkward moment between the kid and his amazingly thoughtful dad, the gourmet cook who could have whipped up *boeuf bourguignon* in between seeing patients."

Jack said, "You always loved this dish."

"Actually I always said that just because I preferred it over the boxed gunk Mom made."

Jill snickered. Connor grinned. Jack grimaced.

Connor said, "It's not that I totally dislike it, Dad. Thank you for a homemade meal. I really do appreciate it."

"Do you want pizza?"

"I'll run down to Giorgio's. Pickup is faster than delivery." He bounded off.

Jill said, "I had no idea that wasn't his favorite dinner. Shall we talk while he's gone? We probably need to set some parameters for wedding planning."

Jack sighed.

"What?" she said.

The sigh must have been loud. "Nothing."

"Please don't say 'nothing.' That gets us nowhere. What did the groan mean?"

He nearly groaned again.

"Jack."

He held up a finger and closed his eyes. He wanted Connor gone before they went any further. When he heard the front door shut, he looked at her.

And almost gave up being forthright.

Jill was the best friend he had ever had. She was still pretty, her voice still sensual. He liked her casual hairstyle. What did she call it? Sassy. It suited her. Her blue eyes, focused on his face, still produced a flood of longing in him.

Then she opened her mouth.

"Jack." The voice went from sensual into clipped command mode.

"It meant," he said, "that I am tired of you micromanaging."

"Micromanaging? All I said was—"

"What you always say. 'Let's do it this way, Jack. Let's get a system going here so I can document it. Then I can use it later. You don't mind, do you, Jack? I'll just jot a few notes while we talk. Or turn on my handy-dandy palm-size voice-activated recorder.'"

She blinked.

"Correct me if I'm wrong," he said, "but hasn't that been our life for the past ten years or so? Every single thing we do is like a scientific experiment. We eat, talk, entertain, argue, watch a movie, and make love in a laboratory. You set the parameters and take notes. I'm the rat finding his way through the maze. Or not."

"You never said you minded."

"And Connor never said he minded tuna and noodles." He paused. "He didn't know it was a big deal until he comes home after months away, finds a casserole made in his honor, and feels cheated."

"You cannot compare tuna to marriage."

He felt his jaw drop. "You compared seven recipes to marriage and had it published! Your radio program is called *Recipes for Marriage*!"

She frowned. "That's different."

Jack went on. "I didn't know living in a lab was a big deal until I read about my sex life in a nationwide chain bookstore!"

"That's what this is all about? I mention candlelight and music— highly common romantic ambience enhancers, by the way—in the same sentence with your name, which I might add you signed off on, and you want a divorce?"

"No." He searched for words and calmed his voice. "No. It was the car accident. I was listening to the station. Heard your ad for the book. I opened the window because I was so upset I was suffocating. I started driving around, going too fast on the ice. And then I slid through the intersection and cracked my head."

"You're upset about the ad?"

"No. I'm upset because when I heard your voice, I realized that this is not what I signed up for."

"Me on the radio?"

"You're not doing it right."

"Not doing what right?"

"You're supposed to be listening, not interrupting and reacting while I'm trying to explain something."

"Yeah, well, this is us, not some fabricated scenario to toss out as an example on how to communicate."

"Exactly." He folded his arms and wished he could undo the smug set of his mouth, but he couldn't help it. She had just talked herself into a corner by agreeing with him.

Jill glared at him.

Neither one of them spoke.

At last she said, "What didn't you sign up for?"

"A wife who has all the answers. Who rates every situation and person as right or wrong, perfect or imperfect. Even me. I can't keep up with you anymore. I don't want to."

"We need to see a counselor."

"So he can tell me what I've been hearing all along? We've got the communication skills down pat, Jill. We've practiced them ad nauseam. I could run them in my sleep."

"But you never told me this stuff!"

"I didn't know this stuff until now. Something snapped after my accident. I needed time to figure out what was going on. The way I see it, we've totally missed the real game of marriage, of life together."

"Then we figure out how to find it now!" She sounded too hyper.

He bit back a smart remark about how that effort would be nice fodder for new material. "Jill, you've grown into an important communicator. Even if you only talk to your Sunday school ladies, you need to be out there just the way you are."

"I'm a wife first!"

"Who has all the answers and a husband who doesn't want to hear them any longer. You have my permission to blame this all on me. Your teaching isn't wrong."

"Then why are we at this point?"

Jack forced himself to breathe deeply. He looked around the kitchen, at the doorways leading to other rooms, to the garage. It was a good home, overflowing with memories, twentysome years of family and friends, joys and difficulties and simple everydayness.

Where and when had their paths diverged?

He said, "We're here because in all our talking, we lost each other.

We lost our friendship. And that, I think, is what the goal should have been from the beginning."

Jill spun on her heel and marched from the room.

Jack leaned against the counter. He had just spoken his mind without first running his thoughts by that little voice that always told him what Jill wanted to hear.

It felt . . . oddly freeing.

CHAPTER 44

—— ❦ ——

"Viv." Jill lay down on her bed, phone at her ear. "Viv!"

Her sister's response remained a muffled weeping.

Jill blinked back her own tears. "Hey, the empathy is appreciated but it's not what I need right now!"

Viv sniffed loudly. "You need to talk to a counselor instead of me. I thought you liked your pastor. Call him."

Jill had just relayed the entire evening to her sister. Jack's awful declaration that they'd lost their friendship. Poor Connor's anxious looks at them during dinner. Jack's upbeat attitude and ability to eat pizza while Jill nursed a throbbing headache.

Jill said, "I can't call him, Viv. He'll tell me Jack's right. I don't want to hear that. And the fact is, Jack's right."

"Yes, hon, but he's also wrong. You're right and wrong as well. Why don't you both just fess up? You've shown major disrespect and he has been a wimp. I mean, you can be a self-righteous prig and you are hard to love, but that's Jack's job and he quit on it. He should've told you when you went too far, when he felt like he was a lab rat."

"He said he didn't know until his accident, almost six weeks ago."

"That's just when he admitted it. He could ignore it because he checked out ages ago when he should have been paying attention."

"I pushed him away."

"Don't take all the blame. Marty pushed me away when he kept prioritizing work and sports ahead of me, when he stopped really seeing me. But I'm the one who decided to have an affair."

Jill winced. Jack had pushed her away and she had looked at Ty Wilkins differently.

Viv said, "Stop the blame game. Both of you need to admit you're wrong, forgive each other, and get back to it."

"He doesn't want to get back to it."

"Then get on your knees, girl. Only God can change Jack's mind." Viv chuckled. "I read that in a book. It had something to do with Rockin' Roast."

Jill burst into fresh tears. How could she have been so flippantly ignorant?

❧

The following morning, Jill and Connor chatted while he drove them through a neighborhood not far from their own. A pewter-colored March sky seemed to touch the rooftops, threatening to unleash another round of snow.

"Good grief, this weather!" she said. "I miss the desert. And I've never felt that in all the twenty-five years I've lived in the Midwest."

"You do have a few things on your mind, Mom." He glanced at the GPS. "Promise not to freak out."

"Why is it I think you're going to add one more thing to my mind?"

He smiled and turned into a parking lot. "'Cause I know you."

Jill looked out the window at slushy concrete, bare trees, a lovely old stone wall, and a sign. She blinked but the words did not change. *Grace Community Church.* "It's . . . it's . . ."

"The *rival*," Connor whispered in a furtive tone and turned off the engine.

She cleared her throat and met his gaze. "There's no such thing as rival churches."

"Are you sure?" He kept his voice hushed and his brow furrowed. "Their youth department has always been larger than ours. Kids from all over the city go here."

Jill squirmed. At one time, there had been hard feelings at her church about teens switching over to GCC. Connor visited with his friends as often as she allowed it, which wasn't often.

Connor smiled and spoke normally. "I know you're not too keen on their teaching."

"Did I say that?"

He nodded. "You referred to it as pablum."

She wanted to crawl under the seat. "Oh. Well. That was a long time ago." It could have been last week. Scales were dropping like crazy from her eyes. It seemed that at every thought she had, God tapped her shoulder. *A little judgmental there, Jill. A little too cut-and-dried. Remember I am mystery. I don't give all the answers. You don't have to either.*

She said, "People worship and serve God in all sorts of churches. I don't know that He cares much where or how. Our expressions of faith are for us, for what suits us best. Personality-wise. Culturally-wise."

"I think so. Emma and I are more in tune with what's going on here. She was raised in the church. She has a relationship with Christ, what you call the abiding kind that I don't have the hang of. She reminds me of you in that way."

"Oh, Con, you don't want her to remind you of me."

"It's the part I most admire." He grinned. "She is a lot quieter about it though."

"Thank God."

He chuckled.

That morning Connor had asked her to go with him to make

arrangements. Still recovering from the previous night's encounter with Jack and dealing with God's shoulder tapping, she hadn't asked what needed to be done. All that mattered was that Connor asked her and that she was available.

Available in every capacity—emotional, mental, and physical.

If she hadn't quit work already for other reasons, she would have today. She might not have always listened well to her son in the past, but right now that was not going to happen.

No matter what happened, she was not going to freak out.

❧

They tried it again, this time in a crowded coffee shop, late afternoon.

Meeting was Jack's idea. Evidently because it had not come from her, it was all right. It wasn't a lab experiment.

While he fetched their drinks, Jill waited at the table, massaging her forehead and considering how to mention his unfairness.

"Headache?" Jack set two lidded paper cups on the small table and slid onto a chair.

"Yes." She took a sip of the sweet coffee drink. Uncharacteristically she had ordered the works: three shots, cream, caramel and chocolate syrups, whipped cream on top. It had been a day of choosing uncharacteristically, but this choice was sheer coping mechanism.

"Is it related to the accident?" His doctor tone annoyed her.

"Just regular tension."

"Did things go all right with Con?"

Jill refocused. There were too many other things to discuss. Jack's tone and attitude were not at the top of the list.

She said, "We had a good day." As she told him about what she and Connor had accomplished in preparation for the wedding, she tried to read Jack's body language.

And kept getting stuck on how good-looking he was. His eyes were red and creased with fatigue, but the hazel color was as attractive as ever.

His striped, long-sleeved dress shirt hugged his shoulders just so. He had nice shoulders. Just-right shoulders.

When was the last time she had really noticed them?

Jack smiled. He seemed to enjoy hearing her tidbits about wedding errands. "What's Reverend Nelson like?"

Jill smiled. "Young and cheeky, but solid. Not the watered-down version of a pastor that I imagined. And I'm not saying that because he has recommended my show to couples."

"Major points."

"But the best part is he insists that Con and Emma meet with him for premarital counseling."

She filled Jack in on other details. Schedules, music, flowers, dinner menu, guest list, dress code. "No tux required."

He pulled on his earlobe, a telltale sign he was puzzling over something.

"What are you trying to figure out?"

"Hm?"

She touched her own ear.

He lowered his hand. "The guest list. It's family only?"

"Except for two of his college friends and their wives, who live in the area. Viv promised to come. Mom and Pops put up a good front but they're not in the best of shape for travel. I doubt they'll make it. Naturally Emma doesn't have anyone here except her parents."

"What about our friends?"

"Connor and Emma really want to keep things small and intimate. Where would we start and end a list? Between church and neighbors and the station—" she shrugged—"too many."

"My office?"

Jill went cold. She managed to swallow and not say anything.

Jack shifted his weight. "Think about it. Con spent three summers and school breaks working there."

Connor really knew only two people well enough to consider inviting. Baxter was a jerk who thought women were toys. Sophie was . . .

Jill's problem, a source of petty jealousy for no other reason than she spent so much time in close proximity with Jack. Childish yes, but that was the way it was. Under the present circumstances, Jill was not in a giving mood to go to bat for Sophie or Baxter.

Jill swallowed again. "You'll have to ask him."

"It seems that if some family members don't come, then local friends might and it'd still be small."

But not the same. Not intimate.

She was getting good at biting her tongue. "Ask him."

Jack nodded. "Did he tell you about the best man?" His eyes suddenly lost their tired look.

"Yeah, he did." She felt mushy.

Jack said, "It makes sense, though, since his best friend is in Japan and can't make it."

"Don't sell yourself short, Jack. He wants you for his best man because you are the best man in his life."

His eyes held hers. "Thank you. We have a special son."

She nodded.

"Well, we did it, Jill. Made it through this conversation intact. I'd like to keep things on an even keel for Connor's sake. I'm sure you're with me on that."

"How do we do that? Fake it?" She felt a bristling as if the elephant in the room had brushed up against her. "Pretend like it's a normal thing to live separately and to meet in a coffee shop in the middle of the day?"

"It's five o'clock. I had a light load today."

She bit her tongue until it hurt this time.

"I get your point, Jill. It's not going to be easy to act normal when nothing is normal right now. We don't fake it exactly. We avoid subjects that may upset us, things we will need to address later."

"Will you talk to Lew with me?"

"No."

"Will you move back home for now and be there while Emma's parents stay with us?"

"No. I can't."

Upset as she was, she noted the storm cloud on his face but pressed on. She and Jack would part ways at any moment. She needed to find out now. "Will you file for divorce before he gets married?"

Before the question was past her lips, Jack was standing and yanking his coat from the back of his chair and talking.

"Jill, this is the stuff we keep off-limits. We will not address our situation until after Connor leaves. We will not speculate about anything. We simply have to table our marriage for a few weeks. Okay? Okay." He rushed off.

She sat very still, hands on her lap, her muscles frozen in place. Her face felt hot. It would be bright pink.

The conversation had not quite left them intact.

CHAPTER 45

—— ❧ ——

THE TRUDEAUS SWEPT into the Galloway household like a blast of March wind laced with hints of warmth and sweet scents of green grass and red tulips.

Or was it Chanel No. 5?

Jill inhaled a classic perfume fragrance while Emma's mother embraced her as if she were a long-lost friend. She went momentarily speechless.

Emma and her parents, Michelle and Philippe, were delightful. Adorable. Charming. They all spoke at once, smiling and hugging, lavishing her with compliments about Connor and the house and her hospitality and her hair. They were not what she had expected at all.

Nothing like the band of anti-American, wine-bibbing snobs she had conjured up.

Euww. Despite Connor's insistence to the contrary, that had been her image of these strangers who had captured her son's heart. Not only had another woman replaced her in her son's life, another family was occupying a lot of space in Connor's world. Jill had been feeling pushed off to one side.

And stingy. And ticked at Connor for not letting her and Jack know months ago about developments in his romance department. Not to mention sorry for herself, the marriage expert abandoned by hubby, left alone to get the house ready for guests and to greet them, an apparently healthy, solid family of three.

She breathed in the perfume again. It wasn't her grandmother's brand but still reminded her of Grandma Ellie. The effect soothed her.

"Jill." Michelle turned the name into a lovely sound with a soft *g* and a long *e*. "I am so happy to meet you at long last."

Michelle and Emma resembled each other. Dark eyes and straight black hair. Slender. Impeccable makeup. Red lipstick. They would look stylish in ratty old sweats.

Michelle clasped Jill's hands. "I am so sorry. Connor has told us everything. I want to say that Philippe and I have been married for thirty-two years. We have had our own troubles. You are not to be ashamed. And you are not to lose hope."

Odd how after knowing the Trudeaus for about three minutes Jill could fall so completely and utterly apart in their presence.

❧

Michelle hung a little black dress in the guest room closet. "You are so kind to invite us to stay in your home. I must admit I am so very tired of the hotels."

"I hope you are comfortable." Three bedrooms had always seemed spacious enough except when she had to give up the one designated as her office. She patted the futon that normally served as a couch. Connor had helped her open it and shoved her desk into a corner. They had carried armload after armload of papers, books, and file boxes from here into her bedroom. Moving Connor's belongings to the basement family room in order to give Emma his room had taken less than half the time.

A sense of defeat weighed on her shoulders. She was getting further behind on work by the hour. The process of quitting the broadcast meant countless e-mails, calls, letters, and whatnot. She couldn't even pass one whatnot off to assistants at the station until she first handled it herself.

She hadn't handled anything in the days she'd been home except the stress mounting over Jack.

Michelle sat beside her. "I have a solution."

"To what?"

"Your worry."

"It's obvious?"

Michelle smiled. "Why would it not be obvious?"

"Because Christians are not anxious." She winked. "Right?"

The woman laughed. "The misconception is alive and well among my friends too. Paul writes not to be anxious and so we pretend that we are not. That is—what is the phrase you like? 'That is so ridiculous I can't even comment.'"

Jill laughed. "How do you know I like that?"

"I hear you say it often! Connor helps me to listen to your programs. Your son is so smart. He somehow found recordings on the computer. He knows computers like my Philippe, and he knows art like my Emma."

"Like you also must know art."

"Oh no. Our children know art. I only know about it."

"But you're a docent at the Louvre."

"*Oui.* I practice my English and my German. I tell visitors which artists' work is in which gallery and how to find the *toilette*."

"I am sure you underestimate yourself."

"You must visit Paris and see for yourself." Michelle smiled. "About the solution. I understand why you are anxious. You talk much about making marriage work and now your husband's actions make your good teaching to go kaput." She shook her head. "You must be real in your public role, Jill. Women respect real. They do not want perfection. Who can relate to perfection?"

Jill nodded. She could accept that. "Thank you, Michelle. I agree it is the solution. It would be better for me to be more real."

"Oh, that is not my solution. No, no, no. The answer to your worry is to explore Chicago with us. This is our first visit and we have two weeks before the wedding. Plenty of time to play, *n'est-ce pas?*"

Jill pictured the to-do piles on the floor in her bedroom. Time to play? She cringed inwardly. The idea went against every grain in her body.

But . . . what had she learned in the desert? That her mother thought she was precious and not a *whoops*. That she did not have to win approval by burying herself in something tangible like correspondence or writing lesson plans or listing talking points for a show. That God did not require her to be perfect.

She smiled. "*Oui*, Michelle. Plenty of time to play."

CHAPTER 46

—— ❧ ——

SAN DIEGO

The bells above the door of Vivvie's Tours clanked harshly, announcing the arrival of a customer.

At her desk in the back office, Viv stopped talking with Dustin about schedules. "What happened to the pleasant tinkle?"

He shrugged. "Must be some burly guy swinging open the door. You better go see who it is."

"You're receptionist today." She poked a pencil along the inside of the cast on her arm. The itch was driving her crazy as evidenced by her shortness of temper. "You go."

"Knock, knock." Marty appeared, filling the doorframe.

Dustin laughed. "Gotcha, Aunt Viv."

Marty clapped his nephew's shoulder and took the chair vacated by him. "Lock up on your way out."

"Sure thing. Bye."

Viv gazed from one to the other, unsure of what was going on. "He knew you were coming. He kept bugging me with silly questions. I couldn't get away."

Marty grinned. "A raise might be in order."

"Well." She smiled. "Hi. You're supposed to be playing softball."

"Nah." He set a manila envelope on the desk, leaned across, and gave her a quick kiss. "I'm supposed to be here saying, 'Happy anniversary.'"

She blinked. "It's March 27. What anniversary?"

"Twenty-six years ago today we met."

"You made that up."

He shook his head slowly, a small smile on his face. "On the contrary, I figured it out."

"No way. All right, maybe we first saw each other in March that year. If I remember correctly, it was not long after my dullest ever St. Patrick's Day."

"It was exactly March 27. I was discharged on March 31. I celebrated early, on the twenty-seventh, with some buddies. On the twenty-eighth I nursed a hangover. On the twenty-ninth I wondered about you. On the thirtieth, the day before my last day, I asked the guys where we were when I met the gorgeous chick with the long, wavy hair and the sparkly brown eyes that kept showing up in my dreams."

A tickle went up and down her spine. She hadn't heard the gorgeous chick and sparkly eyes reference in forever.

She and Marty had bumped into each other, literally, in a restaurant's bar. She was meeting clients for dinner, a sweet elderly couple who wanted to book a special tour for their entire family and insisted on the dinner treat.

It was one of those fluke moments, or—as her sister might call it if it hadn't happened in a bar—a divine appointment. While waiting for the clients, Viv chatted with a friend of a friend who worked as the hostess. Marty walked by as she took a step back. He caught her before she fell. Their eyes met, and that was that.

Except he kept staring at her and the hostess noticed, as did one of his buddies, who'd had his eye on the hostess. It hadn't been too difficult for Marty to track her down.

Marty called. She remembered the cute, rough-and-tumble guy too looped to interest her. She said no thanks. He persisted for weeks.

Viv said, "Marty, it was summertime before we really *met* met." She hadn't agreed to a date, but he had gotten wind that those mutual acquaintances were organizing a tailgate at a Padres game, an event she had already planned on attending.

He grinned. "The first time is the first time."

"You really think it was the twenty-seventh?"

"Positive. I dug out my discharge papers and worked backward."

She smiled slyly. "My, my. Aren't you clever?"

"No. Just really, really grateful that you're all right." Since the bus accident, the man had come close to sappy.

"Does this mean I get something?"

"Naturally." He opened the manila envelope and pulled what looked like Web site printouts from it. "Tickets to Chicago for your nephew's wedding. Reservations for us to stay downtown at the InterContinental, three nights."

Tears sprang to her eyes. She had planned to go alone, stay for two nights at Jill's.

She wasn't about to protest.

Marty said, "But all that doesn't count, because it's a week away. So for tonight, on the twenty-seventh, the exact date of our meeting, I got a room for us at that new fancy resort in Sweetwater. We'll spend the night there and then—" he paused to smile—"tomorrow we'll bring home your bus."

She gasped. "It's ready?"

"Rats. I knew you'd be more excited about the bus than room service for dinner and making love."

"The bus is tough to compete with." She grinned. "But then you didn't mention dinner and lovemaking."

He shrugged, all nonchalant, his eyes warm and crinkly. "Gotcha, Viv."

"You sure did." She sighed. "Whew. Talk about a schpate night."

CHAPTER 47

———— ❧ ————

CHICAGO

What first struck Jack about the Trudeaus was their air of authenticity. The impression that they were real and regular people deepened with each encounter.

And there were many encounters. It seemed no one wanted to miss out on the short time the families had to spend together. Even Baxter and Sophie weighed in, urging Jack to take off work and rescheduling appointments without his knowledge. He found himself available and grateful for it.

The days became a whirlwind of sightseeing, shopping, eating, and talking at the house.

At Jill's house.

Jack almost forgot he didn't live there.

He almost forgot he wanted a divorce.

Every once in a while he found himself watching her. She was her old self, but not quite. He couldn't pinpoint what was different.

She lived up to her dad's nickname of Jaws. She jabbered away, making the visitors feel at home and acquainting them with Chicago as thoroughly as if she'd spent her entire life there as a tour guide.

She booked activities, from the river architectural ride to a visit at her radio station to the art institute and various galleries. They walked the city like they hadn't in years. They ate ice cream in the middle of the day and linguine at midnight.

Through it all she treated him politely if not warmly, yet always maintaining a certain distance.

Not that he blamed her.

"Jill, can we talk?"

It was Saturday night, after eleven o'clock. Everyone else had gone to their rooms, exhausted after a full day. Jack lingered, helping her straighten the kitchen, preparing the coffeemaker for Philippe, who was always up at the crack of dawn.

Jill pulled out her earrings and set them on the windowsill by the sink. "Your timing for talking really does stink, Jack."

Aha. That was what had been different. He hadn't been chastised in days.

He said, "I am such a doofus."

She walked past him, touching his arm briefly. "I'm sorry. It's late."

Her apology rang sincere. The pressure of her hand was familiar.

Familiar in a pleasant way.

He watched her exit the kitchen, heard her footfalls on the staircase. All the lights remained turned on downstairs. The news still flickered from the small television on the countertop. He heard the furnace and doubted she had turned down the thermostat. He was always the one to shut down the house at night. He wondered if it got shut down in his absence.

Suddenly tired of the situation he had created, he bounded after her, taking the steps two at a time. He tiptoed past the other bedrooms and at the end of the hall paused at the closed door of the master bedroom.

Their bedroom.

Her bedroom.

His and hers.

They were still married.

He could not imagine not being married to her. Not really.

He rapped once and stepped inside, shutting the door behind him. "Jill."

She was in the bathroom and did not reply. He turned off the bedroom television, pushed aside clothing on the overstuffed chair, sat down, and waited.

It was a nice corner room. East-facing windows caught the morning sun, south-facing ones kept it bright throughout the day. It was large enough for a king-size bed, two nightstands, double dresser, and a small desk that usually did not hold the piles that lay on it and under it now.

The curtains were drawn. They matched the coverlet—abstract designs in Southwestern pastels. Much as Jill griped about living in the desert as a kid, she never had completely let go of it.

"Jack!" Jill walked into the room. Her hair was brushed, her face makeup-free. She wore flannel pajamas.

She would be cold on a March night without him beside her, even with the furnace still going.

"You scared me!"

"Sorry. I called out but . . . I know my timing stinks but I need to talk. Just listen for a minute. Please."

Muttering to herself, she yanked the bedcovers aside, shoved pillows into a stack, and got into the bed. Leaning against the pillows, she pulled up the covers and crossed her arms.

Her pose was familiar.

Familiar in a not-so-pleasant way.

"Jack, what do you want? We have such a full day tomorrow. We agreed to postpone this until—"

"You know what I like about Philippe and Michelle? They're authentic. Genuine. What you see is what you get. I feel like such a fraud."

"Why would you feel like that? We haven't hidden anything from them. They know we have issues. That you don't live here."

"Basically I feel like a fraud because you've always portrayed me as the perfect husband."

She uncrossed her arms and wrapped them around her knees, leaning forward. "But you are, Jack. You are perfect in the sense that you are a good and decent role model for husbands. Well, up until now anyway."

"We both know I'm not perfect in any sense of the word. I don't come close to being a good role model."

"Why won't you believe me?"

"Because in private I'm the lab rat."

She sat up straighter. "I never meant to—"

"Jill, I don't want to blame you anymore. I accept responsibility for running the maze all these years. It was my choice to avoid the Crunchy Casserole stuff. I am so sorry for not caring enough to notice that the way we were living was driving a wedge between us. We've been going separate directions for years."

Tears glistened on her cheeks.

He stepped over to the bed and sat on its edge.

"I'm the fraud, Jack. I've been living behind this public persona for so long I don't see the mask in front of me anymore."

"Oh, honey." He pulled her into his arms. "You're adorable in the limelight. Somebody has to be out there giving the answers."

"Stop it." She wiped her eyes with his sleeve.

"I'm serious." He put a finger under her chin and raised her face. Her skin was soft. "I'm sorry for hurting you. For hurting us."

"I'm sorry—"

"Shh. This is my turn to talk."

She gazed at him with those big blue eyes of hers wide open. Her lips were relaxed, not pursing together to form more words.

"Jill," he whispered, "I am sorry. Will you forgive me?"

She blinked once. Twice.

She would not enter into forgiving lightly. She taught about forgiveness. She understood its nuances, its implications. It meant she would let him off the hook and never again expect an apology for his actions.

She would forget that he had looked the other way for years and years, letting the wedge grow between them.

He would give many more apologies; he was sure of that. But she would wonder what he was talking about. She would forget. It came part and parcel with true forgiveness.

Jill nodded. "I forgive you."

He sighed. "Thank you." He kissed her beautiful mouth, gently at first.

But she had been away for weeks and, before that, been busy, busy, busy for a long time. A long, long time.

"Jack."

"Hm?" He looked at her.

"We have guests," she whispered.

"Mm." He cleared his throat. "So?"

"We don't live together."

"We're still married."

"But what if—?"

"Jill. We are not taking notes tonight."

She swallowed. "I'm sorry."

"Can you forget everyone and everything except for the two of us right now?"

She smiled. "I can try."

"Maybe I can help you forget." He kissed her again.

She kissed him back.

His mind strayed. Forgiveness had been asked and given. Where did that leave them? Back together? He had no idea. He knew only that love for his wife overwhelmed him.

She touched his ear. "Hey, where did you go?"

"Uh, Sizzlin' Spinach, I think."

Her smile removed all doubt.

"Jill, may I stay the night?"

She took his face in her hands. "Jack, you're my husband. You don't have to ask to be my knight in shining armor."

He smiled. Forgiveness was a beautiful thing.

CHAPTER 48

———— ❧ ————

JILL WATCHED JACK as he slept, his head on the pillow next to hers.

The morning sun highlighted strands of gray, making his brown hair appear even lighter. It had grown and almost covered the jagged red line left over from his accident. Would she always see that scar with the memory of his hurtful words? *"I opened the window because I was so upset I was suffocating. . . . When I heard your voice, I realized that this is not what I signed up for."*

He had not signed up for what their marriage had become.

She had to let go of the hurt and yet not deny the truth. Their marriage needed a major overhaul.

Lord, please help us. Please give us insight. Please don't let go of us.

The laugh lines around Jack's mouth were pronounced. She called them his doctor creases because he smiled often, happy about eliminating pain for his patients. His was such a pure goal. She had always admired it.

After twenty-five years, she accepted that a wife's love was more verb than feeling of infatuation. Last night had been both.

He had been hesitant in his lovemaking, though. As usual. As usual since when?

Since she started taking notes about it?

Lord, I'm sorry.

He opened his eyes. Their hazel color glimmered. "Hi."

She smiled. "Hi."

"Angel."

Her smile lessened. When was the last time he had called her angel? When she started telling him how to run the maze.

"What's wrong? Oh no!" He gasped. His brows rose. He opened his mouth wide, melodramatically. "The jig is up! The houseguests know I have spent the night here."

She couldn't help but laugh. How silly to agitate over the Trudeaus' opinion. Michelle would probably congratulate her on reconciliation. "If you leave this room, they will know for sure. I've heard them all up and about. I smell bacon."

"And yet you're still here?"

"Didn't want to miss this moment."

He smiled. "Thank you."

"Thank you."

"Uh, what's next?"

Her heart sank a little. *Kiss me? Move home? Say you can't live without me?* "Bacon?"

"Okay."

They looked at each other for a silent moment.

She said, "Then church?"

He did a slow blink. "Okay."

"Connor said they would come so I could show off him and Emma."

"Yeah."

"It's a big place. We'll skip adult classes and get lost in the shuffle before the eleven o'clock service."

"Mm-hmm."

"You don't have to go for my sake."

"How about I go for my sake, to worship and thank God for you?"

She smiled. He had such a good heart. Still, certain people with certain attitudes were known to bother him. "You know there is probably some gossip about us. We might want to consider possible reactions."

"Not a problem. I can handle it."

"Okay." She paused. "Jack, I am sorry for making you feel like a lab rat. For putting you on display. Will you forgive me?"

"Yes."

"That was quick. You must have already given it some thought."

He smiled.

"Will you . . . will you . . . ?" The questions burned inside her. Would he move back home? Was his crisis—midlife or otherwise—over? Was last night simply a *guy* thing, a thing he needed? Or was it a seal on reconciliation, a promise that he wanted to work on them? "Jack, where are we?"

He lifted her hand from the sheet and kissed it. "I don't know, Jill. For today we are at bacon, church, the meet and greet with my parents, dinner here, prepared by yours truly. We will take it one step at a time."

We will . . . It was a statement, not a question, not even a suggestion. Good news, in a sense. It meant he was breaking out of the maze and making his own decision, not trying to please her.

The bad news was that he hadn't rescinded that other breakout decision, the one that had to do with divorce.

***

In the end they decided that Jack would skip the bacon and meet them all later at church. His early morning presence in the same clothes he'd worn the night before might be a bit much for their son, who, like most kids, really did not want to consider what the parents were up to in private.

"I almost forgot." Jack winced. "I have to feed the cat too."

"Cat?"

"It's Sophie's. I offered to catsit while she nurses a stray back to health. The two felines did not get along."

Sophie. Sophie. Sophie.

With a shake of her head, Jill dismissed the office manager and the fact that Jack did not care for cats. She would instead think about the past few days with Jack. Most especially she would think about the past eight hours with Jack.

Warm fuzzies came over her, and yet . . . it was almost a bit much for her too. Had they done something wrong? What activities did estranged spouses engage in? Her focus had always been on married people living together. This was brand-new territory. What author or counselor might offer insight to her and her listeners?

That sounded close to note taking.

She trailed behind Jack as he went downstairs. Michelle was the only one to see him slip out the front door.

She smiled at Jill. "Progress, no?"

"Progress, *oui*."

I hope it is anyway. Jill wasn't exactly sure. They had taken a step, no doubt about that. An enjoyable, sweet, affirming, restorative step. Was it toward reconciliation? or simply a short detour off the path of their current situation?

CHAPTER 49

———— ✿ ————

THEY WENT TO church. It was their first Sunday back since that awful day when her world flipped upside down.

Greetings and welcome-home hugs were showered on them. Jill kept a check on her emotions and a close eye on Jack. Either one of them might fall apart at the attention. She detected no heads tilted askance, no expressions of concern. Jack did get an extra big hug from Lew. He seemed to handle it fine.

Connor and Emma shone, typical young people wearing infatuation like another layer of skin. No tongues tsked at the news that Pastor Mowers was not marrying them. The Trudeaus attended as well and won everyone's smiles with their friendly conversation.

So far, so good.

After the service they went to Charles and Katherine's place. Jack's parents loved Connor and were as sociable as Philippe and Michelle. A short visit was not going to happen. Jill rode with Jack to get take-out lunch for everyone.

They sat outside the restaurant on a bench in a patch of sunshine, waiting for their order. No trees were budding yet, but recent warmer temps had thawed the ground and filled the air with an earthy scent and faint sounds of trickling water through drainpipes.

Jill said, "Your mother—" she closed her mouth and then she opened it again—"looks well."

"Yes, she does." Jack paused. "I overheard what she said to you."

"Oh." Jill thought she had stopped herself in time to miss his radar, but he knew her too well.

She had decided that morning that for once she would not tattle on her mother-in-law. Katherine was not overly fond of Jill. Jill had come to accept that truth about the time Connor was five years old and had his first crush on another girl. But still, the woman remained an issue for Jill. Typically Jill unloaded her frustrations about his mother on Jack.

He said, "She told me the same thing a few weeks ago, that it's up to me to fix us. I don't know how she managed to make that your responsibility today, but she did."

Jill knew exactly how she did it. Katherine had said, *"You realize, Jill, that marriage is not a two-way street. You don't want to travel in opposite directions. If you simply turn and go the same direction he is going, then you'll be able to respond to him. He can't fix things without you right there at his side, giving him your full support."*

It came from page 23 in Easy Eggs, chapter 2 of *She Said, He Heard*. Verbatim.

Jack said, "So tell me about these knights in shining armor. How do I join up?"

She stared at him. His face was turned upward toward the sun, eyes shut. He leaned back against the brick wall.

Self-doubt plagued her. It had been escalating ever since his divorce announcement. The past week and especially last night should have been a confidence boost. Right?

Wrong.

Instead his tenderness only added to the unraveling of Jillian Galloway, teacher, speaker, author, marital expert. It snowballed at church. Hugs from old friends and whispered encouragement hadn't helped. Singing praises to the God who had forgiven her for turning her home into a laboratory hadn't helped. Katherine's echo of her own drivel clinched her demise.

Who did Jill think she was?

"Jill." Jack was looking at her now. "I don't want you to stop talking. Silent is not who you are."

"Oh, I think it's high time I got very silent. I told God just this morning that I would stop providing answers. We were singing that song about giving everything up to Him."

"I don't know that He would ask you to give up, to quit."

"You did."

"Not the same thing. Not even close." He blew out a frustrated breath. "I just didn't want answers for questions I wasn't asking. But now I'm asking for one. How can I be a knight?"

She turned toward the parking lot. Dirty snow piles were melting. Puddles were all over the place.

"Jill, last night you said I was your knight because I was your husband. But I get the feeling that I've missed the mark in this department. I mean since you had to tell me, I assume I don't get it."

"I suppose it's one of those things we lost along the way. Honestly, Jack, I don't know what came first: if you gave it up or if I took it from you by my lab experiments."

"So knighthood is a husband's role which he might choose to abdicate?"

She glanced at him. "Do you want to listen to a program about it? I can give you the date it aired. I probably have the CD at home."

He smiled softly. "No, I'd rather hear this firsthand."

She studied his face. "You don't look like a rat running around a maze."

"I'm not. I really am asking you for an answer."

"Okay." A lump was forming in her throat. Unwittingly he was leading them back to Hollywood, to the reason she so desperately wanted to revisit their meeting place. Long before his divorce announcement, she had planned for them to go there because she knew they needed to touch base with this very thing.

She swallowed. "You were a knight in shining armor the day we met. You noticed me. You spoke to me. You teased about my hands not fitting Shirley Temple's prints but later you understood that there was more to the idea that I wanted to be like her. You smiled like you cared, with the corners of your mouth all dimpled in. And then, wonder of wonders, out of the blue you asked me to dinner. You knew exactly what you wanted and you went for it. You were confident but not arrogant."

"What did I want?"

She held in an exasperated sigh. "What do you think?"

"You looked like an angel. I wanted to get to know you."

"Yes. Which made me feel so special and so desirable. It made me feel like a damsel in distress."

"And that's a good thing?"

"It is, in a quirky sort of way. At the time I was independent and basi-cally happy living and working with Viv. But then you walked up and suddenly, fireworks are going off inside. On some level, I was in distress."

"Love at first sight. Nobody can live in that space all the time."

"No."

"Then how does a guy keep functioning as a knight?"

She took a deep breath. "He notices his wife. He speaks to her. He smiles a special smile just for her. He knows her deepest heart, the place where she dreams big dreams. He confidently does whatever is for her best. He intuits that she is always in distress because that's just the human condition. But he alone can comfort and console and make life easier for her."

Jack stared at her for a moment. "That is one major daunting job description."

"Shining armor and a white steed help." She shrugged. "I'm not blaming you, Jack. Like you said, we kept going our separate ways until this wedge developed between us. No more knight and damsel."

"How do we get back to them?"

About sixteen ideas scrambled to be spoken first. *Counseling! Move back home! Tell me you love me! Take a vacation with me!* But Jill pressed her lips together. She didn't think Jack really wanted an answer this time.

He took her hand and squeezed it. "Lots of water over the dam in twenty-five years. I better go inside and get the food."

On second thought there was probably only one answer: they both had to *want* to remove the wedge between them.

❦

"Mom." Connor caught Jill's attention at the dining table. Then he turned to Jack. "Dad."

They both stopped talking to Michelle and Philippe.

Connor smiled. "Promise not to freak out, guys."

"Uh-oh," Jill said. He never included his dad in that request and certainly not others. This must be major. She set her fork with its last bite of cherry pie on her dessert plate.

Emma placed her elbows on the table and batted her big brown eyes. "*Maman et Papa*, please, do not freak out. Promise."

Her parents exchanged baffled looks, a few words in French, and shrugs.

Connor smiled. "It's good news, really."

Emma nodded enthusiastically.

Oh, dear. They are pregnant. Jill cut her eyes to the girl's physique. Did she seem plumper? Hard to tell in the baggy turtleneck.

"We've been offered jobs, beginning in August."

Parental cheers almost drowned out the shared sigh of relief. No baby! Income to take over when the grants and scholarships ended!

Connor went on. "As museum curators."

Emma pouted.

He chuckled. "I just don't want them to worry."

She shook her head and kissed his cheek. "Finish."

"Okay, not exactly curators. Our official titles are something like assistants to the junior assistants. We'll probably run errands and answer phones. I'm part-time; Emma's full-time. But it is a foot in the door, and it's in art, and it's in New York."

The happy chatter stopped. "New York?"

Emma nodded, a sad-happy smile on her pretty face.

Connor said, "We had interviews lined up before we left Italy. That was our first stop when we arrived in the States. At the Cloisters Museum and Gardens. It's a branch of the Metropolitan that specializes in medieval art and architecture." He sighed. "We just heard on Friday. And, well, we accepted."

Michelle pushed back her chair and hurried around to embrace her daughter. "Congratulations!" She hugged Connor. "It is not Paris or Chicago, but neither is it Moscow or Sydney!"

Jack laughed. "Well, that's true."

Jill got in line behind the fathers to offer her congratulations. She hoped her heavy heart did not dim her smile.

Connor hugged her for an extra-long moment. "Thanks for not freaking out."

"Oh, Con. I am happy for you. This is what you've always wanted, to work in the art world and to paint. Maybe part-time hours will give you both."

He nodded. "You always told me I could do whatever I put my efforts toward."

Her smile felt forced. The son she wanted to hold on to forever was truly not coming home again.

❧

Jill poured detergent into the dishwasher, closed it, and turned it on. Beside her, Jack towel-dried a saucepan. She watched him look at the empty rack above the stovetop as if pondering whether or not to hang the pot there. It was a favorite that he'd brought over from his apartment for that night's dinner.

He shoved it into a cupboard.

It seemed a noncommittal choice.

He said, "It sounds like Con and Emma are still talking in the front room."

"Mm-hmm. We should've put in a back staircase years ago."

He gave her a fleeting smile. "Jill, I think I'll go home—uh, to the apartment. Tomorrow is Monday. I need to work this week. You said you need to work. Viv and Marty are coming in a few days. The kids have more premarital sessions. The Trudeaus said they'll entertain themselves."

"And Saturday is the wedding." She and Jack had already talked about the week's agenda. It wasn't his point. "What are you saying?"

He folded the dish towel, avoiding eye contact. "I'm saying it's been a great few days. Fun and hectic. The next few will be full. It's probably not the best time to make any decisions about us." He laid the towel on the countertop and looked at her. "I'm sorry to table our situation, but I think it's best for now."

Jill placed the heels of her hands behind her on the countertop and leaned against it, all open and relaxed. "What I heard you say was . . . Do you mind if we do this exercise?"

He shook his head.

"It's a helpful tool for me."

"I know."

"Okay." She gathered her jumbled thoughts, willing herself not to freak out. "What I heard you say was that there are too many other things going on that require our full attention, which makes it impossible for us to properly address our marital needs at this time. Did I get that right?"

"Yes."

"Is there more?"

"No."

"So you're saying that you are not moving back home?"

He hesitated before replying. "No. I mean yes, that's what I'm saying."

"Are you . . . are you saying this—this *thing* is not over yet?"

"I guess—yes, that's what I am saying." He stepped over and embraced her. "Oh, Jill, I am sorry. Those are not things a knight would say to a damsel in distress."

She stayed rigid in his arms.

He held her tightly and whispered into her hair, "I'm sorry. Please forgive me, Jill."

She already had. Hadn't she?

Yes. But that was for what went on before this moment, before this new infliction of hurt. Before he offered hope last night and now cut it right out of her heart with a dagger.

Forgive your brother seventy times seven. In other words, keep on forgiving, no matter how many times. Did that cover Jack's ongoing rejection of her and their marriage?

She didn't know.

She put her arms around him and pressed her face against his shoulder. "Your being sorry does not help a whole lot, Jack."

The hug helped, though. A little. Maybe enough to get her through the coming week.

CHAPTER 50

———— ❧ ————

MONDAY MORNING JILL woke up with a start.

Damsel in distress waiting for the knight to saddle his steed?

No way. Nohow.

Forgiveness might cover Jack's ongoing rejection, but his behavior was not going to define hers. His back-and-forth swings from tender, apologetic, concerned husband to self-absorbed ninny made her dizzy. It was like trying to tap-dance to a crazy tune.

"Lord, he is a mess. Unless You fix him, our marriage is hopeless. Show him what his problem is. Please. I think he's open to hearing from You, not so much from me."

She sensed an *euww* in her heart and stopped talking. Some people referred to a still, small voice. For her it was more like a tongue making a raspberry noise at cosmic volume.

"Okay, okay. I get it."

She slid from the bed, got down on her knees, and sang softly until her gonging inner voice hushed up. "Holy God, I am a mess. I can't keep this up by myself. Please make me a better wife. And please, please make our marriage whole again." She blinked and smoothed a wrinkle on the blanket where her chin rested. "Or for the first time."

※

Jill left the distressed damsel on the bedroom carpet that Monday morning and hit the week running. She did not weep nor wail nor even cry herself to sleep on subsequent nights. She did not wallow in anger toward Jack nor in the pain of his abandonment. Whenever those ugly emotional heads reared up, she told them to get lost.

She made progress on the correspondence overload and read one book from the pile. It was about a married couple in the Peace Corps in Africa and wonderfully nonrelatable.

She engaged in mall therapy with Michelle. The Frenchwoman brought new meaning to the phrase. The line between want and need totally disappeared for one entire afternoon.

Jill snagged Connor for an hour's lunch, just the two of them. She spoke to him as she would an interviewee and learned the most amazing things about her son's heart.

She fell in love with her almost daughter-in-law one night as they ate popcorn and watched a chick flick together. They talked into the wee hours and Emma told her about growing up in Paris, an only child, an odd girl who began painting at the age of three.

Emma asked her for marital advice. Jill said she had none. Emma said *au contraire*. Connor had said otherwise. He said his mother was a fountain of wisdom. What was most important? Emma persisted. What must they not ever lose sight of?

The answer was what she and Jack had lost sight of.

"Be best friends," she told Emma. "Stay best friends."

All that and Jill did not freak out, not in any way, shape, or form.

But then on Thursday they all went to visit Jack's office because of course the Trudeaus wanted to see his workplace, and then Sophie's eyes filled with tears when she said hello to Jill.

Sophie. The unmarried, devoted, talented, attractive younger woman whom all the doctors loved because she made them look so good. The one who had convinced Jack to take care of a cat.

A cat.

"Mrs. G."

The cutesy nickname had always rankled Jill. *Dr. and Mrs. G.*

Sophie pulled her aside in the hallway while Connor took the others into Jack's private office. "I am so sorry."

About the cat? Or was there more? Like how did the cat get to Jack's apartment? That scenario required an exchange either at his place or her place. Didn't it?

Sophie's puddly tears clung to her lashes. She leaned in close to Jill and whispered, "Your marriage has always given everyone hope. Please don't give up. I'm praying for restoration."

Jill widened her eyes. "You are?"

Sophie nodded vigorously.

"Oh." It was a whimper. "Will you tell Connor I'll be in the car?" Not waiting for a reply, Jill rushed out the doors, back through the hospital corridors, the exits, and to the parking lot.

She tried to catch her breath.

Of all the crazy things. Undone by Sophie.

They should have invited her to the wedding.

Jill remembered the garbage can, the full-to-overflowing container of her faults and mistakes. She should have added "jealous of Sophie" to it long ago.

Jill got in her car, crossed her arms, and rested her head on the steering wheel. Pain shot through the bruise that remained on her forehead. She straightened up.

"I'm sorry, God. Can't You just give it to me all at once instead of this 'Oh, here's another glob of nastiness to stuff in your can'?"

"Give it to Him." Agnes's voice played in her mind. *"Isn't that what the Cross is all about? . . . Dump that rubbish."*

Jill closed her eyes. Her heart thundered. Wasn't she supposed to carry it with her as a reminder of who she really was?

That sounded like she was proud of her load.

"No, Lord, I'm not. I'm not proud of it. I quit. I dump it all at Your feet."

She imagined shoving the can onto its side and its contents spilling out, building into a black, slimy pile.

"Okay, there it is. I give it all to You. Jealousy. Pride. Shame. Anger. Attitudes that do not belong in Your daughter. Not listening to Jack's heart. Browbeating him and Connor. Not forgiving my mom. Thinking ill of Marty."

The list went on.

And on.

She forced herself to say each and every thing that came to mind.

And there were plenty.

At last her breath slowed. She felt empty of words.

In that split moment between keeping her eyes shut and opening them, she thought she heard a whisper. *"It is finished."*

CHAPTER 51

———— ❧ ————

"He spent the night?" Viv felt her eyes bug out. "He spent the night? Here in this room?"

Jill turned from the full-length mirror and said in a low voice, "Do you think that was wrong?"

Viv burst out laughing.

She was in Jill's bedroom, helping her sister get ready for that afternoon's wedding. It had been their first opportunity to catch up on the Jack crisis.

Jill spun around. "Oh, forget I asked. Just zip me up. It's the least you can do. I can't believe you've been in town for two nights and haven't had time for me until now."

"Whine, whine, whine. Hush up. I'm at a fabulous hotel on my second honeymoon with the man of my dreams." She struggled with the zipper on Jill's dress, her left-hand fingers hampered by the cast. "Or first honeymoon—if you don't count a weekend in a camper in a parking lot at the beach. Which, to tell the truth, I never really did count. Jill, I can't possibly zip this one-handed."

Jill reached for it and shimmied about, trying to get it up. "The dress is too tight."

325

"It's perfect. Formfitting, but not too much." Viv admired the flamingo pink silk sheath. "It looks very Parisian. I'll go get Michelle."

Jill sighed. "Thanks."

Viv walked toward the door. "And no, silly, I don't think a physical expression of love between you and Jack was wrong. From what I've read, Sizzlin' Spinach is a mysterious union of body and soul." She opened the door. "A wondrous fulfillment of—Jack! Hi!"

"Hi." Her brother-in-law greeted her with a hug. "You look great as always, even with the cast."

"Thanks." She met his gaze and saw another apology in the works. She'd heard enough during their long-distance calls and cut it off. "You look fantastic."

He winked. "The wondrous fulfillment of a black suit."

Wondrous fulfillment? Had he overheard her comment? She almost giggled again. "Your tie! It perfectly matches Jill's dress."

"Emma is into color. She did it."

Viv smiled. Jack was as good-looking as ever, as gentle and kind as a man could be. In spite of that other business.

"May I come in?"

Viv moved aside. "How are you with zippers?"

Jack walked in and—no question about it—he gawked at Jill. "Whoa."

Jill stopped battling with the back of her dress and cocked her head. "Whoa yourself."

"You look gorgeous."

"The wondrous fulfillment of silk."

He shook his head. "I don't think so." He loosened the knot on his pink tie. "This isn't right. Connor and I are all thumbs. Will you do it?"

"Of course." She still clutched at the back waistline of her dress, trying to hold it shut. The mirrored reflection showed she was not succeeding.

"Turn around." He touched her shoulder. "I'll zip you first."

Jill didn't budge. "Is Michelle here?"

"No. Marty took the Trudeaus on over to the church. Viv, you can ride with us, okay? The kids wanted to do the traditional thing and not see each other before the ceremony."

"Sure." She was watching Jill. Her sister was about two seconds from flustered meltdown. The effect of Jack in a suit was obvious.

"I can get this," Jill said and fiddled again with the zipper.

Jack put his hands on his hips and looked toward the mirror, where Jill's back was reflected.

Viv kept her mouth shut. Were they the two most stubborn, clueless people on the face of the earth or what?

And then her brother-in-law did something that made her want to do a cartwheel. Without a word, he called Jill on her own bluster. He simply stepped around her, gently moved her hands aside, and easily slid the zipper to the top of her dress.

It was a small gesture that to most people would not have been a big deal. But Viv knew Jill and she knew Jack and she knew that Jack had kowtowed to Jill's pigheadedness far too long. It was indeed a big deal.

Viv almost cried at the beauty of it.

CHAPTER 52

———— ❧ ————

Jill sat in a pew next to Jack's parents, in front of Viv and Marty, a mother-of-the-groom lump in her throat.

The day captured the essence of a world ready to burst into new life. Outside, sunlight shone on crocuses and tulips and pale greens of leaves shedding their winter coat.

The beauty flowed inside the chapel, in its simple decor and in the faces of the small group.

Jack stood at the front, best man to his son, and caught her eye. She did not think it her imagination that their hearts spoke volumes in that momentary gaze.

Connor wore a black suit, white shirt, and white tie. Emma wore a simple white silk dress, tea-length, capped sleeves, and white flowers in her hair.

Michelle, the matron of honor, was as pretty as the bride in a mint green A-line dress. Philippe, in the pew with Connor's friends, wore a matching tie.

The chapel was an odd mixture of old and new. Pastor Nelson and his wife were young. He dressed traditionally in a suit and tie but spoke in the easygoing manner of a guy in blue jeans. She played classical selections on the piano but didn't bat an eye queuing up Connor's rap music on his iPod. Replicas of ancient paintings hung on the walls beside colorful homemade banners proclaiming Jesus as Lord in Spanish, English, and some language Jill did not recognize.

No wonder Connor and Emma had voted for this place. Like their union, it was a crossroads of cultures.

In the shared look with Jack, she knew that like herself, he recalled recent conversations about Connor's plans. No matter that they liked the pastor, they would not have chosen the church for their son's wedding. Jack's glint suggested this was one final swoop of the baby bird flying over the nest he'd just left. She gave him a sad smile in agreement.

Jill thought back to her and Jack's wedding that nearly put Charles and Katherine over the edge. It had been in Sweetwater Springs, a downhome affair at her laid-back church of a hundred on good days and a potluck dinner at the VFW, where the air-conditioning wheezed and coughed as much as the pastor had during the ceremony. Most of the men wore cowboy boots and the women, casual dresses.

She reached over now and squeezed her mother-in-law's hand, grateful that Katherine had, in her own way, accepted Jill for who she was. Katherine gave her a knowing smile.

As Connor and Emma exchanged their vows, Jill listened carefully. The couple had chosen to say the timeworn ones, the ones she wanted to hear again, the ones she and Jack had spoken.

The ones they had let go by the wayside.

"I promise to be true to you in good times and in bad, in sickness and in health. I will love and honor you all the days of my life."

I promise.

It was a choice.

Jill stared at Jack, willing him to catch her eye again.

This time he did not look back.

CHAPTER 53

———— ❧ ————

JACK LISTENED TO Mrs. Stanton complain about her feet and made a mental note not to see her again first thing on a Monday morning.

"So." The sixty-two-year-old with the severe pageboy spread her hands. Several large diamonds caught the overhead lights. "I'd like to have the surgery within the next two weeks. Any later would interfere with our annual trip to Palm Springs."

"I thought you had decided not to have surgery."

She blew out an exasperated breath. "Why is it you doctors and your nurses take copious notes and never refer to them again? You wrote it down the last time I was here. It's in the file."

Jack took the folder from the countertop and opened it. He was certain she had been adamant about no surgery. They had discussed it for at least a couple of years.

She huffed. "I said I was reconsidering it. Well, I've reconsidered it. I want to wear cute sandals and not have ugly feet anymore."

Jack flipped through papers. Normally he was pretty good with patients he saw regularly, even if the visits were scattered. People and their feet were his favorite pastime. He knew this woman did not want the hassle of surgery.

"Mrs. Stanton, when did I last see you?"

"How should I know? It was cold outside. It was winter. There was an ice storm."

He found the page. His heartbeat thumped once in his throat. "February 10."

"Whatever."

February 10.

He read the notes he had taken. They weren't copious. *Might do surgery!!* The exclamation points were because the woman had insisted for years she would never go through with it. She was fine managing the pain by wearing practical shoes and having calluses trimmed regularly. She hated, absolutely hated, the thought of surgery.

February 10.

With apologies, Jack sent Mrs. Stanton out to the scheduler and then made a beeline for Sophie's desk. He put his elbows on the counter and leaned over it. "Will you pull my files from February 10?"

She stared at him. "The day of your accident."

"Yes!" He spoke too loudly, too intensely, but couldn't stop himself. "Please! I need the folders. Can you do it now?"

"Sure."

"Now."

"While you wait?"

"Yes, while I wait!"

"Dr. G, this will take a while. I have to pull up that day's schedule and then—"

"I need them now. Right now. As in *yesterday* now."

She glanced beyond his shoulder and called out, "Dr. Baxter."

Jack gripped the edge of the countertop. He felt Baxter brush up beside him.

Sophie tilted her head toward Jack. "We have a situation."

"Okay." Baxter's voice was full-on bedside. "What's up, bud?"

Jack wondered how long he could hyperventilate and remain upright on two feet. There was probably a formula. Height plus weight plus—

Baxter grabbed his arm and began to steer him down the hall.

"I lost the day, Bax." He exhaled the words, one at a time. "I lost the whole, entire, stinking day."

❧

Jack sat on the couch in Baxter's office, his head between his knees. His breathing was almost back to normal, but the room kept spinning.

"Jack, didn't you realize this after the accident? that there was this gigantic hole in your memory bank?"

"No. I don't think I even gave that day a thought. I mean, it was probably like any other at the office." He shut his eyes and straightened. "In the days after the accident I was a little preoccupied with a headache and the business of leaving town. Then with the business of not wanting to leave town. And then the actual not leaving town." He opened his eyes. The room stayed put. "I did not revisit that day. Apparently I had nothing to revisit."

"What *can* you remember about it?" Baxter's jaw went rigid. "And tell me the truth this time."

Jack sighed. "I remember Jill's voice on the radio while I was driving. I remember that it upset me."

"News to me. And when did you remember this?"

"That night you and I talked at my apartment. It came to me later, after you left. The next day was the MRI."

"So you don't really remember going to the dry cleaner's or the accident itself, do you?"

"No, only what happened after the impact. I noticed the dry cleaning in the car and deduced where I'd been."

Baxter cursed. "Jack, why couldn't you admit that to me before? or to the ER doc? What is it with you? Always the facade. All is well with the Galloways; just ask them."

We are perfect, the poster couple for happily married couples. Just ask anybody.

Baxter wasn't finished. "You can't even admit how angry you are at Jill. You just walk away from her."

Jack tuned him out. Reading his own handwriting in Mrs. Stanton's file and not remembering the act of writing the note scared him. Was his brain damaged?

Baxter paced. "These things happen. It may remain a black hole for the rest of your life. At least we've got files as far as your patients are concerned, so your professional side is covered. Other than that, it doesn't matter what you ate for lunch." He stopped in front of Jack. "Right?"

"I guess not."

"Right. You do remember your life before that day. Childhood, mom and dad, wife, son?"

"Yeah."

"Okay then." He clapped Jack on the shoulder. "You'll be fine."

"What you just described doesn't feel fine. A black hole?"

The door opened and Sophie walked in carrying a stack of folders. "Dr. G, this should be all of them."

Jack took them from her. "Thank you. I'm sorry for yelling at you."

"I understand. This must be frightening." She sat beside him on the couch. "The sheet on top is that day's schedule. You had a consultation with someone, but I can't find any record of it except here." She pointed to a line. "I fit her in between Mrs. Stanton and Mr. Childers. She did not make another appointment. I assume she required nothing further, so you didn't start a file on her."

Jack couldn't bring the paper into focus. "Where is it?"

"Here." Sophie tapped the sheet. "At 11:20. Mrs. Dena Wilson."

Memory returned, a bolt of lightning slashing through him, illuminating every single crevice of his mind, annihilating the black hole. It tore his breath away.

"Ratatouille." He looked at Baxter. "That's what I had for lunch that day."

Baxter stared at him.

"It was left over from Sunday. New recipe. Very tasty. I'll make it again and share some with you two."

Sophie said, "Dr. G, you're white as a sheet. You should go home."

He nodded and that set the room in motion again. "Yeah, maybe I should."

❧

They wouldn't allow him to drive. Baxter drove Jack's car; Sophie followed in hers.

Baxter walked him to his apartment door. "Shall I call Jill?"

"No. No thanks. Not yet. I need to get used to, uh, um . . ."

"To that day's memories?"

"Yes."

"Jack, who's Dena?"

"My wake-up call." He smiled crookedly. "Or death knell."

"Jack—"

"Not literally. I'm good. Really. That's the truth."

"Don't say that just because it's what I want to hear."

"I promise. No more of that."

No more of that.

Jack repeated the phrase as he watched his friends drive off. He went inside. No more telling Jill what he thought she wanted to hear. No more responding to anyone in that way.

Jack greeted Sophie's cat, who flicked her yellow tail and walked off in reply. He made himself a cup of Assam tea. He sat in his mud-brown recliner and put up the footrest.

And he revisited every single moment of February 10.

CHAPTER 54

—— ❧ ——

MONDAY AFTERNOON JILL sat at the dining room table in a sea of mail, the hard-copy sort of mail that came on paper and now littered her table and floor. Her laptop was open to the other sort of mail that came through cyberspace, untouched by human hands, hovering above her, waiting for a click of the touch pad to pounce on her head.

"Honestly, Gretchen," she muttered into the phone, "whoever invented reality checks anyway? They should be locked up and forced to eat peas and liver morning, noon, and night."

"You only have yourself to blame for these feelings."

"Is this a pep talk?"

"Let me try again. Every cloud has a silver lining. The darkest hour is right before the dawn. Nothing succeeds like failure. If you have a field full of manure, you know there's a pony in there somewhere."

"Much better."

Gretchen chuckled. "Call me if you need more."

"Right." She turned off the phone and picked up her coffee mug. It was empty. Did she need a third pot?

It was her own fault, yes. Reality checks overwhelmed her because she preferred not to engage in them on a regular basis.

"Back up, Jaws," she spoke aloud to herself. "That's not exactly the truth. The truth is you've never engaged in one, period. You only think you do because you equate them with taking notes on your marriage."

Euww.

This nonstop in-her-face routine was tough business. She saw no other way to get on with her life. She could not know if it would be with Jack or without him. She just had to get moving, to take care of herself.

The Trudeaus, Viv and Marty, and the newlyweds left on Sunday. Before the overwhelming emptiness set in, she got to work putting the house back in order. Bedding changes, laundry, moving her office back into the office, pitching leftovers she would not eat. She even found Jack's saucepan in the cupboard and set it out.

In case he wanted to take it back to his apartment.

The physical activity released the happy hormones. Well, maybe they were more like the not-as-wretched-as-it-seems hormones. Happy seemed a long way off.

Jack had not called, and it wasn't because her phone batteries were dead or the lines disconnected. She knew that because she had checked them once or twice.

She woke up Monday morning to Connor's phone call. They were in Rome. He sounded joyously ecstatic.

That was when Jill decided to have an official, honest-to-goodness Reality Check Day and not hide behind running errands and lunching with Gretchen. Her son lived in Italy. Her husband lived in an apartment. Her life needed attention.

And so she began to read accumulated mail.

And she did not—as she usually did—toss or delete the negative ones.

She flinched and argued out loud and explained herself to the unseen finger pointers, but she did not destroy their letters. Instead she printed the e-mails and put them in a plastic tub with the other paper mail. She saved every unequivocal declaration that her work was worthless, that what she wrote and taught and spoke was sheer nonsense.

Nonsense? More like abominations. Or worse.

The cordless phone at her elbow rang and she jumped. She turned it over to see the caller ID.

Jack.

Jack. All the proof she needed to say that her work was indeed worthless.

The phone rang again.

Not now, Jack. Not now. I have enough going on here.

She set the phone down. The man could have called twenty-four hours ago when she was dealing with an empty house. She didn't want to hear from him now.

She counted ten rings before it quit. Two more and voice mail would have picked up.

Jill carried her mug to the kitchen sink and saw the stray letter she'd left on the windowsill. The stationery was pretty enough to frame, lavender curlicues at the top and bottom. The lovely handwriting hinted at gentleness and thoughtfulness. The content wormed its way into her heart, where she imagined it might stay forever, word for word.

Dear Mrs. Galloway,

I've been a faithful listener to your program since the beginning. Was that eight years ago or so? I still remember your voice—fresh, young, eager, and a little unsure. I adored the sweet blend of spunk and vulnerability in it. I felt I could trust you.

And trust you I did. When you agreed with the expert you were interviewing, I did as well. When you disagreed with one, so did I. You always backed your opinions with Scripture. What was there not to trust?

I recently found out. It was the underlying message of your programs. You never said it in so many words but it was always there. "If you do such and such, your husband will be happy and faithful."

My husband left me. He wasn't happy. I don't blame you. I don't blame myself. I don't blame God. I don't even blame my husband.

I do blame that underlying, subtle message that suggests a wife is responsible for her husband's happiness and therefore the success of a marriage. For me that twists the truth of our call to respect into a call to manipulate husband, self, and God. If I behave a certain way, God is bound to make this man happy and keep him just the way I want him: at home, taking care of my desires and needs.

God is larger than that, don't you think?

I pray you will never feel a hint of the despair that is now my life.

Anonymous

Anonymous with no return address, postmark too faint to read. She should thank God for it.

"Thank You, Lord," Jill whispered and then she tried more loudly. "Lord, thank You for this Anonymous."

And the others. And the others.

She sighed.

"All right. Yes. And the others. I do thank You for all of them. Bless each and every dear heart who tried to show me I was wrong or incorrect or, at the very least, off base. Thank You for speaking to me through them, for adjusting my lenses and giving me a clearer picture of the great God You are. I am sorry—"

The phone rang again.

Jill closed her eyes. "I am sorry for losing sight of Your awesomeness. I am sorry for thinking I could explain Your ways like I have an inside track. I am sorry for being so totally, self-righteously, priggishly black-and-white."

340

The phone stopped ringing.

"It's not that I expect everyone to agree—well, maybe I did. I won't anymore. And I won't tell You how to do things. I take my hands off of Jack and my work. I give everything and everyone up to You."

The phone rang.

Jill sank to the floor and covered her ears. She needed to hear from the Holy One who loved her and liked her and would never let her down—before she heard from her unhappy husband.

❧

Late the afternoon of her Reality Check Day, Jill washed her face. Her reflection in the mirror showed an extra five years settling into under-eye bags, sallow skin, and tired hairstyle. *Help me, Lord.*

Her stomach rumbled and she headed downstairs to the kitchen, determined to finish out the Reality Check Day with dinner by herself. Both Gretchen and Nan had offered to meet her at a restaurant, but she felt the need to complete the day as she had begun it: alone. No time like the present to get accustomed to that new reality.

The doorbell rang.

She went perfectly still, bent over, eyes level with a carton of milk inside the fridge.

It was dark outside but early yet, a cold, early April evening. Maybe kids were selling something, raising funds for school. Maybe a neighbor needed a cup of flour. Maybe the teen across the street wanted Jack to look at his ankle again.

A new unease settled over her. She was home alone. She was a sitting duck for predators.

Did she have to answer the door?

No way was she answering the door.

All the neighbors had her phone number. She should turn the ringer back on.

There was a faint sound of the dead bolt clicking open.

Someone had a key!

The door opened.

"Jill!" It was Jack's voice.

"Oh." Heart pounding, she shut the refrigerator and leaned against it. "Oh."

"Jill?"

"In the kitchen." She pressed a hand against her chest and struggled to breathe normally. What was he doing using the front door? He always came in through the garage.

He walked in from the living room. "I wasn't sure if . . . I'm sorry. Did I scare you?"

She simply looked at him.

"I tried calling. You didn't answer."

"Why are you here?"

"To see you."

"What if I don't want to see you?" Her heart thudded harder against her hand. "Huh? What if I don't want to talk to you? You get to move out and not call and decide you don't want to talk until *whenever*. I'm here in our house where you don't live but have a key to and can come in whenever you feel like it."

"I'll come back another time."

"Don't do that, Jack! Don't quit on me!"

"I don't understand."

"What's to understand? Our marriage has gone to hell in a hand-basket and you're leaving again. Stay here and talk to me." Her throat felt like it was closing shut. "Stay here and address us, whatever that means."

"You said you don't want to see or talk to me."

Jill wanted to scream. "No, I did not say that, Jack."

He spread his arms wide. "I'm lost here. Care to explain?"

"I am simply emoting. It makes no sense. You are welcome to be the voice of reason here."

He lowered his arms. "I should know this one."

"Chapter 2, Easy Eggs." *Everyday female stuff. We emote.* It was a lost cause.

He walked over to her and gently thumbed a damp spot on her cheek. "I'm trying."

Whatever. She noticed then his blue jeans and ecru cable-knit sweater. "Why aren't you wearing a coat? It's freezing outside."

He glanced down as if to see what he wore. "It's been a strange day. And I would like to tell you about it."

She took a shaky breath, pretty sure that she did not want to hear his voice of reason.

CHAPTER 55

———— ❧ ————

JACK SAT ACROSS from Jill, both in their recliners in the upright position, mugs of tea on the end tables. The gas fire emitted heat, but the chamomile was growing cold.

He asked about her day. She declined talking about it. He wasn't sure where civility fit in this new space.

He told her about his day, beginning with Mrs. Stanton, his loud fussing at Sophie, his fear, the scene in Baxter's office . . . and the trigger point that unleashed his memory.

Jill said, "Dena. Your old girlfriend from college?"

"Yes."

"You didn't tell me."

"I just remembered today."

"Oh, that's right."

"This is confusing."

"What did she want?"

"This is where it gets really confusing."

"I'm listening."

He nodded. "Jill, there's something I never told you about Dena."

345

She stared at him. He could almost see her imagination clicking into high gear behind those blue eyes.

Jack had told Jill almost everything about Dena, how they dated as students at the University of Illinois. She wanted to be a nurse and so they shared a common interest in medicine. They had briefly lived together. Junior year they drifted apart. He was accepted into podiatry school in North Chicago; she left at the semester break to go home to Ohio and care for her mother.

That was what he had told Jill.

"What didn't you tell me?" she asked.

"Dena got pregnant. She had an abortion."

Jill sat up straighter, her eyes large. "Your girlfriend had an abortion and you never told me?" Disbelief filled her voice.

"I couldn't. At first it was because I was ashamed. Then time passed and I buried it deeper and deeper until I'd convinced myself it had nothing to do with us."

"A major decision and hurt in your life and it had nothing to do with us?"

"As a twenty-year-old it was more of a major relief."

"Jack, I can hardly believe that you wouldn't tell me."

"I *couldn't*. You can't relate. When have you ever done something so sickeningly regrettable that you can't even admit it to yourself? You haven't. So don't judge me on that count."

"I'm not, but it is a betrayal to me."

"It is and I am deeply sorry for that."

Jill's lips were pressed together. He had never seen her so angry.

The burden of secret-carrying lifted, but he was filled with such remorse for everyone involved, his stomach ached. "Dena left school because of it. We never tried to contact each other after that. She told me that she married and was never able to have children. The doctor I drove her to and paid for caused internal damage. She and her husband eventually adopted three children."

"Why did she come to see you now?"

"She needed closure. I mean we never even said good-bye. The weird thing is she came because of you. She listens to your program. It changed her life, especially the teaching on forgiveness. She wanted to tell me that she had forgiven me."

"Good for her. Good for you." The bitter tone spoke volumes. Forgiveness was not on Jill's agenda.

He leaned forward, elbows on his knees, wishing he could be the knight she wanted, wishing he could comfort her. "Dena's visit brought me to my senses. I saw what a fool I've been to play the guinea pig. Honestly, how could I not tell you the truth? It wasn't because I was afraid you wouldn't forgive me. It was because of what you would do with it."

"Do with it?"

"You'd turn it into a lesson plan."

"That's unfair, Jack!"

"Is it? Why wouldn't you? The thing is, every time you make us an example, I am reminded of how I don't measure up, of how I'm not a knight in shining armor. Never was, never will be."

They stared at each other, not saying a word.

"Jack, what do you want?"

"I don't want to snap in two. We had something good once, but it's dead and gone. I can't live with who we are anymore. It's over. I want out of our marriage."

Jill stood. "Please leave the key when you go." Her voice was cool. Calmly, she strode from the room.

CHAPTER 56

———— ❧ ————

JILL WATCHED THE sweep of the second hand on the large clock on the wall and mouthed its clicks.

Five, four, three, two, one.

The minute hand touched the twelve.

"Good morning and welcome to *Recipes for Marriage*. I'm Jill Galloway, your host. Our topic today is Honoring Our Husbands. This is a prerecorded program, so we are unable to take your phone calls at this time.

"Speaking of husbands, I'd like to say something to mine on this twenty-seventh day of April. Happy birthday, Jack. This one is for you, honey."

The more Jill talked into the mike, the less she warbled. The less she warbled, the more confident she felt. Maybe she really and truly could do this.

Viv, Gretchen, Nan, and Pastor Lew all believed in her ability to do this, to record a program again. It was her first since the craziness with Jack began. It would also be her last.

Nine days ago Jack walked out of their marriage. Unlike his first pronouncement in February, this one was final. Unlike that time, it had come within hours of her prayer. *I take my hands off of Jack and my work. I give everything and everyone up to You.*

Sometimes God's replies made no sense whatsoever.

In the desolate days that followed, she remembered Agnes's words: *"God loves to draw us closer to Himself, close enough to hear His heartbeat."*

The thing about hearing a heartbeat was that it meant her ear must be very close to the source. She imagined herself at the breast of God, enveloped by the Almighty's arms, a lullaby being hummed above her.

Nourished and strengthened by the extraordinary image, Jill put one foot in front of the other and arrived at this moment, back at her microphone.

"Two dear friends are here with me in the studio today. Nan Zimmer is the station manager and Gretchen MacKelvie is my agent. Between us we have something like sixty years of marriage experience. Welcome, ladies."

Jill listened to her friends chat and fiddled with the control panel. She noticed the engineer in the hallway, a hovering grandfatherly type. They were all there ready to catch her if she fell.

But in her mind she focused on one person. For the next hour she would speak directly to her. Anonymous remained nameless, but Jill had given the letter writer a brown ponytail, a pleasant fortysomething face, three teenagers, and a resolve to move on.

Now Jill introduced the subject of Connor and Emma's wedding vows. She asked Gretchen and Nan about their own vows. She recalled that she had stated to Jack a commitment to honor him.

"Those of you who are regular listeners know that I'm all about being personal here. That I am candid to a fault at times. Those things may make for snappy radio dialogue, but I believe they also led to the dishonoring of my husband.

"I want to publicly apologize for treating him like a guinea pig and then airing my test results on this program and publishing them in my book. Jack, I am sorry for dishonoring you in private and in public."

She had no appropriate segue after such a statement. *"I hope you'll forgive me while we take a break?"*

"Okay." She more or less exhaled the word. "It's time for our first break. When we come back, we'll explore the flip side. How do we honor our husbands?"

Gretchen slipped off her headset and sighed loudly.

Nan's brows rose.

Jill shrugged.

Nan nodded. "Succinct and heartfelt."

Gretchen said, "Flaming perfect."

Nan's eyes narrowed.

Gretchen grinned. "What? The mike's off."

Jill looked at the clock. She needed to stay on task, to work as if they were live.

Nan touched her hand. "I'll do the blah-blah part."

"Okay. On five, four, three, two, one."

Jill let Nan introduce the next segment and refocused her thoughts. *Here we go, Anonymous. Are you listening?*

They talked about definitions of the word *honor* as it applied between spouses: to respect, to esteem, to treat with courtesy.

"How do you see yourselves doing that with your husbands?"

Gretchen said, "Honoring can be as simple as treating him like a friend. I listen, make eye contact, give him the benefit of the doubt, buy him gifts, let him choose the restaurant sometimes. I tell him he's wonderful."

Nan said, "I keep a list of his attributes."

"Really?" Jill interrupted, surprised at this tidbit her friend had never mentioned.

Nan chuckled. "After thirty-five years, it's easy to take each other for granted. I need reminders of the positive. Otherwise I tend to dwell on his imperfections."

Jill played recorded voice mails from women who answered the same question. Several had called in during the past week in response to an e-mail she had sent out to the listeners in her address book. Their variety of replies had made her laugh and cry and wish she had done an in-depth program on the subject ages ago.

She had so much to learn about being a wife who honored her husband.

At one point Gretchen held up a note: *Can we talk about bedroom perks?*

Nan ducked her head under the table, laughing.

They took an unscheduled break.

Eventually Jill asked the question for Anonymous. "Why do we want to honor our husbands?"

Gretchen said, "Why wouldn't we? We're in this relationship. I'd rather spend my time living in sync than butting heads."

"In other words you do it to keep him happy?"

Gretchen blinked. "Nah. That can't be it because I am not able to make him happy. Not my job."

"Then you honor him in order to keep the peace?"

Nan said, "It doesn't guarantee peace either. He still might act like a jerk. We're not talking abuse here, but people are people, imperfect to the core."

Jill played the voice mail responses to this second question. There weren't as many as for the first because most simply said, "Because God said to do it."

She saved her favorite for last.

The woman's voice was thoughtful and confident. "Honoring him is how I love him. It's how I affirm him as a man. I think this is my unique role as his wife. I'm in the best position to see him as God does, full of potential and perfect in Christ. Sometimes that disturbs him because it reminds him that he falls short. So no, I don't honor him in hopes that it will make him happy or even feel good. I honor him because that's what a friend does."

Jill said, "I'd like to end by piggybacking on this listener's insight. As a wife, I have the opportunity unlike anyone else to honor my husband. I am not called to an impossible task of making him happy or to ignore his weaknesses. I am not called to accept abuse of any kind. I am called to simply remind him as best I can that he is a cherished human being. What he does with that is up to him."

It might even mean he wants a divorce. I can honor and love and forgive but there is nothing I can do to stop him from moving out.

Nan took over and wrapped things up. "Before we go, I need to make an announcement that for me is personally sad. I know many of you will feel the same. This has been Jill's final *Recipes for Marriage* program with us. She is taking a sabbatical from radio. We will miss you, Jill."

"Thanks, Nan. I will miss everyone here at the station and all of you listeners. Thank you for your love and support through the years. And, Jack, happy birthday. I love you, old friend."

❧

Jill went home, relieved to have completed the final program, tearful good-byes at the station, and a last supper with Nan. She had visited her in-laws, enjoyed a rare exchange of honesty, and received their blessing—and Katherine's tears—on her plans. She had made the difficult call to Connor, who said with a new maturity that he was sorry.

Barring a surprise call from Jack announcing that he wanted to kiss and make up, she had only one task left to do.

She phoned Sophie at home.

"Sophie, it's Jill. Galloway."

"Mrs. G! Oh, how are you? I have been so concerned."

"Uh, thank you." What a nincompoop she'd been to waste energy being jealous of this woman simply because she happened to work in Jack's office and saw him more than his own wife did. Jill could have worked in Jack's office if she'd wanted to. She hadn't wanted to.

"Sophie, I have a favor to ask, for Jack."

"Anything. You two are, well, you're just really important to me."

Yes, major nincompoop. "Thank you. I taped a program today and I'd like Jack to hear it. It'll be aired on the twenty-seventh."

"His birthday, at eleven o'clock?"

Again Jill was taken aback. Sophie knew the date of course, but the time of her program? "That's it. Do you think you could arrange for him to listen to it?"

"No problem."

"Wow. Just like that?"

"I run the place, Mrs. G." There was a smile in her voice, no conceit. "I am the keeper of the schedule. If you want him in his office by himself with the radio tuned to your station at that time on that date, consider it done."

Jill sighed. "I can't tell you how much this means to me."

"Will you try to tell me?"

She heard the worry in Sophie's voice. "What has he told you?"

"Not much. He went home last Monday looking ill. He said he remembered the day of the accident. Dr. Baxter and I considered that a good thing, although probably exhausting. He called in sick on Tuesday. On Wednesday, a week ago today, he met with me and Dr. Baxter. He told us that he . . . that he was not moving back—" sniffling noises came through the line— "back home. Since then he's been his regular self. Well, sort of. It's hard to explain."

That about summed it up. It was all hard to explain. Jill had not talked with Jack since that night. He had left one voice mail, saying that if it was all right with her, he wasn't ready to discuss divorce details. He had opened his own bank account but would continue to deposit his salary in their joint account. He named a small sum that he would keep to cover his own rent and expenses.

His tone had been nondescript, as if he were talking solely about banking and not the splitting apart of the life they had shared for almost twenty-five years.

Jill said, "This program was my last one."

"Oh, Mrs. G."

"Will you call me Jill, please?"

"O-okay."

"Thanks. Anyway, I can't exactly keep up this show about how to make marriage work when my own isn't working."

"I always thought it was more about how to communicate better."

Jill felt her eyes widen.

"I mean, you know of course that I'm single. But I picked up priceless gems on how to relate better with my parents and friends. Even patients. And now I'm dating this guy and, well, thank you."

"You listen to the program?"

"Some. Not all the time. I have to admit that it was intimidating to hear you on the radio, knowing your voice was broadcast all over Chicagoland and beyond, and then to take messages from you for Dr. G."

"Hm." She had no other response.

"What will you do now?"

It was the question that woke her up in the night. The answer never changed. As Nan had announced, she was taking a sabbatical. It couldn't happen in Chicago in her house with no work, no Connor, no Jack.

She cleared her throat. "Just between us? I have to be the one to tell Jack."

"Not a problem. You have no idea how much I don't tell him. For his own good."

Jill had to smile. "I'm going out to California. Indefinitely." Definitely no more than two weeks at Viv and Marty's, though. She was already apartment hunting online. "I'll help out my sister in her tour business for a while."

"That sounds like a break you probably need, but I hope you'll write and speak more. Your book is fantastic. And I'm not just saying that because you're my boss's wife."

Jill shook her head in surprise and smiled. She had wanted to burn all the copies, but the publisher refused to pull even one off the shelf. It was selling. Gretchen thought current blog gossip about the Galloways' breakup accounted for some of it.

Sophie said, "I've started my own recipe collection for talking with patients."

"You have a cookbook in the works!" Jill laughed. "Tell me more."

They chatted, the old barriers of jealousy and intimidation melting away to nothingness.

CHAPTER 57

JACK CHECKED THE caller ID on his ringing cell phone, saw Jill's name, and took a quick internal survey.

It seemed a stupid habit, this emotional temperature check. He hadn't felt like snapping in a long time. Was that because he hadn't lived with Jill for two months and hadn't talked to her at all recently? or because he had confessed everything to her and neither she nor God had struck him dead?

He muted the television. "Hello."

"Hi, Jack."

Silence—on both ends.

He scratched his head.

"Awkward moment between the 'rents." For good reason. Where could they pick up after their last conversation in which he said he wanted out of the marriage and she said, "Leave the key"?

She said, "How are you?"

"Okay. You?"

"Okay. I'm sorry about the key. It's just that you scared me that night."

"I know. Actually I still have a garage opener."

"Oh."

Household details like this were unending and driving him nuts. Bank accounts, bills, credit cards, some of his clothes still there, some cookware, tools, boots, golf clubs.

He said, "I won't come inside without telling you first."

"It's still your house too. I was just scared."

"All right."

"Well, I, um, I called to tell you that I'm in San Diego. Just arrived. So you can go inside the house whenever you want."

"San Diego? Why . . . ? What . . . ?" He couldn't get his mind wrapped around what she had said.

"The truth is, Jack, you can move back into the house. I don't want to live in it."

"But where would you live?"

"Out here. I'm staying out here for a—a while. I can work with Viv. She's coming into the busy season."

"Jill, why would you do that?"

"Why wouldn't I? You don't live with me. Connor's moving to New York."

"But your work here—"

"Is changing and that's not your fault. It's time for me to talk less and listen more. Jack, I want to say once and for all that I forgive you for keeping the abortion a secret. I understand why you couldn't tell me. I never meant to make you think that you had to be perfect, but I know I did. I hope you can forgive me. I do love you, but I'll sign divorce papers. Send them to Viv's. And . . . and that's all. Good-bye."

He felt dazed, as if her rushed words circled his head, searching for a place to land.

"I said good-bye, Jack." She hadn't hung up.

"Uh, uh—"

"I have to go. Viv's here now."

"Uh, okay. Bye."

Now she hung up.

"I forgive you. . . . I hope you can forgive me. . . . I do love you. . . ."

Jack set down the phone. He didn't feel anything like a rubber band stretched to its snapping point. He wasn't sure what he felt besides empty.

He hit the Mute button on the television remote and let his attention drift again into the history of wildlife on the Mississippi River.

⁂

In the harsh light of morning, Jill's news struck him like the proverbial two-by-four to the side of the head.

Their marriage was over.

The sense of finality chilled him to the bone. It filled his veins with ice water.

He cut himself twice while shaving. He dropped his full coffee mug. It shattered and splashed across the kitchen floor. He let it go and sat on the couch. He stayed there for at least an hour, unmoving, his thoughts frozen in place.

And then he called Lew Mowers.

He sat now in the pastor's office. There had been no waiting for an appointment for Jill Galloway's husband. Lew and his wife adored her as did hundreds of congregants.

Why didn't Jack?

Lew was a big guy, a man's man with steel gray hair cut in military style who somehow exuded an almost-feminine compassion. His jovial smile had yet to appear. He nodded and hummed agreement throughout Jack's story.

Jack ended with Jill's news. "It's what I wanted. But it's not what I wanted. I sound like an adolescent."

"Or, some would say, like a man having a midlife crisis. I don't like labels myself, but you are in midlife and you are having a crisis of identity." He shrugged. "Back up to the time period you and Jill interacted while preparing for Connor's wedding. What was it like between the two of you?"

Jack felt himself blush. They had been intimate. Biological need or loving response to their shared days? "Uh, we put the divorce question on hold and focused on other things." Not counting that one night. "And, uh, Jill was in a good place."

"Her usual self?"

Her usual self. As in freaking out, stressing out, bossing others, interviewing-slash-interrogating everyone, recording ideas for future lesson plans? No.

"No, she was not her usual self. There was a . . . softness about her. She was relaxed."

"She'd been through a lot up to that point. Your wanting a divorce. Connor and Emma's surprise. The accident and seeing her friend die. Planning a wedding, which throws most women into a tizzy. What was up with the relaxed persona?"

"I have no idea."

"Stress like she experienced usually brings out the worst in a person. Unless it breaks them and God works a healing."

Jack blinked. Jill had not been at her worst, but . . . "It seems a little pat."

Lew shrugged again. "At any rate, it's her story, not yours. God can remake her until the cows come home but that's not going to change your story, is it?"

Jack returned his gaze for a long moment. "My story being that I blame her for my guinea pig lifestyle and now it's her fault that my only feeling toward her is a rubber band stretched to its limits."

"Oh, it's already done snapped, Jack. It's over. The past is over. From here on out is your choice. Choose life with or without God's forgiveness and healing."

Tears sprang to his eyes. "How do I choose with?"

Lew smiled. "Spend some time on your knees and then do what He tells you to do. Want me to help you get started?"

❧

"Dr. G!" Sophie practically jumped from her chair as he entered the office. She called out across the counter into the waiting room, "Where have you been? It's ten forty-five!"

"I left a message—"

"Hours ago!" She was behaving un-Sophie-like again.

Jack stole a glance at the gawking patients and hurried through the door into the back area. "Are you all right?" he whispered.

Strands of hair had escaped the bun and hung about her mottled face. "And where is your cell phone? It's in your pocket, isn't it? Turned off, isn't it?"

"Oops." He pulled the phone from a deep pocket of his raincoat and glanced at it. Eight missed calls, most likely from Sophie. "I'm sorry. What did you need?"

"You! Just go." She shooed him down the hall. "Oh. Happy birthday."

"Birthday—It's my birthday. I hadn't given it a thought. Thanks."

Sophie pointed toward his office. "Hurry."

Smiling, he walked down the hall. Sophie was flustered because it was his birthday and he was behind her surprise schedule. She remembered everyone's day with something special. He expected to find balloons tied to his chair, a wrapped gift and a cake on his desk, a homemade carrot cake.

He entered his office and noticed nothing out of the ordinary. Odd, but then everything had seemed odd since kneeling with Lew earlier. Odd and amazing. The world looked different, almost off-kilter and yet more right than ever. He'd never be able to describe it to Baxter.

Jack wasn't quite sure how to transition into doctor mode. He hung up his overcoat and put on his lab coat. Maybe that would help.

"Knock, knock." Baxter entered his office, a radio in his hand, Sophie on his heels.

She shut the door. "Happy birthday, Dr. G."

"Oh yeah," Baxter said. "Birthday greetings, bud."

"Thanks. Is that my gift?" He nodded at the radio.

"It might be." Baxter smiled and set it on his desk.

"Sit, Dr. G." Sophie nudged him toward his chair while Baxter plugged in the radio. "Now—" she took a deep breath and smoothed back her hair—"since you are so late, we have to skip over staff gifts and go straight to this." She pointed at the radio. "This is a birthday gift from Mrs. G. She asked me to make sure you heard her program today."

Jack sank into his chair. Jill had set something up for him? And he thought his time with Lew was a surprise.

Baxter turned on the radio and adjusted the volume. "We're going to listen with you."

Jack gave them a puzzled look.

Sophie sat and straightened her skirt over her knees. "Because we don't know if this is a good thing or not. She didn't tell me that part."

Jack smiled. "Of course it's a good thing. It's from my wife."

※

It was both a good thing and not.

Jack's smile waned a bit as he met Sophie's tearful gaze and Baxter's somber expression. He said, "She loves me."

"It was her final show?" Sophie sounded as if she could not believe her own ears.

Jack said, "I think she meant it. That she still loves me in spite of everything."

"Her final show?"

Baxter said, "Sophie, you're repeating yourself. Change is part of life. If we're not changing, that means we're dead and somebody ought to bury us."

Sophie frowned.

Jack said, "She told me the other day that her work was changing and that it was not my fault. Although my actions did have an impact, she is okay with moving on."

"How about you?" Baxter said. "What are you going to do?"

His smile returned, an involuntary action caused by a sense of unfathomable serenity. "Remember those weeks of vacation I didn't take?"

Baxter laughed. "It's about time."

CHAPTER 58

——— ❧ ———

Daisy crossed one leg over the other and swung it briskly. "Do you think he's heard it yet?"

Jill eyed her mother across Viv's kitchen table. "Mom, you're perfectly capable of figuring out the time zone difference. If it's ten o'clock Pacific time, it's noon in Chicago."

"Jillian, I know the program aired already. That is not my question."

Jill bit her lip and looked through the patio door. Her father paced the sunny backyard, back and forth, back and forth, his ball cap pulled down low over his eyes.

Viv carried three glasses of iced tea over from the counter. "From everything I've heard about Sophie through the years, my bet is yes, Jack has heard Jill's formal apology and expression of love."

Daisy said, "So why hasn't he called?"

"Because it's two minutes past the hour."

Jill said, "I don't expect him to call."

Daisy shook her head. "And you were always the optimistic one."

Jill made an effort not to roll her eyes.

When Viv had told Skip and Daisy that Jack and Jill were officially split up, they drove over from Sweetwater to be there when she arrived. At first, Jill appreciated their loving gesture, but soon she realized that besides offering comfort, they were in need of it themselves. She felt depleted.

Daisy reached over and patted her arm. "You were always the chipper one too."

"I'll be fine, Mom. I need some time to rest."

"By working with Vivian? I don't call that rest. You should come home with us. Pops and I can wait on you, hand and foot."

"I need to walk." *Or pace.* Jill went out the sliding door and shut it. She spotted the stack of printed pages on the patio table. The top papers fluttered in the light breeze.

It was the transcript of her final show. She had given it to Viv, who read it and passed it on to their parents before she could stop her.

"Pops."

Skip stopped his pacing, placed his hands on his hips, and waited for her to walk over to him. "You gave in, Jaws. You let him take your voice away."

"I did not."

"You quit the vocation that you were gifted to do."

"I quit that particular show, that format, that eight-year focus on marital communication."

"You were forced to, considering that your marriage went south."

"I wasn't forced, Pops. Not really. It wasn't so much my marriage as the work that went south. It had taken on this nuance of rule keeping and manipulation and guarantees. Like, if you tell your husband twice a day that he is the most wonderful and smartest man who has ever walked the face of the earth, he will be fulfilled and contented and probably happy. Or if you greet him at the door wearing lipstick and little else, he will fall at your feet and give you whatever you want."

Skip's chin dipped and he squinted. "That last one has some merit."

"It's borderline prostitution."

"What is wrong with you? No, don't tell me. You and Jack have problems with—with . . . you know. I hear there's medication and stuff."

She held back a smile. He was endearing when he got flustered. She kept going. "The last time I tried that little lipstick-only enticement on Jack, he said he had a headache and he really was not interested in planning a trip to Italy to see Connor."

"This is too much information."

She grinned. "Pops, you need to calm down."

"Oh, ha-ha. I think you're the one who needs to calm down. Jaws, you just talk too much sometimes."

"Listen to one more. Seriously. This is my favorite. If you go to church every week, tithe, pray together, and argue according to certain guidelines, then nothing can touch your marriage. You are set for life. Happily ever after."

He pursed his lips and blinked.

Oh no. He was going to cry.

"Jillie, that describes you and Jack. That was your way of life."

"Yes, and I encouraged every married couple to live likewise. Obviously, they are good things. They enriched our relationship. But they are not the guarantee I sealed them with. We are flawed human beings, Pops. I never wanted to admit that before. I wouldn't let Jack admit it either."

He nodded. "All right. I get it."

"So." She tilted her head. "You want to know a secret?"

"No thanks. I've had my fill for the day."

She smiled at his quick answer, but he was her dad, the only person who had ever handled her difficult side with compassion. "I was getting bored with the show."

"Since when?"

"I don't know. It was something else I refused to recognize. I was too scared. What would I do instead of the show? Who would I be instead?" She shrugged. "Now I'm back where I started, working with Viv, one of the Wagner sisters carting senior citizens around Southern California."

"Jack will get his head screwed on right again. You two are going to be fine."

"Let's not count on it, Pops. I did the program to publicly apologize for the way I publicly dishonored him. I think he'll appreciate it, but it's not going to catapult us into a new marriage. We've been going separate directions for too long."

"Don't you want to go the same direction?"

She spread her arms. "Pops, what else can I do? He left me."

"I said, don't you want to go the same direction?"

She frowned. "Of course I do. But he doesn't want to!"

"Then we keep on praying that he changes his mind." Skip wrapped her in a hug in time to catch her first sob.

CHAPTER 59

———— ❧ ————

JILL CHECKED THE side mirror and steered the twelve-passenger van into the left lane. No one honked at her freeway maneuver. "Hallelujah."

"Hm?" Beside her in the passenger seat, Viv shut her cell phone.

"I said, how's Dustin doing on his own with the bus?"

"Fine."

"You shouldn't keep texting him while he's driving."

"He shouldn't keep texting back while he's driving."

Jill groaned to herself. Viv was a bundle of nerves over her bus in Dustin's hands without her along to chaperone a trip to the Safari Park. It had been Viv's own decision, though, a totally unnecessary one from Jill's point of view.

But she did not tell her sister that. After several days of depending on Viv and Marty's gracious hospitality, she was not about to judge the whys and wherefores of Viv's tour planning.

Still, this day's itineraries were skewed. Jill could have driven the van to the park with a handful of adventuresome seniors who planned to do the zip line. It could have been her first solo, an easy forty-five-minute drive.

Dustin could have driven the bus with the six Casitas Pack members now packed into the van. Viv—cast-free but not yet ready to drive a tour—could have gone with him to supervise his drive through busy Los Angeles—

"Oh no. I am so dense." Jill was not being flippant. This was a fact. There had been several indicators in recent days of nonworking mental facilities. Disengaged from work and overly engaged with getting accustomed to life without Jack, her brain had gone into some limbo space.

Viv said, "What did you miss now?"

"Why you insisted I take this trip. We're not going to the art museum, are we? We're going to Grauman's. You think I need to return to the handprint and then I'll get over what happened there the last time."

Viv turned toward her, eyes hidden behind sunglasses. "Yes, you are way dense if you just now figured that out."

"Viv. I do not need this! I am doing fine."

"Sorry." She cocked her head toward the back. "We disagree. We think it's time."

Jill looked in the rearview mirror. Some of the ladies must have overheard. They smiled at her reflection.

How she missed Agnes! She might trust Agnes with this crazy idea. But—

Someone touched her shoulder. It was Cynthia, seated directly behind her. "God knows how much it hurts. But there is healing in going back and facing it. And we'll all be with you."

Jill kept her eyes on the freeway traffic. Go back to where she first prayed to love the world in a big way? to where she first met Jack, the man who encouraged her to pursue her dreams?

No way. Nohow. She did not need to be reminded of her failed plot to fix their marriage. Waking every morning in her sister's house was reminder enough of that.

※

Jill figured she would drop the ladies off at Grauman's Chinese Theatre, park the van, and find a coffee shop. Agnes's friends could shower all the love in the world on her, but she was not going to intentionally set foot in the place where her dreams were born and then crushed to smithereens.

But Viv didn't exit with the ladies. She went with her to park the van, and then she pulled on Jill's arm to get her to move down the crowded sidewalk, hissing in her ear.

They must look ridiculous.

"Jill, if you won't do this for yourself, do it for me. I cannot stand your moping any longer. I can't. I simply can't."

"Well, excuse me for being real with you. I'll move to a hotel tomorrow. Tonight even."

"You can't live in a hotel."

"I can't live with Mom and Pops. But anyway, I'm not moping."

"Of course you're moping. The last you heard, Jack wants out. Why wouldn't you be angry and heartbroken and mopey?"

"Why don't you rub it in?" She was out of breath, trying to keep up with Viv's long strides. "I am doing better though."

Viv stopped and looked at her, hand still gripped on her elbow. "Yes, you are, Jill. And I think I am too. But it's just so hard. We're all hurting. Even Marty feels bad." Tears shimmered in her eyes. "So will you please, please give this a try? Go in there and put your hands in Shirley's prints and remember how you wanted to have a heart like hers."

"Vivvie, why are you making me do this?"

"Because this is where you get your dreams and it's time for a new one."

Jill wiped her blouse sleeve across her face. "You are the crummiest little sister."

"You're the crummiest big one." Viv kissed her cheek. "I love you."

For a moment Jill took in the scene before her. People milled around the forecourt, bending over, reading the famous names, touching the impressions of hands and feet and autographs, talking and laughing, calling out to one another. The red pagoda with its fierce dragons loomed skyward.

Maybe Viv was right. Maybe it was time for a new dream.

Jill walked the familiar route, over the names of actors famous when her grandparents were alive. Thinking of how many times she had visited and how it always thrilled her, she couldn't help but smile. Other people had grand cathedrals or mountaintops or forests to speak to them. She had a silly tourist attraction.

At Shirley Temple's slab of concrete, she paused.

Oh, well. Why not?

She knelt and placed her hands in the little-girl prints. She read the inscription: *Love to you all.*

Lord, whatever is next, I just want to love You.

"They almost fit."

Random moments from the past week suddenly joined together in a pattern. Viv's quick phone hang-ups, Dustin's uncharacteristic stammering and blushing, Viv and Marty's secretive whispering, Marty's quirky smile that morning, today's illogical driver arrangements, the senior ladies' effusiveness beyond their typical style.

Jill's breath caught. She leaned back and looked up into the kindest eyes she had ever seen. The man's smile finished her off, though. It was absolutely perfect with lips not too thin or too full, the corners of his mouth dimpling inward and upward just so.

Jack held out his hand. "Actually I think they fit perfectly for a woman who has loved the world in a big way."

She placed her hand in his and he pulled her to her feet. Still trying to catch up to the moment, Jill felt dazed. Jack was there. What did he want? She had things to do. An apartment to find. A van to drive.

He smiled again. "Hi. I'm Jack Galloway."

It was an echo from twenty-five years ago.

"Hi. Jill Wagner."

"Hello, Jill. I've honestly never done this before, walked up to a complete stranger to ask her if she'd like to go to dinner."

Jill smiled. "Are you asking me to dinner?"

"Yes, I am."

"On what grounds?"

"You look like an angel." He touched one of his own cheeks. "The Raphael-type cherub."

"That's enough?"

"It is for me."

"It's original anyway." She heard her coy tone.

His smile diminished. "You're in a relationship?"

She wanted to see the smile again on those wonderful lips. "Oh no, not at all. I have to tell my sister. We rode together."

"All right."

Jill glanced around and saw Viv, right where she had been that first time. She waved her over. "Viv, this guy wants to take me to dinner."

Viv slipped out of character, burst into tears, and hurried away.

Jill said, "She's no fun."

"That's okay. I forget what came next."

"Viv said, 'Take her to dinner? Only dinner? You can take her for good.' And then you looked like you were having second thoughts."

"I love you, Jill."

"That's not what you said."

He stepped closer to her. "I'm having second thoughts about us. I don't want to be separated from you. I don't want to be divorced."

Jill looked at his hazel eyes, the pronounced crow's-feet around them, the laugh creases at his mouth. He had aged in the last few months. Something else had come with the deeper lines. He seemed more real. Solid. Wiser?

She had to ask. "Why now?"

"Well . . ." He paused and seemed to wrestle with his answer.

"Jack, I'm not taking notes. There's no reason to hold back anymore."

He smiled. "Yeah, I guess that's the whole thing. In a nutshell, the truth finally sank in. I know I am loved and forgiven by you and God. Can you imagine the freedom in that? I don't have to cross my t's and dot my i's in order to be accepted."

She smiled at his echo of her words to him. "You didn't know that before?"

"No. I mean, I did in my head, but not in my heart, not where it changes me and makes me new. Jill, I have so much to tell you."

"Hm." Where had this man come from?

"I couldn't call you right away. I had a few things to process. You may not realize it, but there's a lot to becoming a knight. Lew's been helping."

Knight? Pastor Lew?

"And the flip side is I love and forgive you. You're free to be you and I realize that means teaching and speaking—"

"Maybe not—"

"We'll figure it out later." He cupped her face in his hands. "Do you remember me saying that I didn't sign up for this?"

Despite the comforting touch of his hands, she winced. "You didn't sign up for a wife who has all the answers."

"I'm sorry. That wasn't accurate. What I didn't sign up for was losing my best friend. Jill, can we start over? become friends again?"

"Oh yes." She sighed. "I'd like that."

Jack kissed her, right there at Shirley's handprints, surrounded by hordes of strangers, some of whom began to clap.

CHAPTER 60

——— ❧ ———

Jill watched Jack drink his orange juice. The morning sun shone in his mussed hair, highlighting the gray strands. He wore a white terry-cloth robe with the hotel's logo embroidered on its front.

He set his goblet on the table and rested an elbow on the balcony railing. "What?"

"I'm a little gun-shy." She tightened the belt on her robe.

"Understandable. The last time we spent the night together, I left. Not to mention I moved out and said I wanted a divorce. Jill, I promise that's not ever happening again."

Her smile wobbled. "It'll take some time to trust in that."

"I know. I'll give you all the time you need. I'll say it as often as you need to hear it."

"Okay."

They had talked all yesterday afternoon and late into the night. Mostly Jack talked. She moved as if in a daze. Not only had Viv and everyone been in on his surprise, her sister had packed an overnight bag for her and announced that her arm was fine and of course she

373

could drive the van home. She had even informed their parents of Jack's scheme, although not early enough for Daisy to spill the beans.

Her husband's scheme had included dinner at the restaurant where they had eaten that first time and a reservation at a fancy hotel that had nothing to do with their history.

Jack said, "I'm gun-shy myself. Every once in a while I wonder if I'm saying or doing things wrong."

"And that I'll correct you and then talk about it on the radio."

"Yes." He smiled. "We may be at this for a really long time."

"I think it's called life."

"We don't want to avoid that." He reached across the table, between the empty plates and the vase with its one rose, and took her hand. "I don't want to avoid any of it, Jill."

They had not yet talked about tomorrow and the day after and the day after. He had addressed other things. Lew's insights. The support of Baxter and Sophie. His ugly apartment. His determination to be real with her. And his birthday, the best ever.

Jack said, "I don't want to avoid the big question either. How do we guard against growing apart again? Once we go home and jump back into regular life, there it goes. I love what I do. I'm not ready to quit, but I have been a workaholic." He squeezed her hand. "Mostly because it was a means to spend less time at home."

Jill's emotions raced through the whole gamut. Anger, chagrin, regret, pain. She reined in the torrent. "That hurts."

He nodded. "I promise to cut back my hours. If you'll have me."

This new side of Jack was growing on her. She narrowed her eyes. "I'll think about it."

He grinned. "Okay. Also, I don't want us to avoid your giftedness."

"Yeah, well, that's up for redefinition."

"Perhaps, but there is something already in motion that we can take care of."

"What?"

"The book."

"The book."

He said, "The one that mentions candlelight and Vivaldi."

"I know which one."

Jack lifted her hand, kissed it, and held it under his chin. "Gretchen is working on a tour schedule that includes the husband. She even thinks women might like me to sign the recipe section."

"Hm."

"Hm."

Her imagination had been like a dead battery for months. Now Jack's words were like jumper cables. Power sparked through them. The engine popped back to life. Ideas raced, eager to be put in gear.

She said, "What about speaking?"

"I'll sit in the back and cheer you on." He had never, ever sat in on one of her sessions.

"I could call on you."

"O-okay."

"Don't worry. You'll be fine. Knights are always welcome." She grinned. "Especially if they're wearing robes like that one. I'm sure it would boost sales too."

The joy in Jack's laughter filled her with new hope. Their marriage would always be a challenge, always an uphill climb with downhill tumbles. To embrace the journey as committed friends, though, offered the hope that it would also be a thing of beauty.

EPILOGUE

———— ❦ ————

EIGHTEEN MONTHS LATER
CHICAGO

Click. Three. *Click.* Two. *Click.* One.

Jill flipped a switch and spoke into the microphone. "Good afternoon and welcome to *Recipes for Midlife.* I'm your host, Jill Galloway, and with me today is my husband, Jack. Welcome, Jack." She smiled at him across the table and felt the tingle that always accompanied the sight of him in the studio.

"Thank you, Jill. It's great to be here."

It had taken some practice not to pause after they greeted each other. Listeners would hear dead air while the two of them grinned at each other like loonies, lost in a moment of wonder. *Is this for real?* They were working together. Jill got to yap to her heart's content. Jack, the kind doctor with no sense of clock watching, was a natural chatterbox.

She said, "As some of you know, whenever Jack shows up, we're going to talk about our travels."

"Excuse me, honey, but we're talking about pasta."

"We're talking about Italy."

377

"There's a difference?"

"Well, let's find out. Stay tuned, folks. I'm sure the chef has a recipe or two in store for us."

Off-air for a minute, they slid into their loony routine.

Eighteen months ago, Jill had predicted marital ups and downs, but she never imagined details of the adventure ahead of them.

They had worked hard to redefine life without quashing their dedication to separate careers that were never going to intersect. Although he cut back on hours at the office, it wasn't enough. Although she revamped her radio show so that it was less demanding, it wasn't enough.

In July they declared a time-out and went to visit Connor and Emma in Italy and the Trudeaus in Paris.

And that was where Jack and Jill discovered how to devote undivided attention to each other. They learned again the meaning of being friends. Away from home, they were forced to set aside their work. Everyday household details were nil. What else was there to do except be together?

When Connor and Emma moved to New York in August, Jack and Jill went there.

After that, they began to explore their own city, then the state, then neighboring ones. Eventually a new idea was hatched. Why not share stories of their travels on Jill's new show? It fit the revamped program. She interviewed people from all walks of life on all kinds of topics. Why not her husband?

The Jack-with-Jill segments became a favorite. Jill listened now as he described a scrumptious Alfredo sauce they had discovered in Venice. In a few minutes callers would be asking him questions and contributing their own recipes, sometimes about food, sometimes about life in general.

She smiled.

For her the show wasn't about the recipes or hotels or places they had found on their trips. No. The Jack-with-Jill segments were all about how a married couple tumbled down a hill and there, at the bottom, discovered each other.

A Note from the Author

DEAR READER FRIEND,

Desert Gift began with a desire to explore the lives of a married couple who, after twenty-five years, find themselves talking divorce. How does this happen after twenty-five years?

Thus the Galloways were born, a poster couple for an idyllic marriage. There are no looming divisive issues between them. So what's up? Simply put, a separateness has crept into their relationship, a thing that seems to be a common occurrence in our fast-paced culture. There is no one-size-fits-all answer.

I let Jack and Jill loose in Chicago and Southern California, two of my all-time favorite places, to find their own way. Jill's trek to the desert parallels her time of despair about her marriage. In the midst of the vast emptiness, wildflowers bloom and healing buds in her own heart. As always, God is there at work in our anguish.

Thank you for traveling this side road with the Galloways. I hope the journey blessed you with laughter, tears, and a general sense of reassurance that God does indeed love you unconditionally, passionately, and wildly.

Peace,
Sally John

E-MAIL: sallyjohnbook@aol.com
WEB SITE: www.sally-john.com
BLOG: http://lifeinthefictionlane.blogspot.com/
FACEBOOK: "Sally John Books" page

Discussion Questions

As A WIFE and mom, Jill is a version of the Christian woman who cares deeply for her family. She loves God's Word, studies it, and applies it to her family relationships. She believes—probably subconsciously—that if she does everything the "right" way, she and her family will not experience any of life's major pitfalls.

Of course in Jill's case, this good and honorable passion is taken to the extreme. She creates formulas for the "right" way and shares them not only with her family but also with countless others, sometimes in an outspoken fashion. This makes her tumble all the more obvious to us.

1. Do you identify with Jill's passion to be a godly woman? What does that passion look like in your life?

2. What has been your experience with tumbles? What has gone awry and taken you by surprise?

3. Jill is all about succeeding at marriage. She fears what will happen to her public image if her marriage fails. What are you "all about"? What is important to you? What would happen if you failed at it?

4. Do you see Jack and Jill's growing apart as inevitable? What might either of them have done to prevent the demise of their marriage?

5. Compare Viv and Marty's marriage to Jack and Jill's.

6. Describe Jill's relationship with her son, Connor. Are there areas in which you identify with either of them?

7. In what ways are you like your mother or father? How do you feel about that?

8. In what ways have you "married" your parent?

9. Healing in the present often begins with a visit to the past, to heart places where forgiveness has not yet been extended or received. Jack and Jill cannot heal as a couple until their individual needs are addressed. What does Jill learn about herself that stems from old wounds? What does Jack learn about himself that must be healed before moving on?

10. The desert is often used as a metaphor for a difficult time in one's life. Describe Jill's desert. What was Jack's desert? Talk about your own desert experiences. What gift did you receive to take with you?

About the Author

WHEN THE GOING gets tough—or weird or wonderful—the daydreamer gets going on a new story. Sally John has been tweaking life's moments into fiction since she read her first Trixie Belden mystery as a child.

Now an author of more than fifteen novels, Sally writes stories that reflect contemporary life. Her passion is to create a family, turn their world inside out, and then portray how their relationships change with each other and with God. Her goal is to offer hope to readers in their own relational and faith journeys.

Sally grew up in Moline, Illinois, graduated from Illinois State University, married Tim in 1973, and taught in middle schools. She is a mother, mother-in-law, and grandmother. A three-time finalist for the Christy Award, she also teaches writing workshops. Her books include the Safe Harbor series (coauthored with Gary Smalley), The Other Way Home series, The Beach House series, and the In a Heartbeat series. Many of her stories are set in her favorite places of San Diego, Chicago, and small-town Illinois.

She and her husband currently live in Southern California. Visit her Web site at www.sally-john.com.

don't miss the next book in the SIDE ROADS series

Turn the page for an exciting preview.

AVAILABLE SPRING 2012

PROLOGUE

———— ✿ ————

At precisely twelve minutes and thirty-five seconds past ten o'clock in the morning, Pacific Daylight Time, Teal Morgan-Adams's world ceased to exist.

She knew the exact time because the NPR announcer, Dave somebody, said it after his traffic update, which started with "Slow going westbound on the 10, folks."

Teal snorted. "'Slow going.' Ha. It's a regular parking lot out here, Dave."

She sat in the thick of it, second lane in from the right, windows shut, air on high against the August heat, comfy in her white leather seat. She read e-mails on her smartphone and, in her imagination, dared a CHP officer to zoom up on his motorcycle and ticket her.

"As if moving four miles per hour on the freeway could technically be referred to as driving and thereby a breaking of the law."

She laughed out loud. If her husband were there, he'd roll his eyes and question once again his sanity for marrying a lawyer. River swore her favorite pastime was looking for a fight. After three years, though, his rolling eyes still sparkled whenever he said it.

The radio announcer wrapped up his report. "The time is now twelve minutes and thirty-five seconds past ten o'clock."

And then the shaking began.

As always, the unexpected movement registered about half a point on Teal's scale of awareness. One eye on her phone, one eye on the Iowa license plate of the minivan in front of her, she inched forward and braked. Her body trembled as if she were on a train.

"What . . . ?"

And then her coffee mug jiggled and rattled in its holder. Static hissed from the radio.

"Nooo."

The mug bounced onto the floor.

Yes.

Adrenaline surged through her. What to do? What to do?

Duck, cover, and hold on to a sturdy piece of furniture.

In the car? She was in the car!

Teal dropped the phone to her lap, shifted into park, and grasped the steering wheel tightly with both hands. It shook. Her body quivered. The car vibrated. Her seat belt constricted. The glove box popped open. The world rumbled, a hurtling train on rickety tracks to nowhere.

Her pulse throbbed in her throat. Her thoughts raced in circles. What to do? What to do?

If you are driving, stop. Okay. Okay. *Move out of traffic.*

Out of traffic? Not a chance.

She caught sight of the driver to her right. He clutched his steering wheel, his sunglasses askew, his face scrunched shut. Waiting. Holding his breath.

Teal had learned to deal with earthquakes. She and her daughter had lived in Southern California for fifteen years. Tremors came. She panicked. Maiya grinned. Tremors went. She walked off the adrenaline rush. Maiya laughed. They talked about what they should have done. Life got back to normal.

These tremors should have *gone* by now.

People should be exhaling by now.

She should be out of the car by now, *whew*ing with those Iowa tourists in front of her, exchanging nervous chuckles, talking about Disneyland.

Do not get out of the car.

Do not stop under an overpass.

She stared at the overpass. According to the huge green sign to her right, the upcoming exits at the overpass lay one quarter of a mile ahead. Hers was one of them.

Cars and vans and pickups and semis and SUVs and RVs moved where there was no space for movement. Drivers jockeyed to get out from under the bridge. Horns blared. Metal crunched against metal.

And then the tremors went. The shaking stopped. It was over.

Or not.

In horror Teal watched the chain reactions of vehicles slamming and shoving and sliding into each other not far ahead of her. Straight lanes of traffic were now a massive logjam of cars facing every direction.

And then the unthinkable.

The overpass shifted. It happened in agonizingly slow motion.

The right-side concrete abutment twisted, a giant robot turning, losing his footing, falling, falling, falling. It splayed out over the freeway below, over five lanes of logjam. Then the bridge above it toppled across five lanes of logjam.

The air exploded with shrapnel. Crashing noises reverberated.

Teal burst into tears, released the seat belt, turned off the engine, and ducked. She squeezed herself under the dashboard, covered her head with her arms, and began shaking all over again.

The first aftershock hadn't even hit yet.

ॐ

River Adams gazed up at the rafters of the garage ceiling. If it had been The Big One, he would be buried under those beams instead of a mountain of blue plastic storage tubs.

Teal. Where was she? "Please, Lord."

A sharp pain shot through his right side. It had the familiar *as long as I don't breathe, I'm fine* tug of a broken rib.

Many of the tubs were full of books. Or rather had been full of books before crashing on top of him. The entire set of Anne of Green Gables hardbacks lay scattered about. They belonged to Maiya, his fifteen-year-old stepdaughter, a childhood collection she could not bear to part with.

Teal's panic would be sky-high. Maiya would be laughing. *Whoa, dude! 5.9 at least.*

They would be . . . if they were okay.

River refused to follow that rabbit trail. His girls had to be okay. In the four years since he had met them, they had become the center of his universe. Teal was the epitome of femininity with her big gray eyes, bouncy personality, and short black hair framing a heart-shaped face. Maiya called him Riv and seemed more his own than Teal's in some ways. Her easygoing attitude did not come from her mother, nor her goofy sense of humor.

And the icing on the cake? They adored him.

He needed to reach his girls.

Taking shallow breaths, River pushed aside what he could from his upper body. The majority of the tubs pinned his legs against the concrete floor. From their weight, he suspected they contained Teal's law books and files. When he had moved into her bungalow, she cleared space in her office for him to use for his teaching materials.

He broke out in a cold sweat and lay still.

"I'd say we're pushing a seven, Maiya. Epicenter . . . really close."

It was the worst he'd experienced in his forty-two years, all lived in the Los Angeles area.

Just before the earthquake struck, he had carried a trash bag out to the garage and put it in the can at the far end. As he walked back toward the kitchen door, the world started its belly dance. There was nothing in the attached single-car garage to duck under or hold on to. He covered his head with his arms and made a dash for the house.

The dash ended abruptly. The bins struck him, cannonballs shot at close range and full force. Whoosh, straight out from the wall where they were stacked. He went down, flat on his back.

Slowly, River pushed aside some books and felt for the phone attached to his waistband.

It wasn't there.

He scanned the floor and saw it.

Under the corner of a bin.

Crushed.

He struggled to break free of the trap, his side screaming for him to stop moving, to stop breathing.

They have to be okay! They have to! You owe me, God! You owe me this one!